Praise for Mary Dorcey's
Biography of Desire

"Full of courageous and challenging writing, *Biography of Desire* is exquisitely tuned to the lives of women ... within the social constructs of soc..."

THE IRISH TIMES

"Mary Dorcey has produce... ...er which doesn't shirk the implications ... ...ne."

THE SUNDAY TRIBUNE

"Brilliant, sophisticated and lyrical."

AILBHE SMYTH, DIRECTOR OF WOMEN'S
EDUCATION AND RESOURCE CENTRE, UCD

"It's a brave, brave book."

DAVID MARCUS

"I admire her courage for writing the book and the passion and integrity which comes at you off every page."

JENNIFER JOHNSTON

"With scrupulous honesty, the reader is taken through a tale of betrayal and abandonment, lies and deceits and ultimately, freedom . . . Mary Dorcey's first is arguably the first erotic Irish novel."

THE IRISH TIMES

"It is a wonderful, wonderful book: complex and honest and moving and lyrical and true. All the complexities of the heart are there."

NIALL MACMONAGLE

"It is a gusty, compelling account of a once-in-a-lifetime love that waits to be grasped."

IT MAGAZINE

About the Author

The award winning short story writer and poet Mary Dorcey was born in County Dublin, Ireland.

In 1990 she won the Rooney Prize for literature for her short story collection *A Noise from the Woodshed*.

She has published three volumes of poetry: *Kindling* (Only Women Press) 1982, *Moving into the Space Cleared by Our Mothers* (Salmon Publishing) 1991, *The River that Carries Me* (Salmon Publishing) 1995.

Her stories and poems have been collected in more than fifty anthologies and her work is now taught on Irish Studies and Women's Studies courses in universities throughout Ireland, Britain and the United States.

She has been awarded two Arts Council Bursaries for literature in 1990 and 1995.

She has lived in the United States, England, France, Spain and Japan.

She is at present a lecturer and research associate at Trinity College Dublin and is currently completing a new collection of short stories.

Biography of Desire

Mary Dorcey

POOLBEG

Published 1997 by
Poolbeg Press Ltd
123 Baldoyle Industrial Estate
Dublin 13, Ireland
Reprinted November 1997

The Publishers gratefully acknowledge the support of The Arts Council.

A catalogue record for this book is available from the British Library.

ISBN 1 85371 707 X

Cover photography by Telegraph Colour Library
Cover design by Poolbeg Group Services Ltd
Set by Poolbeg Group Services Ltd in Goudy 11/13.5
Printed by The Guernsey Press Ltd,
Vale, Guernsey, Channel Islands.

Acknowledgements

No thanks are sufficient for the support and inspiration of three people: Grainne Healy, Kate Cruise O'Brien and Philip MacDermott.

My thanks are also due to all the fine staff at Poolbeg.

And to Penhalligan's Cafe, Baggot Street for house of good food and coffee.

For You

Book One

Chapter One

October, Dublin.

On an autumn afternoon, in the first week of October, Nina Kavanagh drove onto the coast road, parked her car at the promenade, between the harbour and the old bathing place, and sat with Lizzie in silence looking out to sea.

The last sunlight of the year, amber tinted, fell across the slate grey waters of the bay. And the slowly heaving swell that washed to shore seemed to ride under the surface so that no fracture showed in the gleaming façade until it broke in noiseless waves against the granite pier. Lizzie was the first to speak.

"Why have we stopped here?" Lizzie asked. "Are we going to go for a walk?"

"No, there isn't time," Nina replied.

Seagulls flew high over the harbour, playing with the wind, testing it. They soared on invisible threads of air, then plummeted and climbed again, in a rapture of flight, so far up they might have been scraps of silver paper tossed into the sky.

Nina looked at the child seated beside her. She was eating an ice cream, sucking the last mouthful from the base of the cone with an air of grave intensity. From the moment they had left the house Nina had been trying to find the courage to tell her. It seemed the hardest thing she had ever had to say to anyone. She thought of all the painful, harsh truths she had spoken to people in the past, the obdurate words of separation and farewell. But of them all, this would be the hardest.

"Who owns that dog?" Lizzie asked. "Do you think it's lost?"

A black mongrel played on the beach below, barking at the distant gulls and snapping at the seaweed that washed lazily back and forth across the small pools.

"No, I don't think so."

"Why doesn't it go home then?"

She had finished the ice cream and was growing impatient. Already she had her hand placed on the door handle, waiting to dash out the moment permission was given.

"Can we go and walk on the pier?" she asked, an expression in her wide, dark blue eyes that Nina knew from experience she could resist only for a few minutes.

"There isn't time," she said. "We have to get to your lesson by four."

"Let's go now!"

Nina looked out to sea, concentrating her attention on the movements of the gulls. They seemed to fly in perfect harmony with the water below them, the curve of their flight reflecting its slowly mounting tide.

"What's that book you're holding?" the child asked.

"It's not really a book. It's more like a diary."

"Who wrote it?"

"A friend."

"Is it a good book?"

"I haven't read it yet," Nina said.

"Why not?"

"I haven't had time. I only got it today."

"Will you read it to me?"

"No, it's private."

"Can we go then?"

4

"Yes, in a moment," Nina said. "I wanted to ask you something first."

"What?"

"What would you think . . ." Nina spoke each word carefully, as though it were a physical effort. She looked down at the child, but not into her eyes. Instead she fixed her gaze on the small hands and the two small bony knees that they rested on. "What would you think if, at any time . . . in the future . . . I was to live in another house – a different house from you and Elinor?"

"What would you want to live in another house for?"

"I might sometime. I'm not sure why. People do, you know. After a lot of years in the same place, people who live in a house together, sometimes, like to live apart for a bit. Try different arrangements."

"Other people or us?" Lizzie asked apprehensively. "Because if it's us – I like it the way it is now."

"Yes, I know," Nina said, "but if it ever changed, if I had to go away to another country for instance?"

"On holiday, do you mean?"

"For longer than a holiday."

"Where would you go?" Lizzie was suddenly excited. "Africa? America? Would you take me with you?"

"I might not be able to."

A dark trough of cloud, that a few minutes earlier had lain motionless above the horizon, blew swiftly across the bay driving back the sunlight, casting deep purple shadows over the water. Even on the finest evening there was the threat of storm. Nina stretched her hand out and laid it on the child's knee: "We had better get going," she said, "or you'll be late for your class."

The house where Lizzie had her music lesson was the third in a white-faced Victorian terrace overlooking the bay. A narrow garden stretched between the street and a flight of granite steps that led to the yellow hall door.

"Will I come in and wait for you?" Nina asked.

"No, I'm all right on my own. You can see me through the window though. Will you watch? It's only my fourth lesson but I'm on to scales already."

"Yes, I'll watch."

The child got out of the car clutching a small wooden case and walked through the garden gate. At the door she stood on tiptoe and reached for the brass knocker to announce her presence. After a few seconds the door opened. A tall, dark-haired woman stood in the doorway. She caught sight of Nina sitting in the car and waved to her with a wide sweeping movement of her arm. The child went in without looking back and the door closed.

Nina sat unmoving. The sea thrashed against the wall within inches of the road. A trawler was coming into harbour, a cloud of kittiwakes flying over its bows. She could hear their harsh, excited cries flung out on the rising wind. She looked back towards the house. She saw Lizzie sitting in the bay window, holding the wooden recorder carefully with both hands to her mouth, her teacher standing beside her. She wore exactly the same expression of earnest intent she had earlier eating the ice cream. She was a serious, highly strung child, proud and vulnerable at once. All through the days that Nina had watched by her bedside in the hospital, distracting her with chatter and stories, she had imagined this moment when it would be impossible to put off, any longer, telling her. She had thought of it with dread and forced it from her mind. Lizzie made that easy because she was so high-spirited and laughed so often.

Nina took the red notebook from the dashboard and held it for a moment in her hands. It had been put through the letterbox that morning in a padded brown envelope addressed to her. A note in familiar handwriting had been slipped between the centre pages:

"When I wrote this I didn't intend to show it to you but now it seems the best way of communicating. I want you to know what I've lived through, alone here, waiting for you. Please be patient. I want you to read it from start to finish. Begin at the beginning and don't make a final decision until you reach the end. Promise me?

Even now it's still not too late for us if you would only tell me what you want. Read this. And speak to me!

Katherine."

Nina held the heavy notebook between her hands weighing its length and depth. Could there be so much that needed explanation? Was it possible that so much could have happened between two people in the space of time since she had first laid eyes on Katherine Newman? She opened the book at the beginning and rested the stiff, hardback cover against the steering wheel. She would do as she was asked – she would read it to the end before making up her mind. If she started immediately she could be well into it before Lizzie came back.

Chapter Two

September, Clare.

Nina, I am here, at last. Waiting for you.

I sit with the curtains open to watch the sky. A great white moon, almost full, is hanging over the lake. Every few minutes it breaks like lightning through the dark encircling cloud.

You'll like the house, it's your kind of place, bare and intimate. Black rafters, whitewashed walls, a stone fireplace, small deep-set windows looking out on bogland and sky. There's nothing to distract me from my thoughts of you. Nothing demanded of me. No effort necessary at all. The clock ticks. The roof creaks. Last night I heard the waves breaking on the lakeshore. That's how quiet it was. In the morning, seagulls. In the afternoon, rooks.

I've books on the floor beside me – novels and my textbooks – but I'm not working. I sit by the fire with a blanket wrapped round my shoulders, listening to the strange melodies the wind makes at windows and door, dreaming of you and counting the hours until I see you again.

I try to imagine every detail of our next meeting when I collect you. I'll take the bus to the station and wait for you, pacing the platform, trying to disguise my fierce excitement. How will you look when I see you first? As you did when you appeared to my astonishment at the airport, a bouquet of freesias and white lilies spilling from your arms and that expression of repentance and appeal in your eyes that I've never yet been able to withstand. No matter how much I think about you, picturing you at every minute of the day, when I first see you this is what happens – I stare at you in astonishment, wondering how it is you always manage to seem more lovely, more acutely alive than I'd remembered? How often have I found my anger, resentment, pride overcome by that second of illumination, banished by the force of your physical presence?

I've no reason to leave the house. I have everything I need for the time being. All the household essentials are provided and I bought enough food on the way up to last me several days. Besides, without a car where would I go? Perhaps I should have driven down after all. But we can hire a car when you come, can't we?

I potter about from room to room, inventing tasks to keep myself occupied, but the place is so well kept it provides almost no distraction. I went out into the field just now, in front of the house, and picked some wild flowers; fuchsia and the blossoms of a lovely violet-coloured shrub that grows just beside the gate. I went back into the house and arranged them in two beautiful vases of dark blue china that I found in the loft. I set one in the sitting-room by the window and the other in the bedroom – our bedroom. Then I took out my typewriter and drew up an impressive agenda of things to do. But all this is only a pretence at diversion. Whatever I do I can't keep my thoughts from you. I dream about the future, and I remember the past.

I've developed a system of recalling events that keeps me busy for hours on end. I am as deliberate as a scientist in my research of our story. I pick a day at random; any day we spent together, and try to picture it scene by scene. I start with waking up in the morning and slowly bring back to consciousness everything I can remember of the next twenty-four hours. I go over it all, how we met. How we came to be lovers. How we grew close. How we lost one another. How we refound each other. I try to establish a pattern, hoping, I suppose, that if I can it will make it easier to predict the future.

I discover pleasure in the least of things. I list and categorise my memories according to the day, the month, the year. I remember how you looked, what you wore, what you said. You wouldn't believe how much remembrance can be stored in these simple things. I enumerate them, sifting and sorting through our life together, sense by sense, loss by loss.

I retreat step by step into my discovery of you, my awakening. That's how I think of it – as a revelation. I know in your cynical fashion you don't believe that love happens by chance. I remember you said once that we create our passions, weave them deliberately from the rag and bone of our own hearts. And yet, in retrospect, all my life before meeting you seems now to have been no more than a long preparation for you.

This afternoon, I became suddenly restless and decided to venture out for an exploration of the immediate territory. I found myself going further than I intended – halfway about the lake and back again. On my way home I decided to buy a newspaper. At the crossroads, the beginning and end of civilisation, two miles from the house there is a shop that serves as a post office, one pub, a church and a telephone kiosk. The proprietor, a heavy-set, blue-eyed woman, fifty or so, with a mane of red hair piled loosely about her head, came out from a back room to serve me. She didn't seem to pay any special attention, but I had the odd feeling that she knew all about me. We exchanged comments on the weather.

"Not a bad day at all now."

"A lovely day indeed, thanks be to God. But they say it won't last. They say tomorrow will be wet again. Worse than last week. And last week was fierce altogether. But sure they could be wrong. It wouldn't be for the first time."

"No indeed, it wouldn't."

When she asked where I was staying, I had the definite sense that she knew the answer and that she asked only to be polite. I told her I was visiting for a fortnight and that a friend would be joining me in a few days time. She looked at me sharply for a second: "Ah well and you'd need a friend," she said. "You couldn't be sitting up there on your own – sure it would drive a mad woman out of her head." She spoke with an air of indulgence and affection as if she knew who you were and why you were coming and could feel exactly my longing for you.

"Have you a car or are you walking?" she asked. She persuaded me to take a second carrier bag for the groceries, in case the first would break.

The rain came on as I walked home. A downpour. As soon as I got in I pulled off my wet clothes and took them in to the hearth to dry. But the glowing turf fire I'd left on my way out I found was reduced to a few smouldering sods. Only then I realised that I'd forgotten to buy more firelighters. It took me half an hour to get it going again with newspaper and strips of kindling I tore from an old chip basket, unearthed from the cupboard under the stairs. I made lasagne for dinner and opened a bottle of red wine, quite good Côte de Rhône I bought at the shop. I hardly moved again for the whole evening.

It's awkward being without a car, I suppose. Maybe I was foolish to come without it. But I like so much travelling by train that it seems worth it. I like being given time to adapt gradually to a change of environment. I love the leisurely pace of train travel, the sense of the measured, phased alteration of the landscape. With each station reached and left behind – from factory towns to small villages circled by high mountains

– one is drawn deeper into the unknown. Each placename painted on a platform signpost is a landmark abandoned as soon as reached.

I slept for an hour or so on the way and felt completely rested when I arrived. I took the bus at the station and from the town a taxi to the house. Everyone of whom I asked directions, from old men to young, giggling schoolgirls, knew the place instantly, but then everyone knows everything, here. I can feel them reading my mind before I speak. After a few weeks, I think all speech would become unnecessary. A sideways glance, a shift of the shoulder, a little movement of the feet, a smile – that's all that's necessary to communicate everything of importance. They're all trained to the use of this finely tuned antenna. It's as though living so close, for generations – everyone related to everyone else – talk has become too blunt, too dangerous an instrument. They remind me of Orientals: this almost eastern subtlety and reserve, the exquisite sensitivity to nuance, the self-containment, the deep hidden laughter. Oh yes, they are laughing at me, I know. Another crazy foreigner come here to find peace and they all mad to get out of the place, ready to go to the furthest ends of the globe to escape it. Every local just back from New York or on her way to Australia.

Last night I had a strange dream about Ma. Extraordinarily vivid, as if she were in the room with me. I dreamed that I was lying in a hospital bed or at least some kind of institution (a prison maybe?) and that she came to visit me. She stood at the foot of the bed and just stared at me without speaking, with a look of intense regret and sadness in her eyes. She said nothing at all for minutes and then at last, shaking her head from side to side, she said, almost under her breath: "So this is what you've come to! I was always afraid of something like this." Then as suddenly as she had come, without waiting for me to answer, she disappeared and I was left calling after her. I heard myself shouting aloud: "But I'm innocent, Ma. I'm innocent." To no avail. She was gone and I lay wide awake with this dreadful sense of having been judged and found guilty of some unnamed crime. What does it mean? Why did she say – I knew you'd come to this? Come to what? And why should I feel guilty?

The odd thing is, though she had such a critical air, she looked young and vigorous, the way she did years ago when I was still living at home. But that's how I always remember her – as a young woman, beautiful and vivacious. How did she manage her good looks all those years – with all that she went through? Huge vanity, needless to say. But I have to admit it paid off. Well into her seventies she could still look regal. I never met anyone, right to her last days, who wasn't impressed and charmed by that glowing, highly polished façade.

You know I'd love it if she could appear in the flesh just for an hour, sit down by the fire and have one of the long rambling conversations we used to have years ago. At the time I took them for granted, with no idea of how I would miss them. But now I'm struck by how well we got on. I feel we'd get on better still, if we were to meet in the present. Even enclosed in this hermitage we'd be able to have a laugh together. So long as she didn't begin to tell me something for my own good. That always led to rows. Not that it was ever easy to have a real set-to with her. Not for anyone. She was much too good at getting her own way and I was always too susceptible to charm. Not the calculated kind – I never liked obvious craft in these things. But the kind of spontaneous, half-conscious charm that Ma suffered from – the inability to displease.

And do you know something, Nina? You often remind me of her. Poles apart though you may have been in all essentials, nevertheless there was a strange likeness – the charm of manner, the grace of movement. Is it one of the reasons you had such instant power over me? Though I didn't recognise it consciously, at least not at the beginning. I wouldn't have told you if I had. But something like a subliminal flash of awareness let me feel it. Ah well, maybe everybody of importance reminds one of somebody else of importance? What do you think? Is every great love rooted from some earlier forgotten one? How else could we discover one another, forgive one another?

The wind rages outside. It hasn't stopped for five minutes since last night. It's so loud I hear nothing else. If I put my hand to the walls I feel them tremble. The roof screams under its buffeting. It howls in the chimney and claws at the windows. I can scarcely open the door. I could all too easily imagine myself the sole survivor of some national disaster, left alone up here, on the mountain side, unknown to anyone.

It's making me nervous and fanciful. I got up just now and walked to the window. I thought I heard a cat crying outside, but I couldn't see one. I wouldn't be surprised if a stray or two turned up before long. You know how often there are flocks of them, half-starved cats and their kittens hanging about the farmyards in these places. But in fact, I haven't seen an animal of any description since I arrived. Except, of course, for the dejected, sodden cattle who stand in the fields, hour after hour, without so much as a proper tree to shelter them. How do they bear it? The rain? The cold? It makes me feel desolate to look at them, so I don't. I look at the sky instead, this marvellous, mercurial, deep-blue sky, full of moving sunlight and great billowing clouds. It's what you love about it, I know – this sense of space and constant change.

How am I supposed to manage, here of all places, without you? Why did I imagine I'd be able to use the time alone to get my work done? I haven't opened a book yet and I've barely

made a start on the proposals. I think about nothing but you. I
miss the sight of you, the smell of you. Yes; I couldn't put it in
words but I recognise it: that special, dusty fragrance of your
skin. I have only to breathe deeply and suddenly I'm filled
with the memory of you, the presence of you beside me. I can
almost feel the pressure of your body against mine. I thought
I'd got over this fever, but it's returned in full force.

I fell asleep this afternoon and woke about an hour later from
a terrible dream, my heart pounding and my body bathed in
sweat. I got up from bed and went downstairs and poured
myself a large whiskey. Yes, alone in the middle of the
afternoon! But I'm still shaken when I think of it. I dreamed
that Malachy had brought me to court and was suing me for
custody of Ben and Luke. I was standing in a witness box
fighting for the right to see my own children! Can you
imagine it? I can still see the lawyer's eyes fixed on me, cold
and insolent. I can hear those pompous, oiled barrister's tones
demanding to know what made me imagine myself capable of
raising two children alone? How could I hope to be
considered a fit mother! With your record! he says
triumphantly and the whole court bursts into terrible high-
pitched laughter.

My record. What a phrase! I can almost picture it as an
actual physical object – the book of evidence. A photograph
album with snapshots of my life. My love life. My adultery. My
abandonment of Malachy.

My God, Nina – what would I do if it ever came to that? If
I was forced to contest a legal challenge, how could I defend
myself? But whatever else Malachy might do, he'd never fight
me for custody of the boys, surely? He'd never be so
vindictive, would he? So stupid? But then that's what Elinor
believed of Tom, you told me, isn't it? All of us, insisting that
our man is different until the very last second. And who's to

say what any of us would do under such pressure. Poor Malachy – how I've made him suffer! I couldn't bear to put him though anything worse. I'd almost hand them over without a word of protest rather than go through another argument. But I couldn't, of course. If it came to the point I would fight anyone for them, do any mean, ruthless thing necessary. Like any mother.

I was becoming morose and depressed so I decided to take myself out for a long, cleansing walk. The place is very beautiful: low, stone walls, thatched cottages (yes, I actually counted four newly done), dark blue mountains in the distance, wild fuchsia at every gate. I walked down to the lake where I saw two swans and three cygnets. The parents sailed along, heads high, the three grey, down-covered young following shyly behind them. When they caught sight of me standing on the wooden jetty, the adults at once swam towards it. They're obviously used to being fed by anyone who passes by. Unfortunately I'd nothing to give them. When I bent down and reached out my hand to one of the cygnets, the female swan lowered her head towards me and almost regretfully, it seemed, hissed sharply in warning. Then, she turned and angrily chased back a flock of mallards who had sneaked up in her wake, also hoping to be fed. I must remember to bring some bread for them, the next time I come this way.

Back in the house once more and feeling much better. Have I told you how attractive it is? With its rafters and timber floor and the original small, square windows, painted bright yellow? There are four shelves of books and music cassettes and some lovely paintings and photographs of the area. It's so much more welcoming – a house that's lived in year round – than a rented holiday home. There's a skylight in each bedroom. I lie in the loft and watch the clouds. Just now I saw a flock of wild geese fly overhead in single file, the movement of their wings as loud as a drum beat in the silence.

I am fighting the desire to go to the clock every few hours and check the time again. Last night, before going to sleep, I went into the kitchen and crossed out on the wall calendar the days already behind me.

Yes, I know. I'm behaving like a schoolgirl. I try to keep a grip on myself and fill the hours with activity, but just when I think I'm succeeding something sabotages my best efforts. Just now I went upstairs to get my briefcase, having done nothing yesterday, but when I opened it what was the first thing that fell into my hand? A photograph of you, of course. That one of you taken by the sea in Sandymount, wearing your black leather jacket and black beret, looking like a freedom fighter except for the daft, delighted grin. Do you remember? I took it the first afternoon after meeting Aunt May. I remember how we talked that day. We must have walked about ten miles, along the Strand and up through Ballsbridge to Herbert Park. It was a glorious autumn day. I remember you saying how you loved the time of year; the smell in the air, the changing colour of the leaves, the great crackling drifts of them blown along roads and pavements. I said you should come to New England if you wanted to see colour in fall. How could this place, with its puny sycamore and beech trees, compare, I thought, but I didn't say it in case it might offend you. I didn't want to risk that for a second. I wanted you to like me, to admire and notice me. I wanted your full attention and appreciation from the first moment I laid eyes on you.

I am haunted by scenes of the past. Stray inconsequential moments of delight. Do you remember meeting one afternoon in Rathmines? At the very beginning? You were walking along the main street one day shortly before we became lovers? Three days to be exact – yes, that's how well I remember! I stopped the car and rolled down the window. You reached out and stroked my cheek; a quick glancing touch that startled me.

"I like the ponytail," you said. "It's very cheeky." These lovely gracious ways. And that smile of yours. Like a burst of sunshine on a cold day. I felt new in your company. Younger, unpredictable. Dangerous even. This was a great part of the attraction of course. How you made me feel. Always the most significant factor, this I suppose – how the lover makes the beloved feel about herself. You said once that I was amoral: "You think only of what you want to do, never of what you should," you said. I was delighted, although I knew it was quite untrue. I didn't want to disabuse you of any notions that pleased you, however misguided. Having learned long ago that any lover's estimation is yards wide of the mark, but it's the illusion-making that counts.

Do you remember? Always this question. As if there were any use to it. But I remember every hour we spent together. The first evening? Do you remember waiting in the casualty waiting-room, blood on your hands that I thought was your blood? Do you remember, weeks later, sitting in your kitchen and you leaning across the table suddenly to say with great gravity: "I think I must have known you in an earlier life. In Limbo, perhaps. I remember you clearly – a fat, brown-skinned baby, naked and smiling." Do you remember my astonishment? I didn't know whether to laugh or take it is as a compliment. But it didn't take long to grow used to these non sequiturs of yours. The crazy, unexpected things you say, with absolute seriousness. The kind of nonsense that transformed my life.

Love is a ridiculous condition, isn't it? What else would have me sitting here in a house on the side of a mountain, with nothing to look at but the sky and the rain-soaked fields, and no company but my own obsessive thoughts? Love makes all this seem worthwhile, even necessary and useful.

How do we come, any of us, to invest such significance in one another? What miracle of perspective makes one human face the only desirable sight on the earth? The analysts would ask me who you remind me of – what relationship I'm reworking through you? What unresolved childhood trauma? The priests would say I am substituting human love for godly. The lawyers would ask if a woman in such an obsessive, unbalanced state of mind should be trusted with the care of vulnerable young children. And do you know something, Nina, when I think of it from that point of view sometimes I wonder. I mean after all, maybe these professional carers have a point. Infatuated as I am, almost anything that comes between me and my thoughts of you seems an irritant. It floods me with guilt to acknowledge this, even to myself. I find it hard to credit and yet somewhere in my brain is this whispered thought – maybe I'd be better off alone – free to be with her whenever and however often I wanted? I'm ashamed, but that is what I think sometimes.

What's brought on this fit of paranoia? Is it my hidden fear of identifying myself openly as your lover? Have I been too unsure of you before this to picture the consequences of a life lived with you? But I suppose I need to face the fact that, however decent Malachy may be, if a case were ever taken to court I could hardly expect any lawyer to give up such a heaven-sent opportunity. I can exactly imagine the field day he would have with me.

"Mrs Newman, how would you like to describe to the court your extraordinary behaviour – this obsession that has destroyed the happiness of your husband and children?"

"It is not an obsession."

"And what would you call it then – this affair that caused you to abandon your own children?"

"I did not abandon my children. I took them with me."

"So, your children lived with you in a rented house and

this woman lover came to visit? Is that correct? And may we ask if you consider that this was a healthy atmosphere for young boys?"

"Yes I do. They were very happy."

"You cannot, surely, expect to have them live with you while you openly flaunt this abnormal liaison?"

"It's not abnormal."

"And how would you define it then?"

"I don't know that I want to define it, but if I had to I'd say – the irresistible force of destiny."

"Would you indeed? In that case perhaps you would tell the court what you consider the origin of this extraordinary force?"

"The origin?"

"Yes, perhaps you could say what first inspired it?"

"Her eyes . . ."

"I beg your pardon?"

"I said, her eyes. Her black startled eyes . . ."

What could I say, Nina? What could I possibly tell them? If I were to stand in a witness box and attempt to justify in a few stark sentences my passion for you? Could I say how it began or why? I could say anything. Give any reason. Would it make a difference? I could offer any of a hundred qualities of yours – your looks, your brilliance, your wit. I could say that you embody something essential for me, some archetypal female quality; generosity, sensuality. I could say I was infatuated with your political vision, your radical spirit. Any of those things. All of them. But nothing of this is what matters to me. Or is it?

So many images crowd my mind when I think of you. A brilliant collage, arranged at random, heaped together, one on top of the other, like old photographs in a forgotten drawer. When I sift through them, I find I've stored a picture of you in every characteristic mood and pose. I see you standing, naked and voluptuous, framed in the doorway of my bedroom, pausing for a moment, on your way to the bathroom or the kitchen. Or I see you sitting in bed in the morning, propped against the pillows, holding a cup of coffee in both hands. I see your lips jutting forward, to meet the brim of the cup, as you lift it to your mouth; in the childlike way you have. I see the upper half of your body revealed above the white sheet, your full, brown breasts, your wide shoulders. And I see your black, intent eyes watching me. I see all their expressions: their mischievous gleam, their sadness, their gaiety, their angry passion.

All of these images fall together in my mind, mingled and confused. Only one stands clear from the rest, separate and completely distinct: the first snapshot my mind took of you – the evening we met, in the casualty waiting-room of Baggot Street hospital. Our meeting there was an accident in at least two senses of the word. Earlier that afternoon after driving Ben to his sailing, I had slammed the car door on my thumb and tried to persuade myself that it wasn't broken until the pain became unbearable. At seven o'clock I gave in and drove myself to casualty.

When I think of that evening, now or at any time, I see a precisely composed picture, formal as a studio portrait. It's so vivid it seems like an eternal present. I see you sitting just inside the door as I come in, on a red plastic seat, your legs crossed, your face very white, in the garish light of the casualty waiting room. You are dressed in what looks like a man's tuxedo: black trousers, a black satin waistcoat and a beautiful white starched evening shirt, open at the neck. Your dark blonde hair, the curls tousled, cut short over the ear. You're leaning forward, hands resting on your thighs, your head lowered. You're smoking a cigarette, under a no smoking sign. The only available seat is beside you. I see everything that happened as if it were taking place at this very moment.

21

"Is this seat free?" I ask, knowing it is. You look up startled and apologise about the cigarette.

"I know I shouldn't. I've given them up, but I can't get through this place without them." You drop the burning cigarette onto the floor and stub it out with your shoe. When you speak I'm struck first by the strange quality of your voice, low, musical, with something hesitant in it like a faint stammer fought against. Then I see your eyes – turned full towards me – for the first time – those dark eyes that are sometimes black and sometimes amber – almond-shaped eyes, spaced wide apart – the deep soft darkness of them, the dark of the earth, something complete and final, that can't be altered by surface tricks of light. Extraordinary eyes – black and startled.

I sit beside you. I see there is blood on the sleeve of your shirt and on your hands. I want to ask what happened and if you're waiting to see a doctor. But I'm afraid to ask.

You notice the direction of my gaze and maybe my concern and you smile and stretch out your hands to study them.

"It's not my blood," you say as though to reassure me. I don't understand. If it's not your blood then whose? I wonder if you have a child, but I don't inquire further.

"And what has you here?" you ask softly, probably feeling the need to be polite. I hold out my thumb to show you, swollen by now to twice its normal size. You laugh and then apologise. You say you don't mean to be unsympathetic but we must look like a pair of prizefighters. When you say it, I feel a sudden, unexpected pleasure in the way the phrase draws us together, links our experience. You tell me that you hate hospitals. You say you've spent enough time in them recently to last a lifetime. Again I'm curious but awkward. I don't know how to learn more without seeming rude. "Are you a nurse?" I ask at last, feeling foolish. You make it worse – you laugh out loud and say: "No way. Never. But as it happens the

22

woman I live with is and her little girl Lizzie suffers from asthma, so between the two of them I've seen the inside of a lot of hospitals."

I'm amazed by the way you mention so casually that you live with a woman – though why shouldn't you? I know at once without asking that you mean a lover. How? I don't know. It's not that you look obviously gay – whatever that is (and I should have some notion because I have had gay friends in the States) – despite the man's evening dress which in fact serves only to heighten your womanliness, your sensuality.

"I see," I say, seeing almost nothing. Sensing my awkwardness maybe, you ask if I'd like a cup of coffee and you get up and walk across the hall to the canteen. As I see you cross the floor, just as in the words of the song – *something in the way you move* – your long, loping stride, your head thrown back, the thick mane of hair, something of an animal's poise in your gait, sinuous and cat-like, rouses an inexplicable longing. This woman has kept herself alive, I think to myself, kept herself complete, independent, particular. This is how she would have looked in childhood, innocent and worldly-wise at once, setting out against the world.

When you reappear you're carrying two cups of coffee and two sandwiches.

"They gave me very doubtful glances in the canteen," you say, inviting me into your perspective as if we're old friends. "They're not sure what they think of a woman in a tux. Should I have told them I was on my way to a fancy dress party?"

"Were you?" I ask and I'm further surprised. What kind of party would end with you looking blood-smeared like this? And then I get it – suddenly: "Did you have a car crash?" I ask abruptly.

It's only then that you tell me what's brought you here.

On your way to the party you stopped to pick up Elinor at the hostel where she works and one of the young women there had just slashed her wrists and with your car still running at the pavement you said you'd drive her down to casualty. As soon as I heard the name Elinor – maybe even before that – I realised that I knew who you were.

"I think I know your friend Elinor – is it Elinor Fitzgerald?" And it is, of course. You look astonished – you had obviously expected no such connection with me. I explain to you that I'd met her a couple of times the previous winter when I visited the hostel – not saying what I'm suddenly ashamed of, that I'd been delivering some old clothes at Christmas (that was how ordinary I was – I gave to charity at Christmas and looked with admiration from afar at the people who worked at it all year round). And immediately I tell you this, you warm towards me. You put out your hand, you shake mine, you tell me your name is Nina and I think, yes – that's exactly what it should be. I introduce myself and we work through an impromptu list of other people and places we might have in common in the way everyone does in this country, knowing that with patience they'll dredge up a shared cousin or former classmate.

"Are you American?" you ask.

"Yes, I am. But I've spent half my life in this country."

"You still have a slight accent."

"Have I? I thought I'd got rid of it by this time."

"No, you haven't. But why would you want to? It's so much nicer than ours – so unself-conscious and direct."

You are friendly and flattering, paying me an attention you'd hardly have shown if I hadn't been able to claim friendship with Elinor. And aware of this I have the vague sense of making use of her in some way that was unworthy. You might well say that I poached on that acquaintanceship from the outset? Yes, I can make no claim to virtue of any kind in my feelings for you. I would have done anything, broken any rule, stooped to any depths to bring you into my life.

When your young friends returned, the injured woman bandaged and ready for home, you turned to me to say goodbye, and just as you were leaving you added lightly, as an afterthought, to be polite: "Why don't you drop over some day? I'm sure Elinor would love to see you."

And that was it. You had asked me – of your own free will you had extended an invitation to me.

So it happened that you came into my life and changed everything. Yes, that's how it was. The first moment I saw you I knew my life was altered, radically, irrevocably. As you strode away from me down the hospital corridor, with your loose careless walk, entirely unconscious of me, absorbed in conversation with your friends, watching you I recognised a crossroads cut clear across my path. Cut between past and future. I saw myself standing at the edge of this turning point as distinctly as if I was looking at someone else: a stranger glimpsed from the window of a passing train.

I stood staring after you and the words that formed themselves in my brain amazed me. They seemed to be spoken in my ear by someone else, someone standing next to me. I almost turned round to find the speaker. I want you, the voice said. As stark as that. I want you.

I gazed after you, my eyes travelling from your legs, to your hips, to your shoulders and back to your face that was half turned in my direction. And the longing that swept through me was so fierce no one word could contain it. Not lust, or need, or love. It was like a power outside me. As though a stranger had spoken in my head. As if God himself had stepped down and whispered in my brain. Gazing after you as you walked away from me down a hospital corridor, the longing that swept over me had nothing to do with fantasy or

25

premonition. At the same time, in that split second of my regarding you, some other part of me thrilled with a sense of power. I felt triumphant. Gleeful. Capable of anything – of whatever might be required of me to bring this extraordinary future to pass.

Sitting here, in this desolate mountain place, waiting for you, I remember that evening, that extraordinary moment of revelation as vividly as if it had happened yesterday. But that's not true. I remember it better; a thousand times better.

Chapter Three

October, Dublin.

"Come here to me, my little fairy. How's my darling?" Aunt May said when she saw Lizzie come through the door. She was sitting by the fire in a rocking chair of carved black oak she had brought thirty years ago from America. "Didn't you give us a terrible fright with your asthma attack? I'm too old to be traipsing back and forth to hospitals worrying about you." She set down the letter she had been reading and lifted her cheek for a kiss from the child.

"I didn't have an asthma attack. I had a seizure," Lizzie corrected her. "But I'm better now, amn't I?"

"Yes, you are. You look right as rain. I think you were only having us on. Come and sit by the fire and tell me all your news."

The child sat down at May's feet and launched into a detailed account of her last morning in hospital and all the things she had done since coming home. Nina turned away from them and walked slowly across the big softly lit room to the high Georgian window on the far side. The room was so large that one end was barely in earshot of the other. She stood silently while the child chattered, gazing down into the narrow walled garden overgrown and luxuriant as it was when she first came here. The rhododendron against the back wall, still in bloom, the lavender and pink heads heavy with rain,

27

the mallow by the gate with its wild profusion of violet flowers. She looked at the trees she used to play in, the beech where she had made her tree hut – the best in the neighbourhood – and the old sycamore from which still hung a home-made swing; two lengths of rope and a lopsided wooden seat that May had rigged up for her so long ago as a temporary arrangement. A black cat sat on the roof of the return. She watched it sniffing at the lip of the gutter and then stealthily easing itself over the edge of the roof and slipping down the drainpipe onto the grass below.

"You're very pensive today," May said, "what's wrong with you?"

"Nothing," Nina said. She turned round and smiled at her aunt. "I was just thinking how little things change here."

She let her eyes travel round the big shadow-filled room, with its dark furniture and photographs in gleaming silver frames. Everything was in its time-honoured place; every article of furniture, every ornament exactly as she had last seen them.

She crossed to the fireplace and sat down in the high winged armchair. She looked at May's rugged handsome face, the blue eyes delicate and bright as small wild flowers starting from stony ground. She studied her in silence for a few minutes, marvelling at how little time had altered her. She had grown thinner with the years, of course, and her once blonde hair was now almost white. The smoke-filled voice that was her trademark had grown huskier, but, although she used a stick these days, she carried it, she said, only so that people would know the unsteady gait was a permanent affliction and not the result of a few whiskeys too many. Her mind was as sharp and quick-witted as ever. Nina had to take great care if she were to keep any secrets from her at all.

"How's Elinor?" May asked. "Is she over the shock about Elizabeth yet?"

"What shock about me?" Lizzie asked. She was sitting on the hearth-rug and having taken her recorder from its wooden case was blowing silently through the mouthpiece.

"Going to hospital, of course," May said. "You gave your poor mother a terrible fright. She seemed very subdued when I spoke to her today. She must be worn out."

"Yes, she is tired," Nina agreed, but added as if suddenly conscious of a need to defend herself, "but you know Elinor, it's impossible to make her rest. She's strong as an ox and as obstinate."

"What's an ox?" Lizzie asked.

"A big cow with straight horns," Nina said.

"Well some people can be too strong for their own good," May said. "Too much can be expected of them." She lit another of her small brown cigars and blew twin streams of pale yellow smoke from her nostrils.

"You shouldn't inhale those things, May, you really shouldn't," Nina said looking at her aunt and smiling.

"Of course not." May gave her sudden hoarse chuckle. "Which reminds me, I saw a cartoon the other day I should have kept for you. Two old ladies walking along in a nursing home pushing their walkers in front of them. One says to the other: 'To think Dot, if we'd given up smoking we would have missed all this!'"

She got up from her chair and walked across the room to the sideboard.

"Will you join me in a little stiffener?" she asked her niece, "I have a very good bottle of Scotch here."

Nina turned and smiled at her. "I will of course, I'd love one." May's easy-going kindness pained her suddenly. She felt undeserving of it. And she thought, as she watched her pour the drinks, she was ageing after all, her hands shook slightly, and her voice seemed unnecessarily loud, as though her hearing was beginning to fail. She felt a pang of remorse that she spent so little time with her these days. She wished she had been kinder – had done more sometimes or said less. Small things seemed cruel now: becoming impatient with her for smoking too much or because she didn't take the trouble to cook properly for herself. Because she was so fiercely independent and never asked for help it was all too easy to overlook her needs. She knew May would have hated to think that Nina felt any obligation to her. But she did and any neglect made Nina feel guilty. She always had so little time, that was the trouble. Always rushing. Always saying "Next week. I'll take you to the cinema next week. I'll take you to the races next week." May's beloved races where they had spent such wonderful days when Molly was alive. And when had Nina last managed to go with her? A year? Maybe more?

"Can we look at your photographs, Aunty May?" Lizzie asked suddenly. Whenever they came here she wanted to take out May's box of photographs and sort through them. She was fascinated by the discovery of Nina as a child no bigger than herself and to find that even Aunt May had once been young. She took from the middle drawer of the sideboard an old biscuit tin marked "Special Selection Box". She didn't know that the name referred to the biscuits that had filled it one Christmas, and not the faded snaps that were such a delight to her. They were heaped together with no attempt at organisation. Aunt May was sublimely indifferent to chronology. Lizzie plucked them like sweets from a jar and held them aloft to study under the lamp. Many of them were mottled and yellowed, curling at the edges, and some in bright new Technicolor.

"Who's this?" she asked, holding out a photo of a small girl not unlike herself.

"That's Nina playing on the swing in our garden in Cork."

The child's questions were always the same and so were the answers.

"How old was she then?"

"Seven. Almost the age you are now."

"When did she come to live with you?"

"When she was five."

"And was that when you came home to look after her?"

"Yes."

"Why did you come?"

"Because there was no one else. Her mother was dead."

"I wouldn't like my mother to die and to have to be looked after by an old aunt." Lizzie squeezed up her face in distaste.

"I wasn't old then," Aunt May said.

"You would have liked living with May." Nina had been silent for a few minutes letting the child's questions flow over her, using the distraction of the photographs to steal surreptitious glances at the notebook she held in her lap. "May would have fed you ice cream and marshmallows every day, the way she did me."

"Well then, if my mother dies can I come here to live?"

"And why would your mother die, pet?" May protested. "When she's a fine healthy young woman?"

"Well, if Nina goes to live in another house can myself and Elinor come here then?"

"Why would that happen, child? Aren't you all perfectly happy where you are?"

"Yes," Lizzie said doubtfully, "but supposing if . . ." She picked another photograph from the box. A black spaniel stared out disconsolately from the arms of a dark-haired girl. "He's like Solomon, isn't he?" she exclaimed showing the picture to Nina.

"What put this notion about moving house into her head?" Aunt May asked, looking over the child's head to catch Nina's eye.

31

"I don't know. Probably some book she's been reading or something on television."

"Speaking of books," May said, "what's this book that has you so absorbed? You've hardly a word to throw a dog."

"It's not a book," Lizzie said, "it's written by a friend of hers."

"Oh," said Aunt May. "Is that the truth now? Well her friend must be a very good writer to keep our Nina so engrossed."

May's regard was quizzical, but Nina determinedly resisted the pressure to offer any further explanation. Aunt May, seeming to know when she was beaten, made a show of changing the subject.

"How's your friend Katherine?" she asked. "Wasn't she going off to Clare for a few days the last time I saw her?"

"Yes, that's right."

"And is she back yet?"

"I'm not sure," Nina said, turning away from May's eye. "I haven't seen her."

"Well, she certainly seemed in wonderful form the afternoon you brought her here. High as a kite, in fact."

"Did she?"

"Yes, I was glad to see it because the last time we met I thought she was very troubled."

"Was she?"

"Yes, she was. Did you tell me her husband has a new job? In Galway?"

"Yes, he's an architect and he's just landed a commission to design new apartments and a leisure centre in the city."

"And will she be moving there with him?"

"No, she won't. She thinks she'd prefer to stay here."

"I hope now you're not going to tell me that she's separated?" Aunt May sounded genuinely alarmed, her face taking on an expression impatient and regretful. "Every friend you have seems to be separated."

"Well you know how it is . . ."

"Indeed I do. I know only too well," May said in the tone of one resigned to the madness of the world. "But it's the children I worry about. Who are they going to live with?"

"She's sharing the care of them with their father," Nina said feeling a need to allay May's anxiety. "It'll be fine. It's a very amicable arrangement."

"What's amicable?" Lizzie asked looking up at Nina.

"It means friendly," Aunt May told her, "though if it's so friendly I don't know why people do it."

"Do what?" Lizzie demanded.

"Go and live in different houses from each other and have children running from pillar to post." May picked up the poker and rattled it through the bars of the grate, rousing a shower of blue and yellow sparks that danced their way up the chimney.

"Sometimes it's the only thing to do," Nina offered uncertainly. "The best of bad options."

"Sometimes, of course, but why does it happen so often these days? No one has any patience or tolerance. Life was never meant to be easy all the time."

"What's a pillar and post?" Lizzie asked, her clear blue eyes fixed on the elderly woman who had set her chair rocking slowly to and fro, the hinges squeaking faintly at each turn.

"It's just an expression," Nina answered. "It means moving from one place to another. One house to another."

"The way you said we might, if you went to America?"

Aunt May slowed the motion of her chair to a standstill: "What's this about America?"

"Nina might be going to live in America," Lizzie went on determinedly.

"Now I didn't say that," Nina objected, conscious of a

blush rising to her cheeks. "That's not what I meant at all." She stood up and walked to the window. The rain was still falling. She could see the orange glow of the street lights and the same cat sitting motionless on the wall in the wet.

"Would you like to go upstairs and get my medicine?" Aunt May turned to the child and smiled. "Do you know where I keep it, pet?"

"On the high shelf in the bathroom?"

"Yes, that's it."

The child ran from the room letting the door bang shut behind her.

Nina was still standing by the window looking out.

"Would you like to tell me what's on your mind?" her aunt asked. "And don't say 'nothing' because I know you too well. You were always the same."

"I'm a bit abstracted I suppose – the worry about Elizabeth, and work is difficult at the moment."

"What's all this about America?"

"Nothing. She just got mixed up. I was telling her I'd like a holiday, that's all."

"Didn't sound like that. Is she worried about something?"

"Well, she had a hard time. We all did."

"Sometimes when life is hard it's not wise to make it any harder." May threw the butt of her cigar into the fire and stretching out her hands under the light she studied her faintly yellowed fingertips.

"What do you mean by that?" Nina stared at her.

"The pelican attitude – that's what I call it," May answered without looking up.

"And what is that?"

"The pelican pierces her breast with her beak until she draws enough blood to feed her young." If Aunt May thought this was enigmatic she didn't show it.

"And who's the pelican in this case?" Nina asked.

"Isn't that self-evident?" May began. Just then they heard the sound of the child's leather-soled shoes clattering down the stairs and across the timbered floor of the hall.

She came back into the room, her cheeks flushed, breathless from running up and down stairs. "I couldn't find it anywhere," she said, gasping. "I looked in all the usual places. Will you come with me to look again?"

"Never mind the medicine now, love. Let's have some tea instead."

"Oh can we please? Can we have it now?"

"Yes, right now. Not a moment later. Come with me to the kitchen."

The child danced round May excitedly. "Let's have tea and toast and sandwiches and boiled eggs and sausages and fruit cake and chocolate and marshmallows and can I carry the tray?" she said as she skipped out of the room.

"We'll see," said Aunt May.

"Can I make the toast then?"

"We'll see," said Aunt May.

Nina looked after them as they went from the room and she heard herself give a sudden harsh sigh. She went across to the fire and threw herself into the big shabby chintz-covered armchair. For a long time she gazed idly into the flames, unmoving, her hands resting on the wooden arm-rests, her legs stretched out full-length before her. So, May had noticed how happy Katherine was the last day they had come here? she thought. Although who wouldn't have? High as kite was an understatement. They had taken a risk coming to see May because she was bound to notice the change in Katherine's mood, but Nina couldn't resist the impulse to show her off, even though she knew how foolish it was and disloyal to Elinor. But besides that she needed Aunt May's assistance however unwittingly given. She had always been conscious

35

that, in May's house it was harder for anyone to be critical of her. Katherine had said once that whenever Nina wanted someone to like her better she brought them to visit May, and it was true. She knew she was at her best in May's presence because the old lady drew out a different side of her, a self that was more childlike, more innocent.

She had been so desperately nervous that day, she needed all the help she could get. When she had surprised Katherine at the airport, she had feared at first that she had made a mistake. She thought her vaguely hostile and withdrawn, but by the time they were seated at May's fireside, her mood had altered totally to one of radiant good humour. Nina had been very careful to make no move towards her that day until they were standing in May's kitchen. Nothing had happened until they went down to the kitchen to make tea.

She was feeling very cautious, partly because she was unsure of Katherine's reaction, but also because she was genuinely doubtful about getting involved with her again. One side of her wanted to think they could learn to be affectionate friends and that the atmosphere of May's house was the best one to get them on the right footing. But she hadn't reckoned with Katherine. Could she have forgotten in such a short time how reckless she was? How ready to follow her immediate instincts? And so it had happened at last when they were standing in May's big draughty kitchen with its old range and flagged floor. Katherine was taking down cups from the dresser and Nina was sitting on the table watching her. Katherine turned with her hands full, walked across to the table and put the cups and saucers on a tray. She had to stand in front of Nina to do this. Nina remembered that moment perfectly because it had taken her such an effort to surrender to it, to the risk of allowing it to start again. To risk the fear of rejection and the danger of acceptance. Katherine reached out her arms and slipped them round Nina's waist. She pulled her close to her and kissed her neck softly, and then her lips. Nina's heart hammered against her ribs and she felt so panic-stricken that for a moment she thought she wouldn't be able to go through with it. But it was Katherine who rescued them. Or damned them. She took her hands from Nina's waist and slid them beneath the loose cotton of her sweater and reached for her breasts. She looked into her eyes and said without a tremor in her voice: "As soon as we've made this tea, let's go home to bed."

So much had happened since. But the longing Nina felt at the memory of it was as poignant as ever. And more painful.

Conscious of the heavy beating of her heart, she opened the diary and began to read again the closely written script, not knowing what she might discover. Knowing even less what she would like to.

Chapter Four

September, Clare.

That was the beginning, of this astonishing time; the start of a
metamorphosis, a long journey that's carried me out of one
life, as an ordinary wife and mother, into a new, totally
unexpected world or a new way of being in the old world.

After meeting you in the hospital, I took you up on your
invitation and began to visit your house; at first careful to
find a good excuse, but very soon forgetting to invent one.
Within weeks of getting to know you I'd become addicted to
the special atmosphere of your house: the spontaneity, the
sense of freedom and space, generated by yourself and Elinor
and all the friends who dropped by and stayed to argue about
work, and politics and love affairs. I tried to make my
interest in you seem normal, relaxed, like any other casual
friendship. I tried to conceal my fascination, my preoccupying
need to draw close to you. But from that first visit I was in
thrall to you, enchanted by every word you spoke. And as
soon as we were left alone, I found it impossible to control my
curiosity.

I recognised you at once as an essential force in my life,
almost like a force of nature. Though you weren't like anyone
I might have imagined, if it had occurred to me to conceive of
you in advance. You weren't made according to any image I
had: the image shaped by those I'd loved before you.

38

Everything about you was new, unexpected and took me completely by surprise. And my response to you was the most unexpected thing of all.

I plagued you with questions, wanting to know every detail of your life and upbringing. Who did you play with when you were a child? What did you play? What name did they call you then? Did you like it? Where was your first school? What was your teacher's name? Did you have a favourite subject? What did you wear on your first day at school? Who was your first lover? Who gave you your first kiss? The first deep sexual kiss? What was he wearing – the boy who first kissed you? Was it a boy who first kissed you? And before this – before adolescence and love and sex – who did you love? Who were your parents? Where did you live? By the sea? In the country? The city? But even as I showered you with these absurd demands, I had the sense of knowing the answers. I felt I could picture you exactly as a little girl. This is how she would have been in childhood, on her way to school, sitting eating tomato sandwiches in her aunt's kitchen. This same compact self. Igneous and sceptical in the same moment. An ancient soul – that was what sprang to mind; that clichéd phrase from eastern philosophy took on new meaning.

But more important maybe than all of this, is how I, immediately, became inspired by your politics, your social vision. It's not an exaggeration to say that for me the world you and Elinor shared seemed to be filled with a special air. When I listened to you and your friends talking and debating political issues, I had the sensation of finding answers for the first time to life-long questions. All my ill-defined criticisms and frustrations with the social order made sense to me at last. And I began to see what I could do about them. Before this, politics had no interest for me, or at least not the abstract, patronising posturing of so much that passes for political concern. But your convictions were something entirely different, not generalisations about other people's lives or empty speech-making, but beliefs rooted in practice, in everyday personal experience. Ideas and action seemed inextricably linked. Or rather growing out of each other, like soil and root. But, then all your beliefs have this organic quality about them, that makes your way of life seem inevitable, predetermined.

Yes, I know, this sounds pompous and grandiose. Am I deluding myself, lending high purpose to what was no more than an inflammation of the senses? Greed and gluttony and blind craving seizing control of me so that I was helpless in their power and had to invent these rationalisations to save a vestige of dignity? Blind craving – that much is true if nothing else. My need for you was from the start fierce and predatory, generous, ruthless and high minded all at once, from the start. Maybe it's because I've had to fight to gain you, because I've had to destroy lives before I could connect mine with yours, maybe because of this I've needed, more than most, a gloss of idealism and vision about my feelings. Who knows? Anyhow I know the last would be your favourite explanation because you like to think yourself ordinary and pragmatic. Plodding from one necessity to the next. Because the things that appear inspired to others seem just the necessary practical steps of each day to you.

How long had I known you before I heard that you painted?

When I met you you told me only that you worked as a radio presenter, doing a live phone-in show on a local station. When you told me its name I realised that I'd heard it before and I said with too much eagerness and an awkward attempt at teasing: "You're quite a star – I know people who stay home just to listen to you!"

You shrugged your shoulders in your sceptical way and dismissed the flattery.

"A big fish in a very small tank. There's nothing exciting about being stuck in an underground studio, listening for hours to people you wouldn't give five minutes to at a bus stop." This cynicism was good-humoured and deliberate. I saw that you were determined to appear ordinary, as unremarkable as this solid façade suggested.

It must have been Elinor who first told me about your painting and told me why you had given it up. She took me upstairs to see your work – you had hidden it away out of sight from visitors, but the bedroom and one small studio at the back of the house were crammed with pictures. Dozens of canvases, of all sizes, abstract and figurative paintings, landscapes and domestic interiors. And, running the full length of one wall, a series of vivid portraits of the female nude: a young woman with broad shoulders and a strong, sinuous body, standing at a window, light streaming onto her face and yellow hair. Elinor told me then that you'd spent one entire year painting your own head and body from every conceivable angle and position. Every day you'd stood in front of a full-length mirror and painted yourself. Every bone and muscle sketched and painted separately until you had built up a total, comprehensive portrait. Then, abruptly, when the series was complete you abandoned the studio for good.

I stood gazing at this powerful, intense work covering the walls and was unable to find anything appropriate to say. I was afraid of sounding ignorant, which I was. After a few minutes, I asked shyly why you'd given it up. Elinor looked at me with an expression I couldn't fathom and held out her hands, palms upwards in a gesture that said who knows? She seemed impatient or irritated and I wondered how many people had asked her this.

Long afterwards, you told me how you felt about it. You said that after years of obsession with it, having studied in London and for a while at the Beaux Arts in Paris, you had finally seen sense. You had come to admit your own limitations. Besides, you had grown steadily disenchanted with the whole notion of art making and the grubby world of art selling and management. You'd grown weary of what you saw as its pretensions, its demands, its lack of consequence. You said you wanted work that you could measure every day, something effective, useful. Art had begun to seem an escape to you. You loathed the petty rivalries of artists, their self-absorption and the driving egotism that they concealed behind pious slogans about culture. For you, painting was about communication. If there was no one to see your painting, there was no point to it, and yet in order to paint, it was necessary to forget people, ignore their needs, make yourself inviolate and self-contained. You told me you did your best work in the year that you lived alone and saw no one. You let a cousin die without visiting her so that you could get on with a commission. That's what it took, you said. And this abstraction, this rejection and fleeing from the world frightened and appalled you.

I remember you said much later, when I had known you for several months, that you didn't think you could ever fall in love while you were working on a painting or even planning one. Because the creative energy necessary to fall in love – to create the romance, the vision, the illusion, went into the work instead. Only when that energy was free, set loose to wander where it would, were you able to sustain infatuation. Needless to say I didn't want to agree with this. I could hardly accept that you only loved deeply when other forms of self-expression were blocked or denied to you. After all, I don't think you believed it yourself. You liked so much to pontificate, to shock me (who was so easily shocked) with your passionate denunciations.

But you did seem to believe that romance was a kind of illusion-making you had indulged yourself in for years. You liked to boast that you had fallen in love at least every five years since you were seven! You gave me exact and detailed accounts of your first childhood infatuations. With girls, of course, even then! You claimed to find it astonishing that I could recall nothing to match them. You said, for all the good it had done for my childhood, Freud might never have existed! Not to this day would I dare to say whether even half of your stories are true, or whether you simply made them all up on the spur of the moment to dazzle me.

If your theory about your own romantic patterns was accurate, you were more than overdue a new love affair by the time you met me. You and Elinor had been together for seven years already. The strength and persistence of this passion persuaded you that your old ways were a thing of the past, that falling in love was a phase, like your love of painting, that belonged to a stage of life you'd outgrown.

So what was it about me that had the power to explode this long-sought-after stability? What did I have that was capable of distracting you from the woman who seemed to be the love of your life? What made you risk your happiness, your whole accustomed way of life? How could I know and should I want to? Some things are better left unspoken, safe from scrutiny.

Of course no court of inquiry would accept this kind of shirking. Balance, impartiality would be demanded. What could I offer? The usual excuses. All the things you told me. The flattery and the crazed inventions. Once, you said you thought you liked me so much because I contradicted all your preconceived notions of the good Yank! And then you said that, whatever you claimed as the reason, no one could love me for myself and not my auburn hair! You said we were so different that our attraction had the magnetic force of polar opposites and that it gave you stability. You told me the things other people have told me, of course, and things nobody had ever said before – that even now I don't want to confide to paper for fear of damaging them. You said you loved my blue eyes, my easy laughter. You said you loved my hands. You said my touch had a magic power for you. The very first time I casually put my arm around your shoulder, you had felt a force like an electric current pass through you.

You also said I was the first person you'd ever been close to whom society would give a clean bill of health. If this was a nice way of saying I was ordinary, I didn't mind because it's true. A secondary school teacher, a mother, a wife, a nice middle-class girl who married a nice middle-class man. I know how well I fulfil the stereotype. I seem to have travelled always, without any conscious effort or design, the centre track in life. But when I said this, you at once protested loudly, saying you meant only that I knew how to pass. It was a conjuring trick, a brilliant disguise. I created a surface calm – with my serene Grecian profile (yes, I salted away this delicious flattery for just such a rainy day as this), but that underneath this stagecraft the currents were as turbulent and unpredictable as in any other life. People like myself, you said, the outwardly normal, were the wildest of all when faced with true temptation. What were we hiding, you asked, behind this pretence of calm? Fear of insanity? Fear of evil? Fear of great success? Or fear of arousing envy?

Anyhow, the truth is I didn't care what you said. I didn't mind why you liked me, so long as you did. And, besides, I was afraid of giving myself away by seeming to take you seriously because I could never tell your teasing from your most sincere beliefs.

But this isn't the way to tell our story. To do us justice, I ought to start somewhere else entirely. I should start where love stories always start. In doubt and confusion. With a series of happy accidents. Why else would we say "falling" in love?

We fell into one another's grasp in hardly perceptible

stages. All through that autumn, walking side by side, heads lowered in shyness, exchanging stories of heartbreak and loss, the bad times, the foolish times when we were young and knew no better; promising ourselves never to fall victim again. Analysing our failures, each confiding to the other the fundamental flaw we recognised in ourselves; the flaw that unravelled the pattern time after time. While we talked, because we were only friends, because you were in love with Elinor and I was married with two children, we were quite unguarded, incautious – we said anything that occurred to us, granting each other a licence impossible between lovers.

I allowed myself a vulnerability with you I didn't show or experience with men. With men I had always been too much in control of events. Too sure of myself. Untested, untried. It seems to me now that the absoluteness of their desires kept me safely at the shallow end of the pool. Something fixed in their natures, opaque and unexplored, made life somehow formal and concealed even at the most intimate. You said, of course, it was always like this. You said it was the pleasure of heterosexuality; the way the set boundaries between men and women in our culture kept each gender safe and sound; their identity fixed and immutable. Like creatures gazing at each other across a fence, allowed to see and smell one another, even touch, but never capable of exchanging places.

You didn't encourage me. At least, that's to say, you didn't try to seduce me. Even though you were the experienced one, the confirmed lover of women, you didn't try to persuade me. In fact you had this strange quality of patience or detachment that I'd never experienced with men. I felt baffled by it at first. I remember thinking one day that I was like a butterfly which had landed in your open hand, and if you had made the slightest movement I'd have flown off at once, in fright. But you didn't – you were too clever for that. Or too sensitive. For the first time in my life, I was really free to choose. It made me the subject of desire instead of the object. It was I who must make the first move, speak the first words; words that very nearly cost me my life to pronounce.

I remember you trying to talk me out of it. Telling me that the life I was sailing into so blithely wouldn't be easy. You said you sometimes wished you could give it up yourself. Return to the straight world, as you called it. I remember how you talked about it. You said society made it so difficult at times, that you thought you'd give it up. That the intensity between women lovers made you nostalgic sometimes for the ease of life with men. You wished you could take refuge in normality, in the leisurely conquest of men. Men with their simple desires. Their ready, reliable satisfactions. Your relationship with men (and you'd certainly had your fair share when you were young) had been so easy by comparison. You said you'd always felt at home with them, and felt you understood them. Probably because you'd always been aware of your desire for women, you hadn't needed their sexual attention and, sensing this dimly, they were fascinated. They pursued you constantly, and you were for a while happy enough to be the object of their affection. As Aunt May confirmed to me, you'd always had some adoring man trailing after you.

You talked of the sense of relaxation you had in their company. The sense of social acceptance. You wished you could retreat sometimes to this safe harbour of public approval. To be envied and admired by others. To walk in public with your arm about your man, and see strangers smile at you. To please your mother, make your father proud. Excite the envy of your friends. To have them say – "don't you have all the luck?" To have them ready to weep for you when things went wrong. Congratulate your successes. Ah – the fruits of acceptance; the careless, unthinking, complacent reward for being normal. Restored to the bosom of your family, the respect of your neighbours. All this in return for a little fucking.

That's what you told me. It didn't make a blind bit of difference. I didn't believe you for a moment. You said it to free yourself of the responsibility of leading me astray. You had told me the worst. I could never say I hadn't been given fair warning!

I find it hard now to believe there was ever a time when I didn't know you physically, a time when making love with you was not the central preoccupation of my existence. But we did negotiate a slow, circuitous journey from friendship to love. I remember vividly, in those early weeks, the sense of tension between us, the total absorption in your presence – unable to take my eyes from you for a second while you were in the same room, hanging on every word. I should have known long before I did what was happening. Any fool could have seen it, watching us together. The slow teasing courtship of looks and glances and secret laughter. All the hanging about doing nothing in particular waiting for it to happen. Waiting for the moment that would make it inevitable.

Chapter Five

October, Dublin.

"Be careful now. Don't fall!" Aunt May called out, keeping a wary eye on the child. They had finished tea and cleared the table. May refused to hear of washing dishes, but Nina had slipped down to the kitchen when she wasn't looking.

Lizzie had drawn a chair up to the bookshelf and, standing on tiptoe, was trying to reach down a box from the top shelf.

"There's another biscuit box up here. Are there photographs in it as well?"

"Oh, there might be some I suppose. Bring it down to me if you want and we'll have a look. But be careful."

Lizzie took the box in both hands and jumped off the chair. She carried it across the room holding it out stiffly before her as though it was a glass of something she might spill. She sat on the hearth-rug and pulled the lid off. The box was stuffed with photographs and letters.

"These are all different ones. New people!" she cried excitedly. She dug her hand down into the middle of the pile and drew out a small sepia-coloured snap.

"Who's this – the man with the black hair?"

"Oh, that's an old flame of Nina's."

"What's an old flame?"

"A boyfriend."

"Did you have an old flame ever?"

"Oh yes – years ago, pet."

"Is he dead now?"

"I think so."

"Why didn't you marry him?" Lizzie asked gravely.

Aunt May smiled, but there was a note of real regret in her voice when she answered. "There was a saying we had long ago – I met the man I'd marry and the man who'd marry me. But they weren't the same."

"What happened to Nina's boyfriend?"

"Oh, he went the way of the rest," May said. "She left a trail of broken hearts behind her. She could charm the birds from the trees, I'm afraid, so everyone spoilt her."

"How do you charm birds in trees?"

"Oh, that's a question for your mother, child, not for me," May said, her eyes brightening.

Lizzie made no response to this, but went on sorting through the photographs in silence, picking them out at random. When she spoke again her mind had moved to another topic.

"Nina said she'd take me to see her new office tomorrow," she said.

"I didn't promise," Nina said, "I don't know if I'll be free."

May watched them from her vantage point by the fire. She lit another of her fine, dark cigars before she spoke again.

"You work much too hard," May said. "You need a holiday. Weren't you thinking of going away?"

"Yes, but with Elizabeth in hospital I had to cancel things."

"Why don't you go to see your friend Katherine? That would relax you."

"It's too late. She'll have left. Lizzie got sick and . . . "

"When do you start work again?" May asked.

"Next week."

"Well, at least you have some days to rest." May shovelled more coal on the fire roughly, so that a cloud of smoke billowed into the room.

"I was listening to your programme this morning," she said. "The girl who's filling in for you is very good but she doesn't compare with you. She's too brisk. She sounds as if she has better things to do than be listening to everybody's troubles.

And why wouldn't she? Who'd have the patience to sit day after day listening to them all? I don't know how you do it. I can't understand why it is that they want to expose the most intimate details of their life on the national airwaves. And all the work it makes for you. All those letters they write you. I don't know how you manage to get through them."

"Some people have no one else to talk to," Nina answered. "And it can be easier to tell a stranger."

"Yes, but three million strangers?" May asked in bewilderment. "It's the modern world I suppose – this insatiable thirst for scandal and confession. But sure someone has to take the place of the priests, I suppose."

Nina smiled but made no answer. She sat quietly, the notebook open in her lap, and let her gaze wander round the big softly lit sitting-room that she liked so much. She knew every inch of it, every ornament, every stick of furniture. She knew how the light fell at any given hour of the day, the shadows cast in alcoves, the particular smell of each room. She watched her aunt talking to Lizzie, entertaining her, distracting her attention without seeming to, allowing Nina a little time to herself. And she reflected, not for the first time, how fortunate she was to have been raised by May. Although so much older than Nina and so different in outlook and upbringing, they suited one another remarkably well. May made no claim to liberalism and, despite her direct and outspoken manner, when it came to personal matters she believed, in the way of her generation, in discretion. But underneath this outward show she was naturally tolerant. She allowed for the mitigating influence of circumstance and believed that in any conflict between the heart and convention the heart should rule.

Above all Nina felt a debt of gratitude to May for her readiness to understand her lifestyle. In this she was more accepting than many people years younger than herself, people who liked to believe themselves progressive. May didn't say much, but Nina felt that she treated her relationships with great respect. In her understated way she made clear that she thought Nina's way of loving as worthy as any other. She had always made her friends welcome to the house and asked no questions about the exact nature of the relationships. She invited them to tea, played cards with them, gave them her best whiskey and the chosen few she invited to the races. But when it came to serious gambling Elinor was her favourite companion. They went to all the big race days together and May swore that her luck was always in when Elinor drove her. She treated her like a second niece and Elinor responded in kind, fussing over her, indulging her, listening to her stories and making her laugh.

"I've never seen this one before," the child remarked holding out another photograph.

"Yes, it was taken at Powerscourt when I was twenty-one."

"Who's that man smiling at you?"

"Nina's father."

"He doesn't look like her."

"No, she takes after her mother."

"Do I take after *my* mother?"

"You know you do."

"Did Nina ever see her father?"

"No, she didn't."

"What's his name?"

"Robert."

"That's a nice name," Lizzie said.

"Yes."

"Is he dead yet?"

"Yes."

"Everyone you know is dead," Lizzie said and began to pile the photographs back into the box, gathering them up in handfuls.

Nina sat with a glass of brandy by the window. She had her back turned to the others but she could hear Lizzie's eager questions and May's patient answers. She heard Lizzie begging to be told once again the account of Nina's life in the orphanage and about the day Aunt May came to rescue her. She delighted in this story for some reason and asked to hear it almost every time they came to visit May.

"Where will I begin?" Aunt May asked.

"Begin at the beginning," Lizzie said.

"Nina lived in the orphanage until she was five."

"Why did you not come for her before that?" Lizzie asked. Her voice was tense with concentration when she spoke and she listened with a kind of eager apprehension to every word. "Why did you leave her all that time?"

"Because I didn't know she was there. I didn't know she had been born until her mother wrote and told me just before she died."

Nina stroked Albert the cat and half listened to May telling the complicated narrative in her brusque practical way. She had heard it so often she knew every word by heart. She listened now as if it were a story about someone else, a story in a book. It seemed to have so little relevance to her present life. But then only one subject held any interest for her. Her thoughts returned obsessively to Katherine. With every page of the journal she read she grew more anguished. The sensual memories that filled her head tormented her. What was she to do with this desire? She felt herself growing angry with Katherine. Resenting the power she held over her, the ease with which she invaded her mind and space. Even here in her aunt's house as she sat drinking brandy and listening to Lizzie's chatter, here where she had always before found peace of mind and contentment, she was distracted and impatient. She struggled against the feeling – half fear, half longing that at any moment she might appear beside her and, bending down, place a deep kiss on her lips as she had in this very house. Then, just as unreasonably, her mood changed, her irritation with Katherine switched to her surroundings and to the presence of Aunt May and Lizzie. With a new sense of guilt she found herself wishing them gone, wishing she were alone so that she could read undisturbed, and surrender herself to reverie.

Chapter Six

September, Clare.

Night falls so quickly here. After a brief, burnished sunset when the sky turns crimson, then violet, and the clouds gold, suddenly, like a great black curtain, darkness descends, obscuring every field and ditch.

I took the road by the lake on my way home and very nearly lost my bearings, staggering in the sudden darkness, the road so black I couldn't see my feet. The wind hurled around me and made strange wailing noises in the bare fuchsia. At one point, as I neared the brow of the hill, it forced me to a stand-still. I stood leaning into it, gasping for breath. Then, for a few minutes, it subsided as if taking pity on a stranger and I managed to walk the few more yards to the gate. The path leading to the house has turned to a marsh. The stream in the ditch has burst its banks and the water cascades across the road. I stumbled through the slushy mud that gripped my boots as if unwilling to let me go. Everything here seems to have an independent life. A will of its own.

"What would you be wanting here for two weeks at the end of September?" Máire McCarthy asked as soon as she had me alone in the shop this afternoon. I was standing near the door, shaking the rain from my hair, glad of her welcome and glad to be inside the sheltering clutter of the small room that was packed with an extraordinary range of goods. Everything it was possible to offer for sale seemed to be stacked on the shelves or hanging from the ceiling: from wellingtons and beach balls, to detergents and expensive bottles of French wine. I edged myself between the frozen food compartment and the stacks of briquettes, to reach the rack of picture postcards, wanting to choose one for the boys. As I tried to decide between two (the conventional image of a heavy headed, pensive donkey looking over a stone wall or the new style of parody, a photograph of camels trekking across a yellow desert beneath the caption "Greetings from Ireland,") Máire Mac added: "You'd need some reason out of the ordinary to endure the weather here. But then maybe you don't notice it. You Americans have such romantic notions."

This annoyed me, need I say – this easy dismissal of a foreigner's whim. And it aroused in me, suddenly, an extraordinary temptation to tell her the truth. Why? I don't know. It certainly wasn't because I thought she'd be sympathetic. Maybe it was just a bout of perversity. Or because I need so badly to talk about you I'd seize on any excuse. Whatever it was I almost heard myself saying, "I would be wanting Nina. I'd be wanting her here for a month, for a year, for a lifetime." Yes, I very nearly looked her in the eye – shrewd, sceptical and tolerant as she is, leaning her heavy breasts on the counter while she regarded me with good-natured, lazy curiosity: "I'm waiting for Nina Kavanagh, my lover, to come from Dublin. I'm waiting to hear that she has told the woman she lives with that she loves me and wants to be with me."

Then, with the uncanny telepathy they have she seemed to pluck the thought from my head: "Ah well and sure you won't be so lonely when your friend arrives," she said, and asked, as if to take any harm out of it, if the house was warm and had I enough briquettes to be going on with. As I took my firelighters from her and a litre of milk she said, seemingly apropos of nothing: "It's unlikely now you'd be comfortable enough for visitors in that place above. Sure isn't it no more than an old cabin fixed up by the Germans?"

"Dutch," I said.

"Well Dutch or German – isn't it all the one? Aren't they all mad for any old ruin they can lay their hands on? And wouldn't they pay any price for the old stone and a few slates? Isn't it well for them and they having nothing better to do with their money?"

When I got home I found a stray cat crouched on the windowsill crying pitifully as if it hadn't been fed for days. What did I tell you? Don't I always attract them? She's a beautiful grey and black tabby. She rushed into the house, as if she knew it well, the second I opened the door and sat yowling at my feet. Of course I gave in. I poured her a bowl of milk and when that didn't seem to content her, I chopped up some of the blue cheese I'd bought from Máire Mac. She accepted it with delight.

I sit by the fire and read over the last pages of this journal. What am I doing, I wonder? I don't know why I feel compelled to write all this down and address it to you as if you didn't know anything about it, as if you were a stranger or a newly made confidant to whom I wanted to confide the story of this passion. But I am compelled. It gives me a deep sense of satisfaction to put it on paper, to address it to you as if it were a love letter I might post to you. (And who knows, maybe I will?) Anyhow, setting our story down in writing seems to give it an air of permanence, as though our life together was something fixed and safe from alteration.

What do you think a court would make of this chronicle, so far? Would they find it melodramatic? Self-indulgent? They'd certainly consider it dangerously abnormal. They'd say that women don't fall in love with their friends unless there is a predisposition to the state. These things don't just happen, do they? Why did they spend so much time together? Why did they not take some action to avoid what was happening between them? Where were their husbands? Oh no, this won't stand up to scrutiny at all. They would demand the facts of my life – my actions – where I went and what I did in the last twelve years of my marriage to Malachy. Actions not feelings are the proper concern of the court.

"So can we ask you to give a brief outline of your extramarital affairs, Mrs Newman? You had relations with other men during your marriage, is that correct?"

"One, only, your Honour."

"But, a few years later you fell in love with a lesbian whose lover had been a personal friend of yours?"

"Yes."

"You then began a relationship with her during which you left your husband and children and moved into a house on your own where you waited for her to join you?"

"I told you before I didn't leave the boys. I took them with me."

"She did not join you, however, did she, Mrs Newman? She frustrated your desire and expectation by remaining with her lesbian lover?"

"Yes."

"Would you please tell the court whether you consider the way of life just described could be said to indicate a stable personality, a responsible one? Would you consider such a woman capable of caring for two vulnerable dependants?"

Good God, this all sounds damning, doesn't it? Surely I can manage better than this? If it please the court . . . The facts? What bits and pieces, flotsam and jetsam of experience could I haul together under that heading? When you came into my life, what was I? Who was I? A married woman – yes. A happily married woman? Yes. This is true. I loved my husband. I still love him. I was a happily married woman with two young children. (Or is this only what we all pretend? All of us presenting this bland face to the world so long as we are not actually deserted or beaten.) But I did love Malachy. Yes, I did, even if I knew the happiness of love had been lost somewhere long before.

I know many people will find this hard to accept. They'll demand at once – if you loved him why did you leave him? And, if you really loved a man how could you be satisfied by a woman? They want to believe that a married woman in her middle thirties who falls in love with another woman must have been essentially lesbian to begin with – not a "real" heterosexual. This makes it seem less threatening, easier for them to tolerate. Even some of your friends would share this view, wouldn't they? And describe me as "latent" or "closeted". They suspect women like myself of playing it safe – denying our real nature until we've established ourselves in the conventional roles of wife and mother. But in my case, at least, they're wrong. I was genuinely attracted to all the men in my life. I want to say that at the outset. I want it on the record. I was entirely and contentedly heterosexual. Yes, that's true. (Apart from that one adolescent infatuation when I was at convent school which I'd forgotten until I told you about it.)

So what happened to cause such an extraordinary alteration in my way of life? Did I fall in love with you or fall in love with women? Did I grow tired of Malachy or tired of men? I'm not sure I can (or want to) answer any of these questions. But I know this much, at the time I met you I was already searching unconsciously for some revelation, some radical transformation. I recognised very well that I'd come to the end of the road with Malachy. We loved each other still, deeply, but their was more pain in our feeling than pleasure.

Whatever the motive when I told people I was going to leave Malachy they thought I must be out of my mind. What more could I possibly want, they demanded. They were impatient, even resentful. Of course I couldn't satisfy them because the question I asked myself had no answer. If I couldn't love Malachy what man could I love more? Yes; this was the problem. Even now, when I remember what we used to be to one another I can scarcely believe how far we've travelled.

If I had to sum up in a word the root of his appeal for me, I'd say – abundance. An abundance of all life's gifts, good looks, class assurance, self-belief. "Don't worry – I'll see to it!", were the first words I ever heard him speak and they seemed to cast a spell over me that lasted for years, reaching into some hidden chamber of my psyche, some half buried folk memory of bereavement and offered to heal it and to make restitution.

He came from a wealthy, Wasp family who hadn't known want for generations. Rich, generous, easy, he had always known he could get what ever he wanted. I remember my first experience of this class inheritance, when, shortly after we met, he terrified me, one summer's evening after a day spent swimming and sunbathing at the beach, by walking barefoot into the dinning room of the Shelbourne Hotel and with unshakeable sang-froid asking the waiter for a table for two.

How seductive this arrogance was to me – an Irish American convent schoolgirl; middle-class but never able to take either class position or money for granted. Haunted as we were by memories of scarcity and banishment. My parents lived a reasonably stable, comfortable life. But they couldn't learn to be careless of it. And they didn't want their children to be.

Malachy by contrast was generous to a fault and blithely optimistic. He seemed to hold out the promise of plenty in all things; emotional and material. He made me feel safe and protected. In his company I felt immediately approved of by family and friends. Even by strangers passed in the street. I'd had lovers before I met him, of course, one or two I felt seriously about, but none had anything resembling the force of his appeal to me. None of them gave me the one thing I needed at that stage of my life – self-confidence. They were too self-obsessed, too demanding. And the more I saw of other men the more attractive Malachy became. One man in particular, a man much older than myself, paved the path for Malachy. He was the kind of guy I suppose every woman needs once in her life, someone to wreck herself on – charming, fragile and manipulative. But this isn't the place to talk about Harry. I'll tell you about him some other time.

I think I'd have liked Malachy whenever we'd met but meeting him then, nursing my first serious disillusion, he seemed like light after darkness, the antithesis of all I had come to take for granted with men. We met at a party given by an old school friend of mine. I remember exactly my first impression of him because it exemplified that special mix he has of artlessness and arrogance. Easy and sophisticated he stood out at once from the men around him with his slightly offbeat "preppy" look – the tweed jacket, the denim shirt, the baggy fatigues, his characteristic air of negligent style. The record player had broken down and no one knew how to fix it – the evening teetered on the edge of disaster when suddenly Malachy appeared in the doorway and said – "Don't worry I'll see to it." And selecting one of the better bottles of wine from the kitchen table he left the house. Ten minutes later he was back again, smiling triumphantly brandishing a new recorder player and speakers.

"Where on earth did you get them, at this time of night?" the man I'd arrived with asked him.

"Oh, I just went next door for a minute and asked one of the neighbours very nicely, if she could lend me one." He smiled, a big self-confident, ingenuous smile. "She was delighted with the wine!" he added and shrugged his shoulders as if it were something anybody would have thought of doing.

That's how he was. Is. He carries things off. Splendidly. Effortlessly. Nothing daunts him. Those first words I heard him speak: "Don't worry – I'll see to it," express his personality exactly.

Immediately, that evening, I fell under its charm. He was witty and entertaining, a great story teller. And, as he was the first to tell me, also a very good lover, because he really liked women and loved to give pleasure. He enjoyed showing off, in bed, of course. It was a matter of pride to him, his fitness, his magnificent physique, his total suitedness to the role. He had the same happy vanity about his prowess as a lover as he had about everything else. He was good and knew it so why shouldn't he smile and be generous? We'd go out to dinner in the evening after a day in bed, my mind dazed, my body aching so that I could hardly sit still. He would catch me shifting from side to side and laugh in delighted complicity, stretching out his hand to squeeze my thigh under the table.

I remember one afternoon in July in his mother's house, fucking on his mother's bed while she was down at the beach. Covered in sweat, our flesh sticking together, making small squeals of complaint at each movement away from the other. The sun shining through the half open shutters casting our shadow on the wall beside us. Or rather his shadow: the shadow of his small round buttocks rising and falling. I watched lazily the perfect mirror image of the action taking place on my body. The eager flesh moving in this fixed mechanical rhythm. Clear as a photograph. Perfectly adjusted. Mindless. Set for all time, made perfect by the centuries. And recognised that this was what I wanted, this is what appealed to me in sex with a man. The annihilation of personality. The sense of being in thrall to the species; compelled by an archaic primeval ritual. Beyond choice or individual responsibility.

Joined with the blind instinctive striving of the planet. The urge to life itself. Absurd and pointless. Perfectly executed. Terrible in its individual intensity.

Afterwards walking arm in arm along the river bank, I felt myself draw the gaze of the fishermen and passers-by, smiling approval. The whole world encouraging, applauding. A handsome couple. The joy of life. The pride of youth. And I was still young enough to be proud of myself for doing it so well. The emblem of adulthood. Proud of being at last that amazing ordinary thing – a woman. And this fucking was not the only living proof of it but the very core, its nature and foundation.

For years I lived cocooned in Malachy's devotion. His great plans, his enthusiasms, his certainties, his needs. I was safe. I was busy. I was happy. A lovely son, a wonderful husband, the envy of others. And then . . . very slowly, year by year, it began to dawn on me that I was losing all sense of my former identity. Gradually but ineluctably. I began to doubt that I existed as a separate person. I began to feel a projection of his love rather than an individual in my own right. I began to seek out new relationships. I flirted with men and got entangled in intense romantic friendships that gave me a sense of myself outside my marriage but because they weren't sexual I pretended they did us no real damage.

Then, shortly after coming to Dublin, when I got the teaching job in Sandymount, I found myself getting unexpectedly close to one of my male colleagues, Richard Farrell, who taught English. Richard who had this disconcerting habit of saying exactly what you wished he wouldn't. Like the afternoon he gave me a lift home when my car broke down and he looked up at the house when he parked on Breemore road and with that sad clown's smile that he specialised in and said, "How is it a woman who seems to have everything has this air of never having had the one thing she most wanted?"

I laughed at him and told him not to be so clichéd and then I asked him in for coffee.

He was funny, easy to talk to and a good listener. We found that we shared a love of traditional Irish music, an enthusiasm I'd never been able to share with Malachy who liked to dismiss it, delightedly, as being all about beards, beer bellys and nationalist bravado. So when a few weeks before Christmas, Richard told me he'd got some tickets for a concert at the Point – how could I refuse? And why would Malachy want to come with us?

Well you know the rest of story or you can imagine it. Why did I let it happen? I can't pretend I was swept off my feet. Was it somethimg special in Richard? His quietness and self effacement after Malachy's ebullience? Or the fact that he was such a good listener and made me feel important? It has to be said he wasn't all that good in bed and yet we had three months of total physical infatuation. Maybe I was just trying to send a message to Malachy with the usual subtlety. Was I daring him to stop loving me? To relinquish the image he clung to so stubbornly of the idyllic partnership? I know I was beginning to feel stifled by his relentless love of me, his unwavering determination to have the perfect relationship whatever the cost.

Three months of physical infatuation and then Malachy found us out. Or I stopped wanting him – not to know. He was devastated, amazed and desperate to win me back. I remember exactly what he said to me, sitting in bed one Saturday morning, because it was one of the those landmark moments when you know you're doing the right thing for the wrong reason but can't stop yourself or care enough to do otherwise.

"Whatever he gives you," he said, and it was typical of Malachy that he could say what he did without seeming either pitiable or arrogant, but with the self-confidence to be totally unguarded, "I can give you too – if only you'd ask me."

I was guilt stricken and contrite, of course. I agreed to everything he suggested, without a word of argument. I gave up Richard and went back to my marriage. Tried harder than ever before. We both did. We thought everything was back on the rails. We even said sometimes – isn't it better than before: more honest, more real?

But a shadow had fallen over our lives; a small, chill shadow of mutual doubt and self distrust. And nothing we said could erase it.

I found a bicycle in the outshed this morning and rode down to the shop. Máire Mac is gradually extracting from me all the relevant facts. We begin with a lengthy preamble that's intended to soften me and dull my attention so that when the real inquiries are made I won't find them intrusive. She leans over the wooden counter and gazes off into the distance as if seeing a reality hidden to others.

Today she set about getting my matrimonial position clear. She proceeds with great subtlety, making false statements that I feel obliged to correct: "Well and isn't it grand for you that you can stay as long as you like and with no family to worry about!"

Of course, before I can think I find myself rushing to set the record straight: I have a family – two young boys and while I think of it – does she sell phone cards because I need to call them today? She feigns great surprise, at hearing this.

"Sure they could be no more than infants and you so young."

"No, I'm afraid not. In fact, they're almost teenagers – ten and twelve."

"Well now and I'd never have thought it. And I suppose your husband is looking after them in Dublin?"

"As a matter of fact he's in Galway. He's just got a new job there."

"A teacher is it, like yourself?"

"No, he's an architect."

"Well now Galway's a fine place, I suppose, if you like it. And have you a house found there yet, it can be very expensive I'm told?"

At this I pulled myself together, at last. Surely, I wasn't going to tell her the whole story of the separation? I steered her artfully, I thought, away from the subject and back to the weather. She noticed, at once, needless to say, but was happy to pretend not to and indulge me for a little. "The weather was fierce altogether, yesterday and another bad day expected tomorrow but the weekend will be good by all accounts." And so forth.

After a bit more of this she returned with discreet persistence to the subject of my background: "Sure when you're American and know no one, you can do what you like, I suppose." I was glad of the chance to put her straight.

"Actually, both my parents were Irish. I was brought up in the States but I was sent to boarding school in Dublin and I've lived here for the last six years."

She greeted this with great pleasure – she stretched her hand over the counter to shake mine and smiled broadly:

"And sure you're almost one of ourselves so. Where would we be without Americans who loved Ireland? Wasn't America always our friend in time of trouble!"

I set off for home with the rain behind me, my groceries in the two plastic bags tied, as instructed by Máire Mac, to the back carrier. Just as I neared the boreen leading to the cottage I caught sight of a man standing on the far side of the road staring at me. A youngish man, thirty or so, with a shock of wild, black hair. As I passed him he jumped back into the ditch and stood with his back pressed against the bushes and his arms glued to his sides. He swung his head away from me and stared into the distance. I saluted him but he made no answer and I went on. As I neared the turn for home I felt his eyes on me still. I looked back and there he was standing as if rooted to the spot staring after me. A bit simple, I suppose. Not the full shilling, as they say here.

Home again, sitting by the fire, the cat making her toilet on the hearth-rug beside me. I'm sitting with the notebook open on my lap, I want to write about you but I find I can't get this awful dream about Malachy out of my head. Why on earth should I be frightened by it? Why did I never worry about custody before? Well, there was no time for it until now. Before I met you again there was no conflict. My future was clear; wretched but simple. I would live alone and share the boys with their father. I'd move back to our house on Breemore road and Malachy would live in Galway. The boys would visit him at the weekend. But that was before meeting you at the airport in Dublin, the lilies and that supplicant look of yours I've never been able to refuse. All is changed.

What will Malachy say? When he finds that I'm with you how will he react? Might he try to make things difficult with the boys? Could I lie to him – pretend the relationship is over? Avoid you for a few months until things have settled down? If I were to be open about my life could I rely on him not to use it against me? And if he were to get difficult, can there be any doubt which of us would be considered the more respectable parent by the law? A professional man devoted to his wife and children or an adulterous wife who left her husband for a woman lover?

"Is it true, Mrs Newman that you had no sooner arrived home from visiting your father in America than you re-started your liaison with this woman?"

"If it pleases the court I didn't know that I'd ever see her again. I had no idea she'd come to the airport."

"That is scarcely credible."

"Well it's the truth nonetheless."

"So she was there to meet you and you revived your affair?"

"Yes."

"With your husband's knowledge?"

"We were already living apart – there was no reason for him to know."

"And the children?"

"They were with him in Galway. They knew – know – nothing about it as yet."

"And when did you plan to inform them?"

When indeed. I'll be calling them tonight to see how they're doing but obviously I won't be telling them about you over the phone. I'll wait until I get to Galway to talk to them both. It won't be easy. As far as they know you've gone out of my life for good and they must be hoping that Malachy and I will get together again. Explaining things to Ben will be nothing as difficult as to Luke. Ben is, in so many ways, a little boy still and in spite of all, uncritical of me, trusting. But then he was always the easy one, from the first. My little dote, trailing the house after me, eager as a puppy, always laughing, always that big bright smile. Monday's child: loving and giving. Loving me better than anyone else. Forgiving me. My heart utterly conquered by him; impaled every time he glances up from under his lashes and gives me that open, happy laugh. When I was kissing him good-bye at the airport in Boston I could hardly bear to part with him. I remember he looked up at me with his big innocent eyes and said very seriously "We'll look after Daddy, don't you worry about him." Tears came into my eyes because he said it with such simple trust. Yet, it's true that even Ben doesn't need me as he once did. After a few days at home Malachy said he hardly noticed my absence. He's growing up – eleven this year, changing like everything else in life.

And Luke? Well I can't afford to let myself think about Luke's reaction. Luke; my grave handsome first born. Luke who was always loving but stern, high minded. I think he still blames me for leaving Malachy. He doesn't understand what led to it. He doesn't know how hard I tried to stay. How I fought against my infatuation with you. I remember how I tried to explain my feelings for you, walking home from school with him one day, and how after a moment's silence he looked up and asked: "Does falling in love with a woman, mean that you won't want to love Malachy anymore?" I didn't know how to answer him because as usual he'd gone unerringly to the heart of things.

If Luke didn't understand I don't know if you ever did either Nina. I mean, I'm not sure you understood what it cost me to leave Malachy. I don't know if you realise even now. How could you? I made it seem easier than it was. I disguised the pain it caused me to cause him such pain. He was so good to me always. I know you've heard this before but I need to say it again. I loved him and could count on his love. His support and protection. I don't mean support in the conventional sense of course. I mean that I could count absolutely on his generosity and his knowledge of me. I felt safe with him, embedded in the depth of this knowledge. Wrapped about in the loose, easy habits of our intimacy, the old familiar patterns, the scar tissue formed across old wounds experienced together, healed together. That scar tissue was a bridge across and a rope that bound us. It hurt to forsake him. It hurt to forsake the life we had built together, the furniture and scaffolding of our world. It hurt most of all to discover that I was a woman who could wound so callously, that I could deliver a gratuitous, near fatal injury to my closest friend so that I might be happy or happier with someone else.

I did try to do the honourable thing. God knows I did try. Twice in the short time you and I have been together I did my best to end things. Even before we were lovers I attempted it because I was terrified of where the obsession would carry me.

When we had been together only three months (after I had left Malachy and moved into Ranelagh) we made a mutual agreement to break it off. To make it irreparable you told Elinor and promised her not to see me again. Needless to say it was a doomed effort. Only a fortnight later we were back together, more passionate than ever. This last time, however, was different. I believed you that the break was final. You needed to do it, you said, because you were worn out by your feeling of guilt and the strain of living parallel lives. I allowed myself to be persuaded yet again that it was the only virtuous course. Broken-hearted but feeling a kind of dull resignation I brought the boys to Boston with me for the summer. On the second night there, sitting in Pa's deserted study – "the important room" – where he used to bring us as kids whenever there was something really big to explain, I told them I wouldn't be seeing you again. Ben took my hand because I was crying and asked me very deliberately: "Does it mean we can't see Nina anymore when we go home?"

I said yes, that was exactly what it meant. If I'd had any sense, I'd have said nothing. But there was no hiding my misery from either of them and to have kept silent would have frightened them more.

You asked me to forget you, Nina, and for those months, going back and forth to the hospital to visit Pa, in that strange city that was once home, a thousand miles from you, I almost succeeded. I resigned myself to a life without you; a life made up of work and family. I was determined not to contact you when I got back.

I didn't want to go home to Boston of course. I didn't want to leave the country. And of course I didn't take the news of Pa seriously; another false alarm I thought. Poor Pa, how many times had he staged it before? No more to be counted on in the business of dying than he was in living. How many times had he summoned us back to keep the final vigil while

he dithered between his half life and slow death? Poor Ma –
how did she stand it? She had said the last time – go back
home, get on with your own life – leave him to me. So we did.
We all left it to her, my sister, my brother and I until it was
too late. Poor father – old and alone – outliving her in the
end.

But this time there was no Ma to take care of things and
when the call came I decided to go out myself. I drove from
our old house thirty miles to the hospital every day. Pa sat in a
wheelchair beside a huge picture window overlooking a lake
and held onto my hand in silence, squeezing it as if it were the
only thing that attached him to life. He couldn't speak and
after a while he stopped trying. But he smiled at the boys
when they came in and big slow tears slipped down his cheeks
when he watched them leave. I visited every day and then I
had to make a decision to go home. If he died once I'd gone
home, I reminded myself, he had two other children in the
country to call on.

I started the process of closing my life there. All of my past,
my childhood, my adolescence, sorted out and disposed of;
packed in cardboard boxes and tea chests. I put the house on
the market and shipped back the few belongings I wanted. I
sent the children home ahead of me and had a a fortnight to
myself. During that time I thought over my time with you and
brought myself to accept what I decided was the inevitable –
you were gone forever from my life and all things considered it
might be for the best.

I told you I didn't want to go to Boston. But after a while
there I didn't want to come home either. Home – such an
easily pronounced word. Such a simple concept. But for me,
moving between two continents most of my life, the phrase is
hopelessly ambiguous. Which house do I mean? Which city?
Which country? I no longer know, if I ever did in the last
twenty years. All I can say for certain is that while I was out

there with Pa, just before the final sale went through I felt this unexpected longing to stay in the old house, to settle again in Boston. I felt a sudden revulsion from this place; the climate the culture, even the smell of it. If It hadn't been for the boys I think I might have stayed in New England. I remember as the plane back to Dublin flew in, over the sea, over the fields and suburbs I felt my heart contract with dread. My will struggling against it. I didn't want to be captured again. Gripped in the inertia. The dense web of conversation, chatter and gossip; the ceaseless word-spinning which is begun to pass the time and ends in becoming time itself – the fact and reason for existence. "One more for the road" – always one more story for the road. Every action, the smallest motion of the will obstructed by this national passion for diversion, speculation and wit. Everything put off until tomorrow. A life made up of endless postponement.

I looked out the window at a small green rock lashed by black water. Was this where so much of significance in my life had taken place? How could this speck in the ocean have made a world large enough to absorb me, a world that had seemed urgent, self-contained, complete? The low sky, the low roofs, the seagulls flying low. The plane landed with a jolt on the narrow strip of tarmac between green fields. I saw faces pressed to the window of the observation lounge, arms waving, children held up in greeting to passengers as yet unseen. I was home at last. Or was I? Was this ever my home? A foreigner of no fixed abode. I didn't know as I walked down the ramp that you were waiting in that waving crowd, waiting to greet me.

Then I came through customs at Dublin airport and looked round for Rosie who was to collect me and saw instead, you. You, standing at the front of the waiting crowd, with that great bouquet of freesias and white lilies spilling from your arms. I almost turned back. If I could have hidden from you I would. How did you know I was coming? I hadn't expected you. I hadn't let myself imagine it. If someone had asked me five minutes before I laid eyes on you what my reaction would be I couldn't have said. My thoughts were in such confusion, my heart in such pain. I couldn't have said, in that instant, which would be worse – never to see you again or to see you every day for the rest of my life. But the moment I saw you, it began again. I thought how is it she looks so good? So incredibly more alive than anyone around her? This radiance about you. Your skin, your eyes, your long confident stride. Always this air of excitement about you, as if when you walk towards me the curtain rises, the orchestra strikes up. I almost hear it. And the feeling at once all over again that anything can happen in your company. Anything seems possible. Probable.

I had no time for thought. No time to prepare an attitude. I made the mistake of looking into your face. And that was it. Lost again the moment my eyes met yours. Months of detachment and self sufficiency obliterated with one look. So it was always. Do you know exactly, the power you have over me? Did you know you had only to turn up unexpectedly and smile, to have me at your command all over again?

After meeting me the airport we drove in to the city. We went to our old place for coffee. On the way up Georges Street we passed friends. I was so proud to be seen with you. I remember that – the rush of pride. They'll think we're lovers again is what I thought. I wanted that. I wanted everyone to believe it even if just for that morning. All that day I was under your spell. Held by the old magic. In a jeweller's window, as we walked along Grafton Street you saw a silver bracelet which you said was exactly the one you'd been wanting to buy since we first met, and even as you persuaded me to come into the shop to try it on I thought to myself why am I letting this happen, letting myself be so vulnerable again?

Because I loved you and knew it but knew also it was possible
to live without it. I could be in love but choose not to express
it if the pain were less. And anything would be less painful
than sharing you again. I was sure of that if nothing else. I had
taught myself the hard way. For those long summer months in
another country, I had lived without you. I had survived. I was
happy even, after a fashion.

Later on you took me to Sandymount to see Aunt May. If I
wanted to stop I should have said no, then. Once, we'd
entered that lovely sitting-room of hers, together, all
resistance was finished. United in her eyes it was impossible to
create division again. She saw the love between us. And we
saw it reflected in her face as if we were looking into a mirror.
She looked at me and said softly: "How well you seem, my
dear. I'm delighted to see you so recovered."

I knew as she spoke that was why you'd brought me there.
That was why you said let's go and see May she needs cheering
up. Because you knew I'd forget myself with her. Abandon
myself for her sake. Let you in close.

Maybe I shouldn't have come home. Maybe I should have
ignored you at the airport. Maybe I shouldn't have gone to
Aunt May's. But I did. And I can't regret it. Not now.

I didn't stop to think about Elinor. You'd told me she was
away and that was all I needed to know. When we woke the
next morning I made a pretence of dressing and preparing to
leave but I knew already that you wanted me to stay and I
knew I would stay for as long as it was possible. How could I
have forgiven you so easily? How could I have allowed all my
resolutions to be swept aside because you smiled at me with
your head to one side? Because you kissed me, because you
brought me to see Aunt May? Somewhere without my
knowing it I must already have decided to give you a second
chance. To give myself a second chance if it was offered. Now,
here I am alone on the side of a mountain in Clare, waiting

for you. Waiting for the fulfilment of something I hardly dared imagine.

Dear God, but how threadbare passion seems, set down in cold blood like this. Its treacheries, its self mystifications, its excuses, its random cruelties. I don't need to be dragged before a court to know how the world would judge my behaviour. I know by heart all their phrases of condemnation – unnatural behaviour, selfishness, abdication of duty. But there is so much else that I feel needs forgiveness outside the truths of law courts and public opinion. If I am to be called to account and judged by my peers, I want my real crimes attended to. I want to confess and seek absolution for sins that have nothing to do with the petty disgraces the law keeps track of. Oh no, my failings are on another scale entirely. Like yours, like any lover's, crimes against the heart that hold no interest for the legal mind. The everyday crimes of betrayal, neglect we all commit in our loving of each other.

Through my fault, through my fault, through my most grievous fault.

If it pleases the court. If I am really to examine my conscience on my conduct in love I'll have to go into greater detail about the gradual disintegration of my life with Malachy. My descent or ascent, depending on the point of view – into sudden depravity or enlightenment.

That evening after meeting you at the hospital I experienced for the first time all that was to come; a haunting that possessed me for weeks. An invasion of my mind and blood. An absolute obsession. Have I ever talked about what happened between Malachy and me in that time? I don't want to even now but I feel I must.

For a few weeks in the beginning life went on more or less as usual. Malachy appeared to notice nothing out of the ordinary. He didn't notice that I could neither eat nor sleep.

That I was devoured by longing – a mad craving that made me irritable by day and wakeful at night. He didn't seem to notice any alteration in my behaviour; my restlessness, my impatience. Nor my physical coldness towards him. I went through the motions of sexual response and he seemed content. Or perhaps not. Perhaps he saw what was happening and chose to say nothing.

But if I'm to be really truthful about this, I'd have to admit that at the start I wasn't physically cold to him. In fact, in a strange way, my passion for you seemed to transfer itself to him. I remember the first time meeting him after talking to you, as clearly as if it had happened an hour ago. I had called him from the hospital to say we could meet in our local once I'd driven Ben home. I arrived at eight o'clock and had the weird sense of walking straight onto a film set. The whole pub and everyone in it seemed to be part of some careful rehearsal, all the usual faces in their appointed places; the office workers and the secretaries, the young lovers in the snug, the three serious, elderly topers at the bar and in the corner a group of newspaper men gossiping loudly with that air they always have – furtive and self-important at once.

I got there before Malachy. I sat on a stool at the counter. The moment he walked through the door I noticed the change. I almost failed to recognise him because of it, even though he looked exactly as always. When he put his head to one side and smiled his odd gleaming smile that squeezes up his eyes, only then did I realise what had happened to him. He had become a stranger: a smiling, handsome, unknown stranger. There he was in all his health and good looks, striding across the room towards me. A stranger. The skin stretched tight across his high cheekbones, his slanting eyes, the bright all-confident smile. A stranger. In the few short hours that had passed since meeting you, my husband had been transfigured beyond recognition.

He dropped into the seat beside me. He stretched out his long legs and tilted back his head, his head of dark silken hair that I loved. There he was chatting and joking with me as if we were old friends, life-long buddies. And for all his animation and humour he might as well have been a statue cut from marble; a perfect, clear cut, three dimensional figure, perceived all the more exactly because it is lifeless. When we stood up to leave he put his arm round me, his hand resting with complete familiarity against my hip. I almost laughed aloud at the bizarre humour of this stranger behaving as if he knew me. As though the woman he was leading from the room was a friend or lover or even a wife.

In bed that night it happened for the first time. The first gesture so familiar I scarcely noticed it. His hand touching my shoulder and slipping slowly down the length of my spine. My skin was burnt white hot by its touch because suddenly it was your hand without warning sweeping across my back and up again to my neck and shoulder. His mouth reaching down to me was yours, his tongue coming into my mouth was yours, his belly lapping mine was yours. And I thought this is how it will be, this is how it will feel – her head against my breast, her thighs on mine. He stroked my back from my hip to the nape of my neck, murmuring all his love words and I felt a sudden burst of gratitude to this strange body that was a friend to mine, that was tender and loving and hungry. The beautiful chest with the straight black gleaming hair, the broad, well-muscled shoulders were my consolation, my protection against this terrible need and longing that had no object. All his flesh given to me was a bulwark against frenzy, against lust that possessed me beyond lust, beyond need or satisfaction. For a moment he was familiar again in his warmth and knowledge of me. I kissed him with love, with gratitude and fell asleep telling him I needed him.

But from that night forward I was never physically close to

him again without knowing you were there between us. Superimposed on my senses, like a double exposure of a negative, one image blocking out the other. Night after night, I cleaved to him, as if he might find the power to drive out the ghost that had come between us. Making love with a violent greed and sensuality. Forcing each time more pleasure from him. He was excited, intrigued. When I kissed him I closed my eyes, I hid my face from him. And the fever with which I responded to him was the force of my need to drive you back from consciousness. My tenderness was gratitude when for a moment it seemed as if he succeeded.

We made love with infinite skill and knowledge in those long nights. But silently. I couldn't speak his name or utter one word of affection. He didn't notice. My body responded to his like a piece of well-tuned machinery. But there was a stiffness about my heart like a hand closing round it. I used his body to conquer my fear of you. For a moment or two I was with him or at least not with anyone else. He was glad and proud, ready to give me hours of pleasure. I was grateful and pitying because he noticed nothing. And finally, resentful and cold.

As for you? I thought it would be easy with you. I thought I had only to present myself. I was arrogant and callow as a schoolgirl. What did I know? Nothing but the love of men. Easy, flattering, unobservant, undemanding. I was arrogant – no – better said I was blind. Blinded by habit, by the old ways of love between women and men made stale by centuries.

Chapter Seven

October, Dublin.

With an effort of will Nina forced herself to return to the present. Aunt May was still telling the story of Nina's childhood and Lizzie was still listening, her bright eyes fixed on the old woman's strong-boned, weather-beaten face, studying every movement of it as she spoke. Nina never knew why the child liked this account so much. She loved stories of any kind, but this one had some special power over her. The orphanage fascinated her. Was it because she hardly knew her own father? Had she some hidden fear that she might end up in an institution herself? But that was hardly likely, she was too secure for that surely? Even as Nina tried to persuade herself of this, the next question she heard Lizzie put to May unsettled her again:

"Why was Nina in the orphanage?"

"Because her mother, my cousin Ellen, had died and her father was living in America."

"Why didn't he come home and look after her?"

"Because he didn't know that she was alive."

"Like my father?"

"But your father does look after you," May protested softly. "He sends you money and lovely clothes."

"And why did Nina's father not send money then?"

"Because no one knew where he was to ask him."

"He had disappeared?" the child said.

"Yes," Aunt May said sadly.

That was how her aunt always answered these questions, but Nina wasn't sure it was the truth. Surely one of them would have told her father? Surely someone would have known where he was? There was so much of her own story that was still kept from the full light of day. Gaps in her knowledge of events that were ignored and dismissed as unimportant. There were two stories – the version that May told – a remote piece of family history, unremarkable and familiar. And there was the story as Nina remembered it, something much less coherent and orderly. But over the years she had learned to tell it as a social chronicle, a dramatic tale – which, from constant repetitions to friends and lovers, had taken on the elements of a settled narrative: solid, impersonal, remote.

She had never known her parents. Her mother, Ellen Kavanagh, a country woman, became pregnant when only twenty-two years of age and unmarried. At that time it was unthinkable for a woman to raise a child on her own. So, when she could no longer conceal the pregnancy, she left home and went to live in Dublin, in a home for Catholic girls, where her baby, a girl, was born a few months later. Almost immediately afterwards the nuns arranged for the child to be sent to an orphanage and the young mother returned to her home town and resumed her old life as if nothing had happened. Perhaps it was no more than an accident of nature or perhaps the sorrow of that abandonment never left the young woman, but, whichever was the case, Ellen Kavanagh contracted TB only two years after giving birth to her child and she died in a sanatorium one year later.

The orphanage to which her child was brought was in the suburbs of south Dublin. The child, christened Nina by her mother, lived there until she was nearly five years of age. Then one day a tall, good-looking woman with an American accent came to visit. She told Nina that she was a cousin on her mother's side and that she had only recently returned from America and learned of the child's existence. Nina fell in love with her at first sight. In all her years at the orphanage no one had paid her individual attention before this and she had never met anyone who claimed a blood relationship. The idea delighted and fascinated her. Her visitor told her as she left that she would come again as soon as possible. Nina lived from then on thinking of nothing but the day when they would meet once more. Then, one month later, on a fine April morning with the sun shining on the world as if in celebration, the tall woman returned in a hired car and Nina was informed by the Reverend Mother that she was to go home with this lady, May O'Brien, and to live with her in her house in County Cork from that day forth.

This was how she had learned to tell the story and it always elicited a similar response: people clucked their tongues and frowned in sympathy. They said how painful it must have been for such a small child and how kind and good her aunt must be. Nina agreed emphatically and offered no further comment. She never spoke of the other things she remembered. The life at the orphanage. The loneliness and the fear. The cold in winter, the damp rooms and dark corridors. The grim faces of the nuns, their harsh voices. The crying of small children in the night. The absence of laughter. The awful smell, as in a hospital, of disinfectant and boiled vegetables. The bad food, hard-boiled eggs every day in summer, mutton stew in winter. The long empty days, with no one to touch or kiss and nothing to think of but the one secret obsessive hope, that one day someone would come, some marvellous stranger who would rescue them from this imprisonment. Together with that longing was the other constant emotion, the envy of those who were saved, the fellow prisoners chosen without explanation from the rest,

79

lifted from their cots and borne away to love and happiness. Nina had one recurrent dream in which she saw a tall, beautiful woman with black hair, smiling as she walked away from her down a long, dim corridor. She walked backwards, smiling at Nina, until the very last minute when she turned and disappeared through the front door. For years she called this figure "the woman who cries when she smiles," and no one hearing her had any idea what she meant.

Then, one day, it had happened, finally – Aunt May appeared out of the blue – out of the mysterious public world and rescued her, like a guardian angel, like the woman in her dream. Only that she smiled and there were no tears in her eyes. Nina remembered still the delicious smell when she was lifted into her arms: of tobacco and perfume and lipstick. She had never met anyone before who wore lipstick and the smell of it was a wonder and delight to her. She could smell its faintly cloying scent to this day.

But magical as the rescue was, the world she entered when she arrived home with May was even more full of wonder and pleasure. An old country farmhouse with hens and ducks and geese, a small river at the bottom of the garden, a marsh, wild flowers in the fields, a donkey. May's kitchen garden, her precious flowers: lupins and hollyhocks, hydrangeas, climbing roses and nasturtiums at the front door.

Nina loved the house and Aunt May from the first day. The distance in their ages lent a special freedom and ease to the relationship. There was an improvised quality to it that suited them both; they made it up as they went along, with no reference points provided by custom or convention. May worked as the local librarian and during the school holidays she often took Nina with her. Nina loved the dark silence of the winter afternoons spent between the high wooden shelves, reading comics and drawing with crayons while May stacked books. One day when she was bored and restless May said to her, "Just start to read – read everything from A to Z and then come back to me". And Nina, who had only just learned how, began as she was ordered, taking the command quite literally. She started at the letter A that afternoon and over the following weeks she continued, moving through the alphabet, until finally she announced to May that she had read every single book on the shelves from A to Z.

The house in Ballybeg was no more than a few miles from the town where Nina's mother had lived. Nina learned from May that her mother had been an only child and her own father and mother had died many years before – so it seemed that May and her sister Molly was her only surviving relative. May's high standing in the town protected her from the criticism of the locals to a certain extent, but not entirely. Everyone for miles round knew Nina's story, that she was an orphan who had known neither her father nor mother and that she had been sent to an orphanage. She never forgot or learned not to mind the jeering she endured from the local children, the names and insults called after her as she walked down the street. The whispers and giggles at school. She remembered how the nuns shamed her by drawing attention to her situation whenever they thought she needed correction. They would shake their heads over her and proclaim solemnly: "You can't make a silk purse from a sow's ear." "Indeed you can't. You never said a truer word, Mother."

Then the library was closed down and May lost her job. They were left with nothing but the farm to depend on. Nina felt instantly the fear of want coming back to her. May did her best, but often there wasn't enough to buy food at the end of the week. She remembered too how May put her pride in her pocket that first Christmas and went to the local Vincent de Paul official to ask for help. He hemmed and hawed and made them wait. He said he'd have to put it to the board before he could make a decision. Angry and humiliated, May told him that he could keep his charity. She would do without before she'd beg for it. Nonetheless, on the morning of Christmas Eve, a large wickerwork hamper was delivered to the house filled with riches: a turkey and ham, boxes of dates and chocolates and a plum pudding.

Soon afterwards May was offered a job as bookkeeper in the town's hardware store and their bad times were over. But they were both marked by that year of deprivation. May grew critical of the place, of its small-mindedness and petty snobberies. And Nina learned a lesson she would remember all her life: that even respected people, such as her aunt, could be patronised and made to feel at fault the moment they lost the little power they commanded. A small slip became a slow slide downhill. She learned something ugly about people: decent, kindly people enjoyed the misfortune of others; it confirmed the sense of their own superiority, and though they might be generous, they never allowed the recipient of their good deeds to forget the depth of their obligation.

Then Aunt May's sister Molly was suddenly widowed. A few weeks after the funeral she wrote to May and suggested that, as she had no children of her own and was now living alone in a large house, May and Nina should come to live with her in the city. So May sold the house in Ballybeg and she and Nina went to live in the ease and casual elegance of the old, welcoming house on the edge of Dublin Bay. Nina settled at once into her new existence. She loved both her aunts who were outwardly respectable and privately eccentric. Aunt Molly at first seemed very different from May, formal in manner, reserved and soft spoken. She pretended to be shocked by May's loose ways, her whiskey drinking, card playing and gambling, but it was obvious to Nina that she secretly delighted in them. It was Aunt Molly who first developed her interest in painting. She was a dedicated amateur who produced fine, delicate watercolours. She would take Nina with her in summer when she went to

82

paint outdoors, and from her Nina learned the beginnings of her craft.

Where May was blunt and impatient, Molly was tolerant and compassionate. Whenever Nina or Aunt May denounced someone for pettiness or cruelty Molly would remind them softly that one never knew what people might have suffered. It irritated Nina when she was young, but later on in life it often came back to her and she felt the justice and compassion of it with new respect. And so, between these two women, Nina had everything she needed, all the affection and security she could want and moral freedom along with it. They discussed questions of ethics and behaviour in an abstract, impersonal way that encouraged debate. They gave Nina the benefit of their experience, but left her to make up her own mind on all serious questions. Molly's death years later brought her the only real sadness she had known in all her time in this house.

And her father? Many times when she was growing up she asked May or Molly to tell her about him, but their answers were always brief and vague. He had been a visitor to the area, a young man from Dublin who came to work as the doctor's locum. Nobody knew much about him except that he was handsome and intelligent. By the time Nina was born he had already gone to live abroad and was never told of her birth.

This outline of her family history was presented by her aunts as a simple story of hardship and misunderstanding, not uncommon in that period and place where so many were poor and almost all the young people they knew emigrated to England or America as soon as they left school. It was an account that, for the most part, had satisfied Nina. She had felt no real curiosity about her father, although frequently as a child she had taken down the box of photographs as Lizzie was doing now and sorted through them until she found the picture of a tall, sophisticated young man, standing beside an unknown friend on the shores of Glengarrif, something slightly decadent in his air, the angle of his black fedora, the way he held his cigarette, the sardonic gaze directed at the camera. She had imagined that he must have died many years ago, but she felt no need to have it confirmed.

"But why did he disappear, Aunty May? Why?" Nina's attention was jolted back to the present by the sound of Lizzie's small, determined voice demanding an answer to the one question that always returned to her own mind. Why had her father left her mother? Did he not love her? Did he purposely deceive her? Or was there some tragic but benign explanation based on a mutual misunderstanding? She heard May begin an attempt at illumination with the mild, resigned tone she always used for this conversation.

"He disappeared, child, only because he . . ." but before she could get any further Lizzie interrupted her with a sudden burst of impatience provoked by the word because, a word she had taken a great dislike to in recent weeks: "Because because because because because because," she chanted loudly, "because because because – that's the reason for everything, isn't it?"

"For a lot of things, I suppose," May answered, smiling at her.

But Lizzie had stopped listening. She jumped up suddenly from the floor and ran across the room to Nina, who was standing now at the window looking out at the slowly falling rain. She tugged at the sleeve of her jacket and asked:

"Can we go home soon? I want to see Elinor and Solomon."

Nina drew her down to sit on the window seat beside her.

"Yes, love, we'll be going in a little while." She kissed the top of her head and stroked her hair slowly and softly as she had stroked the cat a moment before.

Chapter Eight

September, Clare.

I feel that everyone knows I am waiting to hear from you. I hurried along the road at evening for the afternoon post. I arrived at the post office and tried to maintain my air of nonchalance and ease. Máire Mac seemed to notice my nervousness. She began to talk about the weather and said apropos of nothing that the wind has a strange effect on some people. It plays on their nerves. Some of them run out of it as soon as they arrive. More stay up on the mountain farms and never leave them until spring.

The she added out of the blue: "Nothing today either. Do you think maybe people haven't the right address?" I rooted about on the shelves looking for things I didn't want so that she wouldn't see my face.

As I was leaving she called after me: "I was waiting myself for a letter from my sister that took eight days to come from London. Did you ever hear the like? But sure what can we do only be patient?" She speaks with a kind of motherly indulgence, a rough kindness. But it unnerves me just the same. What does she know? Why does she let me know that she knows?

I went by the telephone kiosk and stood for several minutes in the rain trying to decide whether or not to call you. I held out because you asked me not to and I'm still trying to keep faith with you.

I sit by the fire brooding. The wind has stopped completely.

Well, I always expected too much, my mother used to say. Autumn and the falling fruit. Why do I say that? Autumn reminds me of Ma and reminds me of you. I met you in autumn and my mother died in autumn. I watch the leaves drifting languidly through the dry air and think of you both.

I had a feeling again when I woke this morning that Ma was in the house. I imagined her downstairs getting breakfast. I could almost smell the toast, hear the kettle boiling, and hear the words of the song she was singing as she made the tea. I almost called down to her. Why am I haunted by her in this way? Though haunted isn't the right word because the sense of her presence is entirely pleasurable. She's becoming a near constant visitor. I almost see her walking about from room to room, washing dishes, arranging flowers. Brightening the place up as she'd say.

She'd like this house. It would remind her of home. She was born and raised in West Cork, a landscape more lush, more civilised than this, but not so very different. And though she reacted from much of her upbringing, she never quite left the place behind her. I remember going home to her people when I was a child, walking with her along the country roads, unchanged for centuries, the tilled fields, the milking sheds, hens and ducks at every gate, the great broad-leaved trees, the oak, the elm, the chestnut. All gone now. She loved to walk by a river, to sit under the shade of a tree, the wide, dark branches holding a pool of shade where the cows gathered to cool themselves. No one now seeks shade on a summer's day. Another thing of the past. Have I done my bit in banishing it? Always yearning to drag things into the light.

Just by closing my eyes as I sit here I can imagine her. I can feel her hand closing on mine, lost in its warm dry grasp. I hear the water wandering by us in small straggles of streams we dignified with the name river. The flies buzzing over the cowpats. The trees soughing overhead, wind blown on even the finest summer day. A glorious day. She would be wearing a frock I remember well or at least its style – a kind no one wears any more or remembers – a forties or fifties affair that is forever the essence of summer; sleeveless, a full skirt billowing in the breeze that always blew even on the finest day, the tight bodice, the cardigan thrown over the shoulders in readiness for the chill of evening. This one is white, with a pattern of green and blue flowers, the material, as she would say, cotton. Her arms and legs are bare, lightly tanned, freckles on her forearms and a scattering on her cheeks. I could almost count them, knowing their exact position, the same freckles have made their home on my body. She had the air of going out for the day, an outing, a day off, a special event. A glorious day – the first real day of summer. I can see her too, walking through the streets of the town to do the shopping. And all the other women festive and merry, smiling all of them because of the fine day, because of the freedom it bestowed, the freedom to stroll the street, to leave domestic chores and walk out in the sunshine with something else to consider but the shopping list – the messages as they said. Getting the messages, the axis and pivot of the day – going to do the shopping, meeting all the others at the same thing.

Bringing their children to the park or the beach, calling out to each other with special warmth and affection:

"A beautiful day."

"Glorious."

A glorious day; belonging to a time of endurance, of resignation, of stoicism. A time of bleak winters, ill-heated houses, cold water, the grind of housework, confinement within four walls, bondage to the needs of children and menfolk – then suddenly, one morning in May, liberated by sunshine to walk in the streets in a summer frock, the sun on the skin, the breeze lifting her skirt.

Oh Ma, did I ever tell you how much those days meant to me? How I've remembered them?

I feel we'd get on even better if we were to meet now. Both of us grown older but wiser. But would she think me wiser? I doubt it. She wouldn't approve of my reasons for being here for a start. She'd think it madness to do anything to risk the boys' safety. But I feel she might understand my need to leave Malachy. She knew we were having problems that last year of her life. She'd always liked and admired him, but she recognised much earlier than I the personality traits that made life with him so difficult for me. She identified a quality in him I found hard to name, because even to name it seemed mean-spirited. I remember Ma saying to me one day, when Malachy was hustling me off on holiday to Spain when I ought to have been studying for my exams and I was feeling guilty because I couldn't respond with total pleasure: "Do you know what it is with Malachy," she said and she looked at me with a hesitant smile aware that she was taking a risk, "he's a benevolent despot," she said, "very benevolent, but a despot all the same."

I defended him at once, but afterwards the phrase came back to me – it fitted him exactly. He had always had this way of steam-rolling people with kindness and generosity, making dissent seem churlish. In a very subtle manner he undermined my self-confidence with his constant readiness to help: "I'll take care of it. I'll look after you." Ma saw that long before I could acknowledge it. And though it was the reverse of her problems with Pa she could see in its way it was as maddening as my father's refusal to feel responsible for anything.

So yes, she would be sad for me but she'd understand the break-up with Malachy. On the other hand, if she were to learn that I was planning to live openly with a woman lover? Well that might strain her tolerance. Though there's no doubt that she had her suspicions about my feelings for you. After all there was that terrible night when we had been in the hospital with

Pa when I tried to confront her with it. I was never sure how much she understood or chose not to understand. Whatever she knew there's no doubt that she was charmed by you from the first meeting. I remember when she and Pa came over to visit that Christmas and I brought you to meet them in Breemore road. When you'd left she turned to me – we were clearing the tea things from the table (our best china and silverware, she'd insisted on – a sign of the importance she granted the visit) and gave me one of her long considering looks: "She has the most extraordinary eyes I've ever seen," she said slowly. "Beautiful."

That was all. No other comment. None was needed.

But then we always liked the same people, Ma and I. That was one of the bonds between us. You met several times after that in the time they stayed here. I like to imagine now that she knew and accepted you as a significant person in my life even if my feelings for you were never stated. I can picture you perfectly, arriving at the house on one of those impromptu visits, standing at the door, head to one side, smiling this delighted smile of yours and always holding out a present, flowers or fine food of some kind. You courted Ma of course. Flirted with her and she responded only too happily. When you turned from her to kiss me I could feel this little frisson of jealousy pass over her because your attention was passing to me and the physical passion vibrated between us no matter how we tried to conceal it.

You told me you always loved other people's mothers because you'd had none yourself. You certainly loved Ma. I think you were half in love with her though you knew her such a short time. But after all I should know these things don't take time, do they?

The cat is sitting before the fire making her toilet. How precise and thorough she is. First the mouth and whiskers with quick sweeping movements of the front paws, carefully licked and wetted. Then the breast, then the belly, then the back legs; the front, the back. Two big yawns, a full stretch, a flick of the tail and she's asleep. What a genius they have for comfort and pleasure. She follows the sun round, moving from one sunny patch to another throughout the day. She begins at the fire and when the sun is coming through the front window, streaming across the table, she comes to where I'm writing and stretches out voluptuously like a sun worshipper on a beach. Mid-afternoon she moves to the west facing side window and sits gazing out blinking at the fading strands of light.

I suppose at this stage I ought to give you a progress report? I've a thousand pieces left on the jigsaw I found in a cupboard upstairs (a landscape by Turner, all mists and rivers) and I've finished the history of women painters I gave you for your birthday and the biography of Frida Meyer. As for the rest of my diversions – these apologies, classifications, confessions – whatever they are I'm writing, I'm surprised to find I've covered more than seventy pages in longhand. So I'm gainfully employed, am I not? Putting this enforced separation to good account. By the time you arrive my brain will be washed clear of all this thought. Purged of self-doubt and useless enquiry. I'll have no need to burden you with it.

As soon as I leave my mind idle it returns to the subject of you. Everything I think of sooner or later returns me to you. But I'll fight, courageously, do battle all day if need be until I get the better of it. I concentrate on other things and try valiantly to lengthen the time I can keep my mind from lapsing. So far, I have managed three minutes! For three whole minutes I have succeeded in contemplating something besides you – your smell, your eyes, the feel of you: the exact weight of you pressed against me when we stood in your kitchen, my back to the wall next to the stove as you leaned against me, your arms about my neck, your arms encircling me!

But you see, I'm straying again. I was thinking about Ma, wasn't I? Needless to say in any explanation of my sexual development I'd have to talk about my relationship with Ma. Isn't it the first thing the psychologists ask about? Did I love her too much? Did she neglect me or dominate me? Was she over-possessive or careless? Whichever way about it is sure to be her fault, especially when it comes to loving women sexually it must be the mother's fault. Yes, pretty well everything that happens to us, these days, is laid at the feet of our mothers.

"Would you tell the court about your relationship with your mother, Mrs Newman? Were you close to her? What kind of woman was she? Did you have the example of a loving partnership between your parents?" Such questions, Ma. She would treat them with her usual lofty disdain. She'd smile as she did with many other issues – throw her hands up and say airily: "Well, I don't suppose there's anything we can do about it now."

I wonder why I imagine her always as a young woman. A tall, graceful, dark-haired young woman. Nothing at all like the national prototype – the downtrodden mothers of this country – self-sacrificing and resentful. But then she had lived so many years outside its clutches. Or perhaps she was, as you said when you met her, different by temperament, an original from her first breath. Whatever it was she always had known what she wanted and was ready to fight to get it. It wasn't difficult with so many people enamoured of her, ready to do her bidding, at a moment's notice. Yet with all that she had a hard life. Six children and an alcoholic husband. How she'd hate to hear me say that even now. I don't think she ever admitted it. Not even to herself. She said of him until the end what everyone said – a gentleman – always a gentleman. As if it was so extraordinary and an exceptional thing for a man to be well behaved or good mannered. And if he was considered such, nothing more should be asked of him by anyone. A gentleman, indeed. And he was, oh yes, let it be said. A harsh word never passed his lips. A charmer, a talker, a maker of blandishments. I remember his singing. All the old songs – "My Love is like a Red, Red Rose." – "She moved through the Fair." Sitting in the armchair beside the fire closing his eyes, throwing back his head, a glass of whiskey in his hand. Oh he could sing all right. And dance. My mother said she married him because of the lightness of his feet. That was the kind of reason people of her generation gave for choosing one another. A good dancer – a great bridge player – a fine tenor voice. That was the kind of nonsense they went on with. Though Ma was never a foolish woman. On the contrary, she was as sharp as a tack. And life with my father honed her to a needle. Her eye missed nothing. Her tongue was only seconds behind.

But sarcasm was lost on him or he pretended it was. He went on contentedly smiling and singing: "And I will come again my love though all the seas run dry." Maddening yes – exasperating. But not a man anyone could hate. Not a man you'd have called a drunk either. Not in the rowdy, bellicose style that word suggests. A drop too many – that was it. That ridiculous sentimental euphemism captured him exactly. It gives just the right picture of smiling befuddlement. Harmless inadequacy. No one would have called him a drunk. But I'm not sure I can remember a night when he was entirely sober.

He wore her out, of course, exhausted her in his dying just as he had in his living. But because he did everything with a smile, you couldn't hold it against him. She – my mother, that is – used to say he hasn't a jealous bone in his body. It might have been better for her if he had. He was content to the point of inertia. He left her to handle everything. So that people could think she was hard and he was soft. A gentleman. Oh yes, a gentleman.

It doesn't sound too good so far, does it? Not the kind of parental example they'll be looking for?

"And what effect did your father's drinking have on your mother, Mrs Newman? Did it make her a nag, a goad?"

Indeed it didn't. How did she manage to keep so good-humoured? She was almost always that. A free spirit, a gadabout, always cavorting with her friends, always laughing, forever bringing people home, encouraging us all to bring back every stray who crossed our path. The door always open, the kettle always on. And my father indulged her, smiling from behind the racing page or puffing at his pipe. "Ask your mother," he would say, "your mother knows best." That was the sum total of his contribution to our moral guidance. He admired her high spirits, her good looks, her vivacity. He seemed to think he had no right to ask a woman of her calibre to weigh herself down with domestic chores. "Your mother's a thoroughbred," he would say, "she needs to be given her head!" And wanting so much licence for herself, she granted it to us. Never inquiring, never controlling. Ask me no questions and I'll tell you no lies, that was her guiding rule. As a child I wanted her to be more like other mothers, dull and secure, resentful but reliable. After her own random, abstracted fashion she loved intensely. But she valued freedom over love always. And if I'd been asked to choose I would have chosen my carefree, untrammelled existence with licence to come and go over the security of a love that cosseted me. Perhaps she knew this? Perhaps she was giving me what I wanted? Or did I grow to want what I was given?

I came home from school and put my own dinner in the oven. She had left something in a saucepan to be heated up. She never bothered with sewing or knitting. I washed my own

93

clothes as early as I can remember. All the better for it, my father said. He put no pressure on her to resemble the wives of her day who stayed at home knitting sweaters and scarves, making stew and apple pie. Mothers who were forever present, listening, tending, advising. She had no time to listen. Busy about a thousand things every day. As I opened the door she flew out of it. Just off for a few hours – expect me when you see me. When other mothers were demanding explanations and wanting a detailed account of movement, anxious if a daughter was an hour late, she was sublimely indifferent, riding serenely over triviality. She trusted me, she said. She had brought me up to think for myself. What was there to worry about? And she was right. Though I seemed to flirt with disaster and delight in risks no other girl of my age would have contemplated, it was nevertheless true, as the nuns said, that I had a sound head on my shoulders. Staying out until any hour I liked, going to dances, smoking, drinking, sleeping with boys and yet all the while this restraint about me, this inner caution like a bed of rock beneath the shifting surface, that was inherent in me because my mother waved her hand airily when I came in late and said I hope you haven't ruined some poor boy's reputation? This core of steel because she trusted me, because she refused to ask questions or stoop to interrogation. You're my daughter, I should hope you know better! And I did. All my life.

The truly wild girls, the reckless dare-devils were the ones who were cautious every night of the year but one. The girls who were hemmed in, monitored and controlled in every moment of the day, these were the ones who went to the devil when at last they did break free. The girls who knew there was always a parent at their backs, someone ready to haul them in when they stumbled too close to the cliff edge. So, as soon as they found themselves on the brink over they went, shrieking with fear and excitement. Whereas I, free, untrammelled, trusted, dashed to the edge a thousand times, ran blithely along the cliff disdaining to look down, but held in check by my mother's voice:

"Well it's your life – you must sink or swim in your own way."

Was it because her love was so flexible and resilient that I had been so slow to recognise vulnerability in others? Had I expected every lover to be like her? To wave me off with a smile, hardly turning from her work and calling out "I'll expect you when I see you!" Never tied us down, never made impossible demands – not like you, Nina, with your expectations of absolute devotion. Never ready to accept that if you love two people at once you can't expect to have the whole heart of either. But here I go again, my mind slipping back to you inexorably, slipping back to find you as ineluctably, slyly, as my hand strayed to your body in the morning, finding its way straight to your cunt while I was still asleep, my fingers finding their way home, your juice on my palm before you had even opened your eyes.

Ah Nina, you must ensnare me again like this – creeping up on me from every direction, without warning, without leave. Is there no subject safe from you? Let me concentrate my mind on mothers – mothers in general, my own in particular.

You made me see her in a new light. Or rather was it my loving you that taught me a different way of seeing her? Did it make it possible to forgive her? To forgive her optimism, her lifelong obdurate hopefulness? I began to ask new questions of myself.

Was I afraid to be the kind of mother she was? Is that why I so easily doubt my ability to care for Ben and Luke? Did I try to do everything differently?

"Did you love your mother better than your father, Mrs Newman? Were you closer to her as a child?"

No, I can't agree. On the contrary, as far as I remember I spent most of my time in the company of men. I don't know if it was because the women were less attentive or because I sought out the freedom and the privilege of the male way of life. I liked the ease men had, their careless ways, their self-confidence. But yes, certainly I held a special place in my heart for my mother. As a child I remember how much I also liked her women friends. The sweet smell of their hair, the brush of their skin as they swept down to kiss me. The sudden heat and softness of their flesh when they drew me up into their arms. The laughter in their voices. They never seemed quite serious. Even while they praised and flattered – isn't she a marvel, isn't she a dote! What will you do with her at all? For every small baby was a wonder to them beyond description. What was the source of this gentle mockery, this sense of absurdity that was different from the men's mischievous teasing that held a note of self-satisfaction in it. Amused by their own plight and your mother's for being responsible for me? Because to be held accountable for this new, innocent life was a matter so grave and daunting that they must laugh to lighten the load. After kissing me they called out, "What can we do to help?" And followed my mother into the kitchen.

The men had more time for me because they had more time. They sat together in the sitting-room or out of doors on a wall or a bench. They sat at ease, sprawling; their legs stretched out, their arms behind their head. They sat circling the fire in winter, shutting off the heat. They lit their pipes with a flourish, lighting up with a cloud of yellow smoke, asserting their right to colonise space and even the air we breathed. They took me on their knees and bounced me about. They threatened to let go and drop me into the ocean. They were rough and hearty and good-humoured. Easy and detached. The night was theirs. Dinner on the way and nothing asked of them but to amuse the child, smoke their cigarettes and exchange profound ideas.

Oh I can hear them . . .

"Would you tell the court, Mrs Newman, whether you have always hated men or is it a new attitude induced by your involvement with a deviant?"

"I don't hate men. On the contrary I've spent most of my life loving them."

"Have you, indeed? You have a strange way of showing it. Would you consider that you loved your father?"

Did I love my father? How would I answer that? Everyone loved my father as I've said. He was a man of his time, I suppose. You would have to view him in context to judge him fairly.

"And what was the context, Mrs Newman?"

The context I guess was the atmosphere and ethos of his era, a style of life shared by all the men who populated my childhood – the fathers and friends and uncles, the strangers and the passers-by. They seem, in memory, to have been more affectionate than the women, more expressive physically. Why was this? The women seemed to acknowledge a mother's rights as so great they didn't like to trespass. They kissed me briefly, they leaned down and talked to me, but it was rare for them to take a child on their knees or in their arms. They were taken up with care of their own children or else they were spinsters unused to the handling of them. Men had more freedom and self-confidence. A male lap was never encumbered by its owner's offspring. When I wanted affection, among a group of chattering adults, I'd wander over to the nearest male and climb up on his lap. I stole his comb and cigarettes. I hid stones and marbles in his breast pocket. I pulled his ears and drummed my fists against his thighs which were too hard, he boasted, for me to make the least impression. This was a lie and so I continued until it hurt. I stuck my fingers in his nose and pulled the long hairs that grew there. I asked to see the hair on his chest and when he wouldn't show me I called him a sissy. When I wounded him he lifted me high in the air and shook me till I shrieked and then it was quits and I was at last ready to be quiet as the women begged me to be.

I liked the company of men. I liked their toughness and their carefree ways. I liked their loud laughter, their hard thighs that were good as a vaulting horse. I liked the smell of their tobacco and their rough tweed clothes. I liked the money in their jackets on the far side from their hearts. I liked to take out the crisp bank notes and count them. I liked the sweets they bought for me. I liked them always having money to buy me sweets. I liked how, when they'd enough of me, they simply set me on my feet, slapped my bottom and told me to run home to my mother. I liked their never being too cross or too tired. They had no need to be cross. They had so much time and so many ways to spend it. They played in gardens and in boats, in forests and on rivers, on railways, in stables, in studies and building sites, on golf courses and football clubs. They had tools and instruments of every description. An endless assortment of playthings. They had rakes and hammers and chisels and lathes, sledgehammers and lump hammers, screwdrivers and scythes and pickaxes and oars and paddles and rods and lines and tackle and saddles and bridles and blinkers and paint-brushes and rollers and turpentine and whitewash and tilly lamps and gas lamps and blowlamps and billy-cans and kettles. They had cars and carriages and bicycles and motorbikes and ships and trains and planes and horses and carts and donkeys and desks and tables and trestletables and workbenches and magnifying glasses and cameras and binoculars and telescopes and shotguns and shooting sticks and pistols and typewriters and pens and paper and journals and books. They had sheds and studies and outhouses and workshops. They had wagons and buggies and yachts and dinghies and trawlers and sails and trailers and mangles, reapers and binders and cement mixers and tractors and jeeps and pick-up trucks and dump trucks and forklifts and mechanical diggers. They had instruments and appliances for every action known to humans, for every need and impulse. For every part of the earth they had a tool to make their desires material. What they wished for they could accomplish. What was more they could teach others.

Women, on the other hand, had nothing but their kitchens. They had knives and forks and spoons. They had tablecloths and sheets and towels. They could feed the children, get them ready for school and put them to bed. They could gaze out the window over a sink and dream of other things. They could sing a song while they washed the floor. But they were always too busy to spend time experimenting. Always there, making the centre of things, taking care of and for, rooted and permanent, but too busy to play, too busy for a jaunt or a gallivant, too needed to go out into the fields and streets looking for fun.

I played with the men and profited from their licence. I revelled in their self-indulgence, their devilment, the self-importance of their diversions. Everything they did took on the grandeur of necessary labour and, if a child were fortunate to be welcomed into the circle of their pleasures, then no woman would pass judgement. You were with the men. Honoured by inclusion in the weighty concerns of their existence. Special, chosen, singled out.

And yet it was women I loved most. From the first it was they who held mystery and fascination. Women who lured me. Women who fired my imagination. Women who must stay behind in the kitchen who could not be trusted elsewhere. Is this why, so many years later I would fall in love with a woman and fall from grace. Fall from power. Fall from exemption.

Does this sound like the sort of thing they want to hear?

Apart from the last few lines, it could be considered to draw a picture of a balanced and healthy outlook, don't you think? A normal childhood?

It's so quiet here when the wind and rain stop. Uncanny silence. I sit bathed in stillness and watch the slow movement of the day from one window to the next. Every window has a different outlook. It might even be a different season. Rain from the west, the sun shining in the south and grey clouds in the north. The sky and the amazing changing light is one's whole existence. I sit gazing, as the cat does, following the day from one window to the next. I dream of having you here, sitting opposite me. I imagine you talking. I try to hear exactly what you'd say, to see the expression on your face, the movements of your hands. I picture it so intensely that at times I imagine you're actually in the room.

There was a knock at the door a moment ago. One of the local men stood on the threshold with the rain-water pouring down his bare head. They never bother with umbrellas or raincoats here. They refuse any concession to the weather. He asked me if I could move my car because it was blocking the boreen and they were bringing cattle through. I told him I didn't have a car and he said "OK so, we'll try below," and he smiled this smile they have and turned and walked off into the downpour again. As he went out the gate I saw Michael, the simpleton, standing gaping up at me, his strangely round eyes staring from under a peaked cap. The man spoke to him as he passed and I heard Michael answer: "I'll drive them to the bottom field, so," he said in what sounded a more or less normal voice. So he can speak if he wants to? In which case why does he wander about pretending to be simple? A few minutes later I heard the cattle streaming by, their hooves thudding in the soft mud, bellowing to one another in fright.

And the shouts of the men after them and the barking of the sheepdogs.

The wind is blowing from the south today, not so harsh as the days before. It reminds me of Ma – one of her favourite songs.

"Blow the wind southerly,

southerly, southerly.

Blow the wind southerly,

my true love to me."

Hearing the rooks shrieking in the fir trees reminds me of her funeral. The churchyard, the yew trees and the rooks. She always disliked rooks, thought them harbingers of misfortune, but on that last day, though they flew through the air, they were silent as if in deference.

Death and burial – the last memories of my mother. What was the first?

She was brought home to be buried as she had wanted, to the churchyard at Drumkeen. I took the train down and went straight to the church. You wanted to come with me but I thought it would be easier without you. All the way down on the train I thought of you and within minutes of leaving the station regretted that I hadn't let you come. I dreaded meeting all the relations, the uncles and cousins I hadn't seen since childhood. But I knew how much it would have meant to Ma to have me there. How much she would have enjoyed it. "Ah, there you are," she'd have said. "I knew you wouldn't let us down. Leave everything to the last minute, but you rise to the occasion when it counts."

Yes, she would have been delighted, full of fun and excitement. And because the rain was falling softly she would have passed me her umbrella and said: "Here take mine, you'll get soaked, love."

I would have slipped my arm through hers and linked together we would lean close, drawn tight under the small protective circle of her umbrella. We would have walked forward to her graveside in step, calm and contented.

"Now who do you know? Let me introduce you to everyone."

She always enjoyed a good funeral. And she'd have greatly appreciated her own. Full of chat and gaiety she'd have been afterwards. "Where did they come from?" she'd ask as soon as we were clear of the church gates. "I didn't know the half of them, did you?"

We would walk back together, laughing, going home for the last time, to open up the house, lay out the food and drink.

"But sure what matter," she'd say, "wasn't it a marvellous send-off?"

And it was. None better.

But we would not have walked home together that morning, my mother and I. No, we would have driven in the sombre, black limousine hired for the day. Let's do it in style – we'll never do it again. Driving together on the richly upholstered back seat in the dark, secluded comfort of the car as it travelled sedately through the hushed streets. There they go now, whispered from the footpath, that's the daughter, the eldest down from Dublin. As we bowled gracefully along my mind would return from the last journey to the first, although it was not the first but the first remembered.

Travelling through the streets of another town, she and I together. I lying face up in the warmth of my pram, watching the world go by. Women friends and neighbours coming to look, their faces gathered round me, their eyes smiling, their lips, the bright scarlet painted lips in the fashion of the day, shaping endearments and flattery, the brown eyes smiling. (Why do I always remember brown eyes?) Among this bobbing sea of faces my mother stood out smiling down at me from the unknown contentment of the adult world: creatures who travelled upright on their own feet instead of bowling along on the flat of their backs sky-gazing. And my face reflected in her smile seemed to play its part in her calm contemplation of the day before us. I was pushed forward into the unseen world leaving it up to this woman to guide me. Knowing from her expression that all was well, the road an adventure unfurling before me.

Travelling up-hill, her shoulders leaning into the handles of the carriage, her breath coming more quickly, smoking on the air above my head, her cheeks growing warm and ruddy. The trees outlined against the sky, the stark black branches of winter, the white skies, the roaring of the sea beyond and the wind through the empty trees. The brow of the hill. The brief rest at the summit. Then the descent, free falling all the way down, gathering momentum on the first bend, the laughter torn from her trailing behind us, her shoes clattering as we rushed pell-mell, bursting together into the future revealed to me, snapshot by snapshot, second by second, framed in the hood of the pram. She saw it coming, I saw it fly into the past.

"We joined the navy to see the world and what did we see? We saw the sea!" There we were at last beside the seaside and her arms reaching down to me, pulling back the shelter of covers and swinging me up into the cold of the air, my fists clenched, my feet wool shod. We joined the navy to see the world. She bore me down to the shore, tight against her breast, and I twisted round to face forward to see the world for one second, in the same second, and not always behind her shoulder.

There it was; the sea, crashing itself to shore, foaming at the mouth, gliding its tongue over slimy green rocks, exhaling with a mighty breath, breathing with ours. There it was, the smell of the sea, the lime on the rocks and the seaweed swirling, pricking our nostrils. Borne closer until I felt the hail of spray against my cheek like small sharp pebbles, the sand crunched underfoot, the cold nibbling at my eyelids and my lips until I shrieked and she swung me up high towards the sky above the reach of the seething, growling water.

Then it was cold and time to go home. She opened her coat and held me against her breast, my hand holding fast to her warm flesh. Time to go home. The covers wrapping me again, my feet squirming free for a last time, my cheek towards the scented, embroidered pillowcase. Her foot letting off the handbrake and we lurched forward, going backwards now, into the future.

"My bonny lies over the ocean,
my bonny lies over the sea,
my bonny lies over the ocean.
Oh bring back my bonny to me."

My lips closed over the thumb and I was quiet and calm, moving into the sleep that is not quite sleep, the best sleep. The wheels spinning below me, driving me into the darkening future, I no longer bothered to watch as it flowed behind me backwards into the darkness over her shoulder, as I sucked warmth and quiet from my thumb, letting it flow like the clouds above me into the long gone, over, the never to come again past. Blow the wind southerly, southerly, southerly. Blow the wind southerly, my true love to me.

You see, I can remember everything but the moment of standing at the graveside. A hole in the earth and inside the hole a wooden box and inside the box my mother's body. Then the clay falling and my sister and brother and I turning our backs on her, once more, for the last time and walking back alone for the first time into the make-believe world of everyday life.

Chapter Nine

October, Dublin.

"Do you know what Elinor's doing this evening? Have you phoned her yet?" Aunt May asked suddenly, looking up from the photograph she was studying.

"No, I'm not sure. Can I call her now?"

"Since when did you need to ask?" May answered lightly, but she was still regarding her niece with a quizzical, faintly troubled gaze.

"You don't have to ask when it's your own house, do you?" Lizzie joined in.

"That's right, pet."

"And this is Nina's house, isn't it?"

"Yes."

"Will she live here when you die?"

"May isn't going to die for a very long time," Nina said looking over her shoulder as she went out of the room to the hall phone. "She sold her soul to the devil at a card game, years ago, in exchange for immortal life."

"Did you Aunty May?" Lizzie gazed at her with new admiration. "Will I live forever too?"

"Much longer than that, pet. You'll outlive us all." May reached out her large mottled hand and, laying it on the child's head, she stroked her hair as Nina had done a moment before, from the crown to the tips of the bright blonde locks falling on her shoulders. "You'll outlive us all, pet."

A few minutes later Nina came back into the sitting room and resumed her place at the fire without speaking.

"Nothing wrong I hope?" May asked. "Did you talk to Elinor?"

"No, she's out. I left a message," Nina spoke lightly, but she kept her eyes averted and seemed to be preoccupied with some other subject.

"Why is she out?" Lizzie demanded. "She said she'd watch *Superman* with me tonight."

"She's only out for a while. You'll see her later."

"You seem worried about Elinor," May said.

"No, I'm not, I just need to speak to her about something."

They sat in silence, Lizzie lying on the hearth-rug playing with the cat, Nina and May gazing into the fire. After a while May looked over at Nina and, with the air of one moving the conversation to happier subjects, she began to question Nina about her radio programme. She asked her how many days she had taken off recently and did she always listen to the programme when someone else was covering for her? Nina told her that fortunately it was not necessary to subject herself to them all. They were recorded at the studio and she could listen to a sample later on.

"I see," May said and fell silent. In the sudden quiet of the room they heard the ticking of the clock on the mantelpiece and the crackling of the cat's electric fur as the child's hand moved over it. After a few minutes May began to speak again in a slow, meditative voice as if her mind had wandered naturally to a disconnected subject.

"There was an interesting story on your programme, a few weeks ago, on one of the afternoons when your friend was standing in for you. Did you hear it, I wonder? About two sisters who fell in love with the same man?"

"No, I can't say I remember. But there are so many," Nina answered absently.

"Well, it was an interesting story. A sad one. It was an elderly country woman who phoned in. She said she'd never told anyone before. But she needed to talk about it. She didn't tell the whole story, of course. She wanted to spare people's feelings. Even now there might still be people listening who'd recognise it, I imagine. But she told the main part of it – how in the small place they were living, a quiet country town, two sisters had been courted by the same man. She said that that wasn't an unusual thing in those days – most of the young men had emigrated and it was common enough at that time for friends to go out together with the same man. But in this case it led to tragedy because both young women grew to feel deeply about the man who was courting them. He was very charming and handsome and considered a great catch for any young girl. He was a solicitor by profession and he had come to the town to work in the local man's practice.

"For weeks he took them both out together and on their own. They went for walks and to the cinema and to the local dances. He flirted with them both. One night he would come over with flowers for one and a few days later he would be back to make eyes at the other. Neither of them knew which he was really interested in."

May paused in her story. She looked over at her niece whose head was lowered over the open book on her lap as if she might be reading. Was she listening or not? May couldn't tell. But Lizzie was looking up at her with great curious eyes. Slowly she began to speak again: "When it had been going on like this for a year or so, the woman telling the story said she could no longer hide from herself the pain it was causing to both her sister and herself. She knew that one of them would have to make a decision and she decided it should be herself. With great pain and regret she decided she must stop seeing the man. She felt it had to be a completely clean break so she made arrangements in secret and in due course left her home

107

place and went to live in England. But after a while the man she loved came after her. He came to the city where she was living. The woman thought that perhaps he felt something special for her after all. But then . . ." suddenly she stopped. She stared at her niece with annoyance: "Are you listening to me, at all?" she asked: "Do you remember this story?"

"No I can't say I do," Nina said, "but it sounds vaguely familiar."

"Oh, I can see I might as well be talking to myself. It's plain you haven't been listening to a word I've said." May sounded unusually impatient. "You're like a cat on a hot tin roof tonight. Where is it you want to be off to?"

Nina looked up and spoke very quickly and almost under her breath, "I was wondering if I might just call over to the shelter for a moment to see what's Elinor's doing. Is that all right, May?"

"Of course, child." May sounding resigned to the inevitable. She was disappointed, but anxious to please Nina. "You can go anywhere you like."

"Can you take care of Lizzie for a bit?"

"Yes, love. But don't be too late. Remember I'm an old lady."

"Half an hour!" Nina called out as she left the room.

They heard the hall door bang behind her and then the sound of her car driving off.

"Well," May said with a rueful smile, "that means she'll be gone at least an hour, Lizzie, so we'd better do what we can to entertain ourselves." May took a pack of cards from the mantelpiece and with expert hands began a slow, suave shuffling: "What would you say to a little bit of gambling?"

Chapter Ten

September, Clare.

Why did I come up here on my own? It seemed a good idea.
To come and wait for you. To prepare the ground, to give you
time to work things out and to give myself time to order my
thoughts. It seemed important to be alone. But have I left you
at the wrong moment? Should I have stayed? I feel so far from
you, here.

This morning I almost decided to go back to see you. But
if I were to arrive, suddenly, at your door, who would open it?
You or Elinor? Could I phone you instead? Could I ask a
friend to go over with a message? But no – any contact
would be a breach of our agreement. I must leave you alone,
to work things out in your own way. I must bring no pressure
to bear.

Why haven't you written to me yet? You said you'd write as
soon as you knew what was happening. But what can happen
after all? You have only to tell Elinor and then leave her. You
can't be expecting her to agree with you. Have you told her
yet, Nina? Have you looked her in the face and said you want
to live with me? I think I can imagine your answer. "Not
exactly," you'd say, "I've told her more or less – she guessed
what I was about to say, so I didn't have to finish. She knows."
But that's not the same thing as telling her, is it? You'd say you
can't throw it in her face. Not now. Now when she's happy for

a bit. But if you can't tell her when she's happy when can you tell her?

You are so different from me in your way of handling this. So contradictory, so ambivalent. I find it hard to understand. Almost as soon as I looked at you I knew I'd have to leave Malachy. That's how absolute it was. No alternative, no choice. I assumed you felt the same way – the same blind compulsion. Yet a year later you were still living with Elinor and even now you are explaining yourself to her. What is it between the two of you that is so tenacious? After all, for me the decision should have been much harder. If I delayed at all, it was out of fear for the boys. Well, not only that, but inevitably it was the major part. But for you? What is it Elinor does to you that makes you so guilty, so tentative, trying always to let her down gently, trying to win her forgiveness? I don't understand it and yet I'm not really surprised. In some part of myself I knew all along that nothing would be easy. I knew it instinctively from the moment I saw you together.

I can't pretend I didn't see the danger signals, the red flags waving about you, the reef on which my desire might founder: lovely, gregarious, warm-hearted Elinor. In the first weeks when I still had the strength for caution I tried to resist you, to hold back the tide that threatened to engulf me because I saw all too well the strength of the attachment between you. Not that you concealed it from me. In fact, I remember you telling me, almost as soon as I knew you, that you could never love anyone more than you loved Elinor. But then you told me so many contradictory things. In almost the same breath as you protested your passion for her, you told me that you were no longer lovers in the physical sense. Of course, I took this to mean what it usually means – I imagined that you were no longer romantic or possessive of each other. How long was it before I realised my mistake? I chose to believe that it meant you were free to love someone else. In spite of the closeness I saw between you, I began to imagine signs of strain. I told myself that Elinor had grown impatient with you, detached and critical. As if I didn't know these things can co-exist with passion. I told myself she didn't understand you as I could. I told myself you'd be happier with me. And all the rest of these self-justifications. But I was on the wrong track from the start, needless to say. Misled? Blind? Well, what had I to go on? Precisely nothing. That's exactly where the case for the defence rests. I understood nothing about lesbian relationships. I was walking in darkness, striking matches for illumination and missing everything that occurred in the space between one match and the next. Did you encourage that ignorance? Did it suit you to have me so naïve? Were you perhaps already casting around (half known to yourself) for someone to create a buffer between you and Elinor? Or did I come into your life uncalled for, an unforeseen, irresistible force of destiny? How good it would be to believe the latter. Was there a time when I did? Oh yes, Nina, I was naïve and arrogant enough for any foolishness.

Time has taught me to modify my faith, but at the start I certainly believed in destiny. The first day I called to your house after our meeting in the hospital, I told myself it was a force beyond my control that was driving my actions. I dropped over one afternoon, pretending that I needed to give you something. (I discovered your address by ringing someone who knew Elinor – I didn't dare mention your name – and asking for hers.) At the first house on your street, I pushed open the low, iron gate, and walked the narrow path – ten steps at most – to your front door. I counted to twenty and rang the bell.

A moment later, you opened it. You were, at once, exactly as I had last seen you and utterly changed. Your hair was the same – the beautiful mane of yellow curls, your smile, that goes straight to your eyes, was the same, but whether it was the different style of dress (a loose blue sweater, black leggings and heavy, brown leather boots) or something else I couldn't define, you appeared startlingly unknown and unapproachable as you stood in the doorway of your own house looking at me, not in welcome but surprise. I proffered the book I'd brought over for just this moment – a hardback, first edition of Adrienne Rich. Her name had come up in the conversation at the hospital and I had said I'd like to lend you my copy. Was I also wanting to show myself as being on relaxed terms with American lesbian literature?

"I just dropped by to give you a book," I said sounding almost normal.

"Ah yes," you answered, "of course, the book." And you took it out of my hand and glanced at it but made no comment. Then you smiled suddenly as if relieved that there was some actual reason for my appearance or because you knew there wasn't.

"Well, I was just passing . . ." I said, my heart pounding.

"Ah," you said and hesitated. And then you spoke the magical words I had been waiting for: "Would you like to come in for a minute, have some coffee? We make almost American coffee in this house."

And that was it – as simple as that. My fate was sealed by that simple remark, sealed forever, as you stood back from the door and waited for me to pass through it.

All I remember of the rest of that afternoon was my terror. Terror at being suddenly completely alone with you, as you led me through the house and into the kitchen, where you began to make coffee while I made absurd small talk, trying desperately to sound casual. And my even greater terror when we were suddenly interrupted by Lizzie, who appeared at the window giving onto the back garden, looking like a nymph or water sprite, her white blonde hair seeming to fizz round her head, her great blue eyes staring in excitement. When she came into the room and sat on your knee, I had the extra burden of finding things to say that would sound normal to a child's acute ear. Somehow I got through five minutes or so without an accident and then, just as I was beginning to relax a little, I blew it with one stupid remark. I had been marvelling to myself at the lovely ease and closeness between yourself and Lizzie and I suddenly heard myself saying aloud:

"You're so good with children – have you ever thought of having one of your own?" I wanted to bite my tongue the second the words left my lips.

Lizzie stared at me in amazement for a moment and then in a small, patient voice said simply: "She has me as her own." It made the question seem so gauche and offensive I wanted to leave there and then before I did something worse. But you took pity and rescued me.

"She means other children apart from you, Lizzie," you said and you smiled at me. With that smile I knew I was forgiven. As you were later to forgive so many other blunders of mine, my clumsiness and ignorance, my stupid preconceptions about your way of life.

I waited a fortnight before finding another excuse. After that it began to look natural, to call over when I was passing. I had a justifiable reason to pass your door every day because it was on the way to school for me. So once a week or so, while the leaves fell from the trees and the evenings drew in, we sat together talking in your kitchen, in Elinor's kitchen. I was more at ease in your house than I had felt anywhere else for years. Why – when I had a lovely house of my own with two children in it? But sitting in the warm, flagstoned kitchen, with Elinor piling up fuel in the range and you making endless jugs of coffee for us all and beginning to prepare dinner and persuading me to stay, I marvelled at the special atmosphere you created; a warmth and hospitality, more intense and yet more spontaneous than any I'd known before, exactly because,

I suppose, it was created by the energy of two women instead of one.

It never took any persuasion to make me stay. As soon as I discovered your amazing food (I told Malachy you made the best Indian food I've tasted outside New York city – and it was true) I had the perfect excuse. I'd phone home and tell Malachy to expect me a little later than usual, and settle in to enjoy myself for a few hours stolen from my own domestic duties and routine. I loved your friends, the casual way they came and went, the heated political debates unlike any politics I'd known, the gossip, the delight in scandal, the marvellous wit. And all the time Lizzie, with her astonishingly blue eyes, hopping about like a cricket on the hob, startling us with her strange remarks, her odd whimsical way of seeing things, her passionate enthusiasms. Watching you playing game after game of backgammon or draughts (old-fashioned games I hadn't seen anyone bother with for years), reading her adventure stories, or playing cards, I felt a pang of guilt for all the times I'd been impatient with my own two when they were the same age. But I said to myself it was different for you because you weren't her real mother. You hadn't the same responsibility. You were free to indulge her.

We sat over the kitchen table and under cover of small talk and general conversation I fell in love with you. We sat talking for hours on end, as women do, drinking endless cups of coffee in the late mornings, or sharing a bottle of wine at lunch, eating dinner or last night's leftovers, and all the while gazing into each other's eyes, laughing as women do. We talked about all the things women normally talk about: about our families, about whose was most loving or destructive and was there a difference? We talked about children, why one of us had had them and the other not. We talked about the difference between a child chosen and planned and one you had grown to love by chance like Lizzie. We talked about sex, when we had had it first, for how long, with which gender, how it had been, how we liked it now that we knew the worst and the best? (Although I didn't at that time, did I?) We talked about romance and lovers and giving our all for someone we knew in advance was thoroughly worthless; the rock on which to wreck oneself that every woman sought out once in her life. Or twice. We talked about the lovers we'd deserted, about our cruelty and indifference to lovers we'd outgrown. We discussed the relative merits of being an abandoner or an abandonee. Whether it was worse to be left for a man or a woman. Your best friend or an enemy. We talked about our school friends: the outrageous ones, the ones who did everything better, the ones who ruined themselves with drink. We talked about success and failure and what we'd wanted to be when we were young – and what we'd managed since. We talked about our talents, our faults and our hopes. We talked about our bodies, what was wrong with them and what was right. The one feature we liked. The one everyone else liked. We talked about every illness we had had since childhood and the ones to come. The one that terrified us and the one we could live with. We talked about every friend we had in common. The one who was getting neurotic, the one who just put it on and the one who was outright mad. We debated which was loyal and to be counted on, which most fun to be around, which we would trust with our lives, which we would love, which was dangerous to know and which the worst gossip in town.

We talked about all the movies we'd ever enjoyed. Every book we'd read, the worst and the best, when and where. We talked about food and how we liked to cook it, where we liked to eat it, and shop for it. We talked about sleep and our dreams and our nightmares. We talked about fantasies, the ones we would admit to and the ones we wouldn't. We talked about our secret past, our ambitions, our longings, the most private thing in our life that we'd never told anyone before. We talked about politics, how things should be run and why they were not and why one crowd was worse than another. We talked about ideologies we'd once believed in and how we'd been let down. We talked about money, who had it and why. The difference it made to things, especially to those who didn't have it. And whether we'd would really want it when we saw what it did to the people who had it. We talked about clothes and fashion, the ones we had followed and the ones we had ignored. What looked best on someone else and why. We talked about holidays and travel, where it was we most wanted to live and why we had left somewhere else that everyone else thought we should love. We talked about our most embarrassing moment and about the ugliest child we had known at school.

We talked again about mothers and fathers and again about mothers. We talked about what it was like to have always had parents and what it was like never to have seen them. We talked about the merits of adoption over blood ties and we talked about how our parents had lived and how they died. And about how we'd like to die ourselves and how we were afraid we might and then we talked about love again. We made more coffee and had some freshly baked bread straight from the oven and some cheese and told jokes and laughed until the tears ran down our cheeks and we gazed into each other's eyes and said nothing at all for the longest time we could risk.

And all the while I talked and listened and waited, I envied you and Elinor. I envied, above all, the love and generosity I saw between you. The laughter. You both had a great talent for story-telling. I was new enough to this country to be entranced still by this gift for talk and entertainment. I loved listening to you. One of you would begin some outlandish tale and the other would join in adding marvellous embellishments to the main theme. I remember too my surprise at how often you touched one another. You'd been together for seven years at that time, but to my eyes you behaved like young lovers. You'd lean over and touch her knee under the table when she was talking or she'd lightly brush her hand against the nape of your neck as she crossed to the stove to make yet another pot of coffee. The first time I saw you kissing, standing in the hallway, your arms about each other saying goodbye, I felt such a sudden rush of jealousy that I had to turn away and hide my face. Very soon afterwards I made an excuse to leave.

But even while I admired and envied the rapport you had, the deep closeness, I must already somewhere in my heart have been planning a way to replace Elinor, to dislodge her from your life. If I was aware of this I certainly never acknowledged it. I couldn't because it would have threatened too strongly my image of myself as benevolent and virtuous, a woman who would never have had an affair with a married man, who would never have wrecked another woman's home. So I dodged it by pretending in some way that your relationship was less important than a marriage. By slighting it, by not paying it real attention. I liked Elinor. Maybe I even loved her. I knew the hurt I was going to cause her and I couldn't stop myself. Or wouldn't. I was about to do something – not only on the point of – but actively planning to make it happen – scheming my way into your life, infusing myself, infiltrating your world, your ideas, your interests – something I'd never done before and wouldn't have countenanced if you had been married.

When I say scheming, again, I don't mean that I sat down and worked it all out. I made no fixed plan. I didn't allow my desire into conscious knowledge. I kept it in the dark of instinct, refusing to look at it directly or take stock. I couldn't afford to because, apart from the damage to my self-image, if

I'd taken time to consider what I was doing, I couldn't have made it happen. And I did, however unconsciously, make things happen.

Malachy saw the friendship developing between us. He saw my intensity. He tried to understand. At first he was pleased that I'd found such good friends. At his suggestion I asked you over to dinner one night. The night before you were to come, you phoned me very late and said you were terribly sorry but Elinor had the flu and you didn't like to come without her and you hoped I could forgive such short notice and so forth. I wondered about this – was it an attempt by Elinor to prevent what she saw developing or just an accident? I know I felt relieved because I hadn't known how I'd get through a whole evening with you and Malachy at one table.

Then, as luck would have it, hardly a week later, when I was out having a drink with him one night we met you by accident in Maguire's. Just before closing time I saw you coming through the door with Elinor behind you. I might have dodged you, but Elinor caught sight of me. You went off to order a round of drinks and Malachy launched into conversation with Elinor, but I could see he was looking over her shoulder, watching you while you stood chatting to the barman at the counter. Elinor, with that instinctive kindness of hers, talked with a show of great interest about football and the elections and architecture, wanting to put Malachy at his ease while you and I made small talk.

On the way home in the car I asked what he thought.

"Of what?"

"Of Elinor and Nina, of course."

"Elinor's lovely," he said after a second's hesitation.

"And Nina?"

"Well it's easy to see why anyone would be fascinated." He kept his eyes fixed on the road and gave me no indication of his feelings.

"Is someone?" I asked, conscious of a reckless daring, but unable to resist pursuing the subject.

"Elinor, for a start," he said and still didn't look at me.

We drove the rest of the way in silence. After that night, he never mentioned your name again nor Elinor's. Not, that is, until the day I told him that I was in love with you.

What was the next act of our drama? The birthday party. When? Elinor's birthday. Do you remember? She gave a party. We were all preparing food together in the afternoon. You and I made an excuse to go out to buy more wine and coming back from the supermarket we walked by the canal and I stopped to admire the calm of the evening (stopping so that you were forced to stop too). I leaned my back against the trunk of the last tree growing at the water's edge (one of the elms that has since been cut down). I looked you straight in the eye and with a pretence of surprise and artlessness I said: "Do you know something I've just discovered? I think I'm falling in love with you." Without answering you moved closer to me, so close I could feel your breath on my lips. I thought you were about to kiss me but you didn't. At long last you spoke.

"Yes," you said, "I know."

"How long have you known?" I asked.

"Since the beginning," you said.

"Does Elinor know?"

"No," you said, "and I don't want her to."

The something extraordinary happened. Something I had imagined a hundred times. You stood beside me and put your arms round my waist. "Look at me," you said. I turned to face you. The night was very dark. The water of the canal seemed black and silent. Then a car passed us. For a moment I saw your face illumined by its headlights. It was strangely pale and still. But your eyes were glowing in the darkness, brilliant as a cat's. For a terrified second, seeing your expression, I thought you were going to kiss me, but you didn't. And so, before the moment was lost forever, in the deep night quiet that surrounded us, I kissed you, instead. I will never forget the shock of that first touch, the softness of your skin, literally as soft as silk, and the long, slow kiss that sucked the breath from my lungs and the heart from my body.

After a moment, you took both my hands in yours and slowly, with a meditative considering air, kissed the open palms.

"Let's go back now," you said, and you led me by the hand, and we walked back along the orange-lit streets to your house, without another word spoken. When we reached it, in explanation of our being gone almost an hour, you told Elinor that the local shop was closed for a funeral and that we'd had to go into town for the wine.

As we walked into the kitchen behind her I whispered to you: "You don't mind do you – what I said? It won't change anything?"

But I was wrong. It changed everything. And not a moment too soon.

After that? Well after that we both knew what was happening. There could be no more pretence.

As time progressed – as I grew to know you better – I grew to love you more. I had no idea that it was possible to love anyone as I loved you, so obsessively, so selfishly and altruistically at once. I wanted nothing but the best for you even while my actions risked wreaking chaos in your well-ordered life. I became anxious and fretful, worrying about the future in a way I'd never done before, in case it might bring you the smallest harm. I wanted to give you all the things you needed; the material things and the spiritual things. I bought you presents, I fixed belongings for you, I noticed what might go wrong before it happened so that I could step in and put it right, I ran errands for you. Above all I talked to you, hours and hours of it, in pubs and cafés, starting at lunch and drifting on until early evening. I wanted to know everything about your past. I envied every friend who had known you before I did. I envied your past lovers – so much that I preferred not to talk about them. I wanted to heal all the wounds in your life. When you told me about the poverty and deprivation you'd suffered in your childhood I felt more pain than if it were happening to me in the present. I wished I'd known you then so that I could have protected you, consoled you. I wanted to take care of you. I wanted to make you light-hearted. I wanted to make you laugh. I would have done almost anything to please you.

How long did we try to resist each other? How long did we fight it, trying to be good – for Elinor's sake, for the boys' sake, for Malachy's sake? We'd go for a drink and I'd manage to keep my hands away from you for two hours and then, after only minutes alone, sitting close to you in the dark of the car, all resolution would vanish. This was before we became lovers when just to look at you made me tremble. We'd sit like idiots, love-struck dumb and shivering, gazing at each other and then wrenching our eyes away with a sigh of pain. You'd lie with your head in my lap. You said it soothed you, helped to distract you from your need of me. No gesture could have touched me more. You seemed so vulnerable, so trusting. I looked at your face and stroked your hair and neck with my fingertips. Afraid to do more. Afraid of being overpowered by my feelings. I'd never before felt so much tenderness and desire with so little provocation.

I began to avoid your house. I didn't want to meet Elinor. I didn't want to see you together. I felt guilty of course, but more than that I had become horribly jealous. I resented her place in your heart. Without admitting it to myself, much less to you, I wanted her out of the way. I wanted you all to myself. Of course, I saw how much she meant to you. I saw how happy she could make you. But I told myself that it was a habit of dependence, one you'd outgrow. That you'd gradually learn to depend on me, to count on me for all the significant and the trivial things in life. Soon, I told myself, you'd no longer have the need to confide in her, to turn to her in moments of fear or trouble. For that was what I envied most – the trust you had in each other, the intimacy. Did I recognise this intimacy as the essence of the love between two women? Did I let myself acknowledge that to be in love with another woman, to live with her and to share this profound empathy was the reward for the courage needed to maintain it? I don't think so. I imagine I told myself it was how you'd be with anyone.

The afternoon we became lovers? Did you have it planned? Did you see it coming? You said it took you by surprise as much as it did me. But then, I was lying. I lied about that from the beginning because I never wanted to admit that I knew how I felt about you from the first moment. I didn't want you to think me calculated, scheming. Which of course I was, but not in the way it might seem. I pretended that I discovered my attraction for you only on the night I confided it to you, and not from the start, exactly two months and twenty-six days before I went to bed with you. I counted the days, you see, from our first meeting until that afternoon. That's how bad I was – how obsessive, how designing.

But when it happened at last, it was by chance. At least, the time and place, I think, were accidental. We met for a drink, in a city centre hotel (even now I don't want to name it, for fear that someone else, Malachy or Elinor, might read this, absurd I know – as if the name mattered), intending to discuss the situation between us and decide finally what to do about it. We met on a Friday afternoon, at three o'clock. By five we were both a little drunk. You said there were only two possible courses of action. Either we both went home there and then and agreed not to let this go any further and revert to friendship or . . . You turned and looked at me and, only because you (who never blushes) looked several shades paler than normal, I held my breath in hope and fear: "Or," you continued, looking into my eyes very gravely, "we book a room now, for the evening. And go to bed."

"Together?" I said incredulous, awkward as a schoolgirl.

"Would you prefer opposite ends of the corridor?"

I smiled, but I couldn't laugh. I sat quite still and eventually gathered enough breath to say: "I wouldn't know how to manage it."

You looked at me pityingly and spoke very slowly as though to the hard of hearing: "It's easy. You just walk across the room to the reception desk and ask the woman on the telephone if she has a double room vacant."

"I didn't mean that," I said.

"Did you not?" you said in mock surprise.

In the end it was you, of course, who stood at the desk and booked us in, but I stood beside you, resolute, glancing through the newspaper rack, for all the world as if I did this every day. The ascent of that elegant, wide staircase, three floors up, was the longest of my life. The stairs, the door, the key, three momentous physical realities I could not think beyond. You walked ahead. I couldn't bear to look at you. Now that I was so close to the realisation of all my longing, my legs were so weak they hardly carried me. At the landing you turned and took my hand. I wouldn't have made the rest of the journey without that physical support.

At the door – you handed me the key. I turned it in the lock. We stepped inside together.

A window, a tall Georgian window with the heavy wooden shutters retained, a window like so many I love in this city, yet different from any before or after it. A window looking out on a street I had walked once a week or more since I came to live in this town. A shopfront immediately opposite, a hardware store where I had bought cane chairs for my kitchen. Through the window I saw the light was changing, the marvellous golden light of a winter sunset in Dublin. The sycamore and beech trees lining the pavement, the mountains in the distance, blue-black. I stood at the window, my back turned to you, gazing down into the street below, hearing the hum of traffic, and the clatter of heels on the pavement. I watched a flock of starlings gather on a telegraph wire below and then with one sudden movement rise swirling into the orange sky and fly as one dense cloud over the dark trees of the park. As I stood, surveying all this, I found myself thinking: this can't be happening to me – to a woman like me – renting a hotel room, in the middle of the afternoon, to make love with another woman? But it was. As I closed the shutters on the roar of traffic going home from this town that had become our town in a way I never felt it before, I heard you say my name, softly. I fastened the bolt across the waiting hasp and a shaft of orange light slipped through, bathing the walls in its glow. When I turned, I found you already lying in bed, leaning against the high pillows, looking at me with that expectancy and nearly suppressed desire that is in your eyes each time you watch me undress for bed. You spoke my name and I walked towards you.

And what was the first thing we did in that bare Georgian room with its memories of lost grandeur, its high ceilings and stuccoed walls, what was the first thing to happen when our bodies touched, that evening of evenings never to be forgotten or bettered? What was the first thing we did when I lifted the heavy winter quilt from your shoulders and lay beside you? Was it to lie still for minutes, together breast to breast, thigh to thigh, quiet, without a sound, holding our breath so that nothing would interrupt this first extraordinary meeting of bare skin, your skin to mine along the full outstretched length of us? Or did you lean over at once and kiss my lips and draw your mouth along my neck and throat so that my arms blossomed in gooseflesh as they do now at the memory and must have then. I remember that I paused, before I kissed your mouth, to undo the catch of the fine golden chain (a present from Elinor?) that you wear around your neck always.

"In case I might damage it," I said by way of explanation, as if it were all that was in danger.

I had been terrified that once alone with you, I wouldn't know how to give you pleasure. But I was wrong. You said to me: "Just imagine everything you've ever wanted yourself, everything you've ever dreamed of."

And I did.

Do you remember, Nina? Do you remember it all?

But I shouldn't ask you because I can't afford to remember myself. Not here. Not now. I don't want to think about it. I can't. Alone, missing you, I couldn't withstand the longing it will rouse. It must keep for another day, the memory of all that happened, that winter afternoon in Dublin. All that I discovered with you, in those hours together, that changed my life forever.

But some things I can let myself dwell on without risk. I can let myself picture a much later stage of the night when we lay, finally quiet, exhausted, in each other's arms, between the heavy linen sheets that were drenched with our sweat, your sweat and mine already mingled as if it were something natural and everyday. We made jokes and told silly stories, as lovers do, and laughed for the first time since meeting that afternoon. As I lay on your shoulder, exhausted, blissful, I heaved one last great sigh of contentment and said: "I could die now, this minute."

You looked at me warningly: "Don't! There'd have to be an inquest and people might get the wrong impression!"

And we laughed like hyenas at that, as if it were the funniest thing anyone had ever said.

"People might get the wrong impression!" I repeated again and again, and with each repetition burst into another paroxysm of helpless laughter. The notion of our being found, naked, entwined in one another's arms, and dead, seemed to us both more hilarious than we could bear to contemplate.

So with the sublimely callous laughter of passion, it began; the first fall, the first betrayal. And so, very soon, it continued in sweet, ecstatic deceit. Stolen kisses, stolen afternoons, stolen nights. A hundred different excuses. Sometimes we went to my house and sometimes to yours. We'd sit embracing in your car and on park benches, all the illicit things not done since adolescence. We went for endless walks along the beach, at Sandymount and Killiney. We walked across Bray Head and around Howth Head. We went to the cinema in the afternoon and sat in the back row kissing. We were the first into our favourite pub in the afternoons and the last to leave. But despite all this we still managed to keep it a secret from Elinor. You said it was much too soon to tell her. You said after Christmas would be better, or after your holidays or after Lizzie's birthday and so on. Whatever time it was it was never the right time. We did it to protect her of course, to lessen the blow. That's what we said. But wasn't it really to buy time? To provide ourselves with a grace period? A period undisturbed by guilt and interrogation, by angry scrutiny of our actions and motives? Which of us first suggested that we conceal it? I'm not sure. But I suppose I thought it was up to you to choose your time and place. I remember once growing angry with you because of these delaying tactics. I accused you of hiding behind kindness, I said you were so ready to deceive others to protect them from hurt that you didn't notice it was yourself you were protecting. And you replied that you might hide behind deception but I hid behind the truth.

Why am I talking about honesty and deceitfulness? I don't want to think about your readiness to deceive Elinor. I know that I did it to Malachy for a while, and would again I suppose: fob someone off, tinker with the truth, prevaricate and dissemble to keep life comfortable in the name of sparing someone pain. But as time went on the whole situation made me feel mean and furtive. Here I was, a respectable married woman, a mother, a teacher, and suddenly, when I least expected it, in love with another woman. I found myself cast in the role of the mistress; concealed and kept to the margins of your life.

At the beginning I think I took it for granted that you'd leave Elinor for me. After all I was preparing to leave my husband. It never occurred to me – ignorant and inexperienced as I was – that a relationship between two women could be more deeply rooted and tenacious than a marriage. The fact that there was a child involved I discounted because I didn't see you as an equal parent, but merely as a woman who happened to be living in the same house. Of no more importance than a family friend. I wouldn't have said this to you because I didn't want to hurt you. But more importantly I didn't realise *this* was what I thought. I see now that I patronised you without knowing it. It suited me to overlook the depth of your relationship. I needed to make little of the bonds that tied you. But though it was convenient, perhaps even necessary, the primary reason was because I didn't know any better. It came naturally.

At the shop. I pushed open the door and found myself alone with Máire Mac. We exchanged the usual pleasantries. I figured that if a letter had arrived from Dublin she'd tell me without prompting. Anyhow, I was too embarrassed to ask again. I took the paper and began to glance through it while she gathered up my groceries and packed them. She asked if I would be needing any more vegetables over the weekend because she would be getting a delivery on Saturday. I had the feeling that she was trying to find out if I would be alone much longer. She looked at me slyly from under the reading glasses she seems to wear for effect from time to time.

"Do you not find yourself very lonely in evenings sitting up there alone?" she asked. "What do you find to think about at all?"

Once again, for what reason I don't know, I had this crazy impulse to tell her. I felt like sitting down in the garish brightness of the shop and pouring out my heart to her. Can you imagine her reaction? If I'd looked her straight in the eye and told her that I haven't an idle or tedious minute, because I am lost totally in my memories of you, dreaming of you night and day, longing every minute for your arrival? What would she think of me? Would she understand at all? I wonder was she ever in love? Hard to credit, but I suppose she must have been once. She told me the other day that she has three children, all now emigrated, two in America and one in England and that her husband died five years ago. It seems to me unbearably bleak, to put twenty years into raising a family and then lose them all to another country. What does she do in the evenings I wonder, sitting on her own in the room above the shop, watching television, going to bed early? Then rising at seven to bring in the cows. She's hardly in a position to feel sorry for me and yet she does, I can feel it. She seems to have a definite idea of some misfortune in my life. But she doesn't ask. Since hearing about the boys and Malachy being in Galway she's said no more about them, but she conveys an air of great sympathy as though they had abandoned me.

I turned to leave and wished her goodnight. She didn't mention a letter and neither did I.

The rain falls without cease. It hasn't stopped for an hour

since yesterday. The fields are turned to mud. It hangs in the air like fog. I stay inside huddled over the fire, a turf fire that burns with a brilliant, clear yellow flame. Beautiful to watch. But not much heat. The wind howls in the chimney. It seems to me, in the quiet of the evening, that even the furniture talks. Yes, I know it's mad, but when I sit steeped in the silence of night here, with the fire burnt low and no other living sound, it's then I notice the din of inanimate objects: the squeaks and groans of the table and chairs, the little shufflings cloth makes, the soft breathing of all the wood, the slow inhalation and exhalation of the air in every groove and crevice. I opened the last drawer in the chest of drawers last night looking for a tablecloth and just in the split second of opening it, it seemed to me I heard the air shift back from me suddenly as if in fright.

In this state of heightened sensitivity I find myself convinced for seconds at a time that you are here, that I see you sitting in the room with me, on the far side of the hearth or walking through the door; standing before me, your head tilted, your hands hanging at your sides, palms turned out in the strange vulnerable way you have. What would I do if you were to arrive this very moment? If I could look into your eyes and see you smiling your bright, sad smile, what would I do? What's the first thing I'd do? I'd put my arms round you and pull you close so that I felt the full weight of your body against mine. And with your hair against my face, my mouth at your neck, I'd breath in all the fragrance of your body from the beating pulse at your throat. I could stand in that way for seven nights and seven days.

I miss you. Have I told you yet, how much I miss you?

You see: I am obsessed and desperately longing for you, but nevertheless I have to admit that I feel it's good for me, this period of isolation and waiting. In a perverse way I'm enjoying the intensity of it – the self-indulgence, the introspection.

After all, when did I last have the time to brood and meditate and do nothing? But incarcerated here, idle, frustrated, I am also irresponsible, free. Yes, it may be extraordinary to you but that's the only word to describe how I feel. When was the last time I could say as much? I am completely at liberty to think what I like, to feel as I like. No one needs me. No one depends on me. No one interrupts me. I find myself remembering things I haven't thought of for years. Memories of my past with you lead me back into the far distant past; years I thought I'd forgotten. Thinking about my marriage has stirred up so many memories of my father and mother. I feel now that I've never before given them the time they deserved. Neither in practise nor in thought. I've never really tried to see their lives from their own point of view.

For instance, when I was thinking about Ma I found myself drawn back to my earliest memories, the first years of my life when she was like my second skin, when she carried me everywhere in her arms and I was never more than five minutes from the sound of her voice. It's a mistake of course to let myself remember this because any thoughts now about the female body bring me straight back to you. I'm sure Ma wouldn't be pleased to hear it, but it's true nonetheless. I suppose, if one thinks about it, all the physical pleasures in life must have their origin in the early relationship with our mothers. The sensual pleasures are formed in the womb, and at the breast. How she'd hate to hear me say this – to consider for an instant that she might be responsible for the formation of my sexual preferences – but where else would we learn them?

And Pa? Where does he figure in this? I've done my best to recall something of equal importance about him, something equally primal and infantile, but in vain, I'm afraid. No memory of my father seems to exist before speech. Unless it was the dim sense of his presence on the opposite side of the bed when I lay next to my mother at night or early morning, in my first year. Perhaps I remember his voice from this time also, chiding her for indulging me. And perhaps yes – do I remember his hand reaching slyly across the sheet under cover of the blankets to tickle the soles of my feet – "Can we make the tin soldier laugh?" he might have said as he used to say when I was old enough to understand his words.

And I remember his shoes. The great black polished leather shoes lined up together at the edge of the bed. Too heavy for me to lift. My hands slipped inside, lost in them. Not much to carry with me as the first memory.

Nothing so much became him in life as his leaving of it. Was that Pa's story? So many false starts and Ma nursing him through them all. I remember so well the first stroke that we thought was his last. It seemed he couldn't possibly recover. I remember most of all Ma's unfailing patience. Her love of him. And my envy of it. Because I had just fallen in love with you and wanted all the world to know and could tell no one. Least of all my mother or my dying father. I remember so well when I went back to Boston to be with her and we spent every afternoon together at his bedside in hospital.

Sitting on opposite sides of the bed, I listened to Ma while she talked to him, telling him stories and jokes and family gossip and other intimate things that she had held in her heart for years. She talked about their youth together, about my sister and brother and tales of our childhood. She told the story of my own birth which she'd recounted with relish on each of my birthdays. How I couldn't wait to be born, but had slithered into life onto the back seat of the taxi as it drew up at Hatch Street. "Hatch Street" – I'd never heard the name of the maternity hospital as a small child without laughing. Another maternity hospital was called the "Rotunda" which was a great joke and Holles Street was the name of the third, a name I always heard as "holler" Street and imagined women screaming in the throes of labour.

"You were the most impatient child I ever came across," Ma said delightedly to me and Pa smiled on the good side of his face and squeezed her hand. My mother liked to tease him about my birth because he hadn't admitted to believing that she was pregnant until the final rush to the hospital. He defended himself always by telling her that with her tall, slender figure it was almost impossible to see the change and I knew this was an old flattery that her story was told to elicit.

Sometimes during those days in the hospital Ma and I reached across the fragile mound of his body and joined hands, but mostly she sat with his clasped in hers, his thin claw-like hand that was no more than a series of joined bones between which fat purple veins showed, so swollen it seemed they might burst at a touch. She lifted his hand and pressed it to her cheek. And she would find another stream of words to comfort him: "Do you remember the time we climbed Ben Bulben and got lost in the mist and suddenly out of nowhere a stag appeared in front of us and you shrieked with fright? You were such a coward always."

"Ah . . ." he tried to answer her, rolling his eyes towards heaven, his lips opening and closing and rough inchoate sounds issuing from them and I thought I could hear the words forming his familiar rejoinder: "How did I ever manage at all before you took over?"

In those days, keeping vigil by his bedside, I saw the love between them illumined and revealed. The love they'd concealed behind jokes and teasing and the preoccupations of practical life. Now, it was spoken out in front of me in private words that embarrassed me. Yet I envied their freedom to show their love in public, in front of so many others, sick and dying. It was proud and unselfconscious and understood by all.

And I knew my feelings for you could never be any of these things. Never flaunted, never careless.

Watching them together I remembered them as they were in my childhood. I remembered Pa's way of sitting in the kitchen at evening with his paper held up for camouflage and his pipe sending yellow, scented plumes of smoke into the clean kitchen air. My mother bustling about doing housework she had neglected until the last minute and saying to him with mock impatience: "Would you ever go and smoke your old chimney somewhere else!"

As if he might consider moving. Or as if she wanted him to. And I'd felt even as a child, or perhaps especially then, a quality of restrained sensuality between them. Particularly on his part. His heavy limbs stretched out in absolute self-assurance, the quiet, steady sucking of his lips at the stem of his pipe, the black hairs showing at his open shirt collar, and glancing now and again at my mother from behind cover of his paper watching her with a lazy self-indulgence, the loud rustling of the pages the only mark of his impatience, his hurry to be alone with her. He spoke little; briefly and to the point. So I remembered best his laughter which was so often directed at Ma, who demanded to know why had God made only twenty-four hours in a day when she had to do every blessed thing herself? And Pa replying: "Listen to her now, getting on her high horse. I'd keep well clear of her in this mood, Katherine."

"Indeed you'd better," she'd answer, growling at him, "don't tempt me to reply to you." When I was little I took them both seriously and ran from the room squealing with fright.

The memory of those images lent a horrible irony to the sight of him lying between the stiff hospital sheets, a plastic tube trailing from his nose, the whistling sound of his breath as it was sucked through its thin, slightly trembling length.

133

On the third day of the vigil Ma asked me suddenly if I thought he was suffering too much.

"Is this the right thing to be doing?" she asked me, her face contorted with anxiety and grief. "Would it not be better to let him die in peace?"

I took her hand across the inert mound of his body and squeezed it, but said nothing because I didn't know how to answer her. I imagined Pa saying (as he did whenever she upbraided you): "What makes you think she expects an answer, Katherine, isn't she only airing her thoughts?"

Later on we took it in turns to hold the oxygen mask from his face. It had worn deep, red weals into the flesh of his cheeks. He lay on his side, the ugly plastic cup strapped to his face, his right leg kicking rhythmically under the covers, the way a horse stamps its hoof in pain and frustration. Later still, in the afternoon, Ma returned to the subject that clearly was dominating her thoughts. She asked again what I would do if someone I loved was in as much distress. I hesitated, seeing her face, not knowing whether she wanted honesty or tact, but the moment I heard the question I was sure of my own response. At last I decided to be frank and I said softly: "If it were someone I loved I couldn't let them suffer unnecessarily."

"But if it were Malachy lying here," she persisted, as if wanting to be absolutely sure I meant what I said, "would that still be your decision?"

As she said Malachy's name I realised that when I answered her first I hadn't been thinking of him. It had been your face that had risen before me and made me speak with such certainty. I saw Ma's eyes fixed on me and knew she was waiting intently for me to continue.

"I couldn't bear to let any person I loved suffer like this," I said slowly, carefully enunciating the words. "I'd prefer to have them die than watch them suffer." Ma turned away from me and regarded my father with a look of great intensity. She made no sign of having noticed anything unusual in my way of answering but I thought she gripped my father's hand more tightly. After a few moments when she spoke again she seemed to have entirely forgotten the mood of tension and fear. Her feelings had brightened almost at once in the way habitual with her and her mind had moved naturally to happier thoughts.

"As soon as he recovers and is well enough again to enjoy it," she announced, "we must bring him something really special to eat – oysters and champagne – how about that? Isn't that what he always liked best?" and she smiled at him as though they were alone. Moving closer, murmuring words of affection, she stroked his cheek and as though to protect him from sudden cold, she fastened the buttons of his pyjama jacket to the neck, with the tenderness of a mother or a young lover.

But when we were at home again that evening, eating a hastily prepared meal at the kitchen table, she reverted to the subject I knew had been on her mind since she heard my answer to her question that afternoon. Not that she made this obvious in what she said. On the surface her words had no connection with anything that had gone before, but I knew differently. Before coming to the point she lit a cigarette (she allowed herself just one every evening after dinner) and slowly and with great pleasure inhaled deeply into her lungs. Then she knocked the ash smartly from the burning tip into an ashtray and regarded me thoughtfully. When she was completely calm she spoke: "I hope you're looking after yourself these days, Katherine," she said, "I hope you have friends you can trust and a good social life."

I was on the point of answering immediately with some reassuring phrase when I remembered again Pa saying. "What makes you think she expects an answer?" and I stopped myself and for a moment considered ignoring the question altogether. But my head was full of images of the day spent in the hospital, of hearing her talking aloud to comfort him, private endearments and pet names, her pride in her love, its unselfconsciousness, and I knew I was envious of the easy forgetfulness that made it possible. Because I'd learned almost from the first day with you, despite my natural inclination, to be always watchful, conscious of who was about before I touched you in public, careful of how I did it, allowing only gestures that could pass for friendship or family affection. Simple instinctive gestures and words were impossible: to kiss you on impulse across a restaurant table, to call you darling in front of others, to take your hand walking along the street. All these things I'd come to realise were dangerous, capable of rousing fury in onlookers, causing us to be thrown out of pubs (as happened the first time I kissed you as I wanted, one afternoon in O'Neill's) or stared at with hostile curiosity in hotel lobbies. I felt a huge sense of grievance and anger that we should be policed in this way by society, by strangers who knew nothing about us, and made to behave as if we were ashamed of the love we felt. So when Ma broached the subject I decided I wanted to tell her something truthful about my life.

"I have better friends than ever," I began and I lifted my wine glass and took another mouthful before I continued. "Women friends," I said pointedly.

"Yes, but I was thinking of your whole social circle," she said hurriedly, "not only women."

"And I wasn't thinking only of friends," I answered. Though I spoke softly the words seemed as abrupt and menacing as a pistol shot in the sudden, tense silence between us. Ma said nothing, but she stared over my shoulder as if she had caught sight of something that needed urgent attention at the far side of the room. But I had begun so I must finish, however resistant she was. I couldn't leave the words hovering between us neither claimed nor denied: "Nina, for instance . . ." I said.

"Yes, I know," she interrupted me at once, her voice quick and light, cutting me off in mid-sentence, "I know you have a specially close and good friend in Nina. She's a lovely girl and you know how much I like her." The words were spoken smoothly and affectionately, but I was struck by the over-eagerness of them and I was suddenly conscious that I'd never before heard her sound embarrassed or clumsy.

"That's not what I meant," I answered her, my own voice relentless. I would not spare her, I thought. For once I wouldn't let her fly off on a tangent. I'd pin her down, she who was forever ready to let things drift, to leave them unspoken or half-spoken. She who was always busy about a thousand things, caught up in ordering the physical world, dashing from one pleasure to the next, from one good deed to the next. She'd rush out the door when we were children, calling out after her: "Tell me tomorrow – it can't be so serious it won't keep for a day."

But this time it wouldn't keep for one more night. My father was dying and I wouldn't let her deflect me. She was smiling now, her bright, distracting smile, exerting her charm.

"Yes, I think I like Nina more than you like her yourself. Is there any chance of her coming over this summer by the way? She said she might visit me."

I looked at her steadily and braced myself to say the hardest words I have spoken to her.

"You don't like her more than I do," I said very softly, "because I don't only like her, I love her."

"Yes, of course you do," she said, "she's very loveable."

"I mean, love," I persisted. "I mean that I love her as much as you love Pa."

The words shocked me. They seemed to rise out of

childhood, out of an earlier, simpler time, from some old argument we might have had at the end of a long day on the beach, in summer, when we were all tired and fractious and someone would demand to know who someone loved the best and who was someone else's favourite. The words hung in the air between us like a poison. Ma stood up and began to clear the plates from the table, stacking them one on top of the other against her braced forearm. She crossed to the sink and back again. On the second journey she turned and smiled at me, an imitation of her normal smile:

"Well if that's the case," she said, "you must understand how I'm feeling now." At that second I saw tears welling in her eyes and saw that her cheeks were flushed and dark. And I thought – don't let her cry! Please God don't let her cry! If she hasn't cried in all these days with Pa, don't let her cry now!

As if she'd heard this silent entreaty she turned and walked slowly from the room without another word. We didn't talk about you again after that. Though I tried, I never again found the right opportunity to raise the subject. After another week Pa recovered a little, passed from critical to comfortable and I booked my flight back to Dublin. To this day I'm not sure how much she understood that evening in the kitchen or what she might have felt if I'd pressed her for a response. Who knows? She always understood more than she let on. But whatever it was I won't find out. As she was so fond of saying, "Well, it's too late now to do anything about it!"

What more can I tell you? Only the one thing I have been avoiding all this time. Walking around it. Talking around it. Distracting myself with stories of love and desire because they keep me from thoughts of death. Whatever guilt I've known at abandoning a lover is nothing to the guilt induced by the memory of my betrayal of Ma. But I must speak of it if I'm to make a clean breast of things. If this inquiry of mine means anything at all I can't flinch any longer from consideration of her death. The exact manner of her dying. Have I told you yet? I don't remember if anyone asked me this question, but I don't suppose you want the answer. There's always too much about mothers. Inevitable of course. Everybody's got one, everybody's got a story to tell, inevitable that there will always be far too much about mothers. All of us wanting to tell our own parent stories without having to listen to all the others first. Or afterwards. Fathers too. Yes, far too much about fathers, particularly from sons – nothing can beat the way men go on about Daddy once they get started. Forever lamenting lost opportunity, never really talked, never really understood and the rest of it. But to come to the point. At last. The final point.

My mother died suddenly without warning or preconsideration by falling under the wheels of an oncoming train. Yes, when my mother decided to die she did it properly. Snap – just like that. Just took off in one go. No dry runs, no false alarms, no alarms at all, my brave, clever mother. At ten past one in broad daylight on the commuter train from north to south Boston. These trains run frequently and regularly. They are painted bright orange. They do not allow smokers, or feet on their seats, or spitting on the floor. They are well ordered and appointed. Under just such a train my mother (who was standing on the platform of her local station awaiting the train to carry her in for her afternoon visit to my father – who was still getting up the courage to pass from this life), my mother, who waited every day for this train, perhaps because she was impatient and stood too close to the edge or in a hurry (she was usually in a hurry), my mother lost her footing just as the train burst into the station. Lost her footing and with it her life, on a bright, breezy afternoon. Lost seems the most appropriate word. Snap. No dithering. No messing about. No second chances. Her spine snapped clear in two. Somebody said they heard it.

She fell, but it must be said plainly now before we go further, that it was not like my mother to lose her footing, her grip was always so sure, her grasp on the earth. It must be said (and it was said, in a quiet, green-walled courtroom) it was said that she might have not so much fallen as thrown herself outwards, that is to say that she might have leaped forward as the train came in, to throw herself under the oncoming wheels. Yes, it must be said that it would have been characteristic of Ma to take action, to take control and initiative in the matter of leaving this life.

Perhaps she was weary of my father's hanging about. Forever threatening death and not getting on with it. Perhaps she wanted to set an example. Perhaps she was tired to death of waiting for him, of waiting on him. She didn't enjoy those visits to hospital. Hospitals are not joyous places, though many choose to live in them rather than in the outer world. I know how she felt because I accompanied her so often. I counted the cost. I counted the cost and left it to her to pay. After all, she had married the man, chosen him, I was merely the daughter, an accident, there by chance not design. It was not my business to keep vigil, was it? I had a life to lead as they say. Ma said it. She said you have your own life to live. You must go away and leave this dying to me. So I did. And abandoning his dying I abandoned hers.

My mother shouldered her choice, her burden. She went every afternoon between three and five to sit by her husband's bedside, her husband who could no longer move or speak. She might be going there till this day if it weren't for the train that took her life – and which phrase is the appropriate one – took her life or lost it? Did she think it all out, premeditate it, counting the days, the hours to her release? Did she choose the right time and place? The right train? Going north or

140

south? On its way to bring her to my father or coming back – that she might travel hopefully until the last? Choice or chosen – lost or taken – we settled for lost.

The phone rang by my bed and when I lifted the receiver my sister's voice made the brief announcement every emigrant awaits in fear and trembling – the announcement of a parent's sudden death – a death from which the emigrant was absent. And like all such emigrants, absent from all the crucial moments of family life, I carry the guilt of it still, the price of freedom. How often have I told myself I ought to have stayed with her, waited in spite of everything she said until Pa's death? But then he conspired against us. He didn't die, couldn't die. He lay there still in his half life, waiting for release. Therefore, isn't it really Pa who's to blame rather than myself for my abandonment of my mother? Shouldn't he take some share of the blame? He could afford to, never having done it before. How gladly I'd have unloaded it onto his inert shoulders if I could.

The past, the past. I am distracting myself again. Hiding from the unknown terrors of the future in the safety of past suffering.

Chapter Eleven

October, Dublin.

It took Nina no more than ten minutes to drive through the back streets of the town to the hostel. After a few minutes, applying sustained pressure to the front doorbell, she heard someone come to open it. She waited while the many necessary bolts and locks were undone and climbed the narrow flight of thirty steps or more to be greeted by an anxious young volunteer who informed her breathlessly – before Nina had time to ask – that Elinor had had a sudden migraine attack and had left halfway through the afternoon.

"Do you know where she went?" Nina asked.

The young woman stared at her nervously: "Home I assume? Where else would she go when she's sick?" Where else indeed? Nina thought. She thanked the girl hurriedly and left as quickly as she could, allowing for several stops along the way to talk to some of the women she knew, regulars who had used the service for years and knew that an old friend like Nina was good for a few cigarettes.

At last she found herself in the street in the cold damp wind blowing in off the river. What was she to do now? Where could Elinor have gone if she wasn't at work or at home? Had she really been feeling ill or was it just an excuse? How long was she going to go on with this – avoiding her and refusing to talk? Did she mean to keep out of her way until she made a decision? Did she know how close she had come to that moment? Not that it would be at all surprising if she was feeling too bad to continue work. You would need to be in the whole of your health at the best of times to contend with a hostel for homeless women. The noise of the place was deafening. It was like the tower of Babel. The moment she walked in the door, a tide of sound hit her ears like a wave breaking: women shouting and crying, radios blaring at top volume. The smell of the place alone was enough to make her feel ill. The smell of poverty: stale food, stale cigarette smoke, damp clothes and cheap disinfectant.

The staff did their best, but it was impossible to make the atmosphere anything other than what it was – a run-down institution. At the back of the building there was the remains of an old walled garden, untamed and untended, where wild flowers grew, climbing roses and hydrangeas and daffodils.

This was the one blessing in an otherwise blighted landscape and the young staff made good use of it. They picked the flowers and distributed them throughout the rooms and corridors. In every other aspect the place was numbingly bleak – and soulless. The building which had been provided by the government was situated in the annexe of an old hospital that had long since been shut down, but an air of sickness and regimentation still hung about it. No one who wasn't totally desperate would have stayed for more than twenty-four hours. But because they were worse than desperate, the powers that be could rely on their subjection. The women who came here were the forgotten people, the homeless, the bag ladies, the rejects, the drunks. Women ended up here when they had been kicked out of everywhere else. They were dirty and violent and quarrelsome. No money would pay anyone to work in the place. Yet many did from choice. Elinor actually liked it, found it homely. She liked the camaraderie, the fights, the tears, the reconciliations, the spontaneous parties. She liked the feeling of being at the front line, where life was real, emotional and totally honest.

It was one of the things Nina admired most about Elinor, that she could view the place in this light. Friends and acquaintances told her repeatedly that she was overworked and underpaid. That, working as a nurse and midwife for one half of the week should be enough hardship, and that it couldn't be healthy for anyone to stay so long in such a world. But Elinor ignored them. She worked there because she liked it. Because it was somewhere useful to work. And because on good days the women were an inspiration.

As Nina drove back to Sandymount to collect Lizzie from Aunt May, the night had turned cold and the orange street lamps cast a sinister glow over the dark sky. Driving along by the river, she passed the gleaming façade of the Four Courts – newly cleaned and floodlit, shown off to best advantage. And Nina felt they had at last recognised its importance, the dignity that befitted it, in her mind, as the location of her first sighting of Elinor Fitzgerald. It struck her, suddenly, that large public institutions played a main role in her personal dramas. Was there some hidden ironic significance in the fact that she'd fallen in love with one lover on the steps of the public courthouse and fallen in love with another, years later, in the casualty unit of one of the city's general hospitals?

But then every corner of this town held significant memories for her. The whole territory was like a street map of her heart. Anguish and pleasure waylaid her at every street corner. She remembered that first day meeting with Elinor. It seemed fitting as the start of their life together that it should coincide with one of the significant events in that period of political upheaval, a time of intense public passion, despair and optimism. One winter morning, a group of protestors had placed a picket on the Four Courts to protest the prosecution of some feminists for supplying information on abortion. After the case, which ended in victory for their side, the spectators and supporters came flowing out into the street. The rain was pouring down and each one in turn stood talking on the steps, bare-headed, without so much as a raincoat or umbrella between them. Nina noticed a tall, dark-clad figure, standing alone in the porch. She looked at Nina and said simply: "I hate the rain."

Nina looked back at her. She saw a trench coat with the collar up, a brown hat with a wide brim, almost covering the darkest eyes she had ever seen. And, without knowing why, something in their expression, something haunted and vulnerable, or was it the contrast of her stance, so self-possessed and cool, that struck her with such force? But whatever it was, Nina knew at once that the only thing that mattered to her for the rest of the day was to make the acquaintance of this unknown woman. Afterwards, she realised how exactly like Elinor that opening remark was – I hate the rain. So extreme and dramatic. How could anyone hate the rain and live in this country?

She was glad now when she crossed the river and put the place well behind her. She thought of Elinor making this journey alone, three nights a week, to spend six hours in that grim, desolate building where so much suffering was walled in together. She marvelled at her resilience. Her ability to hold back the tides of hopelessness and despair that overcame others, no less brave, who went as far out on the edge as she did. Nina knew well she, herself, couldn't withstand it for more than a week. But then she didn't have Elinor's sense of purpose, her puritan streak or her generosity. She remembered what May had said earlier about the pelican. The bird who pierces her own breast with her beak until enough blood flows to feed her young. Who had she been thinking of? Had she intended Nina to recognise herself? If so, which of the people in her life did May consider she was sacrificing herself for? Or could she have meant Elinor? The description much more obviously suited Elinor. She was one of those people who everyone turned to for help and for kindness. She wore herself out because she didn't know how to say no to anyone. Sometimes it made her resentful. Nina knew that she had taken Elinor's generosity for granted far too often. Imagining it limitless as it seemed to be.

They had been happy for so long. The perfect couple, their friends said. Suited for each other in every way. Elinor gave her a pride and confidence in herself and in their shared place in the world that she had never found with anyone else.

And then . . . ? And then as always, the years had taken their toll. She had grown careless. She had taken her happiness for granted, taken Elinor for granted. Begun to live as if her good fortune was permanent. She had let herself grow impatient with Elinor. The very things she loved most: her passion, her impulsiveness, her lack of moderation. She let herself think that all that was best in Elinor were the virtues of any lover, whereas her faults were hers alone. She had driven her away. Neglected her. And then, Elinor had taken a lover. A brief encounter with a woman who came to Dublin to study for a few months. Nina had imagined she could be detached. But the strain of trying to be unpossessive almost killed her. When it was over, Nina wanted to forgive, but she couldn't forget. Resentment, at being the only one of whom magnanimity was demanded, stayed with her, rankled. And something perverse in her began to form the notion that the only cure, the only way of healing the wound, would be to do the same thing herself. How could she have thought that this would help? But she hadn't thought. The decision, if it could be called that, was formed in a part of her that had no connection with thought. An area beyond reach of reason or knowledge of consequences.

Chapter Twelve

September, Clare.

Máire Mac broke the news as soon as I arrived at the shop.

"There's a letter for you, I have it waiting for you here this long time." She had it on the counter in front of her and held it out to me the moment I came through the door: "I wonder now is it the one you've been waiting for?" She looked past me as she spoke towards the wellingtons and hot water bottles that hung from the ceiling, but there was barely disguised triumph in her voice – as though it was entirely thanks to her that it had arrived at last. Of course, as soon as I caught sight of the envelope I knew it was yours and so did she. I almost snatched it from her grasp. I'd have liked to open it there and then, but as Máire Mac was clearly waiting for me to do just that I decided against it. I said goodbye and set off immediately for home. It was too dark to read it going along the road so I had to wait the three-quarters of an hour the walk takes me to get here.

Now, having read it, I am overjoyed. Almost sick with relief and excitement. The second I read the word Friday I felt my heart pound. Just one word singled out on a page from all the rest. I can hardly believe it.

You are coming on Friday evening! Only three more days to go! I am counting the hours again. I have seventy-six hours and forty-five minutes to go. What am I to do with them? How can I contain myself? It will be much harder now that I know the exact hour of your arrival. In my mind I'm already standing on the platform, pacing up and down, hungry for the very first glimpse of the train as it rounds the last bend. I imagine you walking towards me, smiling, your head to one side, your dark eyes radiant. I try to picture how you'll look – what you'll wear. I imagine you holding out your arms to me. I run towards you and the whole place turns to stare, as they always do when we embrace in public, but I don't care. Let them stare at us because I know what comes into their eyes after the first shock (I've seen the look so often – in so many women's faces when they look at us): a totally unexpected pang of envy. That's what they feel, because women recognise passion – however surprising the context – at a glance. Wherever they see it, they recognise happiness and, knowing how little of it there is in the world, they are envious.

I'm steady now, almost calm imagining all this. I can almost bear to wait now that it's so close. I can sit back and take pleasure in the slow passing of the hours that bring me gradually, inexorably, closer to you and to the day that we will be together – the first day of our life. I'm sitting here on the bed in the loft, my back against the wall, my eyes closed, letting the pictures of our new life crowd before my eyes. I don't have to think, I don't have to make any effort at all. Life will take its course. Slowly, surely, the time will come. Slowly and surely, like a ship drawing into sight above the horizon – I can see the sails now, the bright red spinnaker appearing first – our future drawing nearer mile by mile.

I have just now, as I sit here dreaming of you, my heart beating with excitement, realised what it is I miss about you. I miss your mouth. Yes, as simple and physical as that. I miss the feel of your lips, the scent of them. (That curious, sweet, almost musk-like fragrance that I catch when I kiss you, that lies along your upper lip. Is it your breath or the smell of your skin? I don't know.) I miss the sight of your mouth, smiling. The look of it, the feel of your lips, smiling, pressed against mine. Your full, laughing lips when you lift your head from between my thighs. Your mouth wet from me, glistening. Your smile of triumph, of provocation, queening it over me. My sweet temptress, my conqueror, my cunning puritan.

Walking back from the shop this afternoon I came upon a pair of lovers, lying together in the tall grass, imagining themselves, like all lovers, invisible (though only strangers could think themselves safe from observation here – any local knows that no city street is as closely watched, night and day as a deserted country field).

Seeing them, I remembered the last time I made love in the open with you; lying in the grass – that evening on Howth Head when a sudden cloudburst soaked our bare skin and our waiting clothes.

But as I watched their slowly labouring bodies, the boy's back obscuring completely his companion's face, his legs pinning hers to the damp ground, I found myself thinking – if she only knew what she's missing! If she only knew what it was like to be with a woman! But no one will tell her. No one tells any of us. Love is this and nothing else. No alternative. I saw her face for a moment shift from under his, turning to the side to take a breath and I saw in her eyes that look I've seen often on the faces of young girls in mid-embrace. A look of boredom and physical discomfort and a look of determination; resolved not only to please, but to act out their part in the hope that practice will one day, at last, make it pleasurable.

What a shame, I thought, as I walked on, leaving them to the pleasures they imagined secret, that sexual exploration is so rigidly defined and hemmed in by convention. We should all get the chance to experiment – to find out when we are young how we really feel. We ought to be bisexual all of us at that age.

149

Men would learn to surrender themselves to pleasure, to let themselves be made love to without fear and women would learn how to please themselves and how to give pleasure instead of waiting passively to be presented with it. And I wondered, not for the first time, how different life would have been if I'd met you earlier. The question asked by every friend who learned about my feelings for you: would I have responded to you at any time in my life or did I fall for you only because I was ready?

You asked this question too, of course, and you were amazed by how vague my answers were. You'd try to prise from me stories about childhood affections and friendships and you found it hard to credit that I remembered almost nothing out of the ordinary. When I thought of childhood, I thought first of Ben's and Luke's rather than my own. It was as if the fact of becoming a mother had extinguished or superseded my own childhood. Whereas both you and Elinor and your lesbian friends seemed to me to have near perfect recall of childhood, adolescence, your first sexual adventures. All of you shared the most intense interest in the emotional and pyschological paths which had brought you to your present positions. The first question any lesbian asks on meeting another and beginning a conversation, seems to be: "When did you come out?" And that's followed almost immediately by: "Does your family know?" Then you enthusiastically start the business of swapping accounts of love affairs and your first experiences of romance with women. I was fascinated by these stories, so varied and unpredictable, recalled so vividly and with such loving detail; about gay teachers and older cousins and friends and strangers who became the object of adolescent infatuation. They revealed to me a vast underworld or overworld of romantic intrigue and adventure – not furtive encounters as straight people like to imagine, but passionate love affairs, all the more pleasureful for being concealed from authoritarian eyes.

You seemed more precocious than the people I knew and

all of you more or less bisexual in your early days. I remember Elinor telling the story of her first lover at school. She fell in love with a classmate at fifteen and the pair of them would slip out at break and hide in the music cells where they would kiss and fondle one another in a corner behind the grand piano, once remaining concealed for an hour, embracing while the dreaded mistress of music, Mother Dolores, carried out a lesson. She amazed me, I remember, by recounting how all that year they kept a hole torn in the pockets of their gym slips so that sitting side by side, they could reach in to touch one another, whenever they were bored.

Another friend, Jane Kinsella, confided how she used to share a bed with her mother's au pair girl in an attic room in winter and how they slowly fell in love and began a delicious, protracted sexual exploration unknown to anyone else in the household.

Susan Kennedy told a story about a nun who fell in love with her at boarding school and who she eventually rejected in favour of another younger teacher which led to agonies of secret rivalry.

Sometimes this sexual initiation was with an older girl, but for the most part it took place between peers – school friends and neighbours; girls and boys (and all of you seemed to have had heterosexual romances too) and among all these passionate retellings no one had an account that wasn't remembered as entirely pleasureful and consensual.

Listening to all this, I was immensely entertained and intrigued, but I also felt embarrassment because I didn't seem able to respond in kind. Had my past been as rich and adventurous as others but forced from consciousness by the demands of my adult life? You said it was repression, plain and simple – though nothing about me was plain and very little simple, you added – just in time! I must have had more ambivalent feelings as a child than I admitted to. Under pressure (coaxing?) from you, I did tell you the story of my

151

infatuation with Barbara and how it obsessed me when I was thirteen. But, though I remembered the feeling and the unhappy consequences (her parents – without ever stating the problem – separated us, sending Barbara away and suggesting to Ma that I'd be better off at home where she could keep an eye on me) the details of the affair had become clouded with time. My attempts at description infuriated you.

"Were you actually physical lovers?" you'd demand.

"What constitutes lovers exactly?"

"Did you go to bed, of course?"

"Yes, I think so."

"You think so!"

"What I mean is – we went to bed but we didn't make love, or at least not fully."

"Not all the way as the nuns used to say?"

"Exactly."

"But did you want to?"

"I don't know."

"You don't know?"

"Well, yes I did want to, but not in the clear, fully worked out way you felt it. It was romantic more than sexual."

"Are all Americans such prudes? Or such poor liars?"

Was I lying? I certainly didn't mean to. I can see, very well, why these questions are of immense importance to women who have grown up lesbian or bisexual, but for me it was different. I had the sense of drifting effortlessly or mindlessly into my expected position as a heterosexual, as girlfriend, lover, wife, mother, in that order. There was no reason for me to examine my motives or feelings in any depth. I seemed to pass from one stage to the next in an instinctive way without any sense of conflict.

Or at least that's how things used to appear to me. But now, becalmed here, passive, my imagination free to wander, I begin, for the first time, to see things differently. Or at any rate to remember them. And the more I write down about the past, the more it comes back to me. Perfect, clear pictures, fully formed and finely detailed. My first boyfriends, my crush on Barbara, my first kiss, my first orgasm and so on.

So you see, I am gradually becoming just like you, and your friends, obsessed with love and romance and erotic memories! In fact, I seem to be experiencing the sensation described as happening in the last seconds of drowning – all my life passing before my eyes in a constant stream of brilliant, perfectly framed scenes. I don't mean only desire for you, but memories of every love affair, every stolen kiss or summer flirtation. I seem to remember the whole history of my erotic life, from my first sexual awakening to now, in a smooth river of images. In this mood, if I wanted, I could set down a complete biography of desire, and do you know – you won't be glad to hear this part – but it seems now, in retrospect, that lovers merge into one another, exchange places and identities. It appears almost as if all lovers were expressions of the one lover. Is it only the process of love, the functioning of desire that gives to each in its time the appearance of being set apart from all others?

If it please the court . . . But it wouldn't please the court. I know that before I begin. They'll see a pattern in all this that reveals me as deeply flawed from the outset. They'll listen and shake their heads, mutter sadly, we told you so! And the first thing they'll want to scrutinise is the evidence of my early capacity to love more than one person at a time – and my affection for my own sex. But I didn't love girls, only, I must admit. No, from my earliest years I also loved boys. Does that make it better or worse? But however confusing, contrary, I'll indulge myself with the truth. I'll step into the witness box and state categorically that the first person I loved was of the male sex. A boy. A small boy. Yes. A boy who lived on the same street, by the name of Peter.

We were very young when we first met. I remember watching him suck his thumb, the sense of delight in knowing exactly how he felt. I sucked mine in response and his eyes fastened on me eagerly. His brown plump thighs. His yellow shorts covered with fishes. His clenched fists, his laughing face. When he laughed he fell backwards onto the grass and rolled from side to side. He didn't know how to laugh standing up. I fought with him. I punched him and he punched me back. I said I never wanted to play with him again – never, ever, never. He ran home to his own garden.

I was angry. I tore the leaves from the laurel bush. I threw stones at the seagulls. I was lonely. I wanted to play blindman's buff, grandmother's footsteps, stagecoach and hide-and-seek. How could I play them alone? I wanted him back. I wandered to the fence. I loitered there as if come just to run my fingers along the wood. To hop from foot to foot, to whistle a tune. He had taught me to whistle and to make Indian calls through a blade of grass. He was sitting in the birch tree. High up, swaying on a plank of wood we had put there together. He was reading a comic. He didn't need me. I waited. He wouldn't look at me. The branch he was sitting on swayed in the wind. His plump legs dangled, his brown feet encased in brown leather sandals. I called out: "Did you ever play Will Scarlet with a real crossbow?" I held my hands behind my back as if I might be hiding one from sight. He looked up so swiftly, almost before I'd finished the question, that I knew he had been waiting. Waiting for me to throw him a good enough piece of bait to allow him to climb down.

But he didn't wait to climb. He took one jump and landed like a frog, legs bent under him on his brown leather sandals in my garden. I took his hand and we ran helter-skelter across the grass, faster, faster, my knees knocking together, my shoulders colliding. We ran on until we fell down, tripped by whose feet; fell down dead shot by a stray bullet, a ricochet, the last Indian hidden in the dry gulch. We fell to the ground rolling into each other's arms. I was stone dead. Happy again. Friends for eternity. For the rest of the day.

When Charley came I didn't know which I loved best. We sat together all three, side by side on a park bench considering the matter. I sat between them holding a hand in each of mine and they asked me which of them I'd marry. I'd marry them both, I said or not at all. This wouldn't be easy. We knew that, all three. Our loyalty would be a difficult thing to keep in the face of the world. In the world of grown-ups who kept the rules and thought what everyone else thought and did what others did because they did it. Grown-ups who stood up when they laughed, who walked with their eyes down, who didn't think of looking even so high as a tree when they were looking for you, grown-ups who knew nothing about the clouds because they never lay on their back on the grass. Who were too tall and had forgotten what the earth smelt like in summer, in winter after rain. Who didn't like muck on their hands or their feet or their shoes or their carpets. Who ate their food sitting down at a table at a set hour of the day whether they were hungry or not. Who wouldn't spoil their appetites or run all the way up the hill just after eating or plunge into the sea feet first from the pier for at least one hour after dinner. Who wouldn't dig up earthworms for bait to catch a fish from the big rock. Or sit for one, two, three, how many hours waiting for pinkeens in the little pools at low tide. Who wouldn't play in the snow until they were blue with cold, throw snowballs until their fingers stiffened. They wouldn't cover themselves up to their necks in sand, fill their mouths, their ears, their pockets with it. They wouldn't climb into a cave and forget to come out even when the whole beach was looking for them. Who could never find anyone they were looking for. And who were always getting the fright of their lives and worried sick and demented looking after you. They wouldn't stand up in under their blankets to make a tent pole with their heads or pull off all the covers and sleep on the floor. They wouldn't eat ice cream till they burst or smear chocolate wet and hot from the sun all over their fingers and their cheeks and their clothes.

They were sad, these big grown-ups. Forever standing, forever in the cold reaches of the higher air, too far from the earth to remember it. Their faces pale and stiff. Their hands dead at their sides. Their sad smiles, their laughter that was only a noise from their nose.

When I grew up, when my body grew taller and stiffer, borne up into their cold forlorn atmosphere, I'd have to decided who I'd marry. It must be one or the other because no grown-up lived with more than one other. They came alone or in twos. They made up their minds between friends. I held Peter's hand. I held Charley's. Charley with his dark eyes and hair and clean white socks. Smooth and clean and sweet-scented. Grave behind his thick eyebrows that met in the middle of his forehead. And Peter plump and bright and rosy as an apple. A baby. I won't marry anyone then I said if I cannot marry both of you. They squeezed my hands. That was a good answer. All of us were relieved. A way out of the puzzle. An escape from the terrible grasp of the grown-up world waiting to ensnare us as soon as our bones grew long enough to carry us into their clutches. Eat up.

Finish your dinner, your bread, your porridge or you won't grow strong and big. I pushed away my plate, refusing their food, refusing their growth. Refusing the long bones, their tall bodies. I would stay down here below out of sight of their sad eyes and their stiff, pale hands. I will marry no one if I can't marry you both. And we got up then all three and ran down to the beach for a swim, laughing because we'd thought of a plan. A way to outwit them.

See? Isn't this almost worthy of you?

As I came out of the shop this morning I saw Michael standing a little way down at the crossroads. I always recognise him by the shock of hair and the odd stiff way he stands, like a soldier on parade. I decided to speak to him as I passed. "Good evening," I said, "a fine evening now, isn't it?" He stiffened even more, drawing his shoulders back and averting his head as if afraid I was going to strike him. I passed on with no further remark. He stayed standing silently by the ditch, but I felt his eyes following me.

Why does he annoy me so much? It's irrational, but I feel almost as if he puts on an act to annoy people. As though he could behave normally if he wanted, but prefers the excuse to go about slumped in this hostile silence. I know that very often in these places the men described as simple are not in fact mentally retarded, but simply suffering from chronic depression. And is it any wonder there are so many; the constant rain, the melancholy of the landscape, the isolation, the inbred families?

Máire Mac mentioned that he was in and out of St Loman's a few years ago but that he'd settled down now. I don't know if she regards this kind of lurking about as settled. For some reason his hangdog look reminds me of Malachy. This is why he angers me, of course. His expression reminds me of Malachy, brooding and self-pitying. Somewhere in my heart of hearts, when Malachy was carrying on like that, I felt he was pulling a fast one, taking unfair advantage of me. Needless to say, it made me feel guiltier still to realise that I could be angry with a man in such a forlorn state.

Ah well, if I was to be fully truthful I'd say I was resentful. There is something enviable about the licence such a man has. Nothing demanded of him, nothing expected. And so much expected of women. What woman could afford to wander country roads muttering to herself? Even if a woman is childless she is always responsible for someone. In the last

157

twelve years there hasn't been a day when I could afford the time to be crazy.

"Mrs Newman, what would you say you have sacrificed, if anything, for the sake of your children?"

"Madness, my lord. I have sacrificed madness!"

But I won't let myself get onto this track now. Why should I be irritable? When everything I've ever wanted is about to be mine. I won't allow myself a single pang of guilt today nor misgivings of any kind.

You will be here in two days' time? How am I to survive? How am I to distract myself? I can't think of anything to do with sex or passion without going off into these obsessive fantasies of you. I want to see you walk naked across the room, your back to me. To see your beautiful ass, the beautiful dimpled flesh at the base of your spine, the hollow immediately above your buttocks that my tongue has traced so often. I want my mouth there now. I want my tongue there. I want to slide it slowly down between your cheeks to your ass and cunt until your knees give way and you pitch forward onto all fours and I follow you and we make love there and then, though we had finished and you were on your way to make breakfast. I want to feel your breasts cupped in my hands. Your breasts that fit my palms exactly. I want to have you turn slowly onto your back so that I can see your face, so that I can watch your eyes as you come. Your eyes slowly widening, slowly changing colour, almost black now. I want you over and over again now today this minute. I want to see you smile like that once more. Just once more. I want to hear you laugh when you come as though astonished by it. As though for the first time.

Oh my God, Nina, keep me from this. Sweet mother of God, Nina, how am I to get through the rest of the days?

The past. The past. The sweet other world of childhood recalled.

I have remembered Sarah. Yes, if I'm to be very scrupulous or very imaginative I could see Sarah as the beginning of all this; a seed planted in careless soil to flower when forgotten, years later.

When I laid eyes on Sarah, I forgot the two small boys, Peter and Charley, entirely. I loved her from the first glance, her black lashes, her freckled nose, her bony knees, her long shins, her dark fringe that drew a straight line above her eyes, her dark blue eyes that were always looking at me, as if she saw me, as if I were someone, as if I had a form, a shape as real as hers. As solid. As enrapturing. Her eyes followed me everywhere. And my eyes would not leave her face. I forgot Charley and Peter. I didn't need to think of marriage and who I loved best. I loved her beyond words or questions, trials or proofs of affection. I didn't need to ask. I wouldn't know how to tell. There were no words for this. We laughed as we gazed at one another. We looked long hours across our school table, she sitting at a green bench, I at a red. Our copy books open and unmarked between us. Our pencils in our hands. She sucked the tip of hers. I sucked mine. She ran her hand over her cheek. She scratched her thigh. Her foot kicked mine under the desk. I kicked back shyly. She smiled a little. Nothing like the smiles I was used to. I followed her everywhere with my eyes. I was afraid to come close enough to smell her skin. I didn't touch her. Not at once. Not for days.

But the sound of her words falling from her mouth, one by one, set loose for me to revel in, like gleaming marbles thrown down from a fist to roll under my gaze. Each word drew my ear. Her voice was not like anybody's. Was it high or low? Did she speak quickly or slowly? I couldn't tell. It seemed to be part of the air about her, a quality in the atmosphere. An element as distinct as water, wind or leaves. I waited for her to be asked a question so that I could listen. And when I spoke her eyes fastened on my mouth and each word was watched as it came from my lips and was like a present handed to her to play with. When I laughed, she laughed. I'd never marry now because I wanted to spend my whole life waiting to see what Sarah would do next. Would she open her book, or eat a sandwich or jump up to write on the blackboard or call out a joke or climb through the window into the garden to fire a paper pellet at someone we hated?

Where she went, my eyes followed. Where I went, she gazed after. Every part of her was a mystery and a delight to me. I couldn't say where she ended and the world began. Was her skin the air around it? Were her eyes the sky? Were her hands the things she touched? She was a separate element from me, distinct and individual, that I couldn't fuse with. She wasn't water nor earth nor air that I could plunge myself into and mingle with. She was a thing apart. In the world but not of it. I must find a new approach. A new language. A new question. And when we collided with each other accidentally, running into the cloakroom after class, I laughed aloud to discover that there was an edge to her existence, a boundary, a rim where her life stopped and my own began.

We walked home together. We walked two inches apart, not touching. Not holding hands or jostling as I would have with Peter or Charley. Not talking even, except when she stopped and pointed out the flowers growing in a garden by the railway bank and told me their names: narcissus and gladioli. Or when we passed the field where the donkey stood and crossed the road to see if we could find the black cross that marked all donkeys since Christ rode into Jerusalem. When we looked at the flowers or the donkey or leaned over the bridge to see the train flying beneath our eyes or leaned back as far as we could go to see the sky above us until we were dizzy because there were faces in the clouds as they rolled above us, then, looking out into the world, we knew we were looking at each other. My heart turned in my side. My soul stirred. I entered into her being that was not myself or herself but some third place that was made up of the two of us being in the world together. A third world that I entered the moment she spoke or looked at me. My heart beat with the first pain of being. A pain that was not one of refusal: not the pain of being told I couldn't have – I must not do. But the first pain of longing. The pain of knowledge. Of desire. Of knowing I was myself and no other, with skin and bone and boundaries to my being. And that she was herself, with skin and bone and boundaries to her being. And she couldn't merge with me and I couldn't enter into her. And when she turned her eyes from me the sun went cold and when her voice moved beyond my hearing a darkness moved over me. It was the pain of existence itself. Of being one person and no other. And having no language to bridge the chasm but eyes and hands and ears. She reached her fingers through the bars of the railings and plucked a dandelion and gave it to me. She loves me, she loves me not.

We sauntered slowly home side by side. Not speaking. Not laughing. Not hurrying. The sky sailed over us. The footpath rode under our feet. The air hummed. She was Sarah, with raven black hair, a black fringe straight across her forehead. Blue eyes that were the colour of bluebells. I was in love as never before. All others forgotten or held in waiting.

I like to imagine us, Nina, sitting as we did one afternoon, on the top of Djouce mountain and seeing the whole coastline from Howth to Wicklow below us, shimmering in a late afternoon autumn light. You had brought a bottle of wine secreted in your bag. And two glasses. We sat together on the brow of the hill, just emerged from the ink blue of the pine forest, and drank slowly the warm, velvet-textured wine. I thought to myself this would be the perfect way to fall in love, the perfect setting for the start of a romance, not

161

acknowledging that I was already far beyond the stopping place in my free-fall through space, into the depths of your heart.

I am sitting there now. I see the water spread out beneath me. I taste the wine in my mouth, I hear your voice. I listen to every word you speak as though the secret of my life lies in their course. It was that day as if you were drawing a map for me – a life chart of my own hidden desires, fears and hopes.

But I mustn't let myself slip back into the quagmire of fantasies about you. I must try to keep my mind in the upper air of reason and analysis. As far from you as possible.

And what could be further than adolescence? Yet in a strange way, in my love of you, I have at times felt returned to those years of uncertainty and self-consciousness. I thought I knew all there was to know about life and love. I was quite world-weary and sceptical. But in relation to you – a lover of women all your life – I was suddenly gauche and inadequate. The culture you live in is so different from mine. It was at times as if we were from different countries, meeting in one foreign to us both and then deciding to go to the native country of one. In this scenario I was the emigrant. I left my people and went to live with yours. No wonder I felt at times adolescent. But that means also that I felt excited, rebellious, intensely alive. New.

After Sarah, what happened to me next? Was it boys then or girls who caught my attention? The years from nine to thirteen? I remember them now, as a time almost entirely given over to female friendship. A time in my life almost forgotten that was once so deeply enthralling, set apart from all that happened before or after. A small universe of its own – friendship between young girls. Though friendship is a poor word for it. Infatuation would do better. A period of infection, madness, delirium, filled with and created by the wild, unstoppable laughter of schoolgirls, laughter that was a way of being, a thing in itself, transcendent and all-embracing. Unbearable to everyone else. Whinnying, strident, manic. Ceaseless. Senseless. In love with life. In contempt of it. In defiance. In celebration.

Running through the streets of the town shrieking with laughter. Running up and down the stairs of the bus, flirting with the conductor. Dancing in the classroom. Smoking in the toilets. Getting sick on chocolate and beer. Racing on bicycles through the parks, dodging our way between old men and dogs, taking their lives in our hands. Sneaking into strange churches on dull afternoons, seeing how long we could stand looking at the crucifix without laughing. Agony. Three – four – five seconds and then again. Delirium. Out we ran clutching our sides. Splashing holy water on our breasts as we fled just in case. Oh just in case. The gambler's nonchalance in all our gestures. An each way bet. And then into the shops, ladies lingerie, to try on the new uplift bras over our school cardigans, waiting for the assistant to pounce and when she did walking away with a horrible limp so that she blushed and whispered: Oh dear I didn't realise. Going into the laundry where fat Miss McKay worked folding the sheets and towels. Miss McKay the fattest woman in the whole town, the dirtiest, who stank of sweat and no one knew what, the stench so strong we couldn't stand for more than two minutes in her company without covering our noses. In we went. One, two, three, four, five – who covered her nose first? Going to the police station to report a pair of knickers stolen from our bag, pretending to be Spanish so that we could not understand their questions. The guards, country lads, blushing and deliberate, promising to inform us instantly if the missing property was recovered.

Into this delicious theatre of the absurd came romance and erotic play. We flirted with all the boys who came our way. The attracting of boys a social necessity. Props to social existence, the key to freedom from home and parents. A right to a private life, closed doors, late nights, dancing, and openly flaunted sexuality. A right to queen it over older women and younger sisters. A weapon against the world. A barrier against childhood that at any moment could reach out and reclaim us still – weeping for a broken doll, a torn dress, falling asleep in front of the fire with thumb in mouth. And we were glad to sink back into its safe folds from time to time; a dull Sunday afternoon at home, indolent and innocent, a father pleased, a mother spoiling – a good girl who had her homework done and tights and blouse washed for Monday morning. But the next day, drawn back to the new world – the attracting of boys – a world challenged the adult who sought to ignore us. The adults who looked from a height and said, what a child she is still, such an innocent really! And made it an excuse for exclusion – sending us to bed early, shutting us out of conversation. Not taking us seriously. Especially in our obviously burgeoning sexuality. Absurd, they said – playing the femme fatale – hardly out of the cot. The women said it and the men mumbled agreement, but the look in their eyes told us a different story – the men of the family. The men of the outside world.

All of them watching, detaining us unnecessarily with a silly joke, told too often. Making an excuse to touch us; a brotherly squeeze, playful. And their eyes bright with lust and nostalgia. And anger over lost chances. Teasing us – our skirts too short, our lipstick too red. At the cinema feeling us up, under cover of darkness. Drawing closer seat by seat. Then stage one, the mackintosh over the lap, then the trembling hand approaching, the hot clammy touch on a knee. We got to know the procedure so well we enjoyed tempting it. Coming into the half-lit auditorium we knew immediately which ones were the most likely and made a whispered bet about how long it would take them to muster the courage and how long before we cried out and exposed them.

For no matter how frightened and guilty these elderly

molesters were in their approach, they nevertheless persisted. From this we learned their sense of God-given right to claim our flesh as their pleasure. And we learned this new game of advance and resistance so quickly it seemed second nature. Like the easy, comradely antagonism between nuns and girls at school; a show game of attack and counter-blast. Only that at school there was the hidden knowledge that the victors would inevitably become losers. The nuns, now powerful and vindictive, would one day be brought low, as girls grew into women and grew out of their charge and into the hands of men. The nuns, each year, cast off by their pupils, retreated sadder and wiser into their cloistered world. Becalmed in the company of women. Ultimately their authority would be less than ours as it was already less than that of our mothers, who lived inside the boundary of male patronage.

Our mothers told us to respect and obey the nuns. But even while they said it we caught the pitying note in their voices. The poor nuns, they'd say. Empty lonely lives without men or children. All this was plain in every exchange and it lent a playful, poignant element to the daily battles over unworn berets and hanging slips and screams in the corridors and giggles in the chapel and food in the classrooms and stolen glances at the gardener – the only man admitted to school territory, free to saunter by the orchard wall, seen through an open window his shirt sleeves rolled up, his lips pouting in whistle. And which of us, leaning desperately from the window would catch his wink, which of us, as Mother Ignatius rushed back into the room, would return his wolf whistle and which of us would be punished and which of us cared so little that we'd do it again tomorrow?

And the greatest crime of schoolgirl crimes was to court a male's attention and the greatest sin of all sins was to win it. For none knew better than the nuns, so many of their kind having been left bereft and forgotten, that the only escape route from their power was alliance with a male. One day the Prince would come and Cinderella would laugh in the face of her guardians. That day must be postponed as long as possible, of this the sisters were determined. Every girl knew the dagger she held to the heart of her teachers and her mothers by flirting with male lust. And so we studied the game and nurtured skill and stamina.

In the years I was engaged in my passionate love of Barbara, I played this social game of heterosexual seduction better than any other. Free of heart, free of need, I played with cool and command. I won all before me. I flaunted my new-found status. The world opened for me. Older women admired a neophyte pleaser of the male and granted me space and licence, leaving questions unasked and homework unsupervised. For if one were destined to be a breaker of the hearts of men so all would go one's way. There was no need to fret over the usual niceties of feminine behaviour, reserved for timid girls or those who had not yet learned the trick of capturing attention; detachment allied to enticement.

I haven't thought of any of this for years, but I'm beginning to enjoy it. Beginning to get into the mood. I've never before had the time or interest. But those fevered, self-obsessed years of adolescence and first love have a new significance for me now. I see them as the stepping stones laid out by fate, the crazy paving that carried me at last into my love of you.

First love? Which of them really was my first love? I think it's time to talk about Barbara. I know I've told you about her before but I've never said very much. I'm not sure why. Did I feel awkward for some reason? My only experience of lesbianism being such a childish, unregarded thing? I fell in love with her when I was sent over here to go to convent school. I was a boarder and she was a day pupil. I used to visit her house at the weekends. We were attracted to one another almost as soon as we met, though we'd never have described it that way. She was a year older than I, mature and provocative. She led me on, in fact, in the phrase the nuns would have used. She was much courted by the boys of the town already and she used to get me to compose love letters for her. She taunted me with her knowledge of the world and self-possession. She dared me to imagine what her boyfriends felt about her and I found it all too easy.

I knew her during the period when I was making my first experiments with the rituals of courtship and dating. She illuminated that bleak time of awkward, hesitant self-discovery. The scenes I remember best were set in the dance halls and discos that I frequented with Barbara that year I was at boarding school when the two of us would go out with a few other friends to the local hop or disco at the weekend.

Why is it always winter in my memory of these nights? Black night. Rain, sleet and snow. The smell of coal smoke in the air from a thousand chimneys, the sky sooty with it. A cold January or December night, my back against the school yard wall after a disco (and why were they always in boys' schools – managed and sanctioned by priests and brothers who provided the premises – school halls and sports clubs and youth clubs). My feet sore from a night of dancing in shoes too tight, the feet of my stockings filthy from all the feet that had trodden on mine, my lips bruised from rough kissing.

All the girls compared notes on the way home or the next day on the telephone and the notes were always the same, the same things happened in the same order to us all. In those frenzied cattle marts that were the permissible courtship grounds for young Catholic girls in that period, the music so loud, so raucous the chest ached and speech an impossibility which forced us to basics immediately.

We all judged the boys in the same way – by their looks – the little of them it was possible to glimpse in a near-darkened room pressed so close to them, no more might be recognised than a cheek or an earlobe afterwards.

By the feel of the thighs and chests pressed to yours, you judged them awkward or timid, greedy or experienced. Where they placed their hands when they danced a slow one most significant – on the shoulders, the waist, the small of the back or at once laid flat along the buttocks. Some grasped you by the hip bones and moved you about like a rag doll and then it was out to the yard, back to the wall, and ten minutes kissing some overgrown boy with clumsy nervous hands, the rain slipping down the back and waiting for him to take his tongue out of your mouth so that you could say it was cold and wet and how about going home which would be walking two or three miles together to take the last bus.

If an older boy was netted there was the much contested prize of the lift home. Which meant sitting in the front seat with a hand kept all the journey on the door handle so that escape could be made swiftly if he turned out to be a rapist (which he might because what did any of you know about him even if he had kept his hands on your waist?). When you arrived at the house (and all of you told the same story the next day), he parked the car (his father's) a few houses down and turned at once to take you in his arms as though you were a taxi with a meter running. And even before he touched you his tongue was in your mouth pushing open your lips, lashing your teeth. So many of these organs made your acquaintance in those years – they seemed almost to have a separate existence, detached from their human habitat – you could imagine them rolled up and laid out in rows as ox tongue in a butcher's window.

This kissing, as it was called, was routine and expected by priest and family though none would have said so. The boys took it as their due for the money paid in at the door and it was given by the girls, as part payment or in the expectation of being asked out during the week for a real date with drinks bought. The weather played its part in deciding how long was spent in the car saying these goodnights, snow and rain keeping you both captive for half an hour or more and clouding the windows so that there was no chance of a neighbour seeing and none could come to the rescue. The closer it was to Christmas, the more drunken and violent were these encounters and the more likely to lead to a cock pushed into the mouth instead of a tongue when some older boy with the foresight to open his flies before parking grabbed your head and forced it down on his lap before you could speak or protest. As soon as you could free yourself you escaped from the car and ran home and avoided boys for the rest of the week to recover your equilibrium. And he knew, even as he did it, that he had destroyed any chance of a return appointment but what matter? There were plenty more when you came from – a whole dance hall of hopefuls every weekend night and no way to get home unless offered a lift by one of his kind. This sort of boy was never seen again; all of you carefully avoiding any place he might go to, and any of you to whom it happened considered herself lucky to have escaped with your life or, at least as important, your virginity, because the one impulse stronger than any other was to avoid getting pregnant.

Every girl told the same story of this – it was as if you lived a collective life – everything that happened to you was in the plural, reflected through the talk and stories of each friend, so that your social life was like a vast hall of mirrors where each one of you looked to find her definition in comparison with the rest.

But the courtship of boys was not always in dance halls and not always winter. The seasons played their part in your lives as surely as they did for all other growing things in the natural world. This you recognised too and recorded any change in setting or behaviour. Your legs weren't always cold in a short skirt in the rain so that the men could admire your knees and

fondle your thighs. It was as often as not high summer –
August or June. It was as often as not a hay field or a river
bank when you stretched on your back, half-clothed, a blouse
pulled off one shoulder or a skirt up to your waist and some
male sweating over you, bruising breasts and lips and
cramping legs and arms. And the scent of the grass and the
flowers and trees were an intoxicant and the smell of the river
or sea and the noise of the birds and the crickets and all the
thousand creeping chirping flying things that come to life in
the heat. Your play was leisurely and sensual under the sun,
with talk and laughter in between bouts of lovemaking, sex
making or just, physical play-making. In the shimmering light
of summer it mattered now what he looked like, this partner
in pleasure, as you became acquainted with the greater part of
his body, knowing the appearance now of his flesh, inch by
inch intimately, the look as well as the feel of it. You knew if
their skin was white or tanned, if their backs were freckled or
spotted, if their feet were washed. And you had immensely
more say in the rhyming and sequence of things in this season,
the male being more timid when exposed to the light. You had
the freedom of open space all round you instead of the sealed
container of the father's car. Fields and beaches and lying
open to every eye and always strangers walking within earshot
and knowing you could call a halt because of their presence or
draw limits to what you would offer in the name of the hunt
for pleasure; how much of your body you could safely yield up
and in what order, so that the enjoyment was greater than the
risk; the risk always in the back of your mind knowing what
not to do if you were to remain free of the disgrace and
calamity of unwanted, unplanned, unallowable pregnancy.

The male being shy in daylight the emphasis was put not
on his pleasure but on yours, you being less timid, far less, to
expose your flesh to the eyes, and so you revelled in your
youth and your readiness and your quickness of response and

the bountiful harvest that was your body on the glimmering threshold of womanhood.

But that year, for the first time, when it was my turn to lie in the grass I felt something that I didn't dare to share with the others, something held back and secret. Even from Barbara or especially from Barbara because we must pretend that we weren't taking each other seriously in any way. Then in the sun-warmed grass, because it was summer, because the birds flocked in the air and every living thing called out for joy and lust for life and because the fruit hung on the branches and the grass was sweet and provocative on bare arms and legs and the sun warmed every inch of the body so that it was full and ripe and heavy with desire, I wanted perfection. I wanted physical beauty and charm and grace. I wanted romance. How was I to find it with these striplings of boys, these young men offering their first, their awkward best with sweating hands and angled hips and elbows? How was I to keep my mind from Barbara and the beauty of her breast at my mouth and her yellow hair filling my eyes, falling like a swathe of late summer grass across my face?

How was I to keep my mind from her and memory of the days with her, that spring, lazy afternoons lying flat on your stomachs across her mother's double bed composing love letters to her boyfriend, a corporal in the army? She described what she wanted him to do and I wrote it down and she acted out her demands and his responses to give me inspiration. She took off her clothes slowly garment by garment so that I could study her body and describe it to best advantage. Her tie, her tunic, her blouse – now what would he say? – she would ask – write it down quickly before you forget!

I wanted her so badly I was sick with it. Sick with excitement and longing but biding my time all the same, not wanting to ruin it, making the right move at the wrong time and having all this lovely heart-scorching intimacy gone for good. She was teasing me, of course, because she knew how I felt and reciprocated it but wasn't ready to say so. I couldn't make out what she felt for her soldier boy that she boasted of one minute and the next scoffed at with lofty disdain as no more than a spotty-faced youth, which he wasn't because I'd seen the photographs and he appeared all that he ought to be, dark and brooding and a worthy rival and she drew my attention to this whenever it suited her.

Once when we were composing a letter she said she'd like to take him to bed and once there offer no more than her naked breast to touch and say that he must be calm and contented with this till morning like a good boy and prove himself like the ancient knights and she said write it down, write down how you think it would feel to kiss my breast, and I said that I couldn't – that it was far beyond the scope of my imagination. She laughed at me and said nothing was, which was only flattery but nonetheless delicious. I regarded her sitting on the side of her mother's bed, sucking at the tip of a felt pen that spilt red ink across her pouting lips and her right breast showed above the lace of her poplin slip which she wore too tight for just this effect and I gazed at her coolly almost broodily, my eyes intent on hers and spoke the bravest words of my life – we could practise, I said – you could show me. She blushed and seeing the red in her cheeks I knew I had won and thought I would faint with terror. She smiled at me gravely and leaning back on her mother's bed she offered her breast to me, holding it between her hands then letting it rest on the rim of the slip that was pressed down by its weight, forcing it higher and firmer than it was, though there was no need, she had perfect firm young breasts with nipples dark mauve. I moved closer to her and put my hands over her hands and lowered my face to her flesh and so it was that I kissed a woman's breast before I kissed her mouth and it was the best kiss to be the first sexual kiss of my life.

How was I to keep my thoughts from her and my longing and make myself content with the given, the acceptable, sources of gratification? For that I must, I knew all too well. They had separated me from Barbara, suspecting something they would not state and sent me home, away from the bad influence that we were to each other. I knew without their saying it that I must learn to live without her, leave childish passions behind and adapt to the real world, the world of pleasing boys and men, the boys and men that would grant me freedom, a home of my own, children of my flesh. For the love of women was a love that could lead only to destruction and loneliness – an old, odd woman abandoned by the world, whispered at in the street. I knew nothing factual of women who lived with women, had never heard the word lesbian spoken. Had never seen it written. But I knew of its existence nonetheless in everything that went unsaid, in the lowered eyes and in the genteel shudders of revulsion for something never mentioned.

I knew also that somewhere there were people who lived differently from my parents and the world they held out to me. I knew that somewhere there was desire beyond the fringe of the speakable. I recognised – in the very intensity and constancy of the urgings towards heterosexuality and procreation: in the ceaseless enjoinders and encouragement to find a suitable mate while remaining of course virgin – the weight of a society terrified of some alternative. An alternative beyond mention. I pictured this alternative, at some bar in Paris or New York (of which I knew nothing at all) where strange men and stranger women crept at night with haunted eyes and nervous steps to gaze at one another with ineffable longing. The hopeless frustration of their needs forever in their eyes, with ugly hair and ugly clothes and mismatched sexual features, the women sporting beards and the men high voices. From where this fearful image came I couldn't tell but it was as strong and clear in my fantasy as all the other shadow things that could not be spoken of, the thousand shames and warnings I heard adults whisper from behind raised hands.

But their existence, unspoken, unwritten, was nevertheless one of the many shadows in the hidden layer of my mind where all the hidden glimpsed-at things were stored for later exploration. I knew beyond a shadow of doubt that this shadow world would never be any part of mine. I couldn't doubt my own health, my so abundant, self-evident physical normality. I would grow without doubt into whatever a complete and total woman was. I need not concern myself or worry over this process. It was inevitable and ineluctable. It was already taking me inch by inch surely and perfectly into what my mother and my sister and my grandmothers were and had been. It was beyond my choosing or consideration. It was an inescapable, natural unfolding, certain as a flower or seed.

Knowing this, I knew also that my love for Barbara was impossible. I must forget it. Forget the rapture of our mischievous play together between her mother's fragrant sheets when each one's body was a treasury for the other, an enchanted garden and our play carefree and innocent.

This I must forget and leave behind. Elysium. It was a memory that fitted nowhere. Had no name. It was a private world of delight with no relation to any other. Certainly no relation to those lost beings and the unmentionable tragedy lived out by their kind in cities I couldn't imagine. It had no place in the normal, the given, the expected of romance and pleasure and sex and marriage and children that all about me was obvious and taken for granted as fixed and inevitable. So my love for her, my desire, I learned to think, was something particular and curious to me alone. A dream sprung from the private complexity of my nature. And so, in some way, by some means, I must turn it to account, feed its potency and poignancy into the accepted channel. It was a tributary I couldn't follow, an offshoot of my nature that was more passionate than the average. So this stream must not be dammed but guided back into the mainstream which was the romance with, and love of, and search for the male. The male – the man of my life. The man who would be all things forever. The perfect one. The one of dream and myth. Companion and soul-mate, the only desire. Knight, warrior, courtier, worshipper. The man I'd love. The man I'd give all my body to in one piece, in one moment. The man my mother and my friends would admire, and envy me. The man who would father my children and grow old with me. The dream made flesh. The word made flesh. Somehow I must find him in these grapplings and clumsy explorations. I must seek him from a world of impersonators, impostors and strangers. I must find him and recognise him instantly in the first moment of our eyes meeting. I must draw him irresistibly and bind him inescapably. He would create me as a woman. And I confirm him as a man. He was out there already, somewhere among these hundreds that I tested and found wanting. He was somewhere on the hidden boundary of my life, just over the rainbow, journeying towards me, guided by instinct and by destiny. I would meet him sooner or later in any one of the possible meeting places, celebrated in romance – by a lake, by the seashore, on a mountain top, in a crowded room, on a ship's deck, in the streets of a foreign city. He was out there searching also, hour by hour drawing closer. He was almost in sight. When he came into my vision, he would banish, utterly obliterate thought of anyone but himself. All other desires would cease. Would evaporate as though they had never been. No name would come to my lips but his. No face desired but his. The girl I loved would vanish from memory and longing. Eclipsed at once and forever by him as the moon by the sun. I had only to continue my rituals of search, the ordained pattern of quest and discovery. He was making his way towards me.

Thus in this certainty I need not worry or fret that I loved Barbara above anyone – that I saw her face in every face that kissed mine, heard her name when my own was called. That the scent of her skin was with me always and the exact expression of her eyes when she looked into mine, laughing. That I wanted none but her and could imagine no longing but for her.

But this, I knew, was what it was to be adolescent. I knew no fear nor foreboding. All would be made perfect with time. Dream and reality, longing and the allowable would one day merge. I believed in this. Anything less was unthinkable, for anything less would make life impossible. Unimaginable. And life then was greater than anything I could imagine. It beckoned to me in all its glory, its radiance and luxurious promise.

And what did Ma have to say about all this? Not very much. It was far beneath her level of attention. When I came home from school that summer she looked at me sharply for a moment at the airport and then she said with approval: "I think you're growing up at last!" As to Barbara's parents' letter, advising that it might be better for me to stay at home, she made no comment at all. She probably suspected a little adolescent flirtation with boys and thought it was all to the good. Her only advice that I remember about sexual conduct was a brief and cheerful enjoinder when I was going away one year on holidays with friends: "If you can't be good, be careful." Anything more she'd have regarded as intrusion and no doubt she wanted to be sure of maintaining her own privacy.

When I told you stories like this you said: "Well, it sounds like she must have been up to something herself!" I dismissed this as more of your feverish imaginings but privately I thought you had a point. I began to remember how excited Ma was that summer – dashing off in the evenings to play bridge, going out at odd hours of the day because she suddenly remembered something she'd forgotten. I thought about the care she took with her looks and the new clothes she bought and I wondered if Pa had more to put up with than he ever let on. At the time if any of us questioned her about her appointments or abrupt departures from home she'd merely smile sweetly and recite: "Ask me no questions and I'll tell you no lies."

Well that was Ma. Vague, illusive, capricious, merry. So much now reminds me of her. So much leads back to her. My love for you, Nina – is that also founded in my history with her? Is it a response to it or a re-action? Certainly I learned from her to love originality and freedom.

Had I really forgotten about Barbara, until meeting you? No, of course I hadn't. But I had pushed her from consciousness, relegated her to the safe world of adolescent adventure. As I've said it was ended by her parents, when they took her away from school. Soon after that I went back to the States and I never saw or heard from her again. I grieved for her all that summer but by the fall time had pulled me past her, new things came into my life almost immediately. New preoccupations. New loves. I set her aside in my mind as one of the strange obsessions of youth, an experiment in passion, a lovely passing phase that had passed. And I wanted it to be past. Oh yes, of that there is no doubt. I was threatened by it. Threatened by the experience and by the memory. I wanted to be healthy, normal, happy. It didn't seem to be possible to be those things separately from one another. I concentrated all my attention on my heterosexual feelings and accepted the world's definition of this adolescent love as naïve and narcissistic.

It was only when I got to know you that she came back into consciousness. Then the memory of her returned in full force, complete and entire as though it had been preserved untouched by the years, immutable in some banished corner of my mind. What a long journey I was to follow before I met and fell in love with Malachy. A journey that was to keep me firmly and contentedly on the path of relations between women and men.

When I went out for a walk a while ago the world seemed so alive and splendid. The air startles my lungs. So pure and clear I could actually taste it on my tongue. I walked to the lake. No one was about but the place was bursting with life. The birds and cats and, somehow, even the grass and shrubs and trees seemed to be busy and urgent at that time of day. How is it the world manages this every day? Always the same trick – the same wonder? Big, slow waves were breaking on the sand. I stood on the jetty and waited for the swans and sure enough, by some instinct, they sensed my presence and sailed in majestically in search of food. I had brought with me a loaf of brown bread (bought from Máire Mac for just this purpose) and for ten minutes I stood happily breaking it into small pieces and throwing it out onto the water, an inch or two in front of their full white chests (too close and they can't see it – too far and it sinks before they reach it). On my way home the cows were ambling along the road, ahead of me on the way to the milking sheds. The farmers sit in their cars and drive behind their animals with a couple of over-excited sheepdogs running ahead to do their work for them. The farms are all divided into small holdings, with people owning patches of land miles apart so the cows must walk long distances from the fields to the milking parlours.

I passed Michael coming up from the beach. I've seen him before wandering about among the sand dunes. I remember Máire Mac told me that he sets traps for rabbits. He was wearing a blue tweed cap worn back to front so that the peak covered his neck, and carrying a bundle of driftwood and some rope. There's a stone shed, with a rotting thatched roof, halfway down the boreen where he seems to store flotsam and jetsam brought from the beach. Sometimes I've seen him standing outside it arranging various bits of debris – stones and wood and even empty beer cans – along the top of the wall, stacking them neatly in rows as if he's leaving them for someone to collect. When I see him do this kind of thing, I think he really is vacant. But at others, when he pops up suddenly from behind a hedge or stands glaring after me as I walk down the road, I feel he's calculated and cunning. He was smoking a cigarette as he walked along – I've never seen him do this before. He put it behind his back as I drew near and turned his head from me but said nothing, as usual.

Home again. How am I to contain myself? I can hardly keep still. I am pacing from wall to wall talking aloud to myself. Almost as bad as the first day. I must find some way to occupy myself. Something to keep my mind busy for the next twenty-seven hours.

I'll return to the story of my sexual development. There are areas of my life that I only pretended to be vague about. People and things happened to me, as to everyone else, that I'll remember always with affection and regret but prefer to seem to forget.

Harry Bernstein was one of those things.

When I was eighteen I fell in love with him, a man twelve years older than myself, a friend of one of my college lecturers. He was my first adult lover and with him I thought I'd left behind childish things, attraction to my own sex and all other adolescent fancies. I thought I'd arrived, all at once, safely and absolutely, on the shores of heterosexuality and maturity. Were they not one and the same thing? Harry, was dark-skinned, dark-eyed, funny, sad and clever. He was a writer and lecturer. He courted me with an intense, persistent, dispassionate admiration that flattered me deeply because it seemed so sophisticated in its appraisal. He aroused an equally intense curiosity and very soon I was completely infatuated.

I would meet him in a bar in Harvard Square in the late afternoon and our profound philosophical discussions would begin. He was always surrounded by brilliant, witty friends but

Mary Dorcey

he claimed to admire me and admitted me at once into his mostly male circle and even among them he flattered me by holding up the conversation to hear my opinion. He told me I was beautiful and he told me I had a mind. No one had said this before. "You must do something with your mind – make use of it. Don't let it rot while you have babies and look after a husband."

In everything he said, he made it clear that he was not husband material himself. He lived in his head. His body was vehicle to transport his mind from one place to another, and to allow for the enjoyment of food, sex, and drink. He taught me about lovemaking and, because he was so cool, so professional, he was an expert teacher. Skilled and thorough. Having loved so many women he had high standards. He had gone to bed with a prostitute when he was twelve and was immensely proud of this. He was cynical and melancholy and tender. He was Jewish and he worried my parents.

The combination of these things to me, just turned eighteen, was irresistible.

I would live with an older man. I would live with a Jew and never marry. I would scandalise my family. I loved the pleasure he could give me. He drove me almost mad with pleasure. Having no other interest when with a woman but amusement and pleasure; not wanting a wife, or children or a home or security or an escort, he could give himself up entirely to indulging his passions: talk and sex. He wasn't romantic, he didn't believe affairs lasted or should be made to. Because of this he had a special feeling for the moment and a kindness, rare in idealists. He enjoyed himself.

I was his mirror, his instrument. I gave myself over delightedly to the passion and skill he had learned in his dissolute, promiscuous past. I loved the fun we had together and I loved him because of it. He also made me take myself seriously, and to use my mind. He would not let me hide in my

180

role of woman and make myself a servant or passive. He kept asking me what I wanted, which bewildered me because no one had ever asked me what I wanted, only told me what was best for me.

I moved into his apartment block, taking a flat on the floor above his (we were to be close, not in one another's pockets). My parents were dismayed. "He is over thirty," my mother said, "and he drinks too much." The only time in her life she seriously disapproved of anything I did. She was right of course – about Harry. He did drink too much. He stayed up all night writing and drinking. He said alcohol loosened the creative muscles. He went to bed at six in the morning and woke in the afternoon and, after a pot of coffee and his first pipe, he had a glass of whiskey to get him started. I loved his way of life, his decadence, his defiance of every bourgeois value because I feared so much my own conformism. I wanted his cynicism that would prevent my eyes from deluding me, my heart from growing sentimental. He said: "All you Irish are sentimentalists. You indulge misery, court nostalgia, wallow in defeat. You avoid all real suffering."

I would have argued but I thought of Pa and said nothing.

So I lived, talking, reading, drinking late into the night, and having marvellous sex. In return I took care of Harry. I cooked and cleaned and did his shopping. I nursed him through his increasingly frequent hangovers. He guided my studies, encouraged freedom of mind and preached the liberation of both sexes from the tyranny of marriage and family.

Then, little by little, a strange thing happened. He began to fall in love with me. Or I began to notice that he was in love with me. Until then I had been the giver, the nurturer, while he stood back aloof and amused but very gradually he began to talk of the future, of a lasting bond, undefined by society but all the more lasting for that. This forced me to look at him, and to consider what I saw. And what I saw when I regarded him in the light of a future life, frightened me. Ma was right. He drank too much. He was not strong or serious. But most of all he was not happy. That is he didn't have the ability to make himself happy. He was deeply, corrosively cynical about life and his place in it. He drank to forget and he depended on me or whoever was with him to help him, to entertain him, divert him, lift his spirits. I had to get him going in the morning, supply a reason to get up and at night, consolation to make it possible to sleep. I began to fear the life ahead of me.

I drew back from him. With that acute instinct he possessed for the feeling of others, he knew at once and retaliated. He flirted with other women, drank more not less and stayed out at night.

One afternoon I went over to visit him and found him in bed with my best friend. As I said earlier, he defended himself by claiming that he wanted me to realise just what he was worth. It was an imaginative excuse and I think it was true. That was where his strength lay – in honesty and brutally clear self-regard. He knew he wasn't what I needed in the long run, he knew my conventional middle-class soul, my convent training and so he shocked me with the only thing that would shock me and drove me off.

We stayed friends for some years after that. We met for a drink occasionally and to talk – and anti-romantic as he was, he embraced friendship and behaved with great civility. I liked to talk to him and he remained a confidant.

When I fell in love with Malachy I wanted to introduce them. But I feared his judgement. With good reason. After spending a few hours together one afternoon over drinks, Malachy went off to the office and hesitantly I asked Harry for his opinion.

"He is exactly what you want – exactly what you deserve."

"And what's that?"

"Passionate, romantic, devoted to you. Sure of the world and his place in it."

"And – the catch?"

"Oh nothing at all – only what Oscar Wilde says . . . "

"What's that?"

"There is only one thing worse, my dear, than to lose your heart's desire . . . and that is to gain it!"

I laughed at him. Put it out of my mind immediately. But I never forgot it. It sent a chill through my blood.

I went to the shop just now to buy wine and candles. I wanted to be sure to have everything we could possibly need so that nothing would distract us in our first hours together. When I arrived Máire Mac was reading the paper. She didn't look up but when I asked for candles and held out a bottle of Chablis for her to wrap she repeated after me as though to make certain she had it right: "Candles is it? And wine? Well now, it's lucky for some."

Then she began to talk about the weather. She said that it looked fine enough at the moment but she had heard on the forecast that things were to get bad later on that evening.

"I'm glad I'm not having to drive anywhere tonight anyhow," she concluded, "the roads can be fierce at this time of year – if you were driving any distance I'd say you could expect bad delays."

She looked at me then with an expression of vague good-humoured interest and waited for agreement or dissent. But I said nothing. I wanted to be gone from her watchfulness. I wasn't in the mood for it. I didn't want any intrusion into the intensity of my expectation.

"Ah well, however long it takes, if you've reason enough to be going somewhere I suppose it's worth it. Good night now, careful on the bicycle . . . " she called after me as I left. I smiled to myself but made no reply. How does she know? It's uncanny.

I thought of walking to the lake but I'm too restless. I feel reluctant even to leave the house as if there was a chance that you might show up unexpectedly and I'd lose a few precious moments with you. I'm counting again. Pacing the floor and counting aloud like the inmate of an asylum. Ten hours to go before I see you again. What am I to do with myself until then? How can I fill the time until I leave the house and go to collect you at the station? I've made everything ready. I've set the fire for tonight with wood and turf banked high. I've made the bed up with clean sheets and pillow cases. I've washed the floors and hoovered. I've prepared the food for dinner. I've set the table. I've put flowers at the window and on the hall table. I've put candles in the kitchen and in the bedroom. I've set two bottles of red wine on the hearth to warm. I've showered and washed my hair. What else? What else can I find to do?

I sit, waiting for you. Waiting for the time to come when I must leave for the station. I could go now and hang about the town instead but I prefer to wait here, where I can imagine being with you. Once you arrive, I want to come straight back here. I hope you'll have eaten on the train because I couldn't endure delay of any kind, not even to eat.

For the next four days, we'll have a luxury we've never known before – four days uninterrupted, sleeping together, waking up together. Nothing to do but sleep, eat, talk and make love. When it's time to leave, we'll go together for the first time. That will be the best part of all – leaving together.

Then we'll go back to my apartment. Together. We will have an entire week alone together before the boys get back. Is it possible to believe in this? Am I ready for it? My whole life has been preparing me for it.

Chapter Thirteen

October, Dublin.

They took the coast road on the way home from Aunt May's. The lights of the bay stretched in a glittering arc in front and behind them. As she drew near the turn onto the main road, they passed in front of the railway station where she had stood, making her last good-byes to Katherine before she set off for the West. They had almost missed the train because they'd spent the morning in bed and couldn't persuade themselves out of it in time. Nina drove like a maniac to the station and then there was a mad rush for tickets. As they ran up the escalator, Katherine had lost her balance and fallen into Nina's arms. Nina caught her and held her close against her breast. She could feel both their hearts pounding.

"Can I count on you to do this every time?" Katherine said laughing as she kissed her.

"What?" Nina asked.

"Catch me when I fall?"

And Nina had answered, yes.

Lizzie sat in the back seat, her eyes closed, singing to herself. A song from a film she loved. "Bright eyes burning like fire. Bright eyes." Nina thought she should tell her before they got home. It would be easier to say it outside the house. If she didn't do it soon it would be too late. She lifted her foot from the accelerator, letting the car lose speed while she tried to think of some way to begin.

Lizzie looked up: "Where are we going now?" she asked. "Why are we slowing down?"

"I thought you might like to stop for a moment, to look at the lights?" Nina replied uncertainly.

"But Solomon will be waiting!" Lizzie sounded shocked. "He's been alone all day."

"All right, I won't stop if you don't want," Nina said, "but I do have to call over to the new office to pick up some letters."

At mention of the office, the child forgot to worry about the dog. She sat up, leaning forward against the driving seat and began a stream of questions about the new office. She wanted to know if it was bigger or smaller than the last? Would there be more secretaries? What was a basement? What kind of computer would she have this time? Nina let the questions wash over her head, allowing herself to be distracted. She felt the tension that had lodged in her muscles begin to seep away from her, as soon as it was clear that they'd have to postpone the discussion.

When she reached the office she stopped the car and turned off the engine.

"Can I come in with you?" Lizzie asked at once.

"OK, but you have to be quiet and not annoy anyone. Don't start asking questions. Promise?"

"I promise."

"If Paul is here or anyone else you like, we're not getting into conversation, all right? I'm just collecting my post and leaving again."

"All right."

They mounted a flight of granite steps and Nina rang the bell.

"Can I use the intercom?" Lizzie asked.

"What did you promise?"

A woman's voice crackled through the machine: "Yes?"

"Hello, it's Nina Kavanagh. I've come for my post." A buzzer sounded, the door opened and they walked through.

"Now remember – no chat." Nina whispered as they together walked up the broad staircase, Lizzie taking the steps two at a time.

She went straight to her own office and collected her letters from Mags, one of the researchers.

"Why do you need more letters?" Lizzie demanded when she saw them. "There's a huge big pile on your desk already."

"Because I have to have them all read before work on Monday," Nina explained.

Mags threw a glance of anxious sympathy towards the child.

"You must be Elinor's little girl?" she said. Then, as they left the room and wished her goodnight, she gave them both an indulgent, considering look. "How's Elinor?" she asked after a moment's hesitation. "I hear she's not well?"

Nina answered politely, saying something about her overworking as usual but, though she kept her voice neutral, she was conscious of a sudden irritation. How was it everyone knew everything in this town? And how come everyone felt sorry for Elinor? Of course Mags was a friend of Karen's and any news of misfortune travelled like bushfire.

"What's wrong with Elinor?" Lizzie asked as they walked back to the car.

"Nothing."

"Why did Mags say I hope she'll be all right?"

"She's just like that – very considerate," Nina answered. Then she stopped and looked down at the small child beside her. She took her hand in hers and smiled, looking into her dark blue eyes: "Don't worry about anything, OK?"

"Don't worry about what, anything?"

"Nothing. Don't worry about nothing!" She swung Lizzie's hand and they began to run together along the street to the car, their feet clattering on the stone of the footpath, the night silent all round them.

Chapter Fourteen

September, Clare.

In six hours time you'll be here. In six hours time the rest of my life will begin.

I sit on my bed, my back against the wall, my hands resting in my lap. I gaze out the south-facing window towards the mountains. The sky, blue-grey and the yellow autumn trees, their leaves falling slowly through the air, drifting on the grass. The grass is green. Brighter than I have ever seen it. Everything is more brilliant, more radiant than I remember. Black rooks are flying from branch to branch. Their blackness extraordinary – that anything can be so absolute! So perfect. I can smell the leaves rotting, I can smell the faint dust of them in the air, I can feel it on my cheek, sharp as a blow. How is it I never noticed the feeling of the air before this? It pricks the skin. I seem never to have noticed anything properly. In a moment concentrating intently like this, for one second, I will catch the smell of your skin. The skin of your neck to the left of your throat.

How am I to pass the time? How am I to contain myself? I can hardly keep still. I am pacing from wall to wall talking aloud to myself. Almost as bad as the first day.

I went to the phone box to call the boys. I got no answer. Though I waited and called again in half an hour. When were

188

they to be back? I thought it was today. I wish I could speak to them. I hate to be out of touch for this long. I wonder what they're doing? How they are? Has Luke got over that cold? Has Malachy bought Ben the books he promised him? How are they getting on together? It's been a long time since they've been alone with each other for such a protracted period. I wonder what Malachy has told them? Have they any idea that I am waiting for you? But how could they – that's an absurd notion. Even Malachy doesn't know after all. Nobody knows. And if they did? But I can't get into that now. I'll face it when it comes. When we're back in Dublin together. All of us. When I have your support. When I'm feeling strong and loved again, I'll be able to explain to them.

I walked home slowly and when I arrived at the house I had the sense of someone's presence. The gate was slightly ajar and I thought the grass had been trampled by the hooves of cattle. I went back out into the lane and was just in time to see a man's figure retreating down the narrow passage between the hedgerows. I shouted out and began to run after him. He stopped in his tracks and turned round slowly to face me. I saw that it was Michael. I walked up to him. I glared, making no attempt to conceal my anger. What did he think he was doing hanging round my house? I demanded. What did he want? What was he looking for? I was so angry I almost struck him across his foolish brooding face. And then he surprised me. Instead of defending himself he stared at me with a puzzled, slightly frightened expression. I noticed how unnaturally pale his eyes were and the slack way his lips hung open. I could see saliva gathering at the corner of his mouth.

"That's no harm," he said speaking at last in a guttural snarl, forcing the words from the back of his throat as if he had difficulty shaping them, "that's no harm."

"Well why were you hanging around my house then?" I asked glowering back at him. Daring him to deny it. He continued to stare at me looking nervous but unapologetic. Then he said something totally unexpected: "It's my house," he said, and stamped his foot, "*my* house!" I was so startled by the anger and fear in his eyes I stepped back from him at once, pressing my shoulders into the wet hedge. "My house!" he said again and then abruptly wheeled about and marched off down the boreen. I went indoors, dejected and faintly guilty. What am I to make of him? What does he mean by calling it his house? Should I just ignore him or tell someone about it? Who? Máire Mac?

Sitting by the fire again, trying to get warm. I feel odd – cold and shivery. As if I'm sickening for something.

It must be the tension of waiting for you. Though I should be used to this cliffhanging – I've known nothing else, after all, since falling in love with you. So many separations, so many reunions. Always having to adapt to something new, telling myself to be patient, telling myself not to be overexcited, not to believe too easily, not to overreact.

From the start my problem with you was that we come from such different worlds. I don't know how to judge your actions.

I've been out of my depth from the first. Confused, overwhelmed. Expecting too much or too little. Until the afternoon we finally became lovers, I was still capable of some measure of detachment I think, some objectivity. But after making love with you all that was over forever. I was totally lost, thrown light years beyond wisdom or sense.

That first evening in bed together, we stayed in the hotel room until long after midnight. Then left in a hurry, with no time even to shower, fastening our clothes as we went out the door. We said our goodbyes on the street. Standing under a tree, the rain falling on our faces and splashing on the glistening pavement. Two middle-aged businessmen passed us, one of them slowed his step and stared, surpise and then anger passing across his face as he recognised two women embracing in the dark. "Bloody whores," he muttered to us or to his companion, as he moved on again, his voice slurred by drink, his eyes livid.

If he only knew, I thought to myself. If he only knew the half of it!

I tried again to persuade you to stay the night. I said I'd phone Malachy and tell him I was with a friend.

"Couldn't you phone Elinor and make some excuse?" You paused. I held my breath. If you decided, in that moment, in my favour, it meant everything would be all right. In my naiveté and arrogance I needed to believe that this lovemaking had been for you the life-changing, transcendental happening it was for me. I waited, my heart in my mouth. You turned to me at last, you smiled, you kissed my forehead, you said, your eyes full of regret, "No, it isn't possible. Not tonight. Not at such short notice." You must have seen the look of sick disappointment on my face.

"Don't worry," you said, trying to reassure me, "I'll call you tomorrow. We have all the time in the world." And you kissed my mouth again. All the time in the world – at the last words my mood took one of the dizzy swings from dejection to elation, with the wild see-saw motion I'd come to recognise as the normal rhythm in your company.

I drove home, dazzled, faint with desire. Every nerve in my body pulsing with its new awareness of you. I don't know what I'd expected to feel, but not this euphoria, this feeling of unblemished childlike pride in myself, as though I had brought off the greatest achievement of my life. And maybe I had. I had become your lover. I had made love to you. I had made you happy. I was a woman and the lover of a woman. What more extraordinary thing could happen to me? I stood on the doorstep of my husband's house and realised suddenly that's how it was – my husband's house – not mine – not my children's, transformed in a matter of hours to the dwelling place of a stranger. For the second time that day, I hesitated before I turned the key in the lock. I looked up at the sky. The moon was flying through tawny furrows of clouds, lighting the street a sudden fluorescent blue, making the rooftops and the water in the gutters shimmer, as if under snow. The whole world seemed gilded. Transmuted.

I opened the hall door and went inside. The light was off in the bedroom. Malachy was asleep. I got into bed beside him and lay rigid, afraid to move, afraid even to breath. I felt as if all the passion stored in my flesh must throw out energy like a force field around me. It wasn't possible that he could be unaware of me. I was terrified that he would wake and begin to question me or, worse still, turn on the bedside lamp and look into my face. But he didn't wake. At last, as the hall clock chimed half past two, I fell asleep.

In the morning I woke early and was busy making breakfast for the boys by the time he came into the kitchen. He was already dressed and shaved for work, looking formal and subdued. He'd slept badly he said, disturbed by dreams. "What time did you get in?" he asked as he gulped down a cup of coffee. "It must have been late. Did you have a good night?"

For a moment I couldn't remember what I'd told him the day before, where I'd said I was going. I dreaded him asking something more precise. But he was late and rushing. He kissed me at the door, "See you this evening. Let's go out to eat. Have some time to ourselves." Then he was gone. A few minutes later Luke and Ben followed him on their way to school. I was alone. I went into the bathroom and stared at my face in the mirror. It must show, I thought, the astonishment, the joy, must be indelibly marked on my features. But they weren't. I looked exactly as I had done the morning before.

I went to the kitchen phone and called you. My heart

pounded as I waited for you to answer. I knew it would be you because Elinor was always out at that time of day. As soon as I heard your voice, without preamble I asked if you could meet me. To my horror, you hesitated. Was it possible you didn't feel the same insane urgency?

"I just need to talk to you," I said. "I need to talk about what's happening to us." I was conscious of no irony when I used the word happening. I did feel that something had taken us over, something outside ourselves that was hauling us along in its wake. But isn't this what all lovers say, or at least the adulterous ones?

After a moment you answered, "I can't today," you said. "It's just not feasible. But . . . " my pulse quickened at that small precious word, "if you like – tomorrow – I'll be here all afternoon? Could you come over about two?" You sounded doubtful as if you might be asking too much of me. You must have known that I'd have gone to Hell and back, at any hour of the day or night, to meet you if you asked.

The next day, at seven minutes past two, I rang the bell of your yellow hall door and waited. I think I still honestly believed that I'd come to talk to you. That with effort we could work out some plan, some way of making safe what was happening between us. As though it were an as yet unexploded bomb which careful talk and planning could dismantle. The evening before, I'd cancelled dinner with Malacy – put him off with some lame excuse about tiredness. I couldn't risk spending an evening alone with him. Sitting opposite him across a restaurant table, I knew I'd find myself blurting out the truth. The habit of confiding in him, of inviting his opinion, was too strong. Instead I took the boys to the pictures and then for pizza afterwards. Playing the good mother, trying to appease my guilt by indulging them, wanting to prove I could make someone happy.

The yellow door opened and you stood before me.

Solomon, the dog, stood guard beside you as always, his tail wagging, his melancholy spaniel's eyes fixed on me. You were dressed in loose-fitting dark blue jeans with a wide leather belt and a tight black T-shirt that revealed your breasts. Come in, you said and your smile was teasing and rueful at the same time. I followed you into the kitchen. The spider to the fly. The table was set for lunch, wine glasses, French bread and a huge wooden bowl of Greek salad, black olives gleaming on a bed of lettuce and chalk white slices of feta cheese. You poured coffee from the pot on the stove. My hands trembled uncontrollably as I took the cup from yours.

You looked at me apprehensively. "Are you all right? Would you like something stronger?"

"We must talk," I said.

"Yes, we must," you replied, "but have a glass of wine first." And then you seemed distracted suddenly. You turned abruptly and walked across the room to the window and stared out into the garden, your back to me. The wine bottle stood open on the table. I helped myself to a glass, filling it to the brim.

"Have you said anything to Malachy?" you asked, without turning round, your attention still fixed on the yard outside.

"No," I said flatly, feeling guilty as though I'd failed you somehow. And then I remembered I wasn't the only one with news to break.

"Have you said anything to Elinor?"

"No." Your face was still hidden from me. I couldn't judge your mood. At last you turned round slowly. You spoke very deliberately. "We are going to have to decide what to do," you said.

"Yes."

"But first . . ."

"Yes?"

I was afraid of what you were going to say. Afraid that

you'd ask me to leave or ask me to make some promise I wouldn't have the strength to keep. My neck and shoulders stiffened. I wanted to look at you but I couldn't. The fear was too great. I waited for the axe to fall. My head was lowered but I knew that you swung round and crossed the room. You stopped in front of me. You put your hand out and touched my cheek. I looked up. To my astonishment you were smiling.

"First I want to kiss you," you said.

You put your arms around me and instantly the gulf I had felt open between us in the last few minutes closed again. I put my mouth to your neck. I felt the pulse that beat at your throat grow faster. I thought, I'm safe. She loves me after all.

"You haven't forgotten yesterday?" I whispered.

You leaned towards me closing the last half inch between our mouths and kissed me, "How could I?"

We stood locked in each other's arms, my back against the kitchen door. I felt your heart beat. I smelled your breath, and the smell of your skin. That kiss – the first since becoming lovers – had a new, startling intimacy. Knowledge made it different, my so recently discovered knowledge of what it promised. Your body close against mine shivered. I felt the heat and strength of your tongue, the lovely easy insistent rhythm of your kissing. I trembled with the intensity of my desire, of my exposure, and my power. I didn't need to ask what you felt. I saw it in your eyes – the same mad urgency, the same recklessness.

You took my hand and led me into the hall.

"Not here," I said, "I can't, in this house."

"No," you said, "not here. Upstairs – in my room. The attic."

And for the second time in two days, I climbed a stairs led by you.

The bed was a mattress under a skylight. We lay down. The sky was a dark blue with smooth, balloon-like round clouds sailing past the small bright frame of the window above our heads. Up there, with the low roof enclosing us, in silence and alone, the white walls covered by the forms and colours of your paintings, sensuous and vivid, I let myself imagine that it was your house and yours only, a private world, created by your energy and passion.

I hadn't thought it was possible to improve on our first night. But it was. I knew you better. I had more confidence. More skill already, learned from you. You were astonished by how at ease I was. So at home in this strange new element, the one I was born for but that had needed the force of your love to reveal to me, to overcome my caution, all my sensible moderation. Your body was the sum of all I'd lived before touching you, the map of my dreams, of my past and future. Lost in you again, in the sound of you, the smell of you, the taste of you, my blood was set on fire, my limbs changed to water.

Up there, under the dark timber of the roof, under the skylight, on one of the golden afternoons of your native city, the wind blowing through the trees, moaning softly under the slates of the roof, I loved you with a new confidence. Different from before. This time I took charge of you. I lay looking down on you, looking into your eyes. I made love to you, in all the ways I had learned. My hands moved as yours would, they journeyed along the same pathways. I made myself patient. I caressed you slowly and softly. So softly that I knew my skin touched yours only by the expression in your widening eyes. As I caressed you, softly, repetitively, I talked to you, using the words you had used. And others that came straight from my heart, never spoken before. I asked you if you wanted me. I asked you if you loved me. I asked you how much. And where.

I caressed your body, your breasts, your belly, your thighs. I had never before felt anything as soft and powerful as your body. The silk of you, the sweetness, the tension. The lovely, easy power of your muscles gripping me as though you'd never let me go again. My hand sunk in you. The milk of your love streaming on my skin, an absolution, a benediction. Slowly, steadily, arousing you, provoking you. Relentless. My tongue wiser than your own need, my mouth giving birth to your flesh. To my own.

I lay above you and watched you come. I watched your head lift from the pillow. Your wide, beautiful, dark eyes changing colour. Your shoulders rising, your back arching, lifting towards me, leaping like a fish upstream. I heard your laughter, a wild heartbreaking laugh. Laughing for joy. Your thighs were like the boughs of a tree tightening about me. Your taut, flat belly against my cheek. I trembled in your grasp, in ecstasy, in fear. The trembling ran through me from head to foot. I began to come with you, through you. Coming as you did, carried by the sound of you, the feel of you. My body as wild as yours, no longer human. Shaken, wave after wave breaking over me. We floundered, lost, spent, helpless, laughing like demons. We rolled from the bed and onto the floor, still laughing.

After that afternoon my life settled into a pattern. There were the days when I saw you, and the days I did not. The days we made love, and the days we did not. There was desire and its fulfilment. Nothing else. I would phone you in the morning when I knew Elinor was at work. We would arrange where to meet and when. Where to make love was our main preoccupation.

I went to your house. I didn't like to, but we went to the attic and I persuaded myself that it was your room only and our world alone.

You did not come to my house. I had only the bedroom that I shared with Malachy and I knew you wouldn't want to share that.

We made love in the car, in the flat of an old friend of

yours who didn't know Elinor and who didn't owe her loyalty. We went to hotels. We made love in the open air, in forests and in fields, wrapped beneath blankets and sleeping bags. We, who had spent three months talking obsessively, stopped talking altogether. Hardly a word was spoken between us except in bed. Love words – provocative, teasing, flattering. Life divided itself into the hours with you and the hours without you. Remembering the last time or longing for the next. My nights were driven by fevered anticipation, my days made up of fulfilment and then longing renewed. I was devoured by it. It's no exaggeration to say I thought of nothing else. Before we became lovers, when I was still yearning for you, I imagined that once we'd been to bed, the hunger for you would be eased. I liked to imagine that after a few weeks I might even tire of you.

But after that second time, my obsession was absolute. Like a tidal wave it engulfed me, sweeping every obstacle from its path. For the first time in my life, I was blind to everyone's needs but my own, utterly selfish. I wanted to be with you every hour of every day. I wanted Malachy out of the way. I wanted Elinor out of the way. In the end I even wanted Ben and Luke out of the way.

I was greedy. However much you gave me I wanted more. It was no longer enough to see you only during the day. I became obsessed with the need to sleep with you. To fall asleep in your arms knowing I had the whole night with you, to wake looking into your eyes. I'd never been with you without the sense of a deadline; a limit set to our pleasures and discovery, your watch ticking at my ear and you consulting it openly while I kissed you, forever on guard lest Lizzie or Elinor should arrive home unexpectedly.

I became prey to all manner of cravings and obsessions. I'd waken in the middle of the night and go straight to the kitchen, impelled by a violent longing for some particular food. I'd open the fridge door and set to work on whatever I could find, devouring the leftovers from dinner or rooting out rashers and sausages to cook a fry. One night I ate an entire bowl of plums, nineteen of them, one after the other, standing in my dressing-gown staring blindly out the kitchen window. Another morning I woke with a desperate longing for a ham sandwich. Nothing else would do. Of course, I recognised all these bizarre symptoms from the times I was pregnant and I marvelled at my perversity. But maybe it was not so strange – I was pregnant after all – pregnant with love for you, full and rich and weighted. Ravenous with this new burgeoning love.

I couldn't stop myself eating and I'd forgotten how to sleep. My body was so strung out with sexual craving that even in bed with you I couldn't let myself sleep for more than ten minutes for fear of forfeiting precious time. At night, I couldn't sleep because I missed you so desperately, the new entrancing sense of your body beside mine.

I avoided Malachy whenever possible. I took immense care never to be alone with him. At night I went to bed before him and faked sleep when he came in. Or I stayed up long after him watching late-night movies on television. I told him I was overwrought and exhausted from too much work. I pretended to be going to the library every day to work on my thesis.

Beside him at night, while he slept, I longed for you, my head full of fantasies, my heart beating like a piston. On the days I knew I wouldn't be meeting you, I felt literally sick with lust. I would wander about the house aimlessly, or go out and prowl the streets, pretending to shop. Or lie in bed for hours dreaming about you. I thought I could spend the rest of my life lying on the flat of my back or my stomach while you played me like a fisherwoman playing out a line. I ached for you, my belly, my thighs, my womb. I was devoured by brute longing. I could have crawled on all fours, but I had to force myself to be still, to be calm. To wait until you called me, until the summons to your house and a few fevered hours in the afternoon.

I wanted, most of all, to go away with you. To have three days and nights together. Consecutively. Time alone, without having to think of anyone else. I wanted to be somewhere that we could eat breakfast together and start to make love before we had finished. I wanted to lie by a log fire, listen to music and make love to you in the light of the flames. I wanted to have the whole livelong day to laze in, to please one another, to drive one another to distraction.

I wanted to lie supine and utterly passive and watch you as you made love to me, as you fucked me in the steady relentless way you had, hour after hour, with the sweat cold on your forehead from the effort of it. I wanted to watch your hand move, loving the exquisite and yet workwomanlike air of the gesture, as your wrist moved slowly back and forth, slowly, thoughtfully, your head held to one side and on your face an expression of rapt concentration as if you were listening for some far-off music, or the deepest rhythms of the body, perhaps to the blood beating through its canals and rivers. Your strong broad hands. I loved to watch these hands at work on me and I loved the expression in your eyes as you watched pleasure consume me, propped on an elbow, gazing down into my face, your eyes so serious and reflective, sad, almost regretful as you watched passion travel over my face, like a kindly passer-by looking down on an accident victim.

I wanted to make love to you, to make you come so often that you cried out for mercy and I would ignore you and go on driving you further and further. I wanted to hear your voice, struggling to say my name, your tongue stammering the syllables as you struggled to keep breath, as your body rose in the air and your head thrashed on the pillow.

I wanted to announce our love to the world. I wanted to walk in the street calling out your name. I longed to tell

Malachy. Every evening when I went home to him after being with you, I felt worse. My guilt deepened. I told you it was killing me to keep it a secret. I said I wanted to be open and proud. I must at least tell Malachy, I said. But you counselled patience. There was no knowing how he might take it. He might issue immediate ultimatums. He might become violent. He might try to separate me from the boys. This last warning, of course, silenced me every time. It was a risk I couldn't take. I asked you when you'd tell Elinor and you said as soon as you thought she was strong enough to deal with it. And, when I pressed you, you said that you couldn't risk telling her until you knew it was absolutely necessary and inevitable. That struck such terror in me that I couldn't bring myself to ask you to explain it. Did it mean you weren't yet sure what you felt for me? Did it mean that you could imagine giving up our relationship?

When we had been lovers for three weeks you phoned me one morning and said you had to meet me, but not in the house. You needed to talk to me seriously. I felt a cold panic gather in my stomach.

"What about?" I asked.

"Let's go for a walk," you suggested. "By the sea. I need to think. And I always see things more clearly when I walk by the sea."

Standing by the shore, on a winter beach, great troughs of rank, brown seaweed covering the sand from the waterline right up to the embankment, the wind racing on the water, sweeping it almost to our feet.

"We can't go on like this," you said. "We must decide what we're going to do. I must find a way to tell Elinor or else . . ."

The very sound of her name sending waves of panic through me.

You must have seen how stricken I looked.

"I'm sorry," you said and you looked into my eyes with an

expression of such tenderness and regret that I was more frightened than ever. "I'm so sorry," you said again, "but I can't do this." You turned and walked away from me towards the water's edge. I looked past you out to the sea blasting itself against the shore, roaring in the hollows of the cliff, pounding the lowest branches of the pine trees where they grew out from the rock face. And I thought what has happened? What has changed so suddenly? Why were you having guilt pangs, all at once? Had Elinor said something to you? Did she suspect something?

I thought, if you do not let me touch you again now it's over. I will have lost you forever. The sea roared in my ears blocking out the noise of my heart.

Then, at the last minute, you saved me, as so often before. I felt your arms reaching round my waist. I felt the words you said more than heard them, the heat of your breath against my ear.

"I love you. I need you. There has to be a way."

I didn't phone you because you'd asked me not to. Not until you had decided on a definite course of action. I lived through those days in a ferment of emotion, thrown from elation to near despair.

Then, when I'd almost surrendered hope of hearing from you, something extraordinary happened. Something totally unforeseen. You rang and told me Elinor had to go away for two weeks to London to do a training course. I chose to interpret it as a sign that our passion was fated, that we were being drawn together, our lives orchestrated by some hidden, but benevolent force.

"Will you come over at ten, after I've driven Lizzie to school?"

And so began our real love affair, our honeymoon. Two weeks of passion. Of delirium. I was working part-time, four afternoons a week. In the mornings, I came over to see you as soon as you had brought Lizzie to school. You opened the door, in your dressing-gown, naked under it, so that not a moment was wasted. We fell upon one another at once, kissing on the way up the stairs, pulling off our clothes as we went, falling into the attic bed.

How I loved that room. There was a painting by the door; a portrait of two women, naked, lying on blue sheets on a vast double bed, eating fruit, one passing it from her lips to the other's. "Breakfast on Dark Afternoons" was its title. I felt you must have foreseen these days when you created it.

We had two weeks. Two weeks stolen from the world, stolen from duty, from affection, from the ordinary sense of what is right, stolen from Elinor, stolen from Malachy. I knew the day of reckoning would come. I knew we would have to declare ourselves, confess our crimes and be separated or complete the final act of betrayal and desertion. But for fourteen days judgement was suspended. And with it reason and guilt. I was lost to everything but my joy in you.

I had never known lovemaking like ours. In bed with you I felt as if I was battling for my life. As if I might die of lust for you.

I knew already all there was to know about the pleasure I could be given, but what I had no notion of was the deep sensual bliss of giving pleasure to a woman. I said to you one day, "No one ever says what the most amazing thing about lesbianism is – the joy of making love to a woman. Men, of course, must have known all along!"

We made love everywhere. On kitchen floors, in bedrooms, in bathrooms. At night and in the morning, before making breakfast, reaching up under the folds of your dressing-gown, your breasts still hot from sleep, mouth tasting of coffee. Behind the doors of cinemas when distracted from a tedious film or in a noisy pub in the afternoon, your back to a toilet door when leisurely talk and a few afternoon pints had made you lazy and sensual. In ships and in cars, in your own big double bed under the skylight and in the beds of friends and hostesses and in hotels and guest houses in city and country when the proprieters had no idea such nice women could possibly be . . . or knew exactly. In fields when cattle came rooting disturbing you with their hot breath, at sea in boats, water lapping at the planks that stretched between you and the water, in forests, pine needles falling in your hair, your cries of pleasure shaking the branches, releasing them in soft flurries on outstretched limbs.

When I talked about the sense of revelation and wonder I had with you, you agreed with me. You said you felt exactly the same way. But how could it have been true? You had been in love with so many women. Whereas for me everything about this was unique. I remember telling you how bizarre I found it – delightful and disconcerting to find myself combining the intimacy I felt with women friends, with intense physical passion. The force of these two worlds coming together, combining in one person, frightened me. One day when we were talking after lovemaking, I remember saying how strange it was that I hadn't ever had a conversation like this before. "Like what?" you asked. "About mothers," I said, "discussing my mother and my lover's mother in bed." You burst into laughter, amazed by me.

Yet, for all your experience, you roused a protectiveness in me. An older sister? I wanted to look after you. Make life safe and comfortable. Why? Because you seemed indifferent to your own safety? Because you took no account of tomorrow, because you lived from hand to mouth, body and mind? It was how you wanted to live, you said. If you had security you'd reject it. You would always find some way to threaten any sanctuary you might establish. You must always have a bridge to cross, a gangplank to walk. You're a kind of trapeze artist.

Balancing on a knife-edge of your own choosing. There's bravado in this, courage and vanity. A vanity that seems to scorn the things other people live for. See, no hands, you boast, as you teeter on the brink. And those who love you gasp, watching from below.

But somehow, you don't fall or, as Elinor said, when you do, you land on your feet. You have the luck of the devil, she says. But you say it has nothing to do with luck – that it's only those who practice falling, who risk it, who learn to fall well. Falling in love was your special forte. You did land on your feet, time and time again. Practice makes perfect, you said. But I had none of your experience, none of your agility. When I fell it was from a great height right down to the bottom of the abyss, a landslide I could never have rehearsed.

What I didn't understand then, or since, was what drew you to me.

I remember you telling me that you never paid attention to married women. Would never have got involved with one. They were trouble as far as you were concerned, complacent and overdemanding. Inexperienced lovers. You had seen it all too often – a married woman falling for a lesbian and expecting to be swept off her feet and borne into a new life the moment she made herself available. And then if things went wrong, as they usually do, she crept back to her marriage, bemoaning her harsh treatment and the callousness of male-identified women. They only call us that when things go wrong, you said, teasing me.

If I'd no idea what I had to offer you, it wasn't something I wanted to question. You talked of so many lovers that they seemed in a way to cancel one another out. If I'd wanted to be jealous I wouldn't have known where to start. It might have appeared shallow, cynical, but that wasn't how it sounded to me. It seemed rather as though you had stored them all in your own being. You were like a solar light, gathering heat from the hours of daylight, converting it to light in darkness. You were rich and weighted with love. Benevolent and generous. Your experience had made you skilful and easy in the giving of love. I was grateful for this. You were exactly what I needed. The perfect person to apprentice myself to. I was doing it all for the first time. That's the only mitigating factor I can offer. The only extenuating circumstance. What was yours, Nina? Experienced as you were, what was yours?

I don't know how long it was before I began to get an inkling of how difficult your way of life might be, to be in love with someone of one's own sex. For one woman to love another. Such a simple thing, so natural and so profoundly threatening to the whole social system. It was weeks before the mists of intoxication cleared enough to allow through a glimmer of the harsh reality of the outside world. Meeting people I hadn't seen for years and suddenly realising when they made normal inquiries about my life that I no longer knew how to answer them.

One day, walking across O'Connell Bridge with you, I bumped into an old friend of Malachy's and mine, from our early years in Dublin. Delighted to see me, he began immediately a barrage of questions which I found suddenly awkward and offensive. How was Malachy? We were as madly in love as ever? We were still famous for the degree of our infatuation. How were the boys? Was it still just the two boys? "No thought of another," he asked and winked at me. "I can't imagine you and Malachy stopping before you had a girl!"

On another afternoon we went for a drive in the country. We were having a drink in the lounge of a Wicklow hotel. Sitting in an alcove holding hands, gazing into each other's eyes, silent and grinning like loons. Like any pair of lovers. Except that we were women. Just then I saw a woman seated across the room, looking at us. I thought I recognised her, though I wasn't sure. I dropped your hand, pulling mine back into my lap. I stopped smiling and began to make loud empty conversation. You stared at me. "What's wrong?" you asked.

"Nothing."

"Are you sure?"

"Yes, I'm fine."

But I wasn't. I felt suddenly sick. Embarrassed and ashamed.

I dropped your hand because I didn't want her to know about us. Such a small thing and it seemed such a vast betrayal. And, for the first time, I understood how hard this life might be. It was not only the fear of being seen by someone I knew, obviously engaged in an illicit affair, but because I would be exposed at once as the lover of a woman.

But as soon as we were alone again, the moment we got outside into the stillness of the night, the rain falling softly on the trees above our heads while we kissed and kissed again, your soft, hot lips cleaving to mine, your tongue sweet and the rain falling on our faces and your hand reaching inevitably, incorrigibly down to my jeans, I had forgotten.

We drove in silence along the dark roads, your hand on my knee, and my sense of pride came flooding back; the deep unmistakable sense of our love being natural, preordained. We stopped the car before reaching my house, at Sandymount Strand, and watched the waves break on the shore, and you took my hand in yours and kissed the inside of my wrist and sucked my fingers, one by one and told me that you had never known such happiness.

That was the beginning of that extraordinary time, my initiation. My revelation. All through those dark, sweet days, the beginning; the long journey of transformation. My entry into a new culture, a new way of seeing, a new way of being in the world.

In the dark afternoons of my love for you, the amber light

of evening falling on the river, drifting out to sink behind the hills that embrace and circle the city. The smell of hops from the brewery, the sweet, heady smell all through the back streets of the city and high on the hill, in the oldest quarter of the town, the cries of the newspaper boys and the children kicking footballs against the walls. And on these dark afternoons I discovered your body and through it the flesh of all women. I discovered the birth of the world, its passage to light and its journey to death.

In the shadow of the Cathedral walls, under the clamour of the bells, the wind wafting the smell of stout and the river through these high perched streets. I became with you, the poorest of the poor. As vulnerable as the most endangered species. I forsook privilege and the remnants of respectability. I made myself with you, one of the despised of the earth, the untouchables. By falling in love with you and renouncing the power of men, I transformed myself into pariah and miraculous being at one and the same moment. There in an attic room, in the narrow, burnished streets, banished and found. Lost and enraptured. Cursed and annointed. Mad with bliss.

The strangest of all was to wake in the morning with all the bells of the city ringing about us. Right there in the centre of town as we were and to feel that they rang for us. That was exactly the level of celebration I wanted, that I felt we deserved.

Book Two

Chapter Fifteen

It came just now – your message – when I was in the garden, a message phoned to the post office at twelve o'clock, written out by Máire Mac, I suppose, on a sheet of white paper, folded in two, and delivered into my hand by Niamh – Máire Mac's young niece – who works in the post office. She seemed excited or frightened, as if she knew more than she should.

"Your friend phoned and said it was urgent." She hovered uncertainly at the door, as if expecting an answer or because she was worried for me. I took it from her hand without a word and went inside. I walked to the window to read it in the light.

"Sorry – infinitely regret – cannot arrive today. Lizzie worse. Phone me tomorrow morning. I love you, Nina."

I knew what you had written before I read it and yet I stood staring at the page in disbelief, desperately hoping there might be some mistake. As if it were possible that I'd misunderstood a word or that you'd left something out. I read it over and over again, turning the page in case there might be a postscript on the other side.

You tell me to phone you tomorrow, but why not tonight? Why must I wait an entire day? If Lizzie is worse why don't you tell me what's wrong? What am I to do? What am I to think? I don't understand it. I can't believe that you're doing this to me again.

I went into the kitchen and poured myself a whiskey. I

screwed the cap back on the bottle tightly and replaced it in the cupboard, out of sight.

I went out for a walk. I walked for an hour in the rain. Right round the lake and back again.

When I got back I made a pot of coffee and lit the fire. I am tired and calm. Sick with disappointment, but calm. I've made up my mind. I'll phone you tonight. It's no use trying now because I know you're never in at this time. I'll phone after six. I'll insist on talking to you even if Elinor answers. I don't care anymore. I don't give a damn for our agreement. You have broken your side of the bargain, so why should I care about mine?

You had better speak to me. I won't take no for an answer. I don't care anymore what Elinor thinks. I don't care who I upset. I want an answer. I want the truth. I don't care how brutally it's delivered. I must know. You must tell me what's really going on. No excuses, no euphemisms, no false assurances.

I'll sit by the fire and wait. In three hours' time I'll go to the phone box and call you. What am I to think about? I must find something to calm me. Some memory of happiness to reassure myself. I have to build up some confidence. If I ring you in this mood of despair I'll make everything worse. I must calm myself. I must think. Perhaps I'm jumping to conclusions. Perhaps it's not as bad as it looks.

What's happened after all that's so terrible? Why should I feel everything is changed and all our happiness endangered? You've sent a messaage telling me that you won't be coming this afternoon, after all. What did you say exactly? Seventeen words written out by Máire Mac in blue biro. "Sorry – infinitely regret – cannot arrive today. Lizzie worse. Phone me tomorrow morning. I love you, Nina."

So? Is it so awful? If I can put aside the sick disappointment and think about what you've written, is it really so bad? You say Lizzie is worse – can it be true? And if it is, is it a sufficient explanation for not coming? Why can't Elinor take care of her? You ask me to phone you tomorrow morning – why not this evening? What reason can you have for putting me off? Is there something you're not telling me? Something worse?

But no – I mustn't let myself get into this – this paranoia, this frenzied scrutiny of your intentions. All that's over and done with. It's all in the past. Everything is different now. I know you love me. I know you want to be with me whatever happens. We have moved into the light – into the clear daylight of our new life together. I mustn't let myself sink back into insecurity when life is full of joy and hope. I have to remind myself like a child at school repeating a lesson. I have to enforce it on my brain. We've just spent those perfect days together in Dublin. After all the pain I've been through I couldn't have imagined that things could be so good again, so quickly, but they were – better than ever. You've told Elinor that you love me. That you intend to live with me, to stay with me come hell or high water. Why do I say that? Why do these images jump up at me unbidden – these clichéd phrases from movies and romantic novels? You've told her already. You told her the first night after I came here or the next day. So she knows now – one way or the other. She's accepted it as final. No going back. She can see that in your face. You're staying with her for a few more days because it's what you agreed together. Because you're waiting to see Elizabeth recovered. And then? Then you'll come here. You'll get on a train and travel back to me. Only one day. I can wait. Having waited months with no hope, I can wait this long surely?

I must stay calm. Not let myself imagine the worst.

What would the worst be? That you haven't told Elinor yet? Or that you told her and she talked you out of it. Or that you've tried to tell her and your nerve failed. You're not good at hurting people anymore. Your history is against you. I remember all the stories you've told me about leaving former lovers – the guilt and remorse you felt for the suffering you caused. You were an abandoner, you said, something or someone every time impelled you to move on. You were always the first to make the break. The blood always on your hands. You told me that you were haunted by the faces of the lovers you'd left; the expression in their eyes at the moment of knowing that it was inevitable. Lovers you deserted for some new and better love that became in its time an old love left again for some other. I remember you said how suffering makes people ugly, how it destroys all charm and beauty. You spoke of the guilt you felt when you looked on the ugly, distorted mask that replaced the features once beautiful, once beloved and knew that it was all your fault – your indifference, your cruelty, your faithlessness.

Thinking like this terrifies me. The more I remember of it, the more afraid I am that you have given in to her. I know how persuasive she can be. How often have you told me that you put off an argument with Elinor over something you wanted until the very last minute to lessen the probability of her talking you out of it?

I went to the phone at five to six. But someone got there before me, a young man just come from the pub as I arrived. I waited over five minutes for him to finish. It was raining of course, the rain blowing in sheets off the sea. I was soaked to the skin and frozen. At last he came out and nodded a mute apology. I went into the box, which reeked of cigarettes and beer, and rang your number. No answer. I waited and tried again. No answer. I waited ten minutes altogether, trying it again every couple of minutes, cursing you for not having the machine on.

Not that I could have left a message anyway, but it would have made me feel better. I'd have had the feeling at least of someone listening, someone knowing I was there.

Back in the house again. Should I try once more tonight? Or wait until tomorrow? This is obsession. But I can't help myself.

I'll have something to eat and make my mind up after that. If only there was a television to watch or someone to talk to. How am I to stand the waiting cooped up alone here?

I've decided. I will phone you again tonight. I have to speak to you. I have to hear your voice. I am beginning to feel mad. As though I invented everything that's happened between us in the last days, invented your coming to the airport, invented our reconciliation, those two marvellous days when you promised you loved me and me only, that you knew your own heart as never before and could not go back on your decision. Do you remember, Nina, do you remember the things you said to me? Tell me I'm not a fool to have trusted you again?

I'll go to the phone again at eight. I forced myself to make a meal – if you could call it that – an omelette with some cheese and mushrooms, and threw a couple of potatoes into the oven and laid a table as if I were expecting company and opened a bottle of wine (laying the table gave me a justification for having a bottle to myself). When I finished eating I took my glass to the fire and spent the last hour reading through this journal I've been keeping. And reading it altogether, in this way, I'm astonished by it. It's like something written by someone else, some other woman, who has chosen me to confide in. What have I been thinking of? Why have I covered page after page with these infatuated reveries, these wandering ruminations on love and romance? How can I have been so blind – so complacent? So ready to forget in the name of remembering? One thing is clear – I can't trust myself – whatever about you.

I must be careful now. I must try to keep a grip on my imagination. I promised myself this summer in Maine that, whatever happened, once I got home I wouldn't pester you.

And I must abide by that now. I know if I once start the whole thing will become hopeless. So when I speak to you I'm not going to ask you for an explanation. I won't ask any of the questions that fear inspires in me. I won't ask what you've promised Elinor. I won't ask if you lost courage and gave in to her. I won't ask if you've slept together again. I won't ask any of that. I won't ask because I don't want you to lie to me. Because I know you won't want to answer. Because I couldn't bear the answers. Not while I am alone here at any rate. So don't think you have to answer any of this now. Don't be afraid that I'm going to interrogate you. I won't utter a word of reproach. I can wait for the right time. For the time being, I'll try to be so good. So calm and generous. I'll stick to the rules. I promise that. Do you believe me? You must.

Maybe I should try to sleep. If I could sleep I might dream of you. I might find some happiness in a dream. But I can't. I'm wide awake. Stiff with misery and fear.

I try to remember some of the loving things you've said to me. Something to console me. At the beginning, sitting among the gorse bushes on Howth Head one day, I asked you (fishing for compliments then also) what you liked best about me – about the look of me? And you said that you loved my eyes, and my hands and my voice. And that was what mattered. It was always these three physical attributes that commanded the heart. These were the touchstones.

They were the perfect words to make me feel secure. I was absurdly proud and reassured.

I went back to the phone this evening at eight and again at nine. Still no answer. Where can you be? Why aren't you at home? What does this silence mean? On the way back, as I drew near the house, I suddenly smelt cigarette smoke in the air. It was instantly noticeable because the atmosphere is so incredibly pure here and because no one comes up the lane besides myself. Who could have called? One of the farmers? The postman? And why? Whoever it was must have left only seconds before I arrived or the smell wouldn't have been so strong. I found myself brooding on this for a good five minutes. But what does it matter who called? It wasn't you – that's the one certain thing. If only I had something to occupy my time, some way to keep busy, I wouldn't be getting obsessive like this.

I made an effort to distract myself just now by finding something totally unpleasant to do – I went into the bathroom and spent ten minutes scrubbing the bath and wash-hand basin and toilet – if this kind of chore doesn't calm my mind, nothing will. Then I went downstairs to the kitchen and made a cup of instant coffee, pouring the milk onto the coffee grains first and then the water, in the way you do. I remember the first time I saw you doing this, I remarked that it was an extraordinary way to make coffee and you said, on the contrary, (emphatic as ever) that it made it creamier if you put the milk in first. And here I am even now imitating you. I can see you pouring the coffee and bringing it to the table, waiting for me to take the first sip and I can hear your voice exactly as you say: "See – didn't I tell you it tastes better this way?"

As soon as I let myself picture you, the questions start up in my mind again. The same weary assault of jealousy and suspicion. Why have you put Elinor first once again? Why did you stay with her? Why did you not come here with me in the first place? It might even have been easier for her and for Lizzie too. A clean break. How can it help to have you there holding her hand, commiserating, asking her permission to desert her? Oh Nina – why do you always try to soften the blow?

My God how I hate you sometimes. How I despise you. How I despise your equivocation. Your desperate need to please. Your wanting to be all things to all people. Why can't you ever let anyone hate you, Nina? Why can't you let go of someone without looking back to see how they're taking it? Why must you always want to console the people you are leaving? Why can't you let them alone? Let them get on with surviving. Why can't you leave them a little healthy anger and hatred to make it possible to part from you. But no, you want to be liked. You want to be well thought of, you want – even in their last extremity – to see them smile, to have them say, see how much I care for you. What is it? Vanity? Compassion? Guilt? What is it? Because you were an orphan, abandoned yourself? Because you can't walk away from anyone as your mother once walked away from you? Because you have to turn as she did not? When she walked away from you down the corridor and did not turn to look back?

Why can't you let that moment go? Why must you go mourning for it every day of your life? Making amends for it. Healing the world.

You don't mind outraging the world, but you must keep the affection of those who love you at all costs, mustn't you?

Yet, if you are so reluctant to wound, to abandon, what compels you over and over to be the one who abandons? Why have you left such a trail behind you, strewn with apologies and departures? But you gave me the answer yourself – having had it happen before, you can't risk letting it happen again – first out – that's your motto. Yes, you told me. Almost at the beginning.

The first time we broke up I remember this. You were going to join Elinor in London for a holiday and I went to the airport to see you off. In the car you broke the news to me. You told me that when you got back you would have to stop seeing me. You had promised Elinor. I heard what you said, but I couldn't believe it. I was certain that you didn't mean it.

That you'd change your mind. Like a fool I waited to see you off. Until the very last minute.

I waited as you walked down the corridor, I waited like a child, my face pressed to the glass of the observation lounge, longing for you to turn, willing you to turn . . . yes . . . no . . . yes . . . no . . . Yes – you turned – at the very last second, as they took the ticket from your hand, you turned your head. I saw the anguished look on your face and for one moment the hope held that you would turn and run back to me, dropping bags, ticket and all. I saw in your eyes an apology, that you regretted this departure as you had so many others. It's not easy your eyes said and then you were gone. Lost to sight. I waited until the plane disappeared into the sky. I followed it all the way up and behind the clouds before I could turn away. As if I hoped you might even then change your mind, turn round and come back to me.

I had only that comfort, that for one second you had regretted it. You had paused and reconsidered.

So many departures. So many renunciations and reconciliations.

But why am I hurting myself thinking of this now? Everything is different since our last two days together. Why am I letting myself give way to fear? Only a few days ago I was so confident – walking on air. You had come back. You would never leave me again. This is what matters. All that matters. In a few day's time we will be together again. Together openly, absolutely. Beyond doubt or regret.

When I was getting on the train that's what you whispered in my ear. I'll never leave you again, you said, even as you left me. I'll never leave you, even as you walked away from me. I knew what you meant and I believed you.

I find myself now wondering about Elinor. If you have told her and how she's taking it – how does she feel at this minute? Stupid question. I know exactly how she feels. She feels what

I felt when you left me. I could so easily be sorry for her, but I'm not. If someone has to suffer, why shouldn't it be Elinor for a change?

Will I go to the phone box now or wait until tomorrow as you've asked me to? It's so late now, it might be easier to wait. And after a proper night's sleep I might feel differently. The situation might look better.

I passed Michael this afternoon. He was rooting about in the old shed where he keeps his things. He stood stiffly by the open door as I passed and spoke not a word, of course. I noticed he was holding a lighting cigarette. He held it behind his back the way they do here, inside a cupped palm to protect it from the wind. I don't remember ever seeing him smoke before. Then, later on this afternoon, I went upstairs to the back bedroom in search of something to read. It's a room I've hardly entered since coming here. It has an air of chill and damp about it. I walked over to the dusty, grimy window and looked out into the garden. There are two apple trees and a pear tree by the gate and just between them, almost hidden from view, I saw Michael standing by the wall near the shed setting out in an orderly row, stones and pieces of wood he brings up from the beach. He lays them very carefully, as if laying a table for someone or putting offerings at a shrine. The next day he takes them away and puts different ones in their place.

I asked Máire Mac about him when I was in the shop, but she only repeated the same remarks about his being a bit simple but having no real harm in him. "Pay him no notice," she said, "and he won't bother you."

When I asked why he hangs about my house all day she said, as though it was perfectly reasonable: "Sure isn't he a neighbour?"

I went downstairs to make something to eat. About an

hour later, I went to the bedroom again. I switched off the light and went to the window. I saw Michael still standing as before, rooted to the spot, staring up at the darkened house.

A ferocious storm last night. It started about eleven o'clock with the rain and wind growing stronger every hour. Gusts of eighty miles an hour or more lashed the house from late evening until dawn this morning. The noise was so intense it drowned out every other sound. I tried to listen to music for a while to calm myself, but after a few minutes I abandoned the attempt.

I went to bed shortly afterwards hoping to sleep through it, but first I pulled the bed up close to the chimneybreast because I've read somewhere that it's the one part of the structure that remains intact if a house collapses. I lay listening to the uproar; the wind shrieking at the windows, bellowing down the chimney, the walls vibrating, the door rattling on its hinges. The rain cascading through the air, turning the water in the ditch to a torrent that burst its banks. I heard the roar it made as it rushed across the backyard.

Finally I fell asleep to be woken again a few hours later. I leaned over to switch on the bedside light and found it wasn't working. I went downstairs, hoping it was only the bulb that had gone, to discover all the electricity had failed. I was terrified. Imagine being alone in this place with wind and rain raging, with no electricity! In complete darkness! I found one candle and lit it, but the light it cast was so ghostly it frightened me more than the dark. Crept back to bed and lay shivering and wide awake until first light. Got up, made some coffee and decided to go to the phone. I thought I would just call your number and put down the phone when you answered. I was frightened, miserable. I needed to hear your voice, to know you were there. I trudged through rain and muck to discover, when I reached the box, that the phone was

221

dead, the line down, I could see it waving in the wind. Good Christ, what a crazy, god-forsaken bloody place! What am I doing here? I will go mad if I stay much longer.

What am I to do now? I can't even phone you. I wish I could get into the car this minute and drive back to Dublin. What's the point of staying? I don't believe any more that you intend to come up again. I've lost faith in it all. Nothing is safe any more. Nothing is clear. Nothing is what it seemed.

The cat is sitting on the windowsill wailing at me. I can't be bothered to let her in. I haven't the energy to feed her.

I have been wandering round the house like a sick animal, desperately seeking some means of distraction. The storm has died down, but the rain is still falling and the ground all round the house is flooded. When I opened the door I was confronted by a small lake. If it rises any higher it will be impossible to keep it from seeping into the house. I am feeling completely desperate: terrified and abandoned. I don't think I could get a car to start even if I had one. And I can't walk to the shop until the water subsides a little.

Do you know something? I'm beginning to forget what you look like. It's true. I cannot bring your whole self into vision. I try to picture you standing before me and I can't. I try to capture you by concentrating on some detail. I try to see your eyes, your eyes that are darker at night than in daylight. I remember that your nose is straight with a tiny white scar on the left side. I remember your wide, full mouth with the faint lines beginning to show above the upper lip. I remember all the details, the individual features I can picture bit by bit, but I can't put them together. I try to see your arm, the lovely round flesh of your upper arm where I've sunk my teeth so many times, but I can't. I see your hands on the steering wheel, I can see the silver ring on your finger. I can see your thigh, the blue jeans covering your left leg as you drive in the clutch, but then the picture fades abruptly like a television screen at closedown. Blank. Nothing. You've vanished.

I distracted myself for a few minutes by going in search of the cat. (I'd forgotten all about her and was suddenly afraid she might have drowned in the storm.) I found her shivering, cold and frightened on a shelf at the back of the bicycle shed. I carried her in and have put her to dry by the fire and given her hot milk to drink. She is purring noisily now and making a great ostentatious show of grooming herself. Throwing me, every few minutes, glances of affection and gratitude.

What else can I do? I am too restless to read. I don't want to eat and anyhow I've no food to cook. I can't go out and there's nothing to do inside.

I heard a knock at the door a few minutes ago. Niamh from the post office with another message from you. She said you'll ring the post office at five thirty. You told Máire Mac that you had heard about the storm on the news – guessed there might be lines down. Niamh was all sympathy about the situation – how frightened I must be alone up here in the dark. She promised me the power would be back before nightfall. Well, Nina? Am I to go to the phone? I haven't much choice now I suppose with Máire Mac expecting me hourly – all agog – scenting drama of some kind!

Dear God I am so tired of all this. Sick to death. Heart sore. But I will nevertheless walk down to the post office in a hour's time.

Six o'clock. How extraordinary it was to hear your voice again. Standing in Máire Mac's backroom whispering so that she could not overhear. So strange to talk to you at long last, but not to be able to say a word I needed to say. You sounded strange – distant or self-conscious. Guilty, I suppose. And now

I don't know what to think or feel. You said you'll come up the day after tomorrow. You said you loved me, though you didn't sound as if you meant it. I wonder were you alone? I asked if you were missing me and you said of course, day and night, every minute. Yet when I asked if you'd told Elinor you hedged – you said you'd told her the most important part – that you had realised you needed to see me again. You told her nothing about meeting me at the airport or arranging to stay with me here, but you did tell her you needed to see me. You said you couldn't risk telling her the whole truth when she is so worried about Lizzie. It would destroy her. But Lizzie is getting better slowly and you'll be able to leave in a few days' time. I listened and said nothing. I didn't know what to say. I don't know what I feel anymore. Is it just normal tolerance and humanity that's being asked of me or am I being treated like a doormat? I can't decide whether I'm angry or wretched or excited. But I'm glad to hear Lizzie is better. I am really. And not only because it frees you.

I am to phone you tomorrow. And if the line isn't restored you'll phone the post office in the evening.

Chapter Sixteen

October, Dublin.

"Do you hear Solomon?" Lizzie asked as Nina put her key in the door. They could hear the drumbeat of the dog's tail against the floor. It was his habit to lie pressed against the door where he could smell them at the first second of return.

"Can we take him for a walk?" Lizzie asked

"Let him into the back garden for the moment."

The child ran into the kitchen, the black dog jumping at her heels and yet arranging his frenzy so skilfully there was no chance of his knocking her over. She opened the back door and the two of them disappeared into the night together. The noise of laughter mixed with the dog's excited barking issued from the darkness.

Nina went into the kitchen to put the kettle on. On the table beside the gas stove she saw a note in Elinor's handwriting. She picked it up and read it slowly, fear gathering in the pit of her stomach.

"Nina,

Will you look after Lizzie tonight? I've gone to stay with Karen for the evening. I want to be alone and I think you need to think things out. There's food in the fridge. I'll be home about three. I don't know what you want, but if you've decided to leave will you go before I arrive? If you do, could you leave Lizzie at Fiona's and I'll pick her up there?

Elinor."

225

She stood at the window and lit another cigarette before reading it again. But there was nothing more to discover. Just seven lines of clear blue script. Flat. Stark. Matter of fact. No word of love. No complaint. But what did she want after all, she asked herself. Surely not pleading or recrimination? There'd been enough of that. And if Elinor maintained this mood of icy reserve and hostility wouldn't it make it much easier for them all? She could leave without another row. Be gone before she got back, as she suggested. Later – when it was a fait accompli – when it was final and things had settled a bit, that would be soon enough to talk and try to reach agreement.

Lizzie came in from the garden with mud on her hands and knees.

The dog followed after her, a palpitating, mauve tongue hanging from one side of his jaw, a tennis ball gripped in the other.

"When is Elinor coming home?" Lizzie asked at once, looking at the note in Nina's hand. "I want to tell her about Aunt May."

"She won't be home this evening, love. She's gone to stay with Karen. She'll be home tomorrow."

"But she said she'd see me tonight. She said she'd read the end of my book."

"Well, she can't make it. So we'll just have to manage on our own, won't we? Will I get you some hot chocolate? And if you hurry to bed I'll read to you for a bit before you go asleep."

Lizzie bounded up the stairs to the bathroom, the dog running after her, the tennis ball still in his mouth.

Nina heated milk in a saucepan and got out some biscuits. When she arrived upstairs Lizzie was lying in bed, her head resting against the dog's flank while he lay stretched luxuriously beside her, his tail beating, his head on the pillow.

"Get down, Solomon, you know you're not allowed on the

bed," Nina remarked for form's sake, knowing he had no intention of obeying her.

She gave the child the hot chocolate and biscuits and sat down beside her, shoving the dog to one side.

She let her eyes travel about the room, dwelling on the familiar inhabitants, the one-eyed teddy bear winking from the chest of drawers, the three glove puppets on the chair in the corner, the lovely silver mobile swaying above her head, hand-painted wooden figures of small animals and fish. Everything in the room was expressive of contentment and security. Not least the beloved dog who lay at her feet now, his black, satin ear, almost longer than his face, draping his eye. A storybook dog and a storybook child. All the trappings of a protected childhood. So different from her own upbringing, she reflected not for the first time. Molly's house in Sandymount, though elegant and comfortable, was yet austere, suited to the tastes of an elderly lady, not a young, boisterous girl. Nina couldn't so much as have imagined a bedroom like this one – designed especially for a child; with brilliant posters on the walls, toys covering every shelf and the ceiling spread with luminous paper stars that mapped the night sky.

"What are you worried about?" Lizzie asked suddenly in the oddly perceptive way she had.

"I'm not worried," Nina said.

"Aunt May said you were. I heard her."

"Well Aunt May is wrong," Nina said flatly, discouraging further inquiry.

"Will you read my story now?" Lizzie shifted key as easily and produced a paperback from under the covers. She could read very well for herself, but she still preferred to have someone read aloud.

"It's *Irish Myths and Legends*," she said proudly.

Nina smiled. "Which one are you on?" she asked.

"Diarmuid and Gráinne."

"I'll read if you promise not to speak one word until I'm finished. Right?"

Lizzie nodded her head gravely and Nina slipped her arm around her shoulders and began to read from chapter five, as bidden, in a low, soothing voice.

"Diarmuid and Gráinne lay asleep in the forest," she began, "and so deeply asleep were they, content in each other's arms, that they did not hear the barking of the hounds and the thunder of galloping horses until the king's soldiers were almost upon them."

"Why did Gráinne leave the king and run away with Diarmuid if it was so dangerous?" Lizzie asked in a severe tone, having totally forgotten her promise of a moment ago.

"Gráinne was the first to waken," Nina read on, ignoring Lizzie's question, "and when she saw the king's horse stamping his mighty fringed hoof on the ground above their heads she cried out with fear."

After a while Lizzie's eyes began to close. Nina read one more paragraph before she laid down the book and asked: "Are you asleep?"

"No," Lizzie answered without opening her eyes.

"Do you want me to go on reading?"

"Please, for a bit more." So Nina began again. She was nearly at the end of the chapter and she wanted to know herself how it worked out.

At last, hearing Lizzie's deep breathing beside her, she closed the book and laid it down beside the child's pillow.

"Do you know how I know you're worried?" Lizzie did not stir, but she opened one eye.

"I'm not worried," Nina protested in spite of her better judgement. If she wanted the child to sleep she should say nothing at all. "Why do you keep going on about this?"

"I know you're worried because I hear you whistling."

"I wasn't whistling."

"Yes, you were. I heard you. Under your breath the way you always do when you're worried about something."

"I do not."

"You know you do. The way that annoys Elinor – you do it just for a few seconds and then you stop."

"Well I'm not worried about anything even if I was whistling under my breath," Nina offered as a compromise.

"Do you know the story about Saint Patrick?" Lizzie asked with an alarming switch of thought.

"What story?" Nina asked before she could stop herself.

"The one in the book of Irish Myths. It's at the beginning. It says that Saint Patrick drove the snakes out of Ireland, all but one that he placed in a casket beside Lough Derg. Before he walked away he ordered the snake to stay there without moving until morning. And it's said that to this very day if you stand by the water's edge at Lough Derg you may hear a low voice whisper – "Is it morning yet?""

"That's funny." Nina smiled and slipped her arms from under Lizzie's head. "Time for you to sleep, definitely and absolutely." She bent and kissed Lizzie on both cheeks. The dog lifted his head slightly. Let me stay for a little while longer, the expression in the half-open eye seemed to ask.

She turned off the light and went downstairs.

She walked restlessly from room to room. She couldn't remember what she had meant to do. She picked things up: a book, a pen, a small, black, china cat; stared at them for a second as if they might remind her and then set them down again. At last she went into the kitchen and sat in her favourite place: the wooden armchair by the pot-bellied stove and propped her feet on a stool. She looked slowly round the room, attentively studying the things she would have to leave behind her. Almost everything in the room was a reminder of her shared past with Elinor, and a statement about their present life: the yellow-shaded lamp on the circular scrubbed pine table, the earth-coloured pottery vase with the big spray of dried hydrangea, the silver coffee pot, the blue crockery on the dresser. The squat wooden armchair, a grandfather's elbows that stood in the corner, the paintings they had chosen together. Everything held memories. And promise of the future. To an outsider it was a room like any other, but to her it was a living organism, a warm skin she could wrap around herself whenever she needed protection. But now it seemed to her to have altered subtly. Furniture and objects had taken on a reproachful air. They sat in their appointed places, stiff and detached as though already withdrawing from her. She looked at the things around her and they seemed to look back as if already they no longer belonged to her. They had become, in an evening, bric-a-brac: pots and pans, crockery, furniture in someone else's life.

She went out into the garden. The grass was wet and glistening in the light from the house. She looked up at the stone wall that bordered the park and the great birch trees and elm that grew within its boundary. She could hear the hissing and soft splashing of the stream that flowed between the back gardens and the park. In the middle of the city, its oldest quarter, and hardly a murmur of traffic. The warm, roasted fragrance of hops blew downhill from the brewery. A mallow bush, still in bloom, grew just outside the door. Elinor had planted it from a cutting and it was already as high as a small tree. It flowered right into November, violet, luxuriant.

Solomon the dog appeared beside her. Announcing himself, as always, with a whack of his tail against her calf. She looked down at him and he gazed up. Why must he look at her in this way? The sloe-black eyes, silken, wistful, supplicant. Who could withstand them? And who would keep him? she asked herself. Elinor, of course. Lizzie could never be parted from him.

She went upstairs to the child's bedroom. She was fast asleep. Her arms stretched up above her head, her feet sticking out from the side of the duvet. She made a faint snoring, soft as a cat's. Her hair lay out behind her on the pillow, fine blond hair like her mother's. Everything about her fine, beautiful. A princess, a fairy princess. Come here to me, my little fairy, May always said when she saw her at the door. Looking at her now Nina thought of the week when she had kept watch at her bedside in the hospital, holding her hand, the child drifting in and out of sleep. Hour after hour. While she sat beside her, the small inert body so slight it hardly showed beneath the covers, she had thought about what she must do in the coming days. She had sat, holding the warm, damp hand in her own and planned her betrayal. At times when Lizzie writhed suddenly, as though in pain, or called out in her sleep, Nina imagined that her thoughts must be transmitting themselves to the fitful consciousness and she felt smitten with guilt. And it was impossible to leave.

Now, Lizzie lay peacefully in her own bed, her hand above her head so small, shaped into a fist. Nina reached out and took it into her own. She held it loosely, letting it lie in her palm like a tiny living creature, like a small bird, come to nest in her shelter. The emotion that filled her heart was the purest love she had known, the least selfish. This child who was not her own aroused the closest thing she knew to devotion. Could she feel more strongly for her if she belonged to her? Could she even contemplate her present course of action if the child were her own flesh and blood? Strange how easily that phrase came to the lips. What did it mean to her? Could she say of anyone that they were her flesh and blood? Even as the question formed itself in her mind, an image of Katherine rose before her; the woman she loved unto madness, the body she loved until she was sick with it, until she was turned to fire and water at the glance of her, the touch of her. Fire and water competing, nurturing each other. Trembling with fear at her touch. As if she held her life in her hands.

Chapter Seventeen

September, Clare.

You are coming the day after tomorrow. You have promised me. One more day.

I feel strange; nervous and disoriented. I think I'm finding it hard readjust to the good news that you're coming after all. I ought to feel excited. But it hasn't sunk in yet. I can't quite believe in it or let myself relax. I got such a terrific shock when I read your message. Blind panic took me over. I think my heart beat is only now returning to normal. Why should so small an alteration of plan have such a devastating effect? I suppose because I thought all this was over – the uncertainty, the abrupt changes of plan, the mood swings.

You said once that we create passion, create the beloved in our own image, weave each other out of the rag and bone of our own hearts. Yet if that's the case why is it impossible to disentangle you, deconstruct you, when I need to? Why can't I take you apart strand by strand, thread by thread? Why in love is the whole always greater than its parts?

I have been blind from the start. Willingly. It's given me such acute pleasure to be foolhardy, to let myself be swept off my feet. How can I complain now? After that first night with you when you let me see so plainly (maybe deliberately) the conflict you felt, even blind as I wanted to be, it ought to have become impossible for me to go on concealing from myself your emotional ambivalence. You made it all too obvious, that evening in the hotel, as soon as I asked you to stay the night with me, how torn you were, how much it cost you to betray Elinor. But I persuaded myself that the pain would grow less and the magical sense of liberation I felt would gradually overtake you.

We had agreed that we'd break the news to Malachy and Elinor when Elinor came home from London and that we wouldn't contact each other until the following Monday morning.

That afternoon I said goodbye to you at three before you left to collect Lizzie from school. I could hardly bring myself to part from you. I knew our sanctuary period was over. Once Elinor was home we would enter completely uncharted territory in which anything might happen. I lay in bed, watching you, afraid to leave the protection of our sheets. All the passionate days between us seemed suddenly such a frail, tenuous bond. I called you back to the bed to kiss me. I asked if you loved me. I made you promise that you'd phone immediately you were alone on Monday morning. You took my arms from round your neck. You kissed my shoulder. You began to dress. I watched you getting ready for the world, slowly reassembling your other self, your wordly self, the self you were when you were not with me, the self you put on for Lizzie, for Elinor. I saw your eyes in the dressing-table mirror as you brushed your hair. I saw the face that others saw, the face that you showed to the world when I wasn't present, when you weren't seeing me. It struck me how self-confident it seemed; resolute and self-contained. A face that knew nothing about me, that lived in a world without me. I turned my eyes from you and got out of bed. I began to dress at once, pulling on my clothes with furious haste. I wanted to be gone from you. Gone from the self who didn't see me.

"Are you all right?" you asked when you realised I was ready and waiting to leave.

"Yes."

"I'll see you on Monday," you said, smiling, as if it was a short time, a period anyone could live through with ease.

"Yes," I said.

So, after two weeks of bliss with you I went home once more. I went home to my own house. To my children. And to my husband.

On the evening of that day Malachy phoned me just after eight o'clock. He was working late, he said. He'd grab a bite to eat in town. He told me not to wait up. Something in his voice made me think that he knew what I wanted to say to him and wanted to put it off as long as possible. I felt sick with fear. But unaccountably angry also. I needed to tell him that night. I couldn't bear to avoid it for even one more day.

I sat in the kitchen drinking wine and reading until I heard his key in the door at five past twelve. I went out to meet him. I kissed his cheek. He put his arms round me and drew me close.

He said: "I thought I'd never get away from those bloody people tonight."

I pulled away from him.

"I have to talk to you," I said.

He smiled. "What about? Something pleasant?"

How could he smile? How could he not notice my mood? I felt as if little sparks were flying from the ends of each nerve.

"Right then," he said, "let's talk in the bedroom. I need to lie down."

"No. Let's go into the kitchen." I knew that if we went into the bedroom I wouldn't be able to tell him. My courage would drain from me, in that place of intimacy, that held all our years of happiness between its walls, the room where I had loved him and only him. So I led him into the kitchen where I felt safe. A room where so many people had come and gone and left their atmosphere, neutralising it, even you.

234

Sitting down immediately at the table and yawning loudly, Malachy poured himself a glass of wine. He lit a cigarette, holding the box in one hand and, with the fingers of the same hand, striking the match – one of his many graceful tricks. He drew on it deeply, sucking the smoke right down to the bottom of his lungs. I could hear the rasp of his breath. I thought, when he breathes out again I'll tell him. I waited. He sat in front of me staring at the glowing tip of the cigarette held between his middle fingers. At last I saw a faint trace of yellowish smoke leave the side of his mouth.

"So," he said, "you have something you want to tell me?" He looked into my face. For the first time I saw the pain in his eyes, the fear and anger.

"Yes," I said and turned away from him.

"Well?" his voice was very low, hardly more than a whisper. Was that what made it so frightening? I hesitated. I tried to decide what part of it to tell him first.

"It isn't easy," I said. "I wish I didn't have to say this . . ."

And suddenly he interrupted me: "Why do you have to then?" he said. "Some things are better not said, don't you think?" He gave me a look of appeal or warning. I couldn't tell which.

"But . . . Malachy, I need you to know . . . I want you to understand." My voice sounded high and false somehow, though I was completely sincere.

"Maybe it's better if I don't," he said softly. He looked at me for a moment with the same expression of fear or appeal in his eyes. I waited in silence. After a few seconds he spoke again, but reluctantly, as if he'd have preferred to say nothing: "How will it help?" He stared fixedly at the floor between the door and the table as if wanting to memorise the exact pattern of the tiles.

"Malachy?" I looked at him, needing him to meet my gaze. But he sat stiff and silent.

"Malachy . . . please, I need to tell you," I said again.

"All right then . . . if you insist . . . if it makes you feel better . . ."

"I want to tell you because I want us, together, to work out the best thing to do . . ." I began.

Then he interrupted again. He spoke in a voice that sounded unnaturally calm and yet abrasive, as if the words were forced through his lips: "Has she been here?"

"Has who? What do you mean?" I was startled for the first time.

He looked directly up at me then, for the first time. His eyes seemed to have shrunk in his head. They were like two small, hard stones gleaming from deep, shadowed sockets.

"Isn't this what you want to confide? So tell me . . . I'm asking about yourself and your lover – does she come here with you?" And there was an ugly grin on his lips now. "Do you do – whatever it is you do – here? In our house?"

"No – of course not!" I said at once, before I had time to think what it was I was denying.

"Of course not? That's an odd phrase!" His tone was reflective, and mildly surprised. "Where do you go then?" he asked after a moment, in the same unnatural voice.

"What does it matter where?" I was growing angry.

"It matters to me!" He stared at me still, sitting rigid in his chair.

"Her house," I said abruptly, to get it over with. "We go to her house. Now are you happy?" And I glared at him.

"How nice of you to ask," he said. He took off one of his elegant, black leather moccasins and shook it as if to rid it of a stone. He put it back on again. He stooped and pulled up the sock of the same foot, drawing it up under the creased leg of his suit. "And tell me," he said finally, "where does her lover go? Elinor – isn't that the name? When you're over there – where is she?"

I said nothing. I was not going to be provoked in this way.

"Are you deceiving a woman, as well as your husband and children?" he said.

"Leave the boys out of this."

"You should have thought of that sooner, shouldn't you?"

The veiled threat I thought I heard in this remark sent little waves of fear about my heart. I forced myself to stay quiet and not make things worse by a panic reaction.

"Malachy – please!" I stretched out my hand and laid it on his. To my surprise he didn't pull it away. "None of this matters."

He stubbed out his cigarette and tilted back his chair, his arms across his chest once more, his head lowered. For a moment he seemed pacified, calmed and when he spoke his voice sounded normal: "What does matter then?" he asked and turned his gaze towards me and for an instant what might have been tears glistened at the back of his eyes. "If not your children and your husband? What does matter to you?"

I stood up because suddenly it was unbearable to remain sitting. I crossed the room to the sink. I stood staring at it. There was nothing to wash, but I turned on both taps full. I stood with my back to him. The roar of the water splashing down, hitting the stainless steel surface, filled my ears.

"What does matter then?" I heard Malachy ask again.

With a sense of immense effort I gathered my earlier resolve.

"It matters that I love her," I said.

"I can't hear you," he said, "turn off the bloody tap!"

I turned off the water, but stayed standing with my back to him, staring into the empty sink. And, as I stared, it seemed to me that I could I remember every meal I'd cooked in that house, every meal I had cleared up after. Every cup and plate washed and dried since I'd come to live there. At last, as if from a great distance, I heard myself repeat: "What matters is that I love her."

I turned round then and regarded him in silence.

He looked back at me with a weird expression on his face. His features seemed suddenly lopsided, distorted, like someone trying to smile coming out of a dentist's surgery.

"And does she love you?" he asked.

"Yes . . . I think so."

"You think so?" As he repeated the words something changed in him, some subtle alteration moved through his body, his shoulders dropped from their stiff defensive position, as if relief or resignation made it possible for him to relax his guard. He stood up and walked over to the counter where the kettle stood. He had to stand beside me and reach in front of me to fill it from the tap. I moved away and sat again at the table. I watched him lift down two china mugs from their hooks on the pine dresser above the sink. I watched him spoon tea from the caddy into the teapot. He took milk from the fridge and poured it into a jug. He filled the pot when the kettle boiled and brought it and the two mugs to the table. Then he sat down again on the far side from me. I watched him with my breath held. I had no idea what he was thinking.

"What do you want to do?" he said finally, in an almost conversational voice.

"I don't know yet."

"Are you going to go on with it?"

"I don't know."

"Are you in love with her?"

"I don't know." I had suddenly lost courage. It seemed impossible to deliberately hurt him more deeply than I had already. But I felt I was betraying you even as I said it.

He looked at me for a moment to see if I was telling the truth. There was still the queer, distorted look about his mouth. I drank the tea slowly, looking down at my hands clasping around the yellow-flowered china mug.

"What do you want me to do?"

"Nothing."

"Nothing? Do you expect me to share you?"

I made no reply. I had no idea what to say.

"Does anyone else know?"

"No." It was a relief to say something that was the simple truth.

"Not even Elinor?"

"Not yet."

"Are you going to tell her?"

"Yes."

He stood up and walked to the door. "I need to get some air," he said. "I'll be back." He walked out of the room and a second later I heard the hall door closing.

When he came back almost an hour later, I was in bed. I lay with my eyes open in the darkness. I heard his step in the corridor. I heard him put the lock on the hall door and turn off the kitchen light. I heard his step on the stairs. I heard him go into the bathroom. The bedroom door opened. Light from the passage outside showed momentarily. He closed the door and walked to the bed. I heard the rustle of his clothes as he pulled them off and threw them on the cane chair by the bed. He got in beside me and lay on the far side, not touching me. After a few minutes he said: "Katherine?"

"Yes."

"Do you still love me?"

"Yes," I said because it was more true than not true.

He turned then and put his arms around me. I felt his beard against my cheek. I thought how foreign the touch of it seemed, impersonal and strange and the smell of his skin was strange also, though for thirteen years his body had been as familiar as my own.

"Katherine?" he said again. He brought his lips to mine and kissed me softly. I returned the kiss because I felt such pity for him and regret.

After a few minutes he spoke again: "We'll be all right, won't we?"

I didn't answer.

"I mean this thing between you and her, whatever it is you need, tenderness or empathy or whatever it is, I'll try to understand."

He kissed my forehead, I felt tears on his cheek.

"I mean, one way or the other, it can't last, after all, can it?"

"Can't it?" I said. For a crazy moment I thought he knew something I didn't. "Why not?" I heard my own voice in the darkness, low and nervous. Afraid that would give me some reason to distrust you. He must have sensed the anxiety. He tightened his arms about me as if to reassure me and we lay face to face, in the darkened room, our breathing the only sound between us. "After all," he said, "it's not as if you're a lesbian. It's not as if you could be satisfied by it . . . at least I know that much." And he laughed for the first time that night.

Something frightening happened here this evening. I went to the pub for a drink. Yes, I know, what's the point of going alone to the pub in a place like this? But I had to get out of the house. I had to do something – anything, to distract myself. It was a lovely clear night when I set off. There was a moon, waning but still high, shining over the water and frost in the air. My feet crunched on the ground, crushing a sweet, warm scent of hay from the grass as I walked down the boreen. I felt my spirits lift a little.

But the moment I reached the public house and opened the door, I knew I had made a mistake. The long, barn-like room with a pool table at one end and a television at the other was almost deserted. The only customers were sitting grouped on high stools at the counter, five big broad-shouldered men; local farmers, obviously, with tweed caps and rough, reddened necks. They turned and stared as I walked in. Their eyes curious but embarrassed. None of them spoke, though one inclined his head slightly in my direction as though in greeting. I felt immediately nervous and self-conscious. I walked slowly up to the bar with a show of indifference and ordered a pint of lager from the young, shy-faced boy behind the counter. The man nearest me said, without turning his head, "Fine evening now." And I understood that it was meant as acknowledgement of my presence. All the others stared ahead, eyes fixed on the bottles of whiskey and gin that lined the glass shelves behind the counter.

"A lovely night, indeed," I answered and I felt the line of shoulders stiffen slightly and the eyes grow more rigid in their attention. No head turned. I got my pint and took it off to one of the seats near the television. I pretended rapt interest in a fashion programme and decided to leave as soon and as discreetly as possible.

When I got up to leave, I felt all eyes turn towards me and gaze after my retreating back. Outside I felt the whip of rain in my face and, in spite of it, I was glad to be on my way home. I heard footsteps behind me. I looked round and there was Michael walking with his odd, limping gait about fifty yards behind me. I kept going, pretending I hadn't noticed him and turned for home at the boreeen without looking back.

At home I made tea and put more turf on the fire. I thought I heard a noise at one of the windows. I was just on the point of opening the curtains when I felt suddenly frightened. I realised that if I stood at the window, anyone outside would see me clearly. So I drank some tea, sat by the fire and tried to forget it. Then, after a bit, I heard the sound of a dog barking. Fred, probably, at the end of the boreen. But why should he bark? He never barks at night. There's never a sound to startle him. I sat in absolute quiet listening. I thought I heard the sound of footsteps on the stones outside.

I decided to go out to investigate. It was raining still and so dark I could see nothing. I walked once around the house, my eyes straining into the blackness. I saw the cat sitting on the wall. It miaowed at the sight of me and rushed to the door. I consoled myself with the thought that if anyone was hanging around in the bushes, the cat would not have been sitting so calmly.

I went back into the house and read by the fire for an hour or two.

Nothing more happened. The dog didn't bark again and at last I felt relaxed enough to go to bed. Nevertheless it was a while before I slept.

No doubt I am frightening myself for nothing. I probably imagined the whole thing, but nonetheless this character hanging about staring at me, following me along the road is unnerving me. But what can I do? I can't report a halfwit to the police, I suppose?

I must distract myself. I'm turning into a nervous wreck. The only thing that calms me is this retelling the story of our relationship.

Turning it into a coherent narrative as if it were a plot in a novel makes me feel secure. I suppose I love remembering the past because it's the one thing we possess for certain. For all time.

And so, to continue . . .

After that that terrible weekend when I talked to Malachy, I rang you. At ten o'clock on the Monday morning. I couldn't wait a moment longer. When you heard my voice you said I sounded strange and asked at once if there was something wrong. When I told you I had news, there was a sharp silence at your end. I took a deep breath. "I told Malachy," I said.

I had thought you'd be delighted. I'd imagined it would bring us immediately closer. But your response was oddly muted. "What did he say?" you asked, after a moment, and you sounded apprehensive and reluctant to speak. Maybe you didn't want to seem too pleased by something that was evidently a cause of pain to me.

"He knew already," I said.

"How could he?"

"He just did. Wouldn't you in his place?"

"I suppose so."

"Did Elinor?" I asked.

"Did she what?"

"Did she know before you told her?" I asked.

"No."

"What did she say?"

"Well it wasn't quite like that."

"How do you mean?"

"I didn't actually get a chance to tell her yet."

"Why not?" I struggled to keep the alarm from my voice.

After a moment's pause you said that you'd tried all weekend, but just couldn't find the right chance. There had been people around all the time, Lizzie and her friends. You'd tried again last night, but she was too preoccupied, worried about work. I asked you how you could be sure she'd take it so badly.

"How could she not?" you asked.

"But she must have her suspicions – like Malachy. And it's not as if it's the first time?"

"No."

"So?"

"So, it's different this time from any other."

"Why?"

"You know why."

"I don't."

"It's different because I love you."

"Do you?" I heard how defensive I sounded.

"You know I do."

I said nothing and neither did you. For about thirty seconds.

Then I found courage again to ask why you hadn't told her if you were so sure of your love for me. You said that was exactly why you couldn't. I tried to make light of it – I suggested you were exaggerating her response but you replied that I didn't know Elinor and, for the first time, I thought there was irritation in your voice. "When will you tell her, then?" I asked, wanting to get something definite from you. But you side stepped, as always.

"When she's feeling a bit calmer. More confident. When she hears whether or not she's got the new job – she'll feel better."

"When will that be?"

"A week or so. Ten days maybe." I didn't answer because I was too disappointed and wasn't sure I could hide it.

But that was when I first realised how different things were for us. You treated Elinor with kid gloves – why was I so brutally frank with Malachy? Because I wanted to be rid of him? Because I'd lost patience with him as soon as I got involved with you? Because my obsession with you made him clinging and self-pitying? Also, of course, because I took for granted you were doing the same with Elinor. Why should I have been surprised that you didn't? Everything about you and Elinor was different, but I couldn't see it. I didn't understand that it broke every code you lived by to betray the lover you'd lived with for the sake of a married woman. I didn't appreciate any great distinction between our lives. As I saw it – we were both married; both ensnared and committed to long-term relationships that had outgrown their urgency and necessity. I didn't know that your roots were so entangled that to cut them would require major surgery and cause near fatal haemorrhage.

Would you have acted differently if you hadn't been so sure of me? If I hadn't told Malachy that weekend? You had me in the palm of your hand from the start, as he said. Should I have made you fight for me – play hard to get while I had the chance? While I had the support and structure of a husband and family? I shouldn't have let you see how easy it was. Even now isn't this what's happening – aren't you indulging Elinor at my expense because you know I'll be here waiting for you whenever you arrive? That morning, just before you put down the phone, you asked me something else. "If it's all right with you," you said and paused for a moment in a way that terrified me. Were you going to give me an ultimatum? If you did, how would I respond. My mind went blank with fear as I waited for you to speak.

"I think it would be better," you continued slowly, "if you didn't come here for a while – that is not until I tell Elinor, at least."

What did this mean? Was it worse or better? I was beyond telling. At least I had the sense to say nothing and wait.

"We could go to Jan's. If you'd feel all right there? She's out all day and she's given me the key."

"Yes, I don't see why not," I said, too relieved and surprised to say anything more. How could you think it would make the least difference to me where we met? What did I care, so long as I could see you?

Chapter Eighteen

October, Dublin.

Lizzie came padding down the stairs, her thumb in her mouth and her hair falling into her eyes.

"Was there someone at the door just now?" she asked.

"No love. No one."

Nina stared at her not knowing what to say. She had counted on her staying safely asleep for the night.

"I thought I heard a man at the door," she said persistently.

"Well, there was no one here. You're thinking of the night when Malachy called."

"Was that the man who came into the kitchen?"

"Yes, Malachy Newman."

"Is he a friend of yours?"

"Sort of."

"Why did he come so late?"

"He didn't have my number, but he knew where I lived, so he came over."

Why was the child so interested in this? Had she overheard something of their conversation?

That night, when she was sitting alone in the kitchen waiting for Elinor to come in, she had heard the doorbell sound. At first she hadn't recognised the tall, white-faced man who stood on the doorstep. The rain was streaming down his face, washing the black mop of his hair over his forehead so that he looked quite different, younger, more vulnerable.

She would have been surprised anyway to find him at her door, but she was all the more so because Katherine had told her he had already moved to Galway.

"I want to ask you if you know where Katherine is?" he said and glared at her. She wondered if he'd been drinking.

"I just want to know where she is," he repeated.

"Isn't she at home at Breemore road?"

He shook his head with an angry motion, sending drops of water running down his cheeks.

"Look, I may be drunk, but I'm not stupid. I wouldn't be here if she was at home." He brushed his hair out of his eyes and drew his head down into his shoulders so that his face was half hidden by the raised collar of his raincoat.

"I came from Galway yesterday expecting to find her at home. But she hasn't been there and she left no message." He still glared at her. "So, would you mind telling me if you've seen her in the last few days?"

"No, I haven't."

"Have you seen her since she got back from the States?"

"I've spoken to her on the phone," she said telling a quick lie of omission. She had talked to her on the phone as well as spending three days in bed with her at Fairfield Road. "I don't know when I'll see her again." She had said that part with conviction because it was the truth.

He looked at her in obvious dismay, his white face seeming to grow yet paler.

"If she wanted to see you, she'd get in touch. She has to see the boys anyway, so she's bound to speak to you in the next few days."

He seemed to be struggling to understand what she had just said. And she was surprised to find that she didn't feel any of the usual irritation with him, but felt instead something very close to pity.

"Why don't you come in?" she said on a sudden impulse, "you can't stand here in the rain."

He followed her through the hall into the kitchen and sat down at the table.

"I'll make some coffee."

"I don't need it."

"Well I do."

They had sat alone together for the first time, drinking coffee in silence. After a few minutes she had tried to make conversation. She asked him how the project in Galway was going and he said the money was running out. That these bloody Irish always thought they could cut corners.

She ignored the edge in his voice when he said this, and asked about the boys instead. Were they settling in? He looked at her from the black holes of his eye sockets with a brooding look that seemed to say, What the hell do you care how the boys are doing? And she couldn't reply, because I love their mother, which was the only answer. A few minutes later he stood up. He knocked back the last mouthful of coffee as if reluctant to waste it before making his way to the front door in silence. She followed and let him out.

"Thanks for the coffee," he said. "I'd heard you make good coffee." And suddenly he smiled. The look of good-humoured self-mockery that spread over his face transformed him. For a second she could see why Katherine had loved him.

She wondered how much Malachy had guessed that night. As they had stood at the door she had weakened, feeling sorry for him and hinted at where Katherine might be. Had he gone to find her? Were they together now? In Galway? And what would she feel if that were the case? Anger? Relief? She didn't know what she thought or wanted. She was paralysed by guilt and beyond choice. Perhaps any resolution would be better than none.

"Can I watch television?" Lizzie asked

"There's nothing on, love. Would you like something to drink? Some milk? Hot chocolate?"

"Chocolate."

"Come and help me then."

"Can we go to the pictures tomorrow – I have a half-day?"

"Maybe."

"When will Elinor be home?"

"Tomorrow."

"Can she come to the pictures with us or will she be working?"

"I didn't say we were going yet."

Nina looked into Lizzie's earnest, upturned face and felt a rising tide of panic. She still hadn't found a way to talk to her. She knew that if she couldn't bring herself to tell the child now she could never find the courage to leave. If she couldn't face Lizzie what was the point of telling Elinor? But how could anyone tell a child, clutching a teddy bear under her arm, that you were planning to leave her? It seemed to her now as if she had made herself a part of both their lives, like the mortar between the bricks of a house, and she didn't see how she could extract herself without shaking the whole structure. After all, it was what she had wanted – to be completely intimate and necessary to them. She hadn't wanted Lizzie to think of her as the friend who lived with her mother. She wanted to be considered her second mother. Not that she thought it was the right way to do it, or because of any particular principle. The only reason was that she had fallen in love with Lizzie on the day she moved in. And, once having encouraged her to trust such an uncertain, erratic character as herself, and having made what some would consider a strange and unnatural lifestyle into a safe haven for the child, how could she tear it apart?

She would have to be told. But perhaps this was not the moment. After all, for Lizzie it was the middle of the night.

She heated the milk and mixed chocolate powder and two spoonfuls of sugar in a tall cup. She put the cup on a big saucer and set it on the table. The child sat down and lowered her mouth carefully to the rim of the cup and sucked the hot liquid noisily into her mouth.

"There's something I need to talk about with you."

Lizzie didn't look up, but she withdrew her lips from the cup for a moment. "What?"

"Something that's been on my mind."

"When do we have to talk about it?"

"I don't know. When would be the best time?"

"If we talk now, can we watch a video afterwards?"

"Remember what I was saying in the car, before your lesson?"

"No."

"About living in different places, me and you?"

"You mean about going to Africa? Are you really going? Will you take me? Do you promise?"

"I didn't say Africa. I don't know where you got that idea. I don't mean a foreign country. I mean just another house. Another street."

"Why would you want to go on holiday to another house?" Lizzie had finished her drink. A dark brown stain circled her mouth. She stuck her tongue out and, with small cat-like movements, began to lick it clean.

"I don't know," Nina answered softly. "Put that way it seems very odd all right."

"If you don't know, why do you want to do it?"

Nina smiled. "You're too logical – that's your problem. And life isn't. Most of us don't know why we do things until after we've done them and it's too late to change.

"What does tulogical mean?"

Nina put Lizzie's cup in the sink and handed her a cloth to wipe her mouth.

"Do I have to brush my teeth again because I had chocolate?"

"No, it doesn't matter. It's too late. Let's go to sleep."

She sat in her bedroom, a room used mostly as a study because she always slept in Elinor's bed. She took out the letters she had collected at the office. She began to read through them. After a few moments she set them down again with a sigh. It was impossible. She couldn't bear to read them. Every page told a story of some great grief or loss, stories of family tragedy and social deprivation. She couldn't face anymore of it tonight. She went over to her desk by the window, opened the top right hand drawer and put the letters into it. It was full to overflowing and as she rooted about to make space a photograph fell onto the floor. A photograph of Katherine. She closed the drawer, sat down and held the picture under the desk lamp to study it. It was one she hadn't seen for a long time. She had to be careful where she put photographs that she didn't want Elinor to see. She remembered when it was taken. A year ago, when they were walking on Howth Head. A brilliant summer's day and Katherine looking sexy and provocative in a black cut-away T-shirt, the skin of her shoulders so brown they looked like polished oak. How many times had she walked up behind her as she had that day, put her arms about her waist and rested her lips against the cool skin of her shoulder?

She felt an ache in the pit of her stomach. An ache so familiar she was hardly conscious of it unless it was suddenly intensified as now. The pain of longing. For weeks she had gone to sleep with it and woken up with it. She thought about Katherine all day. Fantasised about her. She couldn't sleep and didn't want to eat. She was smoking too much and drinking too much. She couldn't understand herself. She could hardly believe emotions could be so perverse and contradictory. How she could be at one moment consumed by longing for

Katherine, and at the next filled with a jealous fear of losing Elinor? The two realities competed with each other in her bloodstream like the germs of some tropical fever. She felt for the first time in her life a real fear of madness – fear that she was on the verge of insanity. She leaned over the desk and held her aching head between her hands.

She imagined she felt the two sides of her brain separating. She felt as an actual physical sensation the two halves; the left and the right, slowly, inexorably begin to move apart. She had the sense of a passage opening between them and imagined a cold wind blowing along it. Her skull felt as if it might burst open with the pressure. For weeks she had expected to wake one morning and find it had happened while she slept – to find blood and grey matter splattered on the pillow. She felt she would like to be able to wear a sweat band like a tourniquet about her temples, to hold the inflamed organ in place.

She put the photograph back in the desk drawer and went in to check on the child. She was asleep. She bent over to draw up the covers and caught the smell of her skin; the lovely smell, like hot caramel, she had at night. She moved her hand just above Lizzie's hair but did not kiss her. She woke at the slightest touch. She stood beside the bed for almost five minutes gazing down at her. She went back into her bedroom and sat down at the desk. She took out a pen and a writing pad. Suddenly she had the idea of sending a letter to Katherine. But what could she say? Maybe it was better if she finished reading this journal of hers first before making any decision. If she stayed up late she could have it finished before Elinor came home the next morning.

As she sat in the dimly lit room, with the soft glow of the one lamp falling on her hands and on the blank sheet of paper lying before her, she heard the murmur of the stream as it flowed over rocks and stones beneath the park wall. The park where she and Elinor had so often walked together, in other times. She sat unmoving. Unable to make a decision. A terrible weight of sadness descended on her.

She no longer trusted herself. From the night that she had first abandoned Elinor for Katherine she felt that she would never believe in the word love again when she spoke it. She had learned what a counterfeit it was. Not until that night had she seen that there was nothing that could not be done in its name. No love so great that it could not be denied. No love so lasting that it could not end. And she had learnt too that it was the lover who betrayed love. Not some outside agent or third party. It was love itself that destroyed it.

In this last year she had learned things about herself she would have preferred not to know. She had learned for instance that she could never again regard any relationship as essential. Passionate, yes, intoxicating, compelling. But not essential. No relationship could transcend circumstance. And she had learned this year that she was not the person she had thought herself. Her real being was lost from conscious sight. She could be little more at any given hour than an uncertain, ill-informed courier from some hidden recess of herself to another.

She lit a cigarette, drew the smoke deep into her lungs, held it and as slowly let it stream from her slightly open lips. Then she ground out the stub in the ashtray on her desk.

Chapter Nineteen

September, Clare.

From the time I told Malachy, I felt as if a great burden had been lifted from me. I no longer had to pretend. By being honest with him I felt I'd given him the means to defend himself. At least he knew now who the enemy was. He deserved that much. I would have preferred to sleep in the spare room from then on, but I didn't want the boys to realise until they had to. (Had they noticed anything yet? I don't think so. As long the rhythm of their lives went on undisturbed, the surface unbroken, they were too absorbed with their own affairs to pay much attention to their parents moods. Or so I liked to think.) Malachy and I avoided one another with such skill that we might have been preparing for this very situation and practising the appropriate behaviour for years. He came home late, I went out early. We slept on opposite sides of the bed, even in sleep careful not to touch. I ate with the boys, he ate before coming home. We barely spoke and, when we did, we avoided each other's eyes. A couple of times after our first conversation I asked him if he wanted to talk about the situation, but he shook his head and said without looking at me, "Just let me know when it's over!"

Did he think if he ignored it it would go away? Burn itself out? At times his confidence worried me and I wondered if he might know something I didn't. But I dismissed the fear almost as soon as it came to me as no more than another symptom of infatuation.

Then one night as we were driving home together from a meeting with one of Ben's teachers (Malachy had tried to get out of it, but the school had insisted that we both went), he broke the long, tense silence, just as we were drawing up at the house and I'd thought I was safe, with a totally unexpected question: "Tell me something . . . ?" he asked with a note of cunning in his tone.

"What?" I said nervously.

"Are you sure you can trust this woman you're involved with?"

I felt a little chill play about my heart. What was he up to now?

"What do you mean – trust?"

"Nothing. I was just wondering if you were sure she was trustworthy, that's all. Seeing as you've handed over your life to her."

"Of course she is – what are you trying to suggest?" I said with barely controlled irritation. "Why on earth shouldn't she be?" I knew I was handling it badly, but I was too frightened by the question to think.

"That's fine then," he said as if relieved. But so calmly that every word held menace. "So long as *you're* sure, everything is all right, isn't it?"

I could have argued it out with him. Tried to discover out what had provoked this, but I decided it was best to say nothing. His jealousy was obviously beginning to get the better of him. The carefully maintained show of nonchalance and complacency clearly no more than a façade. But I realised, at that moment, that I'd no idea what he was thinking and even less what he was capable of.

For a week or two things went on as before, scarcely disturbed by Malachy's new knowledge or Elinor's ignorance.

It was as though time stood still. There was no tomorrow, no yesterday, only the eternal present of my hours in bed with you. Separated from you, going through the motions of everyday life, I felt like a sleepwalker. I remember having the impression of a physical pressure bearing down on my forehead, as if a strong hand were pressing against it, numbing my brain and sending some sedative chemical all through my limbs. I was incapable of introspection or thought of any kind. Dazed and drugged. I drove down one-way streets, straight through red lights, forgot my change in the supermarket, walked out without paying and, one memorable day, I drove all the way from Monkstown to Ranelagh with a bag of groceries on the roof. It was a wonder I remembered to eat or dress myself. Indeed, if I'd walked out of the house stark-naked, it would hardly have surprised me. Clothes, like everything else in the material world that separated me from you, had become an irrelevance, merely an obstacle that delayed the meeting of our skin. In as much as I thought at all, I thought that everything would work out for the best. Our love was so strong I was certain it would triumph over any obstacles set in our path.

Once or twice in that time I raised the subject of telling Elinor. But you forestalled criticism. You turned your dark, glowing eyes to me, full of sorrow. "Would you like me to be the kind of woman who casts off a lover like an old shoe?" you said. "I've hurt her so deeply already – what do you want me to do? Kick her in the teeth and leave her to bleed?" I suggested this was being a bit melodramatic, that you were surely overestimating your importance in her life. You said you wished it were true. But that I didn't know Elinor. And how could I argue? When losing you was the worst fate I could imagine befalling anyone? You kissed me and told me to be patient – I had time on my side and Elinor had nothing. Couldn't I afford to be magnanimous? I made a show of acquiescence. But I had one piece of knowledge that gave me confidence. I knew there was a natural limit set to this period of secrecy: the Easter holidays. Lizzie would be home all day and it would become impossible to conceal your second life.

After last night I decided to try to talk to Máire Mac again. I told her that I was seriously frightened. I told her Michael was hanging about the house all day and now coming even at night. Was there anything that could be done about it? I asked her. I described the way he had snarled at me the other day and insisted that the house was his.

She regarded me with a look of weary concern. "Well, maybe if you knew the whole story it wouldn't bother you so much," she said regretfully.

Then she told me his story from the beginning. I leaned against the counter in the little, garishly lit room and listened while she told me one of the awful tales that are so common in these desolate places. I began to feel sorry I'd asked. He was quite normal as young boy, she said, but things that happened to him since had twisted his mind. She'd told me that his father died when he was very young and his only sister had left five years ago to live in Australia, his mother died shortly after that. But it was events of long ago when he was a child that had caused the harm. Things he had never recovered from. It seems that he had a twin brother who was drowned at sea on a wild night one December when he was out fishing near the islands. His mother was destroyed by it. She never recovered from the grief of it and, from that night forward, she used stand every day staring out from the top window of the house towards the sea where Seán, her son, had last been seen.

Since she died, Michael had taken to going to the house and gazing up at the window where she used to stand. Seán was drowned on the night of a full moon and some people said that the ghost of the mother could be seen standing at the top

bedroom window on the night of the full moon, looking out
to sea.

I felt a shiver pass over me. Reluctantly I asked her the
obvious question, the only information not offered by her.
Where did all this happen? I asked. What house did they live
in at the time of the accident? But I didn't need to hear her
next words to know the answer.

"The house you're staying in now. That used to belong to
the Caseys before the Germans bought it."

"Why did no one tell me this before?" I protested. Why on
earth had they allowed me to be frightened and annoyed all
this time?

"Sure what was the point of bothering you for nothing?
What you don't know can't hurt you. And sure there's no
harm in Michael anyhow. Not a bit."

On the way home I tried once again to contact Luke and
Ben. But still I got no answer. Though I waited and rang on
and off for an hour. Why am I not getting through to them?
They should have been back in Galway the day before
yesterday. Should I write to them? If I had a car I could drive
over for the day. Maybe it's just as well that I can't.

Late one Friday night, (Malachy had just gone out the door
for a walk) you phoned me at home, before midnight. I was
alarmed at once. You never called me at weekends when
Elinor was home. And I'd agreed never to try to contact you
except in case of emergency.

You asked me if I was alone – if I was free to talk.

"Why? Is something wrong?" I knew something had changed
the moment you spoke. "I told Elinor tonight." My heart leapt, I
was at once ready to be triumphant, elated. But I knew better than
to show it. Your tone of voice put me on my guard, it was tense
and halting. There was a long silence I was afraid to break. What
were you thinking? Why were you so serious, so withdrawn?

"How did she take it?" I asked at last, not wanting to hear the answer.

"Badly," you said. "As badly as possible."

"What did she say?"

"She wants me out."

"Out?"

"She wants me to leave . . . " You stopped dead on the last word. For a horrified second I didn't understand you. I thought you meant she wanted me out of your life.

"Leave what?" I asked, forcing myself to speak.

"The house – her house – our house."

"When?"

"At once."

"And will you?"

"What choice have I?" How often I'd longed to hear you tell me this very thing. But I'd never imagined I'd hear you like this – so wretched and self-accusing.

"And do you want to?" For the first time I was grateful that we were talking on the phone and that I couldn't see your face as I waited for the answer.

"It's probably the best thing," you said at last.

"For who?"

"For all of us."

"But you do want to?"

"Yes, of course I want to . . ." you said and you sounded aggravated suddenly and impatient. With me or Elinor?

"Where will you go?"

"I don't know. Share with someone. I think Jan would let me move in for a while." There was a long pause before you spoke again. You were hesitant. Unsure of yourself.

"Could you come over tomorrow and help to clear out my things?"

"What about Elinor?" I asked you.

"She won't be here," you said.

259

The following afternoon I arrived at one thirty. Your car was parked on the street, crammed with boxes of books and paintings. The hall door was open. I went inside. For a moment I thought there was no one in. Then I heard the sound of raised voices coming from the bedroom at the top of the stairs. I stood rooted to the ground when I recognised Elinor's voice. And as I waited, transfixed with embarrassment, I heard it rise into a scream, and a torrent of imprecation flowed like hot lava from behind the closed door. I couldn't distinguish a word and I didn't want to. I stood like a fool unable to decide whether to stay or leave. Too frightened to think. Suddenly the door flew open. You seemed to stumble from the room. You stood on the landing, your back to me, facing the bedroom you'd just left and Elinor, who was hidden from my sight. You were both silent for an moment. Then I heard you speak. The words were as clear as if they were addressed directly to me.

"This isn't how I wanted things to be – I never intended this . . ."

And then Elinor stepped into sight from behind you. She threw out her hands and, for a terrified moment, I thought she was going to shove you down the stairs. But she didn't, of course. She put one arm around her waist, clutching herself as if for support and the other hand covered her mouth. To muffle a scream or to hide her face from your sight? She stood in this way; silent in front of you for what seemed an eternity. Finally, she stepped past you and stood to one side of the corridor. She still clutched her waist, as if to staunch a bleeding wound. At last she took her hand from her mouth; her lips were a livid scar in the unnatural whiteness of her face. She said in a voice so low I scarcely heard the words: "You bitch," and her eyes did not move from yours.

"Elinor, calm down . . . wait a moment," you pleaded with her.

"You bitch," she said again in the same dull, expressionless tone. "Just get out. Get out of my house and don't come back!"

You turned and began to walk down the stairs. At that moment Elinor saw me. I will never forget the expression on her face, or rather on the mask that had become her face – a crude pantomime mask, the mouth open wide but no sound issuing from it. The eyes staring in horror.

Then you caught sight of me. What was it I saw pass across your features in that split second? Anger? Fear? You ran down the last steps. You gripped my arm so tightly it hurt. You pulled me towards the front door in frantic haste as if your life depended on getting us both outside. Just before it slammed behind us, I heard Elinor calling after you. Calling your name. You almost dragged me into the car. You started up the engine and drove off down the road without looking back once. You said nothing. And neither did I.

This afternoon I went to phone you. I dialled the number slowly because of the tremor in my hands. I listened to the familiar ring that I imagine I recognise from any other. Then it's answered – I hear Elinor's voice, her deep, suave tones assuring me as so often before that she regrets she cannot come to the phone but will get back to me as soon as possible. My legs shook as I listened to her. I felt a sharp pain in my side as if a knife had been thrust between my ribs. I went out and walked up and down the road. I decided to wait ten minutes. I stood at the gate of a field and counted the sheep that lay like white stones scattered over the mountainside. When I reached fifty I walked back to the shop. I rang you once more. Elinor again – still regretful but if I'd like to leave a message . . . That was it. What was I to do? Had something happened to prevent you staying in for the call? What's going on, Nina? I can't understand this. I'm afraid to try.

I phoned Malachy's Galway number instead to speak to the

boys. I let it ring for a full minute before I replaced the receiver and walked home.

Back at the house, the moment I opened the door I had the sense of some subtle transformation having taken place in my absence. As though the place had become hostile to me, withdrawn into itself. The air seems to have grown more dense, to have stiffened somehow. I feel it requires an almost physical effort to make my way across the room. I have the uncomfortable sense of being talked about behind my back, as if the table had been laughing at me, exchanging gossip with the chairs and the cutlery. I feel them draw back, shrinking from my touch. I light the fire, put on the kettle, let the cat in and feed her. I put on some music. Gradually I reconquer space, recolonise the room. After half an hour it's mine again, human and domestic. Bidable. But hours later I go to the back bedroom to find a book and, opening the door, I'm suddenly aware once more of the reluctant, grudging feel of the place. This room doesn't know me, doesn't have to pretend as the others do to welcome me. I cross through the cold air hurriedly not looking about me, choose a book and leave, closing the door behind me with relief.

When you moved out, at last, from Fairfield Road, I thought all was finally clear between us. After the great ordeal of breaking free from all the structures that had defined our lives before we met, we were beginning to piece together a new world.

On the days I went to meet you, I'd drive out to Jan Maguire's house in Monkstown after dropping the boys to school. As soon as I turned onto the coast road my heart began to beat faster. There must have been cold, wet, sleet-filled mornings that March as in any other, but I don't remember them. I remember sunlight on the pale green waters of the bay, seagulls hurtling through the sky, sailing boats and cargo ships at anchor in the harbour and the elegant Victorian terraced houses lining the street, with their white façades and discreetly curtained windows, had a theatrical air to my eyes, like a stage set, lit for an nineteenth-century literary romance.

Day after day, I was mad with need for you. I waited obsessively for the moment, the first touch. I wanted to fill you with pleasure, to devour you, exhaust you, to carry you beyond pleasure and back. But even as I sated myself with you I grew hungry again. Fulfilled and ravenous in the same moment. All my senses laid waste.

If I could have any one of those days back again, whole and entire, I'd be happy. If I were to have nothing else in life. If I could have back any morning I stood on the front doorstep waiting, with racing heart, for you to answer the bell, knowing that in a few seconds or less the door would swing open and I'd see you standing behind it, half hidden because you were naked and did not want to waste a moment. You put out your hand to take mine and draw me in and you are smiling your wide radiant smile because we have all morning and half the afternoon and no one to think of and nothing to do but pleasure each other.

Or, I'd like to be returned to the early days, sitting in your living room at Fairfield Road while you move about clearing the table or laying it or putting music on or off or pouring brandy or coffee and I am watching, knowing that at any moment you'll turn and smile at me, or come close and touch my neck in that lovely, glancing way of yours, or look into my eyes with that long, considering, sexy look you have which first seduced me when I sat in your kitchen on autumn afternoons. I'd like to be stretched out by the fire in the afternoon and you kneeling on the floor between my knees looking into my eyes and then kissing my mouth and then bringing your lips to my ear and speaking into it every name you have for me. Slowly and tenderly each and every one of them, your breath hot from your lips into my ear while you say slowly and tenderly each name until at last your mouth is so close I can no longer hear but only feel the words you keep for me.

Most of all, I'd like to be lying in bed with you, at a quarter to three, knowing that in exactly ten minutes you'll jump up and throw on your clothes and run from the house on your way to collect Lizzie from school (which you still did of course and said you would always want to do), leaving me to gather my scrambled wits and clothing before you return. And knowing that we have exactly ten minutes, you ask how we can make the best use of them? What can we do in the time and what can we leave out, to save time? Maybe if we don't kiss at all, not even one kiss? Or maybe if we only kiss and keep our hands by our sides . . . ? If I had just those ten minutes left to us, I'd like to lie between your thighs and kiss slowly the smooth, silken skin of the inside of your leg, from the knee to the top of the thigh.

At three o'clock every afternoon, no matter where we had spent the day, I'd drive home again to Breemore road and try to pick up the scattered pieces of my life. It took all my energy to pull them together so that the surface, at least, looked like the life I used to lead. I knew all too well what was coming. I knew there was no escaping it. But if I could stall for even a little, I would. Then, like an answer to silent prayer, Malachy told me one morning that he had to go away for a few weeks. He had to see his clients in Galway, look over a site and draw up plans for work to commence in the summer.

"If this madness is still going on when I get back I want you to move out," he said the night before he left. Then he turned his back to me and and slept or pretended to and we did not speak again until he left the house.

With Malachy away we began to live something like a public life together for the first time. But there were self-imposed restrictions on our freedom. You were still protecting Elinor. Careful where we went and who saw us together. You didn't want to go anywhere her friends might see us. And so, for the most part, we spent our time together alone. Needless to say I made no strenuous complaint about this.

Neither did I object when you went to visit Elinor as you did a couple of times a week. I accepted it as an inevitable part of the separation process, but secretly I hoped that you'd slowly need to see her less and less frequently. I hoped that I'd grow to fill all your needs and that she'd become little more than a good and trusted friend.

I began to tell my own friends. Or at least my inner circle. They were amazed and embarrassed. Envious of my so evident happiness. They told me I looked radiant. And I must have. They wondered how I got away with it, having a husband and two children and a woman lover. Then, wanting to be sympathetic, they said, but, isn't it very difficult – you can't be thinking of living like that? Like what? I replied, brandishing a delighted smile. Of course, they'd say, getting into the mood, things are different now – attitudes have changed so much. Not all that much, I told them, thinking of the things you had told me. You said liberals always asked the same questions. They always wanted to know what the hardest part was and why so few people were open about it or at least so few women, for oddly it never occurred to them that their own attitude was the hardest part, their wide-eyed ignorance and complacency. When you told them the things that caused pain, when you described the attitudes that damaged the course of lives and drove people into a lifetime of concealment and lies, when you told them of the fear so many experienced, the corrosive influence of rejection and denial they looked at you innocently, and exclaimed: "Really! How terrible! Can it be that bad? I'd never have imagined!" But the truth was they never imagined any of it, you said, because they never needed to imagine it and never took the trouble to try. So, they kept the centre of society intact and things only changed at the periphery.

I began to learn the rules of the game.

I learned that people like ourselves, gay people, had to be extra careful in everything, vigilant and wary and good mannered. No one would put up with us making a scene – that is, making a display of our feelings in public, making obvious the nature of a relationship. They didn't like us to walk down the street holding hands either, or kiss on a park bench or have an argument at a restaurant table, or console the other's tears with passionate embraces or sleep in the same bed when we stayed in a hotel or sit gazing into each other's eyes in public places or embarrass them in front of friends who didn't know (or mightn't feel comfortable). This was quite aside from accepting that it was selfish and brutal to be honest with our family or workmates. If a mother was told, she might die of a heart attack and that would be our fault. If we were open with colleagues, we might make things difficult for them – tarnish them with the same brush or make them the subject of gossip. But in general everything was fine so long as we were discreet, had a sense of humour and kept our private life strictly private. Didn't rock any boats by asking for equality or social recognition. After all people needed time to get used to us, didn't they?

And what was my place in this world I had stumbled into by accident, the accident of falling in love with you? This lesbian counter-culture? Wasn't I a fish out of water from the start? Or do all women feel like that at the beginning; plunged into a second adolescence at middle age? Are all newcomers as wide-eyed, naïve and clumsy as I felt?

I remember how stunned I was the first time I went to a gay bar (a few weeks since becoming your lover but before anyone else knew). I almost left again five minutes after coming in. It was a new, trendy club on the south side of the river. A mixed club that you thought would make my initiation easier. What astonished me was that it was so exactly like any other fashionable night place; the impossible music, the lighting, the crowds, the fevered bodies, the thick pall of smoke. Indistinguishable and yet at once, unforgettably, different. The air of sex was palpable, the desire and the heat of anticipation. I don't know what I expected. Having already met so many of your circle I'd long since abandoned any former notions I had about gay stereotypes. The women belonged to every type and class. Beautiful young girls, students and workers, older women, glamorous women dressed to kill, career women. In spite of myself I looked out for the butchs and femmes and found some but, for the most part, there were no distinguishing marks and somehow this unsettled me. The men surprised me even more. I'd expected young, effeminate men floating about with make-up on their faces and high-pitched laughter. What I discovered were the best-looking men I had seen anywhere. Handsome, macho-looking, of all ages, with athletic bodies and elegant clothes. The most striking thing, for me, was the tenderness I saw between them; a warmth and affection between friends, an easiness of physical contact unimaginable between heterosexual males. My response was a deep sense of confusion. Not fear or excitement at the scene unveiled to me, but a vast uncertainty about my place in it. Where did I fit in? Was I a straight woman having a fling? A bisexual acting out one half of my nature for the first time? Or by falling in love with you had I become a fully integrated member of this new world?

I thought everyone knew what I was feeling. That they could see my self-consciousness and confusion. You all appeared to my eyes so assured and knowing. Among you I felt gauche, suburban, over-sheltered. It wasn't how I liked to think of myself. In my own heterosexual, liberal world, I was used to being rated fairly cool and streetwise. But here – there – in this subculture – outer-culture, I found it almost impossible to establish where the boundaries lay between friendship and sex. The world you lived in seemed not so much promiscuous as made up of constantly shifting limits between desire and liking.

267

A world where women could "come on to" other women in public without apology. A world where they talked of "dykes" and "queers" with pride. A world where they used words I'd have been shocked by men using. A world of frank appreciation of one another's physical attractions, of seduction without any of the romantic trimmings women are said to want. A more passionate world certainly, a world more sensual, more demanding. If I didn't know how to define myself, I didn't really care so long as I was with you. That was the start and finish of it.

That night, I watched you dancing with others for a long time before I had the courage to join you. I saw how closely you danced. What ease there was in your movements. I watched you talking. I saw how you held your cigarette between your middle fingers and each time you brought it to your lips and back it was as though you blew a kiss. I heard you arguing with Barbara Conroy about whether it was possible to be truly bisexual or whether there was always one preference stronger than the other; an argument with which I'd become familiar. Finally, when I knew there was no more than an hour of the evening left, I summoned my courage. I walked up to you to ask you to dance and, just as I reached your side, you turned towards me and smiled as if the idea had been yours, not mine, or as if it had been agreed between us hours before and you were waiting only for a pause in the conversation. We walked to the centre of the room through the crowds. The words of the old Rodgers-Hart song flowed around us:

"And so it seems that we have met before
and laughed before
and loved before
But who knows where or when?"

We danced so close to each other we might have shared the same skin. I kept my eyes open. I wanted to be able to see the others as I danced. To see other women close in one another's arms. To see them smiling. To see them watching us or indifferent to us. To know that this extraordinary moment was everyday and completely natural to them.

The Easter holidays had come. And with them the agreed time of decision. Malachy came back from Galway the following week.

We had chosen the next evening to talk. We sat, Malachy pretending to lounge on the sofa, I bolt upright in an armchair beside the fire, leaving as much space as possible between us, both of us tense and defensive. "Well?" he asked as soon as I looked at him. So he wanted to go straight to the point. There'd be no need for preamble.

"Do you remember that when we talked about this before you asked me if I was in love with Nina and I said I wasn't sure? Well . . ."

"Well what?"

"Well, I am sure now."

"And?"

"I am in love with her."

"I see," he said. He made no movement of any kind. I thought of the phrase – stony silence. His face seemed to have turned to stone; cold and opaque as marble.

"What are you going to do about it?" he said at last, in hardly more than a whisper.

"I want to move out." I didn't look at him, but I felt the change in his attitude at once. I could feel a flame-like anger run through him.

"Have you gone completely out of your head?" His voice was stiff with controlled rage.

"No," I said. I looked at him, not wanting to see his face, but knowing I must. "I've never been more sane in my life."

He stood up from the sofa and walked to the window. He stood with his back turned to me and when he spoke his voice was so low I hardly caught the words. "Don't insult me with this garbage. If you have to act like something from a Mills and Boon novel, go ahead, but don't justify it. Don't pretend you think this squalid affair is sane."

"Don't you dare talk to me in this way!" I was as angry as he was now and I was tired of controlling it. "Don't you dare to describe my life!"

"So what would you call it then – a transcendental experience?" He had turned to look at me and the cynical mockery in his eyes appalled me.

"What can she possibly give you that I can't? What could any woman give you? What more do you want? You have your home, your work, your children." He glared at me and I began for the first time to feel frightened. "And though I have to remind you of it – you have me – a husband who loves you."

"It's not about any of those things, Malachy . . ." I spoke very quietly. I felt that I must try to calm him. I had no energy for arguing.

"What is it about then?" he sneered at me.

"It's about me! It's about growing up!"

"For Christ's sake!"

"Look Malachy, I can't explain it to you. I don't know why I should try," I said. But all the same I knew I had to try, however resistant he was. "I can't fit any of what's happened to me in the last months into your words. Into the words I had for my life before this happened. But I'm not the woman I was when this life was right for me. And I can't fit back again. I've been changed forever. It's not just about love or happiness. It's about a way of being in the world, a vision, a sense of communication and sharing . . ."

"It's about sex as far as I can see," he interrupted me, almost hissing the words out. "Though you don't even have the excuse of not liking sex with men. At least, you can't pretend that with me whatever you say to your new-found lesbian friends who don't know you any better!" He glared at me in disdain. Then he walked over to the drinks cabinet and poured himself a Scotch.

"Malachy – we can't go on talking like this . . ." I

hesitated, trying to find a phrase that would mean something to him, that could connect with the selves we had once been without arousing his fury.

Before I could speak again, he interrupted. He turned to look at me, holding the empty glass in his hand.

"Tell me something . . ." he said softly and for a moment I thought the drink must have calmed him. "Do you think she'll leave Elinor for you?"

I shouldn't have answered him, but I did. "Yes."

"You're sure?"

"Yes. Why?"

"Do you remember I asked you once before if you trusted her?"

"Yes."

"Well, maybe it would interest you to know," he began slowly, "that I saw your beloved friends together a few weeks ago, in Stephen's Green. I was sitting on a bench, at lunch-time, one sunny afternoon, when who should come along but the two of them, Nina and Elinor, strolling arm in arm, laughing and gazing into each other's eyes as if they hadn't a care in the world." A little grin spread over his lips and he paused for effect. "They didn't recognise me of course – they wouldn't deign to notice a mere man. They stopped beside the duck pond, no more than six feet from where I sat, and kissed each other very slowly. Any fool could see that they're still in love."

I stared at him, too shocked by this blatant, desperate lie to find any words.

"If you think inventing this kind of rubbish is going to cause trouble between myself and Nina you're wrong."

"It's no invention – the plain truth unfortunately for you!" He shook his head from side to side and said pityingly: "They're making a laughing stock of you! God help you when your eyes finally open."

Suddenly he swung out of the room and slammed the door behind him. I stood stiff with panic. This was worse than anything I'd imagined. What was I to do? I felt it would be dangerous to stay the night in the same house. For the first time since we met, I was afraid of him.

I went into the bedroom and began to gather up clothes and belongings from about the room, feeling like a thief fleeing the scene of a crime.

Suddenly, I heard him behind me. I had my briefcase in one hand, a grip bag in the other.

"Where are you going?"

"I can't stay here tonight," I answered without turning round.

"Why not?"

"Because I think it's dangerous with the mood you're in."

"Dangerous? What does that mean?"

"It's pointless to go on talking now, Malachy. Let's leave it until we're both feeling better." I looked at him and tried to smile. But his body was stiff with suppressed anger and his face unyielding.

"What did you mean by dangerous?" he asked again with the same ugly tone in his voice. "What's dangerous? Who's dangerous? You?"

"Malachy – forget it. Please." I tried to slip past him, but he stretched out his arm to bar my way:

"Who's dangerous?" he asked again.

"Let me go, Malachy – just let me go."

He didn't move. His arm was stretched out between me and the door.

"Don't cause any more trouble." I lowered my head and tried to slide beneath his arm.

He caught hold of the lapels of my jacket and pulled me up with a sudden violent force. He pushed me against the door and held me there.

"Trouble?" he repeated and his eyes stared into mine with a glazed fixity. "Is that what you want? Is this what you expect me to do? Do you want me to act like a real man? To make you stay, is that it?"

"Malachy, for God's sake!"

"Is this the only thing that gets through to you?" he said, hissing the words through gritted teeth. "For all you say, in the end this is what you expect of a man, isn't it? This is the only language you understand!"

I stood absolutely still, waiting for his anger to subside. I kept my head lowered until he came to the end of his tirade and then I looked directly into his eyes. But they were the eyes of a stranger, obsessed and unseeing.

"This isn't what I want," I said gently, trying one last time. "This isn't why I've loved you. For the sake of everything there's been between us, just let me go quietly and don't say another word."

I felt a sudden change pass through his body. He put his mouth to mine and forced my lips open with his. His thrust his hips against me. His heart was pounding and his face was soaked in sweat.

"Will you get off me, for God's sake," I said, almost screaming. I just stopped myself from saying "Get down – down," as impatient and dismissive as if I were talking to a dog. He fell back from me at once. Almost reeled back. His face turned a sickly, ashen grey as though he was about to throw up. His eyes looked red and inflamed as if they might fall from their sockets. He crouched against the door, his arm over his mouth.

I stepped passed him and walked out of the house.

From that night on I was free of any sense of guilt about him. In one moment his bullying and intimidation had released me. If he had behaved well I might have been unable to let go of him. Shortly afterwards my friend Maggie O'Sullivan told me that she was going to the States for six months and asked me if I'd like to take her house in Donnybrook. I moved in that week with the boys. And Malachy agreed that when he went to Galway in the summer, I should move back to Breemore road.

Chapter Twenty

October, Dublin.

When Nina answered the doorbell she was taken aback to find Paul on the threshold. He must have seen the surprise on her face because he said immediately: "Have you forgotten you promised to give me those scripts for the programme next week?"

"Oh Jesus, yes. It went right out of my head. Sorry, Paul. Come in, come in."

She brought him into the sitting-room and gave him a drink. He sat down, stretched out his blue denim-clad legs, tilted his head to one side, and let an expression of boyish appeal and self-deprecation come into his bright eyes. When he spoke there was no preamble, "So tell me, have you made up your mind?"

"About what?"

"About you and Elinor of course."

"Is that what you came to find out?"

"No, but I've heard the rumours and seeing as I'm here . . ."

He shifted his body further down into the armchair as though settling in for a long evening. She smiled at him. How good at this he was, she thought. So disarming with his look of good-humoured bafflement, his boyish face, the dark lashes flickering against his pale cheek, his full red lips open with surprise.

"I saw Elinor yesterday," he said. "She seems a terrible mess. Have you told her yet?"

"Not totally."

"What does that mean?"

"I haven't made it final yet."

"And Elizabeth?"

"I've been trying to tell her for a week."

"But how can you? How could you bear to leave her? And all this . . ." He made a sweeping gesture with his free hand circling the room from floor to ceiling. How could she answer that? She didn't understand herself how she was to get through it. She looked at him for a few minutes in silence. She wondered if it was worth confiding in him. She had told him something of it before when it first began. He was one of her oldest friends and as good a listener as anyone she knew. But whenever she started on this story – and she had so often in the last year – she was overcome with a sense of futility. Nothing she said seemed to do justice to any of the emotions involved. However she tried to explain it, it sounded trite and clichéd. There seemed to be no language capable of closing the gap between words and feeling. And yet she felt she must talk to someone. So, reluctantly she began. She gave him a brief outline of events, trying to avoid getting bogged down in the detail of advance and retreat that marked all such stories. But even as she tried she felt the familiar sense of inadequacy. Words and sentences seemed to choose themselves from the air. She had the feeling that the story told itself in a certain way each time she began without any conscious direction from her. She was uncomfortably aware that everything she said made her sound weak and vacillating. Shallow and disloyal. She ploughed on without conviction, wanting now just to get to the end of it, to some semblance of resolution.

She told him about Katherine going to the West to wait for her and how because of Lizzie's illness she hadn't been able to join her after all. He wasn't impressed by this, of course. He said at once what anyone would have said, that if she really wanted to go she'd have found a way. Was it true? She walked to the cabinet by the wall and poured another drink for Paul and a double for herself. He regarded her thoughtfully for a moment or two and then said, seeming regretful but also faintly satisfied in the way people often do when events follow a predictable pattern.

"But you still haven't made up your mind? It's the classic dilemma – passion versus security?"

"Yes, it looks like that," she said and she lowered her head feeling shame at the banality of it all. "It's what anyone would think, isn't it?" She paused, she saw his brow puckering, and his mouth draw down at the corners. This was not what he expected to hear, she knew, it showed a lack of conviction which made her all the more culpable.

Was it worth explaining the contradictions she felt? The conflicting currents of desire and attachment? How could she put into words the depth of her need for Elinor: the fascination she still felt for her; their knowledge of each other existing on so many levels that whole areas of her personality were only real in Elinor's presence?

"The perverse part of it is, that in some way the nature of my love for Elinor is the more passionate," she said softly as though not sure she wanted to be heard. "But so much pain is built into that passion," she continued reluctantly. "I'm afraid of it. I'm afraid of how she can hurt me because I'm so deeply rooted. Whereas, with Katherine, I feel free. I can make myself up as I go along, I can be one thing today and another tomorrow. There's no history. And that gives me security."

"I see," he said. But he didn't look as if he did. She felt he disapproved of her. Not for leaving Elinor, but for claiming to feel so much for her still. Well, he was right. It was in bad taste even to say it. And if it were true – all she said she felt – how could she want to leave her?

Suddenly Paul stood up. He tied his red silk scarf loosely around his neck and pulled on his leather jacket. "Well, I'd better be going."

He stretched voluptuously and yawned.

"I'm sorry I can't be of more help," he said.

"You have."

"I wish I could tell you what to do. Wave a magic wand."

"Yes, I wish you could."

They walked to the door. They stood together on the doorstep looking out at the garden which was perfectly illumined by the porch light. Solomon came banging against their legs, thinking a walk was possible, panting and beating his tail from side to side.

"Who'll keep the dog?" Paul asked.

"Oh, he'll stay here. Elizabeth couldn't live without him."

He had seemed reluctant to go without having cleared some doubt from his mind. "If you're so in love," he said to her after a pause, "what are you afraid of?"

She hesitated. Not sure how to express herself.

"I'm afraid that in time . . ." she began, "it will become the same with Katherine. That the amazing easy pleasure we have now will be tainted by my guilt or my lack of faith or my egotism . . ."

"You haven't much trust in yourself, have you?"

"No," she said. "I haven't much reason to have."

"Ah," was all the answer Paul gave. Then, as though hesitating to break bad news, he added softly: "But no matter what you do or don't do – passion fades . . ."

277

"Yes, of course. Put that way the whole thing sounds pathetically predictable. And yet . . . what can I do? I can't live without her. I can't think of anyone but her. I can't sleep at night unless she's beside me, and when I do I dream of her?"

"Of who?" he asked. "Of Elinor?"

"No, Katherine, of course," she said at once, and she shrugged her shoulders, but not with resignation. "I'm trapped – whichever way I turn."

He looked at her for a moment studying her face. "They say a fox bites off its own leg . . ."

"Yes, they do, don't they?"

"So?" he asked softly.

She didn't need time to find the answer. But she hesitated because she knew how glib it would sound. "I'm afraid that if I try to love someone else and it doesn't last . . . I mean that when the first intensity cools, as it's bound to, that my feelings for Katherine might not be any deeper than what I have now, with Elinor." She paused.

"So?"

"And I'll have ruined lives for it."

"Ruined?" He looked doubtful.

"Well, damaged. And for a long time." She lowered her eyes and looked down at her hands. She saw that she had been pushing with her fingernail at the cuticle of her thumb and made it bleed. She put it to her mouth. He was silent for a few minutes in contemplation. Then he reached out his hand to stroke Solomon's head, lifting one heavy ear and letting it fall back against his cheek.

"Has Elinor always been faithful to you?" he asked as though out of the blue. And she was surprised he hadn't asked before.

"No," she answered at once, with a sense of relief at giving the full picture. "She had an affair about two years ago. It hurt so much I think I need to have one myself, as a kind of immunisation."

"But you fell in love?"

"Yes, I fell in love."

"Out of your depth?"

"Yes."

"Did you forgive Elinor?"

"I don't know. I thought I did at the time."

"And do you think she could forgive you?"

"I don't think she wants to."

She looked at his pale, handsome face waiting for some further explanation that she couldn't give. Forgiveness – was it ever possible? If Elinor was prepared to try, what then? If she were to walk in now and beg her – beg her as Katherine had done? What then?

She watched Paul walk down the street and unlock his bike from the railing. He cycled off into the distance waving an arm behind him, like a young boy.

As she stepped back into the hall she heard the phone ring in the kitchen. Reluctantly she went down to answer it.

"Hello."

A voice she did not recognise asked her if her name was Nina Kavanagh. She felt an instant chill of fear. Only bad news began this way.

"Yes, speaking," she said. Her mind raced to Katherine. Had something happened to her? She was flooded by an anxiety and guilt she didn't want to name.

"I'm sorry to have to tell you that your aunt, May O'Brien, has had a heart attack, her neighbour gave us your number. She's here in Saint Mary's if you'd like to come to see her. Although we have made her comfortable now and you might prefer to wait until morning?"

Chapter Twenty-One

September, Clare.

I woke this morning at seven o'clock, just before dawn, and could not sleep again. I lay on my back in the darkness listening to the night, the silence and emptiness of the small hours, when suddenly the sky behind the curtains seemed to be filled with a blinding white light. I had the sensation of feeling it more than seeing it. I lay huddled in the sheets staring towards the window and my heartbeat seemed so loud it filled the room. I was suddenly overwhelmed by a sense of impending disaster. The sensation was not just in my body, but seemed to be taking place in the world outside me. As though some terrible natural calamity was taking place, an earthquake or the sky and earth slowly freezing over.

I had a dream about you last night. The first dream since I've come here. I dreamed that it was Christmas Eve. You and I were driving in a car together. We were on our way home to our new house to have dinner with friends. You put your hand on my thigh and I put mine over it. As we turned the corner for home I saw a familiar figure standing at the bus stop. I looked again and saw that it was Elinor, standing in a long black coat almost to her feet, her eyes searching wildly through the crowd of last-minute shoppers. She looked lost, bewildered. I knew at once from the tragic expression on her face that she had come looking for you. I imagined her asking around the town for you, being directed to our house. Walking in unexpectedly while we were sharing presents with our friends. For a moment I considered ignoring her. I knew you hadn't yet seen her. But I knew the moment I looked into her face that she had come for you. I knew too, that she would seek you out. She would not give up, however long it took. And so I said: "I've just seen Elinor – we'll have to stop." You turned to me and your eyes had a look of immense sorrow and resignation. "Yes," you said, even before you had seen her. "Yes, we'll have to stop."

I went downstairs and poured a drink. Red wine, cheap and bitter.

I am plunged back into the anxiety of yesterday. I have suddenly this terrible sense of foreboding. Why did you not answer the phone? Am I going to receive another message telling me you have cancelled our plans again?

I went out for a walk. I went to the lake. Three swans came to meet me, a male and two females. They swam right up to the little pier and stretched their black beaks expectantly. But I'd come empty-handed again. Their bodies are snow white, but their necks are stained brown from delving in the brackish water. One of the females turned a sad, watchful eye to me and bowed her head. There was a place I used to go to in Kinsale with Malachy. Ma brought us there first. A slipway at the far end of the harbour where a flock of swans came every day. As many as twenty or thirty swans would sail in and clamber up onto the concrete slip and begin to preen themselves. We always brought bread for them and they came to know us well. Malachy had a name for most of them and insisted that each responded to its own. I will never go there with him again. And with you? We had said we would go everywhere together that we had ever been separately, everywhere we had loved in our former lives. And now? Why am I full of this sense of doom?

The swans swam away from me, graceful, stately. After a few minutes I saw them taking off from the still lake with a furious wing beat, the cold water rising in little white waves beneath them. Watching them, I remembered the lines of a poem – one Malachy loved to recite, years ago:

"Never give all the heart, for love
Will hardly seem worth thinking of
To passionate women if it seem
Certain, and they never dream
That it fades out from kiss to kiss."

Oh God. My poor Malachy – how did it all happen? How did it come to this? My charming, guileless Malachy.

With a leaden heart I turned towards home.

On the way I stopped into the shop to buy some bread. At least that's what I pretended to myself, but really it was only because I was desperate for conversation. I found Máire Mac alone. She was leaning on the counter reading the evening newspaper. The small, cluttered room had an air of tranquillity and warmth and seemed like an oasis in the desert after the isolation and tension of my last hours.

We made a little small talk about the weather and the price of newspapers before I got started on the subject weighing on my heart.

I told her I couldn't get through to my boys on the phone and that I was very worried. She was kind to me. She reassured me. She said sure there could be any number of reasons. "Come into the back with me, have a cup of tea and try again in a little while."

I sat in the small dark sitting-room behind the shop and slowly, as she chatted and bustled about the room, fetching tea and biscuits for me, keeping up a stream of small talk, the tension began to ease from my body. I looked at her worn, kindly face. I felt again a longing to confide in her. I needed so badly to talk to another human being. To unload some of the pain. I'd been alone now too long – almost anyone would seem good company to me tonight. But Máire Mac kept up her chatter about the weather and the price of cattle, and the new shop opening in town and the crime rate rising, and the loneliness of the nights here when you live alone, and the death of a neighbour who was killed by his own gun when he was out hunting rabbits. After ten minutes of this it was time to call the boys. This time the phone was answered. I showered Ben with questions, but of course I got very few answers. "Everything is fine – just like always," he assured me. Why was I worrying? he asked.

"Yes, I know it's silly, but when I don't see you for a while I can't help worrying." Then, he asked if I was coming back next week? I hesitated, not wanting to promise if I wasn't sure I could manage it. In that moment of hesitation he grew defensive: "Well, it doesn't matter, Mom, we're all pretty busy next week anyway."

Why didn't I say yes straight away? Why didn't I reassure him? Because I'm still trying to keep myself free for you.

I walked home. Turned into the boreen and seemed to come upon the house suddenly. Desolate now. No welcoming light, no sense of expectation. It was the certainty of your coming that had made these stone walls and low slate roof seem a haven to me.

Inside I lit the fire, drew up my chair and began again on the wine. I thought to myself that there must be something in the house to cheer me up. If I could find something belonging to you – some tangible reminder – to bring your presence back to me, immediate and real. I went upstairs to the bedroom and took out the leather briefcase you asked me to carry down for you. It was filled with letters and notebooks – your work papers. I thought about going through the letters; all the stories of woe that women send to you in hope of consolation.

Other people's miseries might cheer me. But I hadn't the stomach for it. I put them back and took out instead the books you had packed, in the front pocket of the briefcase, two paperback novels and an anthology of Russian poets. You know the one? Of course you do. And do you remember also what you left between its pages? A colour photograph? A photograph of you and Elinor together. You are standing arm in arm in what appears to be a city park. She's looking directly into the camera, smiling. You hands are clasped in one another's. Your head is turned as if somebody called you suddenly. But you are happy. Although your face is partly concealed, I know that. I know it without wanting to. How they wound me – these mementos of your life together. You'd think I'd be inured to them by now, it's not as if you ever made any effort to hide them. They were all over the house at Fairfield Road and when you moved to Jan's you took them with you. But why would you want to bring them here? You can't have intended to – even you would hardly bring down photographs of one lover when you're coming to stay with another?

But so what? That's all over and done with now. Why should I let myself get upset?

I took the books downstairs to the fire and determined to forget about it. I sat before the blazing turf, with my wine glass in my hand, the cat purring at my feet and I was nearly content again and peaceful. I began to leaf idly through the books, first the novels, two Irish women writers I haven't heard of, and then I opened the last one, the anthology. I opened it immediately at the centre page because I wanted to look at the photographs. A card fell into my lap. Do you remember it? Are you feeling the same panic as I did, now that you know the one I mean? Need I describe it? All right – a picture of two dark-skinned women, with black hair coiled about their heads, sitting on a street corner of some Spanish or Italian town, bending their heads over some work in their laps – embroidery or lace, the sun casting the long shadows of a summer afternoon at their feet. For ten minutes I sat holding it in my hand and tried not to read it.

Yes, this is the truth. I saw that you'd written inside it and I knew at once it wasn't meant for me. I don't know how, because it's not addressed to anyone. I sat by the kitchen table gazing out the back window into the fields. I clutched it between my hands; afraid to begin – afraid not to. I watched three crows do battle over an apple rotting on the grass. I watched them stabbing it with their beaks, grinding it to pulp, I heard their shrieks of rage as they struggled for possession and I thought how little different we are – you and I and Elinor. I opened it and looked at your unmistakable, bold, rounded script. As soon as I had begun the first sentence I regretted it.

"My only love,

We will be like this again soon, won't we? When all this is over? We'll find a quiet table, in a side-street café, and drink Pastis on ice in the afternoon. Sitting there, without need of words, there will be nothing more to do. Nothing more to want. Together again, at last. Will you come with me to Florence, my love? Soon?"

I feel as though my heart has been packed in ice. For a few minutes I tried to persuade myself that you might have written this to me and forgotten to post it. After all you might well have wanted to go to Italy with me also. How often have you called me your only love? But I can't fool myself, however desperately I try. I remember, you see (unfortunately) that you told me this spring that Elinor had asked you to go on holiday with her. You didn't tell me where. And you told me you didn't want to go. But I heard afterwards – when we had already broken up in July – that the two of you had gone to Italy together for a month. It hurt me so much at the time I didn't let myself think of it. I pretended she must have bullied you into it.

But now . . . Now I know differently, don't I? Now I know that even before you'd finished with me you were planning this holiday.

I sit staring out the window. I have been sitting motionless for more than an hour. I think I stopped breathing. The same few words repeat themselves endlessly, throbbing in my brain: "When all this is over." All what? When all of what is over, Nina? You told me that you had never made any promises to Elinor about us. That you'd never agree terms with her without telling me first. But what else can these words mean? The same thoughts go scrabbling round in my brain, eating into my sanity, fouling every memory, every hope. "When all this is over!" I have read it twenty times and I still can't credit it. One phrase has smashed my faith in you as nothing else has had the power to do. "When all this is over." How could you have written this about our life? How could you have dismissed all that's between us in this trite, mean phrase?

Have I been mad all this time? Have I been completely deluded to imagine, for one minute, that you'd leave Elinor for me?

I am so weary. Every muscle in my body aches; my head aches, my teeth, the roots of my teeth, my eyeballs throb. Why should it come as a shock that you have lied to me? Why should I feel outraged? I know only too well how good you are at it. How practised. After all, I heard you lie often enough to Elinor and didn't complain. I saw how you carried it off, the little tricks you used: the offhand tone of voice that made a lie convincing, or your way of telling the truth in such exaggerated language it seemed like a lie. And of course there was your distraction technique – how you diverted attention from difficult questions by subtle flattery or a sudden pretence of excitement about some other subject. Oh yes, I can't let on

I haven't been prepared. Yet here I am stricken, furious because you've lied to *me*.

For the last few hours I've been trying to decide whether to write to you. Why should I wait to phone? It might be better to put everything I feel on paper. But what would I say? Does it make any difference? Is there anything left to say? Anything not said? I could say I love you. But does it matter to you? Do you love me? Yes. But how does it help me? Love is no help. It's the love that causes all this pain in the first place.

I am too tired to write anything. Sick with hurt and jealousy. It devours me, like formic acid on my skin. It is a chronic, dull ache about my heart. I can hardly breathe with the pain of it. I do everything in my power to control it, but I can't stop thinking about you. The two of you together. I see you gazing into each other's eyes. I hear you laughing in exactly the way Malachy described when he saw you walking in Stephen's Green that day. Why is laughter so terrible? All the times I've seen you laughing with other people. Your lovely, infectious, deep-throated laughter. How I enjoyed it. How I gloried in it. This rich, open laughter of yours, your wide, beautiful smile. But now I picture you walking along a street, arm in arm with her. She is leaning her head against your shoulder, your thighs pressed together as you walk. She lifts her face to gaze at you, you bend (for you are two inches taller), and put your lips to her forehead, you are laughing. Both of you. I see you striding through the city streets, leaves blowing about your feet, heads thrown back and laughing.

Dear God, I didn't know that pain could be as terrible as this.

I remember now all the things you've told me about her. All the things that have tormented me in the past. When you confided them first, I was in bed with you, blindly secure in your love for me. I let myself listen because I was curious. Ignorant of every aspect of love between women, I felt I needed to be educated. I encouraged you to tell me all about your life with Elinor. Afterwards, when you abandoned me for the first time, it came back to haunt me. Ravaged by jealousy, I couldn't banish from my mind the images you had conjured up. Now it's started again. Worse than before. Unbearable. What can I do? How can I protect myself? It will drive me insane.

If I wrote it down would it help? Could I ease my obsession by trying to objectify it? Would it purge me to set it down in cold blood?

I remember you told me how you loved her body. You still do. You love it like a piece of sculpture made with your own hands. Even after seven years there was still this passionate connection between you.

You told me you loved her and that you could never love anyone more. You told me at the outset. But you also said that she was dangerous for you. She tormented you because you were both so intense, you were like two pieces of live cable sparking at the slightest touch. You overexcited each other. You wore one another out. Neither of you ever knew where to draw the line. You told me that when you first looked at her you knew she would hurt you in the future. You didn't know how, but you were sure she would do you some great injury and yet you could not keep from loving her.

I remember asking you what you loved about her and you could not answer at first. Or did not want to. When I pressed you, you looked away from me and began a long rambling discourse on the nature of long-term relationships. I listened to you, impressed and frightened. I remember most of it. Some of the words and all of the sense. You said you could give any of the thousand reasons for loving someone and you'd still have said nothing. Sometimes you looked at her and could not have said why you loved her at all. Why you loved her rather than the woman she was standing next to or the woman standing behind her. You only knew that when you began to love her it seemed that you had chosen her from a thousand others because of some distinct extraordinary quality. By the time you had loved her for several years it seemed sometimes that you loved her, because you loved her, because she was the one you had chosen to love. Because she was the one who was there to love.

I have to force myself to be calm. To examine the situation. Once again I have to make myself go over the facts. Or what has been presented to me as fact. You've told me that you're staying in Dublin because Elizabeth is worse. Is it the truth? Or is it part of the truth? Is there another reason?

I know that you love Elinor and that you left her for me. That you went back to her and that you regretted it and came to meet me at the airport nine days ago. I know that all you said to me then was true. That you were sincere. You did want to be with me and you did believe that you couldn't continue with Elinor. But that was while you were with me. Influenced only by me. I was a fool to let you go back to her. I should have insisted that you come here with me. You could have written to her. You could have told her on the phone. But you said you had to have the courage to tell her in person. Why did I believe you? I've trusted you so often before and it's always been misplaced.

I used to think, sometimes, when I saw you together that you regretted breaking up with her. When I watched your face when you read a letter from her, or talking on the phone as you did for hours at a time. But I didn't want you to start resenting me. I was always at pains to encourage your relationship. To show you how completely accepting of her I was. I was terrified that you might guess at my jealousy and begin to be guarded with me. I pretended to be always delighted to see her. I went out of my way to speak kindly of her. I think sometimes I succeeded so well that it made her resentful of me, imagining that I was so totally without jealousy. The angel Katherine she called me. If only she had known! Did either of you ever guess what it cost me? Did you ever suspect the effort, the strain it was to live always in her shadow? That's how I felt; in her shadow. As though everything I did was compared with her. As though you had this model of the perfect lover, the ideal relationship and everything and everyone was measured against it. Once you told me that you had found it impossible to live with her not because you had stopped loving her, but because you loved her too much. You were tired and bit drunk when you said it. I don't think you really meant me to hear you. You certainly didn't expect me to remember. But I did, Nina. I did.

Even when you first left her and went to live in Jan's you still insisted on going back to visit her and Lizzie. You saw them two evenings a week. But why did you share a bed with her when you stayed over? If you were friends only why was it not sufficient to meet in the daytime, have a drink together, go for a meal? I never asked you directly because it was assumed I understood. You loved the house you'd lived in together. You loved Lizzie. You thought of her as your own child. You'd spent seven years of your life with her. Yes, I understood all that, but I also knew that when Malachy came to see Ben and Luke, nothing in our shared feeling about them made me want to share a bed with him again.

Tried to sleep again. No use. Got up. Made some lunch. Went back to bed. Could not sleep. Afraid to dream. Do not want to think. Do not want to eat or drink. Do not want to go out. If I phone you tonight what will I say?

This is the last time – the very last time I'll think of you.

There can be no going back on this, the pain is too great. No making a new time, another time. If you do not come back now you must never come back. I can't go through this again. If I do this now I can never do it again. So let us be sure it is necessary. Necessary and inevitable.

I have been through this before, remember? When you left me the last time. Do you know what the pain was like? Have you the least idea? You can't because you went back to Elinor. You went back to safe harbour with Elinor and left me alone. I felt as if I'd had a limb amputated without anaesthetic and been left to recover without pain-killers. I was woken every morning by the pain of you missing from my side. All through the day the agony of it went on, my body hurting where you were not. An ache in my chest as if my ribs had been crushed. I understood then what was meant when people spoke of being broken-hearted. I had always before thought it a manner of speech, a metaphor. But it isn't. It's the plain, unadorned truth.

Chapter Twenty-Two

October, Dublin.

"Any change?" the nurse asked every hour. She took May's temperature. It was quiet now in the room. May had been moved to an alcove at the far end of the ward, separated from the rest of the room by an opaque glass partition. Nina remembered how, years ago, they had moved Molly to the far end of the room when she was dying. The last bed in the ward was always the death bed in those days. But now? She sat beside May's bed, anxious and ill at ease, afraid to take her eyes from the old lady's face in case the change the nurse spoke of might take place without her noticing. How could a few hours have made such a drastic change in her? She was hardly recognisable. Lying between the starched, unyielding sheets, May was a different woman altogether from the one she had left smoking cigars and drinking whiskey at her own fireside. Her blue-tinged skin was stretched too finely over bones that seemed suddenly gaunt and over-large. Her lips had turned a deep violet. Three electrodes had been attached to her chest underneath the emergency hospital smock that seemed to be made of coarse, white paper. The wires were linked to a monitor beside the bed across which a steadily advancing grey line tracked the old woman's heartbeat. A sinister low-key sound accompanied it – bip, bip, bip. Nina tried not to listen. But found herself straining anxiously to hear in case it might suddenly stop. May's breathing sounded normal enough. The awful sound that had come from her an hour ago had changed to a soft hardly audible rhythm. But was this better or worse? Did it mean she was regaining strength or losing it?

It was useless to ask. They told you nothing. All lay people were regarded as feeble-minded intruders to be protected from the facts at all costs. Nina had an exaggerated fear and loathing of these institutions. The moment she walked into the hallway, the warm, sweetish smell of the air made her queasy. It had been as much as she could bear to come and see Lizzie. But to sit alone in this eerily sanitised ward, to keep vigil at the bedside of someone she loved as much as May was her notion of a season in hell. The clamour was the thing that most amazed her. When she first arrived it was like a railway station filled with garish light and constant movement. Even here, in what they called Coronary Care, staff bustled about ceaselessly, looking anxious and hurried. Everyone seemed on their way to somewhere else.

The nurses glided by in their little white caps and plimsoll shoes along the highly polished tiles, their feet seeming not to quite touch the ground. To summon one it was necessary to walk to a control desk at the end of the ward and press a buzzer. It might be five minutes before anyone arrived. The televisions – perched on shelves just below the ceiling – loomed over the room flashing their incomprehensible messages hour after hour, lurid and incoherent. To listen to them, one had to use the headphones that were attached to each bed. The patients lay gazing up at them with fascinated eyes, as if clinging to the normality of these familiar images. So long as there was television there was hope, they seemed to feel. The faces and voices known from years of watching in the safety of home were the only reassurance in an eerie world of ceaseless movement and violent light.

Now at close to midnight it was finally quiet. All the visitors but herself had long since left for home. The nurses had given her leave to stay because of May's advanced age and the unspoken danger that she might not last until the next official visiting hour.

She reached out and took May's hand. It was cold and dry.

"If there's any change call me." That was their phrase – any change – it covered a vast unspoken territory too uncertain or frightening to define. But there was no change. May lay in her fitful sleep. On her side. Her entire body hidden beneath the covers. Her face white and hollow cheeked, the starched, white hospital smock accentuating her frailty. She seemed totally out of place. Out of her element. Her head, buried in the thick pillows, seemed unnaturally small. Her hair, still thick and white, with a little of its original blonde still visible, had fallen across her forehead so that her usual air of authority and order had been vanquished.

She had been sleeping since Nina arrived, but it was a sleep without any sense of rest. She felt May struggling against it. As though to let herself sleep was to move deeper into the place that waited before death. The anteroom.

Every so often her foot moved under the covers and she muttered to herself. Nina leaned forward, bent over her face to catch the words. Sometimes she understood and sometimes not. An hour ago May had said almost clearly: "She's a lovely girl and mad about you." Did she mean Elinor or Katherine? There was no knowing.

The monitor gave out its steady bip-bip and Nina sat gazing in stupefied fascination watching the blue line rising and falling in its ceaseless journey across the screen. She could scarcely believe that this was happening to her. Here she was again sitting anxious and impotent at a hospital bedside. Though she ought not to be surprised. Troubles, as Aunt May liked to say, seldom came single. It was true; grief and anxieties so often seemed to attract more of the same, as if suffering exerted a magnetic force that drew into its path any other free-floating misfortune. But what could have precipitated this particular crisis? When Nina had said goodbye at the doorstep in Sandymount May appeared perfectly well. Throughout the evening she had seemed her normal self: bustling about, smoking her cigars, making jokes, bossy and full of energy. And now she was in a hospital bed, a silent inert mound, beneath a pale blue bedspread, reduced to the status of anonymous invalid. An emergency case – nothing more.

What had happened to provoke it? Or could a heart attack come completely out of the blue – without warning or cause? She tried to remember what they had talked about that evening. She knew Lizzy had persuaded her to go through the old photograph collection again. Had there been anything significant in May's behaviour? Had she seemed worried? Anxious? The truth was Nina hadn't noticed. She had been so preoccupied with her own dilemma all evening. Even now she couldn't drag herself fully into the present. May was lying in a hospital bed beside her and her thoughts were going back obsessively, like a tongue to a bad tooth, to Katherine and to Elinor.

She asked herself, for the first time that night, if May might be dying. Did people always die in the small hours? She didn't look so bad to Nina's eye. But what did that mean? How did the dying look? How many people had she seen die? Only one. And she was a child then. Death was kept well hidden. That was how everyone wanted it. Neat and clean. Preferably out of sight. No one wanted the mess and dirt and pain of dying.

But if she was to die, Nina hoped it would be quick. She couldn't bear to watch her suffer. At once the thought followed – petty and unworthy – something she cancelled even as it flashed through her mind – that it must be quick, her death, because she hadn't the time to watch over a death-bed. She hadn't the time for anything that took time. She shivered violently like a wet dog. She felt, all at once, utterly desolate, alone and abandoned. Chilled to the bone. The reality of May's death struck her with sudden, brutal force. How would she manage without her? She would be more adrift in the world than ever. A true orphan for the first time. No family of any kind. No blood relatives. The outcast she had felt most of her life. She leaned down and put her lips to the damp, straying hair that lay along May's forehead. No one knew what the loss of May would mean to her. If she died, friends would smile and say, "Well, after all, she had a good innings." As if that was a comfort. It would be too difficult to explain. It was not as though she depended on May or looked to her for practical support. She was so much older than the parents of Nina's friends that she had never expected of her the qualities they demanded of their mothers – someone to advise and give council. But, despite this, she had one virtue that outweighed all others in Nina's eyes – May had known her almost all her life. And for her, orphan that she was without brothers or sisters, this was something no one else could replace. May was the only fixed and permanent element of her world. A part of the landscape. The only person in her life who took her for granted. Already, just imagining life without May, she missed her, and all the small routine things they shared; things one gave no thought to until they were gone. The careless routines that held life together like invisible glue. The Sunday lunches that she had begun lately to see as a duty. Their trips to the races. Their arguments. The easy, comfortable talks. Gossip, old jokes, sitting over the fire drinking whiskey. The look of May's face, her sceptical, deep blue eyes. The sound of her walking stick as she crossed the floor. The smell of her expensive cigars. The feel of the old house she had known from childhood.

Guilt came rushing back then, like a dark ink, seeping into her blood. Why had she not done more for her? Why had she not been kinder? She regretted all her lapses: getting impatient, nagging her about her smoking. Not making time to see her often enough. The trouble was it was too easy to overlook her needs because she never asked for anything. She never made Nina feel conscious of duty towards her. But that was a poor excuse for failing to do so many small things she could have done to make her happy. She was always in too great a hurry. Always saying, next week I'll give her more time, next week I'll take her to the cinema, to the races. There was nothing May loved better than a day at Leopardstown or the Phoenix Park. And when had she last taken her? A year ago? Maybe more.

Now there was less time than ever. Now, when Nina's whole life was falling apart, how could she find energy to care for May? If she recovered and went back to live at home she would need someone to look after her. She would need more attention than Nina had ever spared for her before. But attention was the one thing she didn't have. She had no space in her mind for anything but the one obsessive question that dominated her, night and morning.

Chapter Twenty-Three

September, Clare.

"I went to church on Sunday.
  My love she passed me by.
  I knew her heart was changing,
  by the roving of her eye."

I remember you sang this to me once. Driving to Galway together on our first holiday. I listened intently and felt an acute pleasure in the sweet melancholy of the words while we drove though the country roads, united and radiantly in love. If I had known then what I know now.

I dreamed of Ma, or she appeared to me, again this morning. She stood at the foot of the bed gazing down at me with a look of intense sorrow or pity in her eyes. At last she spoke, looking away from me and towards the window where the first light of dawn was beginning to show in a dark sky. "Pray for the repose of her soul," she said, and then she was gone. I woke terrified. Whose soul? Hers? When had I last said a prayer for her? Or did she mean my own soul?

I tried to get back to sleep, but couldn't. I gave up at last. Exhausted, I rose, got dressed, drank some coffee and left the house. I turned right at the end of the boreen and walked towards the crossroads.

A country crossroads – a shop, a pub, a church. The three centres of civilisation in this land. Could I find comfort in any of them? The pub would be full of men, watchful and curious. The church empty and forlorn, dedicated to one man, who was neither watchful nor curious. The shop? Well, I've been there too often. Máire Mac will be getting weary of me.

I chose the church. I've often passed it on my walks in the last week, but never felt tempted to go in. It's a small stone building just beside the crossroads. It stands a little way in from the road, sheltered by a grove of hazel trees and sycamore. A gravel path leads to the heavy oak door, past a scattering of old tomb stones that rise at drunken angles from the long grass.

"I went to church on Sunday.
My love she passed me by."

I pushed open the door and went inside. It must be five years at least since I last stood in a Catholic church. It was newly decorated, brightly lit with fresh yellow paint on the walls; benches of light stained pine and the low altar, facing the congregation, dressed with clean linen and two tall vases of white lilies. Someone must come every day to look after the place, though I've never seen anyone in the vicinity. I'd expected it to be dark and musty, with grimed, stained glass and the smell of stale candle wax and incense. But it smelled of nothing but clean air and new paint.

I missed the dark, soulful gloom of the churches of my childhood, the whispered prayers of the old women, the looming statues, the bleeding hearts, the nailed feet. I wanted the crucifix with ghastly face of Christ gazing heavenward in supplication. I wanted to relive all that glory and suffering. The glamour of penitence – the romance of sacrifice. What was there to inspire me or revolt from in this bland, well-tended doll's house, with its fresh odourless air?

I walked to the little grotto of Our Lady in an alcove on the right-hand side of the main altar – the only piece of imagery that seemed unchanged from the days of my childhood indoctrination. I looked at her pale, white face, her blue mantle, her hands chastely joined, her eyes raised to an indifferent heaven. I took a small white candle from a box attached to the railing and lit it from one already burning. I placed it in a candlestick beneath her bare feet. It burned with a smooth yellow flame. I prayed for help. I prayed to block from my mind the pain of my loss. I asked her to give me peace of spirit, to ease the anger and hurt that devoured me. To grant me some sign that would give me direction. Was I to forget you – once and for all? To drive you from my heart? Or to go on hoping, trusting in you? I recited slowly, with closed eyes, the only prayer I can remember from childhood: "Remember, oh most ever loving Mary, that never was it known that anyone who sought thy help, implored thy intercession was left unaided."

But no sign appeared in the sky. No prayer could heal me or expel the words that were spinning obsessively in my brain, two sentences I'd read on a greeting card: "My only love" and "When all this is over . . .", written to another woman. I walked along the centre aisle and paused before the first station of the cross: Christ is brought before Pontius Pilate. I looked into the leering eyes of those condemning him to death, into the meek, pallid face of Jesus receiving his sentence. How was it possible that anyone found comfort in this gory iconography of suicide and murder? To me it had never been anything but a horror story. I wondered was it because men cannot give birth to life that they're forever held in thrall by these myths of death? The central symbol of their greatest religion – a man offering rebirth to the world through the sacrifice of his own life. And so many of us infected from infancy by this sadistic, life-denying fable invented by them.

And women? What part is offered to us? To weep at the foot of the cross? To carry the corpse to its tomb? To be the witness when the male miracle of resurrection took place? Virgin Mother. Where did that leave us? Which one of us could bring off that trick? Was it any wonder none of us felt we got it right? No, there was nothing for me here.

I opened the door and walked outside, relieved to be in daylight and to feel on my skin the cold, fresh air of the graveyard. I felt the wind blowing in from the lake. I would go and look at the swans for a bit, more inspiring than any church. I walked the narrow path between the tilted, grey tombstones. I read the names inscribed there as I passed: McCarthy, Duffy, Boyle, Gillespie, Black, McHugh. I saw that many of the stones bore two or three names, several generations of the one family listed together; husbands and wives, sisters and brothers, parents and children. When I looked more closely and read the dates I noticed that, in several cases, one death was followed within a few years by another. A child who died at seven was the first name given on one, her father's name dated three years later and her mother two years after that again. Underneath were inscribed the words: "To thee do we send up our sighs, mourning and weeping in this valley of tears." The nuns at convent school had constantly emphasised this grim, morbid picture of the world. I had rejected it fiercely and imagined that I'd kept myself free of their masochism. But standing alone in that windswept, desolate place, I wondered if they had been right all along. "A valley of tears – mourning and weeping." Is this just an accurate description of the way things are? Is life on this earth no more than a slow accumulation of loss?

I remembered my dream and Ma's words. "Pray for the repose of her soul." I had forgotten to say a prayer for her when I was in the church. I knelt down beside a grave where tall grass grew over the stone, the names long since eroded. A flock of rooks screeched in the branches of the yew trees near the gate. The sound of their voices at once mournful and excited. Just as they had at her funeral. When had I last said a prayer for her? As I stood at her graveside and watched the narrow coffin lowered into the mouth of the clay I prayed silently then to please her. And in those last precious moments in her company, before she was swallowed by the wet, black earth, I felt convinced that nothing mattered in this world but the physical reality; the material body. The soul was nothing – a candle snuffed out in one breath. A picture rose up before my mind then, of Ma as she was years before, in her patterned summer frock, her tanned sun burnt skin, her bare arms, her eyes glowing with excitment, and I knew that in these last seconds I was losing all I had loved best in her, forever. Only a few days before, if I had seen her fall and hurt herself, I'd have been full of anxious sympathy and concern. Yet, here I was, watching her body lowered into the ground, left to rot alone, in the dark, rain-sodden earth, enclosed in a wooden box. I couldn't make sense of it. On that cold April morning I wanted you there beside me, to hold my hand, to smile at me across the grave's mouth. I wanted to feel your hot breath and your warm skin. So long as you were alive and breathing, my love of your body was the only thing that mattered; the hot, sweet, vibrant flesh.

I walked to the crest of the hill and looked out across the lake, the wind blowing into my face and blowing my hair out behind me like a scarf. I held my coat close about my knees, clutching it with my hands. I found tears in my eyes. What was I doing here? Here in this place of death. Waiting – when I knew life is too short for waiting. But what was there left for me to do?

"It's not so bad a day now." I heard a voice behind me and turned to see the figure of a woman standing at the grave under a row of dark yew trees. She was wearing a red coat and a patterned blue and red headscarf tied tightly about her head.

I thought how bright, almost festive, she looked for a visit to a cemetery. "We might have a fine afternoon, yet." When she spoke the last words I recognised the voice and then the face beneath the scarf. It was Máire Mac, scarcely recognisable in her outdoor clothes. It struck me then that I hadn't seen her beyond the confines of the shop walls since coming here.

"Máire Mac, you startled me. I wouldn't have expected to find you here," I said, stupidly, because of course she lived in the parish and must have relatives buried here. Why wouldn't she come to visit from time to time? But I felt as I used to as a child meeting a teacher unexpectedly outside school.

"Oh, I come here often enough."

"Have you some of your family buried here?"

"My mother."

"Is she long dead?" I asked making an effort at politeness.

"She is, girl. She died fifty-five years ago."

I stared at her uncomprehendingly. I thought I must have misheard her.

"Fifty-five years ago?"

Máire Mac knelt down at the side of the grave. The wind was sweeping across the hill, carrying sea spray mixed with rain.

"Yes," she said, without looking at me. "She died fifty-five years ago today. The day I was born."

I looked at the inscription on the gravestone in front of her. "In loving memory of Maggie McCarthy, born 1900 – died 1935, dearly beloved wife of Patrick McCarthy, mother of Thomas, John and Máire."

The rooks bawled in the trees and flew in circles just above our heads as though to warn us or to drive us off.

"How terrible!" I said, finding inadequate words.

"Yes."

I stood silently beside her, looking down on the weathered, grey headstone on her mother's grave. I tried to think of some consoling phrase.

"It must have been so lonely for you."

"It was," she said simply. She was kneeling still and her face was hidden from me. "It's a terrible thing to carry for life on your conscience . . ."

"On your conscience?" I could make no sense of this.

"It's a terrible thing to think that you killed your own mother."

I looked at her in horror, too shocked to answer. And she continued, at once, the words rushing from her lips, as if escaping involuntarily.

"I often say to myself that if I hadn't come into the world that day she would have lived and my brothers would have had a mother and my father a wife. No one ever said that, but it's what I felt. Even still I imagine I see her somewhere, walking along a street in town or sometimes when I walk near the lake at evening. I forget for a moment that she's dead. Or maybe it's that my brain doesn't accept it yet. It's as if I'm still, after all these years, after my whole lifetime, waiting for her to come back. As if she had just gone out for a message and would be home again in five minutes. Sometimes when the door of the shop opens at evening when I'm there alone I find myself half expecting to see her come in." She stopped abruptly as though too sad to continue. I remembered all the times I had called to the shop in the last few days and seen nothing but an inquitive, cheerful countrywoman, anxious to make a sale.

"And do you know the worst thing," she added, in a voice so low I barely heard it. "I've no notion of what she looked like. My father burnt all the photographs of her on the night she died."

I felt guilty and contrite as I listened. Why had I not seen any of the sorrow? But I was blinded by my own troubles, petty and foolish in comparison.

305

"Every year since I was a small child I've dreaded this day. I wish I could forget it."

I thought of you. I remembered how you too hated your birthday. You told me how your aunts tried to get you to invent your own day for it, but it didn't work. Whatever day you chose, you said, once it was called birthday you thought of your mother's death.

"I'm sorry, Máire," I said.

She looked up at me and her face softened. "Don't be, girl. It's all long in the past. I only remember it now because I'm telling you." She smiled at me, and for the first time I saw real kindness in her expression, the usual look of quickness and inquisitiveness entirely gone from it.

Dense black cloud rolled across the sky from behind the church. The rain couldn't be far off. Máire Mac clutched the patterned headscarf tight around her head. We lowered our faces from the blast and set out together. We made our way down the narrow path and through the low stile that separated the cemetery from the road. The rooks screamed a farewell to us.

"You seem to be troubled, Katherine?" she said softly. "Have you lost someone belonging to you?"

The simplicity of the words struck my heart with the force of a blow. Again, she seemed to be reading my mind. But, of course, it was nothing of the kind. It was, after all, the conventional thing to say. Katherine – she had never used my name before and I was unexpectedly touched by it. Was that what aroused the same strange desire to confide in her? But after all she had told me her story. And I needed desperately to talk to someone. Even if it was a stranger, a countrywoman who ran a grocery shop. But wasn't that exactly what made it attractive? Or maybe it was only because she was there and we had ten minutes to walk together, on a dark rain-swept road.

"What would you think of a woman, Máire Mac," I began, deciding to plunge straight into it, knowing no other way, "who ran off with a lover and left her husband behind? A woman who fell madly in love with someone else?"

"What kind of husband was it? A husband who drank?" she asked matter-of-factly.

"No, he didn't drink – at least not until after she left him."

"Was he a man who beat her – a violent man?"

"No, not that either. Or at least only at the very end," I added softly. But I don't think she heard it.

"What was his problem then?"

"The problem was hers rather than his. The wife in question. She went off, left a perfectly good husband, because she had found someone else," I said, determined to face the worst in myself.

"A perfect husband – well now, that's something I never heard of until this day!" She laughed aloud. "Wasn't she the lucky woman?"

"Not so lucky. You see she didn't love him. Or at least not enough. She thought she loved him until she met someone else and then she knew that she had really all those years been responding to his love. She had loved him because he loved her, not for himself, you see."

"Well, it's a tall order now if people are to go about asking to be loved for themselves. What's wrong with loving a man because he loves you, I'd like to know? Isn't it the ordinary, natural thing to feel?"

"This woman didn't think so. She thought love should be spontaneous and passionate. She wanted to be overwhelmed. Struck by divine flame."

"And wasn't she the foolish woman? What happened to her at the end of it all?"

"She stayed with him for as long as it was possible. And

then, when she could no longer conceal her love for someone else, she left him."

"And what happened him?"

"He took to drink for a while. He grew violent and resentful."

"God love him. And did the woman stay with her lover?"

"Yes."

"And the children?"

"She took them with her."

"Thank God for small mercies, I suppose. And tell me, were they happy?"

"Who?"

"Any of them?"

"Happy enough. They all did their best to make it work for the good of the children. Even her lover tried to do the best for the children. But it was hard for everyone just the same."

"Well, I don't know why she bothered if it made no one happy. She seems to me a foolish woman. I'd have no patience with that carry-on at all."

"Do you think she should be punished?"

"She should be left to her own conscience. That would be punishment enough for her."

"It is Máire Mac, it is."

We had reached the crossroads. The sun shone on the windows of the shop, throwing bright shafts across the pools on the wet tarmac.

We said good-bye and parted. I walked on alone, the rain striking my face at every step, like a shower of needles.

Chapter Twenty-Four

October, Dublin.

"So many lesbians," May said suddenly, shifting in her sleep and looking up at Nina for one instant with clear-seeing eyes. Every half hour or so she woke and managed to pronounce a phrase or two, disjointed, but not incoherent.

"So many lovely women," she said, "spoiling you." Was there a smile on her faintly blue lips as she closed her eyes and returned to the safety of sleep? The nurse bustled about with a sudden rush of activity to conceal her embarrassment. "They often begin to ramble at this stage," she assured Nina firmly, avoiding her eye. "It's nothing at all to worry about."

"Is that so?" Nina replied with an air of deferring to professional knowledge. But May, she knew, wasn't rambling. She meant exactly what she said. It wasn't said in sorrow or anger. There might even be covert pleasure in her tone. From her vantage point in Nina's life she had good reason to think that there were, every day, more women falling in love with one another, leaving their lovers and husbands.

On familiar terms with so many of Nina's acquaintanceship, she had witnessed more than once the fever-like way these attractions took hold, claiming one life

309

after another, one marriage after another. Yes, May knew all about it, but she couldn't be seen to approve. She was a supporter of marriage, though unmarried herself, and could not be seen to encourage social disorder or home-breaking. "It's the children I worry about," she said when the subject of marital problems was raised. But underneath her sceptical exterior she was a romantic and wherever she saw passion she felt indulgent towards it. The only consistent advice she had given Nina over the years was, "When in doubt follow your heart." That and a few maxims from the racing world: "Quit while you're ahead." And, "Never hedge your bets." She had not always been so tolerant of Nina's life, of course, but she had many years to adapt to its vagaries. Nina liked to tell people that she had been born a lesbian. "With your history!" Elinor protested when she first heard this line – knowing too much of Nina's sexual past. "Ah, but in my heart," Nina answered. "In my heart, Elinor."

The aunts must have been able to see into her heart all those years ago, Nina thought, because they seemed to have known before she told them, though she had tried to keep it from them. And from herself. She had wasted a lot of energy in adolescence fighting her attraction to women. She submerged herself in the theatrics of heterosexuality, the ancient courtship rituals. Practice would make perfect, she believed. (Kept at long enough it might become her nature.) Not that she had to make an effort to enjoy the company of young men. She was at ease with them because she was never in love or deeply engaged. They were her companions and friends, her confidants. They entertained and flattered her. And, because she was so open and relaxed, they found her intensely desirable. Not one of them caught her acting in those years. Not one of them saw the mask slip or guessed for one moment that her sexual identity was anything but the absolute hermetically sealed construction they wanted it to be. But from the first time she kissed boys she thought of girls. In time, this pattern made her very artful in the business because she experienced it as if she were two sexes at once – the girl being kissed, and the boy kissing her. Her first experience of love was when she fell in love with an older girl at school. Their mutual enchantment lasted for almost two years until they decided together, very solemnly, that at fifteen and thirteen they were too young to commit themselves, and they went their separate ways.

She left home first when she was seventeen. Suspecting she was pregnant (after a brief adventure with a boyfriend) and terrified of her family history repeating itself, she took the boat for England. She lived rough on the streets for a few weeks and then in squats. Three months later she had a miscarriage and promised herself that this divine escape would be a lesson she would not have to learn twice. Soon after this, while working as a waitress, she fell in with a Bohemian, artistic circle who persuaded her to go to art college. During her second term there she started a love affair with one of her female teachers and after a few months she went to live with her and stayed until she graduated.

When she returned from England at twenty-three she decided if she was to make her home in Ireland she would have to be honest with her aunts.

She told Molly first. This was a long-established pattern. Molly was soft-spoken and gentle and whenever Nina had anything difficult to say she told Molly first and left it to her to pick the best moment to tell May. When she told her Molly looked grave at first. She said she was afraid Nina was making life very hard for herself. She asked if anything they could have done would have made a difference? And Nina said no, nothing at all. Then she asked Nina if she was happy about it herself and Nina said yes, radiantly. Molly said, "Well that's the important thing, isn't it?" And so the conversation was closed. They had never gone in for long exchanges about personal matters. Molly's understanding depended more on how something was said and the emotional reality she picked up, than any words used.

Talking about it with May was a different story. She made it plain that she was worried. She considered that Nina was going out of her way to be contrary because she was driven by a spirit of rebellion. She said Nina didn't know how hard life could be. "After all," she had said, "it's not as if you were ever treated badly by men – on the contrary, they've always spoilt you." Nina agreed, it had nothing to do with men. Simply that she liked women better. May advised very seriously that she must be prepared to make some compromise to convention. She said that if she gave way on the small things the world would leave her alone, but if she insisted on making a public issue of it they would be merciless. But once having made this forceful view clear, she didn't criticise her. She accepted Nina's life because she loved her and because she saw it made her happy. And to the outside world, she was fiercely defensive of her.

So, in their reserved, formal way, the two elderly ladies supported her. So long as she was happy and didn't shout it from the rooftops (which she very nearly did), they would not object. They welcomed her friends to the house as they had always done and came to love them. They admired, too, the intensity and freedom they saw between these women and even admitted to envy of it, as something very different from what they had known in their dealings with men.

What would May think of her present crisis if she knew of it, Nina wondered? Was it possible that she did? That she guessed at it in the intuitive way she had? She tried to recall their conversation earlier that evening. What had she asked about Katherine? Hadn't she suggested that Nina go to stay with her – that she needed the rest? What was that a euphemism for? But it was hard to imagine that, if she knew, she would encourage any course of action that might endanger Nina's relationship with Elinor. Certainly she had been charmed by Katherine when they met – the direct American manners, her warmth. But Elinor held an impregnable place in her heart. Elinor, who had rescued Nina, as May considered, from a rackety, bohemian life and given her order and stability.

Nina acknowledged to herself that this was largely true. The life she had lived in London and Europe in the gay subculture of the late seventies, before feminism had made lesbianism the semi-respectable alternative life it had now become, was a totally different world from the one she inhabited these days. It might have existed in the last century, so remote was it from contemporary values. For Nina they were years of passion and reckless adventure, lived out in an atmosphere of repression and secrecy and exhilaration. A small, defiant outpost of self-discovery and sexual exploration, proudly flouting convention and the bourgeois morality of her upbringing.

There was a special camaraderie she had loved in the gay world of those days. Because the numbers were limited, no one could afford to confine themselves to the narrow boundaries of a particular social circle as straight people did. In the bars and clubs all classes and age groups mixed together – middle-class housewives, factory girls, students, prostitutes, civil servants and businesswomen. It was a world more fluid and unstable than anything newcomers such as Katherine could imagine.

Elinor, too, had come out in a more recent, enlightened age and took its freedoms for granted. She had a sense of security and self-confidence impossible for women who had grown up in the earlier atmosphere. Her social poise and air of stability attracted Nina from the first. And as the years went by the fact that she had a daughter and lived what anyone (even Aunt May) would consider a regular life, held a special perverse appeal for Nina who had always lived on the outer fringe.

Within weeks of meeting they became lovers. It was a romance to rival all romances that went before it. They might well have invented rapture and sexual passion. In those long, luscious afternoons in the city, the dusty orange air, the gardens basking in late afternoon sun, they lay on in bed until afternoon, (while Lizzie was staying with her father) wine and cheese on a tray beside them so that there was no need to get up until they dressed for the evening, made something to eat and sauntered down to the pub for a couple of drinks before a meeting. They spent a large part of their courtship at public meetings, held in small, smoke-filled rooms above centre city pubs, or in large, draughty public halls, meetings where a few hundred women gathered together in solidarity, the fate of the world hanging on their every word. It was a time of impassioned debate and dizzy rhetoric. Made all the more intense by the constant presence of a faithful entourage of opponents; the opposite camp in little bands about the room, provoking and delighting with their manic tirades, their fevered denunciations of sex and its attendant evils. Reflected in their eyes, Nina and all her friends saw an image they gloried in and vaunted – wild, dangerous women with courage beyond sense, taking the world on, challenging the core of its assumptions and complacencies, breaking it apart to make space for themselves at last.

Only a few months after their love affair began, Elinor asked Nina to come and live with her. Nina made a show of hesitation for form's sake, but she knew, the moment it was proposed, that she would; she would say yes. In June of that year, in a summer of balmy days and long, brilliant nights, she moved into the orderly, graceful house in the southside suburbs.

Soon after this she got a job teaching at the College of Art and, for the first time since childhood, she found herself living a stable, chosen life. She had a regular income. A regular lover. A child to raise. Her friends could hardly believe the transformation.

And Aunt May could not conceal her pleasure.

So, she knew only too well how reluctantly May would accept her break-up with Elinor. Not to mention her concern for Lizzie. She could never approve of Nina jeopardising her life in any way. She wondered if there had been some undertone of anxiety in May's conversation earlier on? Hadn't she seemed particularly attentive to Lizzie? Wasn't she going out of her way to entertain her and soothe her with all the old family history, letting her sift through the photographs, endlessly patient in the retelling of Nina's story? She tried to recall the exact course of the conversation, but she couldn't. As soon as her thoughts returned to May, her mind became rigid with anxiety. She turned away from her, seeking relief, only to be confronted with the sight of the other patients around her; old women, lying mute and fearful, unnaturally still. She wished with all her heart she could go home to her own house and leave behind her this decay and depression. But she must stay and see it out. She must wait patiently for whatever was to come.

Chapter Twenty-Five

September, Clare.

Visiting the church has made a bad impression on me. The pain and anger have eased a little. But they've been replaced by a horrible sense of my own guilt. Máire Mac's reaction didn't help, needless to say. And of course she saw through my ridiculous pretence of talking about a friend. Though she didn't let on. Much too tactful to embarrass me.

I found myself just now trying to remember what we were taught were the necessary conditions for a good confession. A thorough examination of conscience. Knowledge of all one's sins. Sincere sorrow for having offended God. And last – a firm purpose of amendment. "I firmly resolve never more to offend Thee and to amend my ways." Well, that counts me out. Even now, if you were to walk through the door, could I promise to amend my ways? Would I have the strength to resist you?

I ask myself how I am to live without you? It's such a simple-sounding question. Good friends, activity, new places, work. One more frightening than the next. They said the last time – when you left me before – other people, well-wishers – they said I must rebuild my life, assert my independence. She is not doing you any good, they said, you must face the inevitable. This is what they advised, and will again. I can hear them already. "Look after yourself. Get on with your own rich life." Rich? This rotten assemblage – bits and pieces of consciousness I am dragging behind me like a rotten tail – this debris of what was once your life and mine.

What is left to me after you? Where do I go from here? If I am to lose you, what happens to me? Do I look for another woman? What woman could I find interesting after you? How would I begin to look? I've no idea how to go about it. Without you as my guide and partner is there any possibility of my being able to negotiate this strange and disorienting world? Everything with you happened by accident. We drifted from friendship into love. I've no experience of courting women. I don't know if I want to. Maybe my love for you was just a fluke, a passing phase, an aberration in an otherwise normal heterosexual life? But men? I think you have ruined my chances with men. How could I be satisfied with any man after you? And yet it would be easier in so many ways. Men are so much less complex. More consistent and infinitely less observant. The most I suffered with them was frustration and mild boredom. You saw the loss of autonomy, the sacrifice women paid for that security; the loss of self, the pretence of fragility, the sexual passivity.

I remember now all the things you said about them that once sounded cynical. Only a year since I last slept with a man and already it seems that everything you said is no more than the simple truth. Blunt, unapologetic, sceptical, but honest. What thousands of heterosexual women might say if they were to be equally candid – what they do say on a night out, after a few drinks. Life with men was so easy, so relaxing, so long as you were physically available. It was so easy to find a decent man and let him take off your clothes.

To flatter him. To pretend you know nothing of your own need and must wait wide-eyed for him to reveal you to yourself, organ by organ. How easy to call him clever. To say you needed him. To say that never before . . . all the small, unimportant lies to make him happy, to make him capable of doing his job. The solemn difficult work of being a man. Sweet flattery, so that he may be able to get it up and keep it up. Give courage and confidence to his fragile, uncertain organ. Unreliable at the best of times. Always likely to let him down at the worst moment. So much female submission and self-effacement necessary for this – to provide the essential stimulus required. A small price to pay to keep him stiff and masterful. Hard and confident. His closed face, his steel-like flesh. A woman must be prepared to sacrifice something to achieve and maintain this artifice, this tower of ivory, this great illusion, this fragile glory of masculinity.

How could I go back? Knowing all this? How could I close my eyes to all the compromise?

Maybe I'd be better off alone. Without man or woman. Is it better to end relationships while they still have the glow of perfection? You said so once – you said we should break up now while we were still in love with one another. Before there can be any bitterness or bad memories.

I've been thinking about Malachy again and the pain I've caused him.

Understanding it now as I never did before. You have done that much for him. You who never intended him any good or harm. You whose name he would not speak. But then his jealousy of you was fuelled by his unresolved anger for things that had happened years before I laid eyes on you. For all his extremes he couldn't hold you responsible for the unhappiness that had its roots in the early years of our marriage. Does love inevitably fade and grow stale? Is it possible that if I lived with you I might eventually tire of you as I tired of Malachy? Are you right about this? You're not exactly the perfect candidate for long relationships, although you've managed to keep things going all these years with Elinor. At what price? Would I want you at the cost that Elinor pays – the pain of waiting for you to fall in love with another woman? Would I want her life? As for me? Am I capable of sustaining interest in a lover for any length of time? I didn't do so well. And why did I grow so easily irritated with Malachy? Was it his fault or mine or the nature of relationships between men and women?

When I told you about his behaviour the night I left him, you were furious and disdainful. You couldn't understand how I could forgive him. How I could speak to him again, much less like him. But then you didn't know what was loveable in him. You didn't understand the bond that raising children together brings. Yet how can I write that – even now I forget the importance of Lizzie to you.

Can I imagine experiencing the feelings of revulsion with you I had at times for Malachy? I can't bear the notion that all affection is modified by time. Was there ever a time I felt irritated or bored by you? Angry and jealous – yes. But exasperation, physical dislike?

I remember once, after an argument, we drove home in the car, neither of us speaking, and you began to whistle, through your teeth in this awful tuneless way. And it reminded me of Malachy. I thought to myself how extraordinary that you should have the same annoying habit. But my irritation lasted about three minutes because suddenly when we stopped at a red light you leaned over and kissed me on the mouth.

On another occasion, we were to go away for the weekend and you phoned me on Friday night and said you had the flu, and could we cancel it. I said, well, we can just stay in bed for three days. And I persuaded you to come. But all the way to Cork you were coughing and sneezing and complaining of fever and I felt unexpectedly impatient, as if you were putting it on or overdoing it. When we got there you wanted to go straight to sleep. I lay in the darkness beside you, mad with lust, wanting to wake you from sleep and make love to you. Only just able to stop myself. And for the first time I thought I'd some idea how men felt – something I'd never understood before – this impatience, this greedy, almost aggressive desire. I was ashamed of myself and furious with you.

But the next morning you woke up smiling and we had three of our best days ever.

Can I magnify these fleeting examples to imagine long spells of antipathy? No, even ten years from now I don't think I could be annoyed with you for more than a few hours.

Whereas with Malachy, almost from the start, I had these strange protracted periods of resistance to him. I'd fluctuate from passion to some kind of revulsion. Wanting to regain my independence. Feeling smothered by him.

The year I was pregnant with Luke was the worst time ever between us. Twelve years ago now. We'd left Boston to live on a farm in Maine. Malachy had applied for a year's sabbatical to work on his book and we rented an old run-down farmhouse and tried to live the simple life. Almost from the start I began to feel this near frenzied loathing for him. It seemed to descend out of the blue with no warning symptoms. I could hardly bear him to come near me. I struggled against it. I tried to conceal it from him, but the effort made me worse. I was consumed by irritation. What caused it? Was it his fault or mine? Was it some physical effect of pregnancy? Or was it because I had begun for the first time to dread captivity with him? The servitude to female domestic life that I saw looming ever closer with the birth of this first child. Locked up in that place in a terrible winter, it was easy to say I was suffering from what they call in those remote northern parts "cabin fever." But I saw it as marriage fever. I saw myself gradually being transformed, against my will, from an individual, an independent being, a friend, a companion, a worker, into something totally impersonal; an institution, a function. I was becoming a wife and mother. A married woman. Mrs Malachy Newman. In this heightened state of tension and dread I took out my fears on Malachy.

In the evenings, sitting together by the fire, every gesture he made got on my nerves. He'd pick up his black briar pipe and beat its bowl down against the palm of his hand. Then start the whole procedure of filling it and lighting it. I couldn't bear to watch him sucking at it. Like a clumsy child at the breast. Everything he said and did annoyed me in this exaggerated, overstrained way. The sound of his voice, the odd, choking noise he made at the start of each sentence as if the air was blocked in his windpipe. His hands; the lean, beautifully shaped brown hands that I loved, when he began to use them to beat out a rhythm on the wooden armrest of his chair, I felt I'd scream with irritation. I'd kneel at the hearth to fix the fire and poke nervously at the coals, knocking out the dead ash. And then I'd hear his fingers start up their percussion on the chair again, in the same perfectly controlled rhythm. I'd jump up and almost run from the room.

Again and again that year I asked myself how it could

have come to this? How was it possible? I had loved him when we married. I'd loved his humour and his generosity, the strength of his body, the power of his desire for me. His flattery, his need. Making me a woman, making me *the* woman, the only woman. Now all this set my teeth on edge. Everything I loved was turned to ashes. The image reversed. Desire had changed to revulsion. Need to resentment. I loathed myself. And I hated him for changing from the person I'd loved. I felt cheated. Why had he forgotten how to please me? How had he become transformed into this? A pathetic creature, shuffling about, digging his potatoes and his cabbages. Whistling through his teeth. Sitting for hours at night by the fire, reading his manuals on organic farming. And nothing to show for it but a dismal row of turnip and cabbage.

I couldn't bear to watch him in the daytime, pottering about the garden. That was what he had become. A potterer. Half fixing half-broken bits and pieces. Saving up odds and ends that might come in useful. He felt himself the complete pioneer, a true man of the soil, when he went down with his wheelbarrow and pushed it home filled with seaweed. Beaming with self-satisfaction. Rushing in to tell me. Oh, what great things he would do with all this fertiliser. Barrowfuls of it. All free! Natural. There for the taking. Oh, the vegetables we'd have – the marrows and turnips, the lettuce in summer. We'd never need to go near the grocers again. What would we do all day, I asked, without even the shops to visit?

How often did he come up behind me, put his arms round my waist, squeezing my breasts exploratively as he would test a fruit, for ripeness? Sizing me up. Will she or won't she? How soon? For how long? I'd feel his lips draw back from his teeth, his moist breath warming my neck. I'd stand motionless and silent, so he thought he was in with a chance. I'd allow myself to be turned slowly to face him. His mouth would descend on me, quickly, too quickly to deny it. A hot, wet mouth. Why were his lips always wet now as though he could no longer control the flow of his saliva? I was reminded of a dog. A dog hungry for its dinner, the lolling tongue, the beseeching eyes, a dog deprived beyond its normal dinner hour. At night I'd lie stiff and cold on my side of the bed refusing to touch him. After a few minutes, hearing his strained, clumsy breathing in the darkness beside me, feeling his resentment, my nerve would snap and I'd think – right let's get it over with. And I'd turn to him and caress him, feeling like a prostitute, using skill to get it over with more quickly. But why were men so easily manipulated? So easily aroused? So falsely reassured? How was it they could never tell the difference between passion and calculation? Or was it only that they didn't care? How could he have let himself be taken over by this creature? How could he have abandoned me to this? I wanted to kick him. I wanted to bang him over the head and scream at him. Do something. Make me love you. Make me love you as I used to!

I went over the past, ceaselessly. Of how he used to be. Of what we had felt for each other. Trying to see in our past together some warning sign of what was to come. Would he have turned into this whatever I'd done? Was it what happened to any couple if they lived together long enough? Was it inevitable? Or was it all a reaction? The horrible residue of my betrayal. Had I broken him with my coldness, my criticism? Was it possible for one human being to break another? Had I so much power? Was he so weak? Or was he punishing me? Was all this a game – a terrible strategic battle fought out in silence between us? He revenging himself, making himself pitiable because I'd failed to love him. Daring me to complain of the whinging, grasping creature he had made of himself?

When I was pregnant he was ludicrously proud. Patting my belly, gaping at me as though I were a two-headed cabbage. A further proof of nature's bounty. He loved it. Free. Natural. Fertility all about him. Sprouting and bursting. And he scurrying about planting his seeds. Busying himself in the dark of the soil, in the dark of my belly to sprout, to grow triumphantly, and come forth at last, returned to him who had planted, who had believed and trusted. Walking about the house imprisoned by sleet and hail and muck that rose to the knees. The broken-down car that he fixed every week, that could not be trusted to get as far as the town and back. Imprisoned, a pacing, angry tiger behind bars, my belly growing fat and heavy. The clumsy walk, splay-footed as a duck. The ache in my back, the nausea, the acid bile beneath my heart when he ticked off the weeks on the calendar and begged me to practice breathing exercises. I felt that I'd go in an ambulance to hospital and demand complete anaesthesia from beginning to end if it would deprive him of this empty, parasitic pride in his own fertility. What had he to do with it, for God's sake? One ejaculation, one miserable teaspoon of sperm was all he had to manage to give himself licence to go about crowing like a farmyard cock!

Yes, it was as bad as that.

When I confided my feelings to Ma she laughed aloud and said: "If I'd left your father every time I felt like that – none of you would have come into this world!" Then, she put her hand on mine and said: "Don't worry – it's just how marriage is. It will all be different when the baby is born." The maddening thing is she was right, as usual. The cloud of loathing and irritation lifted the moment I saw Malachy holding Luke in his arms. It was love at first sight between the two of them. And his love for our child transferred itself to me. I loved him for the father he became, and very soon afterwards I loved him again for himself. As though he knew he had discovered the key to my heart and approval he made himself faultless in his treatment of the boys. The qualities that make him so good and patient with them are the things I liked most in him. His warm heart, his generosity.

After that we had many bad times, but we always came through them. After all he had his own lapses. Yes, two or three brief encounters (I think) that he told me of and exaggerated in the telling so that he might be seen to exaggerate and so encourage me to think them insignificant, which I agreed to think. He could never accept defeat in his feelings for me. And he had such amazing powers of recovery – the ability to rise, Lazarus-like, from the depths of depression and become again charming, exuberant, hopeful. How many times did he woo me back? I believed, until I met you, that he always would.

Will he be glad to know what I'm suffering now? Would it be some small consolation? Or would it make it worse to know that it was all for nothing? That the wheel we are all bound to, turns full circle, every time. Turning joy into pain.

This is my reward, is it? My karma? Will I ever tell him that I came here to wait for you? That we'd planned to start over again? But he's hurt enough as it is. No reason to reawaken his jealousy and suspicion just when he's begun to relax a little and be co-operative again about the boys. He need never know anything about this. There's no one to tell him if I don't.

Anyhow, there's no point in rehashing our differences. All that happened between us is unalterable now. Nothing remains of what we were but our bond as parents – shared memories and a tentative movement towards friendship.

Chapter Twenty-Six

October, Dublin.

She sat looking at the grotesque tubes battened onto May's chest as if they were sucking blood from her and heard, without wanting to, the sinister beep-beep of her heartbeat translated through the sound system of a machine. And she found herself wishing that May would die.

She wanted something to be over, to be resolved. Death made things simple. Pure. After so much waiting, it would be good to have one thing certain and unalterable. Beyond her responsibility or power of decision. She had to decide tonight. And it had to be final.

She was exhausted. Deathly cold. Though it was like a furnace in the ward, she had been shivering all night. She must do something. Take some action. She began rooting in her pocket for money. She should phone Elinor and tell her about May. But how could she? It was three in the morning. It would seem as if she were looking for sympathy. She couldn't risk that.

She felt sick at the thought of something so momentous happening to May and Elinor being in total ignorance of it. In seven years nothing of importance had happened to her that she hadn't immediately shared with Elinor. Maybe in the morning she could call, first thing.

But what if May died before that and she hadn't told Elinor?

Just then May stirred and murmured something from sleep. Nina reached out her hand to touch her cheek. It was cold and very dry. She was instantly struck by remorse like a blow in the chest. How could she have wished her dead only a moment ago? How could she let herself even think such a thing? Even for an instant? May whom she adored. May who had done everything for her. The only true family she had known. She was ashamed of herself. She wanted her alive and well. Happy. But, if she were to die, she couldn't bear to have it dragged out in public, in pain and loss of dignity.

"Nina, is it you?" May spoke suddenly, without opening her eyes, perfectly clearly.

"Yes. I'm here."

"I want you to know something." May turned her head slightly on the high pillow and then, as if by an effort of will, she opened her eyes. She seemed to be looking past Nina at the wall behind her or maybe the door. Was she watching for someone?

"What is it?" Nina stretched out her hand again and lightly touched the old woman's shoulder.

"I want you to know that your father was a good man."

"I do."

"I don't want you to blame him."

"I know May. I don't blame him," she said in a low, soothing voice.

May heaved a great sigh and her eyes closed. She lay silent.

Nina was frightened. The ghastly blue tinge to May's skin seemed to have deepened.

"Are you in pain? Will I call the nurse?"

The old woman's eyes opened again and this time she looked straight into Nina's anxious gaze.

"It's hard to kill a bad thing. Don't worry about me."

"I don't think I should let you talk. Are you strong enough?"

"Don't worry about me," May said again. She reached her hand out from under the covers and took hold of Nina's.

"I want to tell you this. Just listen." Her voice was very low and soft, but she spoke each word with perfect clarity. The confusion of the earlier hours had lifted completely. She seemed almost her ordinary self.

"It was all an accident, you see."

"What was?"

"He adored your mother."

"Why did he leave her then?" Nina said acidly and regretted it. Why couldn't she be patient, even now?

"She didn't want to marry him," May said softly.

They both fell silent. Nina studied the monitor's screen, watching the line of May's heartbeat anxiously, trying to judge whether it was safe for her to continue talking. But the rhythm seemed exactly as before, steady and strong.

"It wasn't your father's fault, that's the important thing," May spoke again, her voice seeming to gain power.

"Did you know him well?" Nina asked.

"Yes, I did."

There was another short silence before Nina said hesitantly, as though it was a question that was in some way improper of her to pose.

"Did you like my father?"

"Everyone liked your father," May answered, and her pale, blue lips smiled faintly for the first time. "You couldn't help but like him. He was handsome and great fun and kind." She paused again. "But he tried to be kind to too many people. That was his trouble. He tried to please everyone."

"Why did my mother not want to marry him then?"

"Your mother told me just before she died that she knew she had TB," May answered very softly, looking away towards

329

the high window behind Nina's shoulder, "and so she felt she had to turn him down."

"Did he know she was sick?"

"No, she never told him."

"It sounds a very sad story," Nina said and she held the old woman's hand more tightly in her own.

"Well, it was like a lot of stories of the time. You remember the words of the song: 'I met the man I'd marry and the man who'd marry me. But they weren't the same.'"

"You said that already tonight," suddenly alert to some other undertone in May's story. "Is that what my mother felt?" she asked her.

"No," May answered quietly and she drew her hand back gently from Nina's clasp. "It was what I felt."

"What do you mean?"

"I mean that I would have married him if he'd asked me, but he loved your mother, as well."

"As well?"

"Yes."

"Why did you never tell me any of this before?" Nina looked at her aunt trying to keep the sudden hurt she felt from her voice.

"I never told your father either," May answered and paused before adding, "but he knew just the same."

"And did he really care for you?"

"Yes."

"So?"

"As long as your mother was alive he thought it wouldn't be right."

"And after my mother's death? Why didn't he then?"

"He did, he followed me to New York. He asked me to marry him, but too much had happened. After that he disappeared."

"I can't understand why you haven't told me this before?" Nina said again.

"I did try to tell you, child. More than once."

"When exactly?"

"I tried to tell you some of it no later than this very evening. But I don't think you were in the mood to hear. You were very preoccupied."

Nina was conscience stricken.

"I'm sorry," she said. "I really am. I've had such a lot on my mind. I wouldn't have noticed what anyone said tonight."

"I know, child. That's why I was trying to tell you."

Nina reached out and touched her aunt's hair, brushing the damp, grey locks gently back from her forehead. "It's such a sad story, May."

"Yes, it is – a tragedy of errors." She smiled gently and looked into Nina's anguished eyes. "You see, neither of us knew about you until it was too late. But it had a happy ending after all."

"What?" Nina asked in surprise.

"You, of course," May said.

"What do you mean?"

"I mean that I found you." Her eyes closed. Nina felt the grip loosen on her wrist. She looked at once towards the monitor, staring at the movement of the heart line. For a terrified moment she thought May had stopped breathing. But the line was still calm and regular. And just then she heard another soft exhalation, a long slow sigh. "I've always said you were the daughter I might have had."

She closed her eyes.

"I'd like to sleep now for a bit."

"Yes, do," Nina urged.

May looked at her again for a moment. "But don't forget what I said."

331

"I won't."

"I mean don't forget what I said about your father. Don't make his mistake, Nina. That's what I want to say to you. Don't try to please everyone." Her eyes closed.

"Don't talk anymore." Nina drew the covers over May's shoulders. "Sleep now," she said.

"Yes."

Nina bent down and put her lips to May's cold forehead.

"I love you," she whispered.

"Yes."

Chapter Twenty-Seven

September, Clare.

Not a breath of wind now, no sound, no rain. The house seems like a sepulchre awaiting its last occupant. I would have said deserted too and then I remembered my own presence. After all, how can a place be called deserted when one is standing in it? Here I am living and breathing, drawing into my lungs this stale air and expelling it a little more soiled each minute. My body that fills the place with its own odours that seep from every pore and orifice, every cell in my body playing its part in ceaseless exchange and transformation of energies. The labour of existence, such huffing and puffing necessary just to keep the wheels in motion.

Am I imagining all this since I heard Michael's story? Now that I know the suffering that was lived out between these walls.

I went upstairs to the back bedroom and stood for a long while gazing out the window. I don't know how much time passed before I made out the dark shape of a man standing in the same spot by the hedge of fuchsia, staring up towards the window where I stood. I watched him for a while and, as I did so, my eyes began to see more clearly. I could see the way his head tilted to one side, his arms clamped against his body. How forlorn and pitiable he seemed. Now that I knew his terrible story I no longer found anything irritating in him. I felt ashamed of my earlier impatience with him. They should have told me long ago. How desolate he looked standing alone in the softly falling rain. Waiting for what? A shadow at a window? Why did I think he reminded me of Malachy? Is it not myself he resembles more nearly, if I were to be really truthful? Maintaining day after day this hopeless vigil. Waiting to catch sight of a phantom at a darkened window? His habit of lining the wall by the shed with bits of driftwood and stones, the old cans and other debris he hauls up from the beach, I understood now. He has made a shrine at which he lays offerings to placate the ghosts of the dead. Is that any more quixotic than my own behaviour? Any more futile than my gifts to you – the flowers, the letters? This journal?

I see Michael still staring silently at the window. I stand looking down at him. The hours pass.

Yes, it isn't Malachy he resembles, but myself. Perhaps I recognised some distorted image of myself in his passivity, his futile waiting about for something or someone. Whether or not that was the case, I know I feel no more sensible tonight, no less forlorn than Michael out there hovering about the windswept hedges in the rain.

What am I going to do? I am still avoiding this question – the only question in my heart since I spoke to you on the phone. Is there any point in waiting for the next one? When I know almost certainly that you'll say you don't want to come up? What will I gain by talking to you? Even if you tell me that you're coming on the next train, won't it only postpone the evil hour? Would it be better to get it over with? To choose the timing myself?

If I made a decision I could write to you explaining it. I could walk to the post office and give it to Máire Mac. You might have it by tomorrow evening.

I climbed upstairs to the loft and read over again the early pages of this notebook, lying on the floor under the window where the sun falls in a pool every evening, the cat sitting beside me, stretched out in its warmth.

I understand now only too well what Elinor suffered. I understand her at last. Now that I have been deceived and made to suffer as she was – not knowing ever whether an act of trust was normal good faith or blind folly – I understand at last completely what she must have suffered. Loving you as she does all this time, waiting and hoping. Expecting every day to hear the worst.

You were so bound up with one another, it seemed at times impossible for you to think separate thoughts, or feel separate emotions. It was like being in love with an identical twin. When you broke up with me in July and went back to Elinor I couldn't persuade myself that you were motivated by guilt. No, it wasn't that. Simply that you missed her too much to live without her. You missed your shared life, your life with Lizzie. You missed Elinor's knowledge of you, her absolute loyalty. You missed the house. Reading it again I see everything you've written differently. I see the suffering you have been through. The pain I have caused Elinor. I can't pretend I didn't know before what she went through, but I turned my eyes from it.

I remember the day the full truth was forced on her, when she realised that her tolerance and good faith had been exploited. I remember the look in her eyes as she finally understood the nature and extent of your deception. I watched her at that moment and I thought to myself, she is never going to recover. It sounds exaggerated, but that's what I thought. Something essential had been broken in her. Something that would never heal: her belief in people who live by the truth, her belief in integrity.

Oh she did recover, finally, as everyone does. She got over it as we say. Time papered over the cracks. But she did not heal. If by that we mean the whole person growing strong and complete again, then I think you can't deny that she did not heal.

And Lizzie, who I have not allowed myself to consider until now? I understand what you say about Lizzie. I couldn't wish you to hurt her or to hurt yourself by wounding her. Perhaps in the past it seemed I underestimated the importance of the bond between you, but I was conscious of it from the outset. It was one of the things I liked best about you. Your way of life attracted me almost as much as you did. I don't know even now if it's possible to distinguish them. I loved your love of Elinor and Elizabeth. I love your passion and your constancy. I admired the way you had constructed an alternative world and made it work. I like all your friends. I love the sense of community and common purpose between you. My life by comparison – the life of a comfortable, bourgeois individualist (yes, that is what I have been) – even if liberal and Bohemian in some respects – seems narrow, complacent and self-centred by comparison. Considering this, why does it seem inevitable that all I most admire in you is threatened by your love for me? If you were to leave Elinor and Lizzie what would be left of you? Would I be able to live with your guilt? Your nostalgia?

Should I go to the phone tonight and tell you all this? Would you listen? Would you argue with me?

I'm sitting on the top step of the stairs looking out the back window across the fields and towards the mountains. Mount Moran with its strange and beautiful outline, like a woman lying on her side, her hands crossed over her breast. The sun is sinking just below it, bathing it in the fierce orange light so that it resembles a great warrior queen, her head swathed in fiery red hair. The rain is falling softly. The wind is blowing from the east. From the farm I hear the bellowing of cattle at the gate. A terrible pain-filled bawling. I asked Máire Mac about it and she told me they were cows who'd had their calves taken from them.

"The unfortunate creatures," she said, "I couldn't do it myself – it's men's work." Hearing her, I thought, this is how we collude in the brutalisation of men, asking them to carry out actions we can't face and yet are happy enough to profit from.

I can't bear the sound. The mothers calling out and the calves answering. Each calf knowing its mother call and each cow knowing its calf. I suppose if there were fifty children penned up in a yard calling, I would know Ben and Luke's voices from all the rest.

Which brings me back to my feelings for them, my responsibilities. All the unanswered questions. Have I really faced what it would mean to them if I began an open relationship with a woman? If I were to love you, I couldn't ask you to be closeted, to conceal our relationship from them. I couldn't ask you to live as if you were ashamed of the very thing you've been most proud of. You and Elinor were always direct about your way of life and Lizzie learned from you to take pride in it. But then she grew up with it, whereas Ben and Luke would be encountering it all for the first time, with no precedent, no example.

But, despite everything, I did sincerely believe it would work out. I still believe it. They like you so much. And it works with so many other lesbian mothers that I've met. Why should I be the exception? Only because, as you say, I'm not used to having to stand against the tide? It's true that I've had an easier life than you. I've been able to take love for granted, its privacy and legitimacy. I've never felt an outsider until I fell in love with you. I've been free to do the things I wanted in life. I've been secure and content. I've never had to justify myself before or expose myself to obloquy. I suppose this did give me the self-confidence to be blindly sure of my love for you and sanguine about the future. I do feel that things work out for the best, if we are honest and true to our deepest natures. I don't believe in sacrifice or unnecessary suffering. I think people come to terms with what happens and learn to extract what they need. I think change is good, even when it's painful. I believe we can grow beyond the damage of trauma.

Mary Dorcey

I'm American after all, I suppose.

The cat is playing on the stairs. She's found a pine cone behind the sofa. She catches it between her teeth, shakes it like a mouse from side to side, spits it out, catches it again with one paw, flips it perfectly into the air and, leaping up with the grace of a ballerina, claps her two paws together and traps it in mid-air. What am I to do with her when I leave? Who will look after her? But I can't decide what to do with my own life, much less the cat's.

Supposing I say to myself that it's over. Let me try the sound of that. Practice it. Let me hear myself say the words out loud: It's over and done with. I've cleaned out the house and packed my bags. It's finished. Final. The waiting, the longing, the hope, the terror, the unbearable pain of disappointment. All over with. I am done with anger and jealousy.

I'm not going to wait, Nina. I am not going to hang about for a telephone call. Why should I? It's pathetic. And pointless. I'll leave tomorrow. Just to imagine a course of action makes me feel stronger. Isn't any decision better than none? Better to write to you and explain it on paper. How does this sound? Would you accept it? When I reach Dublin I could deliver it in person. Drive to your house, walk up the path, drop it into the letterbox, leave immediately. Or I could ring the bell and hope that you answer. Do I want to see you one more time? Even if it's only to say goodbye? Can I survive without seeing you?

If I decide to go home, to relinquish you of my own free will, what a marvellous ease to my conscience! No reason for guilt anymore! I can scarcely imagine that extraordinary state. A respectable citizen again – a good mother, a normal human being – all with one stroke of the pen!

If it please the court: I am going back to my children, to look after them, to make a home for them. I renounce my lover. I give her back to her family, to her partner, to her

338

child. I recognise her duties and obligations. For the greater good of society, for the greatest good of the greatest number. Of my own volition, being of sound mind and body, I surrender all expectations of her, all claim on her life.

Will you be happy? With Elinor? I don't know what to want. I can't bear the thought of you miserable and yet the thought of you happy with her is worse. How will she feel to have you back again? Will she know how close she came to losing you forever? Will she be as happy as I am wretched? I hope so. I hope someone benefits from this. What's the use of sacrifice if there is no grateful beneficiary?

I've almost finished cleaning the house. I've swept the yard and cleaned out the fridge, to make my decision seem conclusive. While I work I sing to give myself courage. But the only songs that come to mind are sad ones, laments and love songs:

"Shall I forget you?
Or will my heart remind me
how once we walked on a summers day?
Shall I forget you?
Or will my heart remind me
how much I want you back again?"

Ma used to sing this song. I remember her standing at the sink, washing dishes, and the sweet, mournful notes rising through the air of the steam-filled kitchen.

How far I've travelled in such a short space of time. Reunited and already renouncing all claim on you. Would it have been better for me if you hadn't come to meet me at the airport? If we hadn't gone home together? It's useless to ask because, even if I'd known then what I know today, I couldn't have resisted you. The moment I saw you, standing in the arrival lounge, my defences fell from me like snow melting from a ditch. Standing there, smiling your dazzling smile that got you out of every jam you were ever in, what chance had I? You kissed the heads of the flowers and held them out to me.

And I walked into your arms. The flowers fell to the floor. We stood locked in each other's arms. It was like plugging into a direct current. I could fight with you, hate you, long to be free of you, but the moment you touched me I was plugged in again. The light came on, the heat. I was in love again.

I didn't ask why you had come. I didn't ask where Elinor was or what you had told her. I knew by your being there to meet me that you'd turned a final corner. There could be no going back. You wouldn't have done it, you wouldn't have opened the wound, if you weren't certain that it was finished between you, once and for all. You asked me if I'd missed you. Yes, I answered, a little, (an old joke between us – once long ago, you had said when parting, miss me a little, then you'd phoned me and said, "I miss you a little – but every inch of you, a little.")

I went home with you. We stayed in bed for three days. I was astonished by the passion I felt, even though I had hungered for you all those months. I was drunk on our kisses alone, kissing so deep and sweet it left me breathless. It seemed to me as if my whole body wept for you, as though tears that had been damned in me for months were released, disguised, to flow as sexual rapture. But what did you feel? My mistake was to assume always that you felt as I did. That's all. But you had loved a woman before, more than one, and it was impossible that you could feel the astonishment, elation, the sense of returning home to a place you'd never been before.

That afternoon as you lay in my arms, I felt your hot tears run down my cheek, and I said something I'd promised myself never to say, the one thing that couldn't be said between us. "Don't leave me again," I said. "Ever."

Yes, I knew you loved me that day. I know it now. The only difference between us is that you loved someone else as well. It has taken me all this time to absorb it.

I am changed forever because of you. The rest of my life

will be lived in the light cast by this passion. Even if I am never to see you again. I have my memories. Inviolable. Stored in every cell of my body, beyond reach of damage. No words could do justice to all that I discovered with you. If my life depended on it – if I were called to the dock and asked to explain the nature of my love, my passionate delight in you – I couldn't do it. I would have to find words I don't possess. Words that would surpass meaning. I'd have to put into language what belongs outside it, beyond it.

I would ask a question first. I would ask if you remember the sea in childhood. I'd ask if you remember the sensations of sand on skin.

Do you remember playing by the sea on a warm day, I would ask, the sun on your back, sinking your hand as far as the wrist into a pool of wet, warm sand? The sand sucking at your fingers as you withdrew them, the water you had held back gushing in to take their place. The warmth and grip of wet sand, the warmth and silk of the water flowing between your fingers, the sun streaming down, burning a hollow between your shoulders? Do you remember as a child playing at the water's edge? The sea gushing and slipping, advancing and receding. Do you remember building a dam of sand to keep the water back? Building and rebuilding, always losing the battle. The water triumphing at evening, breaking over walls and buttresses, swallowing sand and your body in one sweep of its tongue. The sand washed all about you, clinging in the crevices of toes and fingers. The warm sand growing cold, its gritty pressure under your clothes hours later, reminding you of lost pleasure, its magic when mixed with its opposite element, water.

Your body was like the pleasure of the beach in childhood. The sea playing with mouth and eyes and hair, washing deliciously through all the senses, finding its own course. Unstoppable. Your whole body a vessel for the sand and sea and the air to play with. Blended inextricably, so that it was no longer merely itself, but an expression of all these.

Your body was the sum of these parts and the sum of mine. And my body was the sum of all I had lived before touching you. It was not any one thing about you, not one quality or physical feature that made me love you as I do. It was everything and no one thing. It wasn't your belly or your back or your thighs; the lovely taut muscle of the inner thigh, like taut rope under my hands. It wasn't the silken blue glimmer of the skin of your back where it flowed into your haunches. It wasn't the deep hollow of the armpit with its gloss of dark hair. It wasn't the soft ripeness of your neck, or the full curve of buttocks. It wasn't your cunt, vulva, vagina, what can I call it? The suck and heat and grasp of you. It wasn't the bud between the swollen lips; the clitoris rising like what to the caress of my tongue? Like the beating pulse of my heart. It wasn't your eyes in the ravishing moment that stopped my heart as you travelled to orgasm, eyes like lilies floating on water, widening and contracting, wide with surprise and delighted knowing of their pleasure. It wasn't any one of these elements alone or together that ravished me. It was, instead, the very essence of you, the sense I had of entering through your body into the heart of the universe. Entering through the hot, beating pulse of your flesh into the beating pulse of the earth. Not only that you carried me beyond myself, but more that you gave me back to myself. I entered into my own being, discovered my being at the centre of the earth. I entered darkness, I embraced it. Enclosed by it. Sucked deep down into the beginning of things, the centre of all creation, of all suffering. I tasted birth. I tasted suffering. I played upon them with lips and tongue. I sucked pain from pleasure and delight from anguish. I sank my soul into the start of time. I entered death as I entered birth.

I have my memories. Inviolable. Stored in every cell of my body.

Chapter Twenty-Eight

October, Dublin.

It was seven in the morning. There was a sudden buzz of activity. The nurses on the morning shift had begun their rounds and any patients capable of walking were making their laborious trek back and forth to the lavatories. Breakfast would be served in five minutes, she was told by a young girl mopping the floor. Nina decided it was a good time to go and phone home. She wanted to make sure that Paul could stay on until she got back to make breakfast for Lizzie.

She walked to the lobby at the end of the ward. The only phone on the floor was in use when she reached it. A woman in a pale green towelling dressing-gown had got there before her. A drip plugged into a vein at her elbow attached itself by means of a long transparent tube to a plastic bag filled with clear fluid which hung from a mobile stand. They were faintly grotesque these dispensers on wheels, she and other patients dragged about behind them, like dogs on leads, as they walked the corridors but Nina gave them hardly more then a glance. After one night in the place she had already grown accustomed to the bizarre form of collusion between patients and the medical technology used to treat them.

As she stood at the reception desk waiting for her turn, she had the sudden sense of being watched. She turned round and looked down the corridor. A glass door separated the lobby from the landing and staircase. A woman was standing with her face close to the glass and one hand raised as if to greet someone. She was smiling. Was it because of the smile or the way the light was falling behind her, that it took a second or more for Nina to recognise her?

It was Elinor. Elinor standing absolutely still, dressed in the long black woollen coat and the black fur hat she wore pulled down to her eyes that made her look, Nina thought, like a Russian princess. And it was Elinor's hand raised in that silent greeting as though she had been about to wave but had thought better of it. Seeing her so unexpectedly; seeing her as a stranger might, so familiar and at once so unknown, Nina felt her heart beat with a heavy painful rhythm.

How had she known where to find her? Nina was at once astonished and not at all surprised. Because she had this knack of turning up unexpectedly just when Nina was thinking about her. Intuition or a gift of perfect timing? Certainly it was a special power of being always in the right place at the right time. And that expression on her face – that was so intensely familiar – a look that almost defined her. Nina could see it now in the dark eyes nearly hidden by the rim of her hat and in her lips drawn back in a kind of anguished smile – that look of intense emotion; an expression of appeal and longing, excitement and sorrow all at once. Her face filled with emotion like a glass filling with light. Or sunshine across a field on a day of fast-blown clouds, her feelings blew across her wide open face, revealing her heart to anyone who glanced her way. Conscious of a sudden quickening of her pulse, Nina wondered if it were possible to love someone – to forgive them time and again – simply because they had power to express emotion so perfectly?

She walked to the door, opened it and Elinor walked through.

"How is she?" she asked at once, fixing Nina with a look of absolute concentration.

"Sleeping," Nina answered.

Now that she stood close to her and could look into her eyes, Nina was struck by how different she appeared. What was it about her that was so altered? With a shock then she realised suddenly the change was only that she looked again her usual self. The cloud of anger and resentment that had covered her face for weeks had slipped from her features like a mask. Her own face had returned to view. The face she had almost forgotten. Warm, sensual. Tender.

"How did you know about May?"

"I couldn't sleep so I phoned home. Paul told me. I'm so sorry," she said. She threw her arms around Nina's shoulders. And Nina felt something extraordinary flowing through her – something she hadn't thought she would ever sense from Elinor again – pity.

They stood in silence. Arms close about each other. Nina felt Elinor's heart beating against her own chest and she hid her face at her shoulder not wanting her to see the tears that had come into her eyes. Not wanting her to feel the fear. How much of that fear was for Elinor and how much for herself she could not say. There seemed in that moment to be no longer any dividing line between them.

"Can I see May? Will they let me?"

"We won't ask," Nina answered.

Chapter Twenty-Nine

September, Clare.

I got through at last to the boys in Galway. I asked for Malachy but they said he was out and that Clair was taking care of them.

They both sounded well and in good form, but a little muted somehow. Or embarrassed as though they knew something I didn't. When I suggested I'd ring back later, Luke was emphatic that I should wait until tomorrow. Why? Where is Malachy? Are they covering for him for some reason?

I walked home from the shop about four o'clock. When I arrived at the house I had the sense of someone's presence again. The gate was slightly ajar and the grass looked as if it had been trampled by the hooves of cattle. As I walked up the path I saw Michael, leaning against the wall, smoking. I regarded him for a few minutes in silence before he saw me. What a forlorn creature he was, so alienated from the world, so angry. I tried to think of something to say that might reach through the fog of resentment in which he'd wrapped himself. Something that might make him feel my new sympathy for him. But as I stood hovering, uncertain of how to proceed, he turned in my direction and caught sight of me. I expected him to shuffle off then as he usually did, but to my surprise he stayed where he was, although his body stiffened and his expression grew more sullen.

"Fine evening," I said. He stared at me but said nothing. I drew close to him, close enough to see the tufts of beard on his jaw and the clumsy red wrists protruding from the frayed sleeves of his jacket.

"And it looks as if it might be fine again tomorrow," I offered and smiled at him slightly to lend emphasis to my goodwill though I felt it begin to evaporate already under the relentless frost of his gaze.

Then, suddenly, he said something that amazed me: "The other one was here," he grunted, his hands twitching at his sides.

I stared at him.

"The other one? What other one? Who are you talking about? There's been no one around here but you." He looked at me now with defiance and a suggestion of contempt, as though I were too stupid to understand the obvious.

"The other one," he repeated, "the one who came looking for you."

For a moment, I couldn't take in what he was saying. And then I understood with a sudden burst of joy. I smiled in spite of myself; I felt it break across my face, a daft delighted grin. "You mean Nina!" I burst out. I felt like hugging his thin, angry body.

"The other one," he muttered again, stamping his foot now like a mutinous horse, growing impatient because I seemed not to accept what he was saying.

"All right, all right," I said, smiling. "I understand. But where is she now?"

He turned and jerked his head towards the road behind him.

"The shop," he said. "Gone to the shop."

So! You were here! You were waiting for me! You had come after all – despite everything! How could I have doubted you! I reached out my hand to touch his arm as I thanked

347

him, but he jumped back from me as though I was about to deliver a fatal blow. I turned on my heel and took off down the boreen without another word. I ran the mile to the shop without stopping, my breath breaking from my lungs in great white clouds on the cold air. I burst in upon Máire Mac who was sweeping the floor in front of the counter.

"They have no manners on them at all any more, children," she said, "they'd have the place destroyed altogether with their crisps and their sweet papers."

"Did someone come here looking for me a few minutes ago?" I asked in a rush without pausing to explain myself. She looked up and smiled, a slow satisfied smile of understanding.

"Yes, only ten minutes ago."

"And where is she now then – where has she gone?" I almost shouted at her.

"I said you might be above at the old graveyard, if you weren't at home, because I know you like to go there."

The church! Five minutes in the other direction. Three, if I ran. And if I didn't make it on time I would be bound to meet you on the way back. There is only the one road you could take.

I reached the church without passing you. I was breathless as I pushed open the heavy doors and had to shove hard with my shoulder to make them part. I stood inside, my eyes dazzled momentarily by the relative darkness after the brightness of the street. I looked about wildly, heart pounding. Nothing. No sight of you. My anxious gaze was met by row after row of empty benches and an absolute silence; the heavy, stiff silence of air undisturbed for days. Where were you? Where could you be? If you weren't here, and I hadn't passed you along the way, what could have happened? There was nowhere else for you to go. There was only the one door and the one path to the gate and the one road back to the shop. What could have happened? Why did Máire Mac say you were here if you weren't? Had she lied to me? Had Michael lied? Were they playing some awful joke?

I turned around, studying the interior as if you might be hiding in some corner waiting to jump out at me. I saw the marble baptismal font, the two confession boxes on opposite sides, the wooden crucifix hanging from the far wall, looking strangely life-like, the large, pale eyes staring out from the drooping head. I waited and listened. Not a sound. Nothing. You were not there.

I went outside. The cold rain blew into my face and washed away tears of disappointment. I walked along the gravel path and pushed open the low, iron gate leading to the graveyard. It occured to me that you might have come here and then gone to the lake. I walked through the tall grass, the damp seeping through my shoes. Past the new marble stones, and the old ones of granite, the names eroded from the worn surface, the graves of the long-dead and the forgotten, grass growing high on the heaped earth.

I walked to the crest of the hill. The lake lay wide before me, dark and calm except for the small waves that washed to shore, forming ribbons of yellow froth on the sand at the water's edge. I saw the swans, three tall, full-breasted, white birds, sailing slowly into shore, their heads high and proud. I saw a man kneeling on the small wooden jetty, his back to me, gazing out across the water. I was about to go back. I didn't want to have to speak to anyone. But if you had come here, perhaps he had seen you? I was on the point of calling out to him when he stood up. He turned to face me. He was wearing a long, black coat and dark tweed cap, low over his eyes. Slowly he lifted it from his head, bowed gravely and began to intone with mock formality words I'd heard many times before, long ago:

"Soon far from the rose and the lily and fret of the flames would we be,

Were we only white birds, my beloved, buoyed out on the foam of the sea."

It was Malachy.

How like him to take me by suprise in this awful way. To arrive without any warning when it was you I was expecting, longing for every minute. To have raised my hopes, as he did for that anguished half hour I spent looking for you. Not that he intended to cause this sick disappointment, of course. He's not at all malicious. On the contrary, he always means well. That's the problem. Generous, impulsive and selfish. So sure of his welcome, even now. Never imagining how disappointed I would be – expecting you and finding him! He had driven down that afternoon on impulse, he said. He had to see me before going back to Galway. The boys were fine. Clair was staying with them. Had I not phoned? Had they not told me? Why had he gone to the church, I asked him.

"To find you of course," he said. "First I called to the cottage. No sign of you. Just that crazy hanging about."

"He's not crazy," I said, sounding foolish to my own ears.

"What is he then?"

"He's just depressed."

Malachy laughed delightedly. "Oh I can see you've been here too long. You've become sentimental already – it's not like you! Anyhow that depressed, lonely person who was hanging around the cottage told me you'd gone to the shop. At the shop, they said the church. The church, what could you possibly be doing in a church I said to myself? But they were right of course. Only a week alone in the country and already you're sneaking off to confession in the afternoon! Well, there's no trusting city people in the country, especially dyed-in-the-wool atheists like yourself. You have to be steeped in it from childhood to have any immunity."

I let him rant on in this way with no attempt at self-defence.

I was angry, but trying to hide it. One thought was obsessing me – with Malachy here how would it be possible to see you, if you were to arrive?

"How did you know where to find me?"

"I called over to Nina last night. She told me where you might be."

I was staggered, "You called to see Nina!"

"Yes, why not? She always knows where you are when I don't."

"But what were you doing back in Dublin?"

"I had to collect a few last-minute things," he said.

But why should you have told him? I wanted to demand immediately, but I bit my tongue. I must be careful, tread very gently. I could feel the old anger rising again – that he could be so interfering. So pushy. Most of all that he could go and talk to you when I couldn't, when it meant nothing to him and meant everything in the world to me.

Then, in that second of jealous anger, as I imagined him standing at your door, talking to you, looking into your face, a sudden realisation dawned on me. A thought that at once transformed him in my eyes. He had seen you! He had spoken to you! He might even have some idea of how you were feeling. Of what your plans were! And in that flash of illumination he was changed from a maddening interruption to a most precious emissary. A thousand passionate demands flooded into my mind. How did she seem? What did she say? Did she say anything about me? Did I dare let him see how desperately I needed to know? I tried to sound off-hand, turning my head away from him as if only half interested in the answer:

"How did she seem – was she in good form?"

"It was very late. We didn't say a lot. It was raining. I got soaked through. She asked me in for coffee. The child was there, in bed I think, and that idiot of a dog jumping all over us . . ."

"But how did Nina . . ." I interrupted him, trying and failing to sound patient, "how did she seem?"

"She looked pale, tired. She asked me to come in and I would have said no if I hadn't been drenched to the skin. We had coffee and I asked her about you and that was it more or less . . ."

"More or less?"

"Well, she didn't want to tell me where you were. I knew that. But she couldn't resist talking about you, of course, as soon as I mentioned your name."

"And what did she say . . . exactly?"

"Nothing. I've told you we hardly spoke," he said flatly. My heart sank. I stared at him in disbelief. Could this really be all he had to say about it? And then, as though he felt my desperation and surrendered to its force, he said, sounding weary and resigned:

"She's obviously as much in love with you as she ever was," he paused, "if that's what you're waiting to hear."

Chapter Thirty

October, Dublin.

Elinor walked ahead with her quick confident stride. Even in a strange place she had this air of knowing exactly in what direction she was headed. As she walked, Nina watched her, the straight line of her back, the full, shapely legs in the black cotton leggings, the finely turned ankles. How well she knew her – every inch of her body. From years of gazing at her and only her. Sometimes when she looked in the mirror she was surprised to see her own face and not Elinor's.

When they reached May's bed, Elinor bent over her sleeping form and put a small, light kiss on her cheek. May did not wake, but Nina had the sense of a slight stirring of her attention. She and Elinor sat down on opposite sides of the bed. The ward was quiet again temporarily, breakfast having been served and cleared away in her absence. Nina looked towards the window from which she could see now, in the light of day, a stretch of brilliant green grass with little hills and valleys ringed by tall fir trees – a golf course lending its habitual air of calm and prosperity to the harshness of the hospital world. The rain was falling through a pale yellow sunshine. She could hear birds singing nearby, though out of sight.

Suddenly, she remembered another hospital ward and a

very different occasion. She remembered a few years ago when Elinor had broken a leg and was confined to hospital for a week. Nina had come to visit her several times a day. Sitting talking at the side of her bed until late into the night, the nurse putting up with it because they imagined them sisters. Or at least that's what they pretended for form's sake. One night, when she was leaving, a young nurse came in as Nina bent to kiss Elinor goodbye, a long, lover's kiss on the mouth. And when she turned, the nurse was standing transfixed, an amazed smile slowly lighting up her face.

So many memories. There was such a deeply layered resonanace to their life. They had been everything to one another. They had done everything together. They had wept and laughed and fought and made love. They had left each other forever and come back again. They had stood together against the world, taking on allcomers. From the start it had been possible for Nina to be open and fearless about her sexuality because she had Elinor at her side who was so spontaneously, so unselfconsciously proud of their love. For Elinor, Nina was simply the woman she was in love with and she didn't care who knew. And the world, seeing this, took them at her estimate.

They had been through so much together. The death of Elinor's mother, the death of a former lover of Nina's, the death of friends. They had stood by each other through the death of love itself. Or of love's absence. When they were going through bad times, no one could console Nina as Elinor did. When love returned again, they fell upon it and celebrated, ready to start all over again, ready to forgive one another, to trust, to abandon themselves to the risk and the hope of happiness all over again. But this time?

She recollected then with a sense of painful irony that it had been in the casualty ward of a hospital where she had first met and fallen in love with Katherine. Such a different kind of love. The sexual connection, electric and obsessive. Sparks flying from their skin when their eyes met. And those eyes of Katherine's – those vast, brimming, blue eyes fixed on Nina in admiration and desire. Like twin mirrors throwing back an image of herself that was intensely flattering: Nina the adventurer, the pioneer, romantic and fearless. Could she ever live up to this? Would it inspire or stifle her, the weight of so much expectation?

She wondered at the paradox that life had chosen another emergency room, in another hospital, as the setting for her last farewell to Elinor. Elinor who knew the very worst of her and still loved her.

She looked down at May sleeping quietly between them. Her face had returned to a more normal colour and her breathing, though still faster than usual, sounded easy and natural. She was struck by how calm she felt suddenly. Reassured simply by Elinor's presence. Somehow, with Elinor in the room, nothing seemed as critical. Pain, sickness even death, in her company took on a more natural aspect. She had a way of facing trouble head-on without defence or squeamishness that made it at once easier to cope with, less freakish.

Elinor reached her hand across the bed. She touched Nina on the wrist. She did not speak until Nina turned her eyes from the window and met her gaze.

"What do you think?" she said, looking her full in the face. "Will it be all right?"

"The nurse said if she survived the night there was a good chance," Nina said, reassuring herself as she spoke. "And she looks much better than she did."

Elinor looked away from her.

"I didn't mean May," she said and she spoke so quietly Nina barely caught her words. "I meant us," she added as softly.

"Us?" Nina was startled. She stared blankly at Elinor.

Elinor raised her head and met Nina's eyes once more.

"I was asking if you thought we had any chance?" she said and she flushed faintly as she said the words and averted her eyes once more. Nina realised with a pang the effort it cost her to ask this. She saw the stress and tension in her face. The embarrassment at putting herself once more on the line. And conscious, so acutely, of this, she didn't know how to answer her. What could she say that would be worthy of such a difficult gesture? All the words that suggested themselves sounded hollow in her ears before she spoke them. Phoney, inadequate.

"Is that what you want?" she asked at last.

"It's a question of what you want," Elinor said looking back at her. Her expression held something like defiance and appeal at once. As one who might yet refuse help having called for it, if it arrived too late.

They sat on either side of the bed, their arms stretched over the lightly breathing form of the old woman lying under the blankets, their fingers touching. They sat in silence. And neither wanted to be the next to speak. After a moment, Elinor withdrew her hand, but very slowly so that Nina scarcely felt the movement.

"You must be tired," she said. Her tone was sad and full of concern. "Let's not talk now," she suggested. "Why don't you go home and give Lizzie her breakfast."

"Do you think so?"

"Yes. I think that's the best idea. When you've had breakfast come over again with her. I'll wait until you get back."

"You don't mind waiting?" Nina felt anxious, not sure to what exactly she was consenting.

"No, I don't."

"Are you sure?"

"Yes. I'm quite sure." Elinor paused. Her gaze travelled to the window behind Nina's shoulder where thin shafts of sunlight were making their way now through the shifting rain clouds.

"I'll wait," she said, "as long as it takes."

"Will you?"

"You know that."

"I don't know anything anymore."

"Only because you don't want to."

Nina stood up and kissed May's sleeping face.

"She has to be fine," Elinor said, "she's such a great old warrior."

"Yes, she has to be," Nina answered and she walked softly from the room. At the door to the lobby she turned back for a moment. She looked at Elinor sitting absolutely still beside the bed, watching the old woman's face with an expression of deep concentration as if she might preserve her by the force of her attention.

Chapter Thirty-One

September, Clare.

I walked with Malachy, slowly along the road, between the
hedgerows and the low, stone walls; grey billowing clouds
blowing over our heads, the same endless drizzle that had
fallen since you left, falling now, making the paths and the
grass glitter in the pinkish-blue light of early evening. The
whole landscape had recovered its air of enchantment. The
bare, black-branched trees, the noisy rooks, the mournful
sheep crying in the damp fields.

"I got the car sorted out . . ." Malachy was saying, "I got a
very good price on the trade-in . . ."

But I scarcely heard another word he said. I was listening
instead to the bawling of the cows that came running to the
field gate as we passed, as if in hope that we had come to drive
them to the yards for milking. Leaning their heavy heads over
the iron bars, regarding us with solemn, patiently suffering
eyes. I was listening to the wind through the bare fuchsia that
made the branches rub together and give out a plaintive,
high-pitched squeal that, when I first heard it, I took for the
crying of birds. I was looking at the sky, the always changing,
mercurial sky that was now rearing over our heads like waves
on a stormy sea. You were as much in love as ever! What else
could I want to hear? Malachy had seen you. He had talked to

you! And whose opinion could I trust more than his when it came to judging your state of mind?

When we reached the house Malachy immediately set about preparing dinner. He wanted to make something special. A meal to remember. A celebration.

"A celebration?" I asked him in disbelief. "Of what?"

"Of my succeeding in tracking you down to this god-forsaken hole of course, what else?"

This was a mood I knew and distrusted. He was full of nervous excitement. A sort of bullying high spirits, when he used his enthusiasm to steam-roll any obstacle set in the path of his optimism.

It took him nearly half an hour to unload the car. He carried in seven carrier bags full of groceries and presents from Dublin. Wine, flowers, cheese, smoked salmon, coffee. Even books and records. It seemed as though he intended to stay for days. While he chopped and pared vegetables, rolled out pastry and simmered soup, he maintained a running commentary of excited pronouncements. I would love Galway. It was the only place to live. I would like it better than anywhere we had been before. It was made for me – the bookshops, the pubs, the music . . . The boys had settled in already and made friends with the neighbours. They were longing to see me and show me around. As soon as we got back, they wanted to take me fishing on the lakes. He wove these delighted castles in the air without so much as pausing to consider what I felt about it. I said nothing to dissuade or encourage him. I had learned to ignore this humour. Having come to see it as a form of intense manipulation whether deliberate or not. He made himself so likeable, so generous that it was almost impossible to refuse him. Not to fall in with his plans seemed childishly begrudging and sullen.

"Malachy . . ." I began hesitantly, hours later when he had finished dinner and he was quiet for a few minutes, sitting over the fire smoking his pipe while I cleared up. "Malachy, I think it might be better if we talked about all this tomorrow. Tonight is not the best time for decision-making."

And he assented, smiling sweetly as if he were fully open to suggestion, entirely ready to see another point of view.

He's asleep at last in the loft upstairs, in the bed I'd prepared for you. I can hear the faint sound of his snoring, so I know he's really sleeping and not lying awake staring into the darkness in injured silence as so often before when we have had to go through this conversation.

I know he wanted to talk it all out tonight. To make clear his plans and persuade me into some kind of hasty agreement. He thinks that if he can talk me into going to Galway for a visit, that I'll find it impossible to leave. Seeing the boys again, being in a new place, a family once more, he thinks is sure to win me over. A new start – that's what we need. A completely fresh start, he says. The past behind us. A new house, a new city. New friends. Living all of us together again, but a whole new structure and different attitudes.

He looked so full of hope, his cheeks flushed, his eyes brilliant, carried away by his own eloquence and optimism, I almost believed him. It's so easy to imagine. So seductive; this picture always, of the happy home, surrounded by the people I love and the things I love; friends and money, pleasure, security. I can picture myself, already, sitting by the fire in the evening when the boys are in bed. Remember the sense of contentment. My own hearth, my own roof. The knowledge that my children, my own flesh and blood, are safe and trusting in sleep only a few yards from where I sit. Unheard, unseen, but casting the warmth of their presence all through the house. I can imagine sailing, as Malachy promises, on Galway Bay on Saturday afternoons and fine summer evenings, the light mesmerising, as the sun sinks into the grey-blue waves. I can hear the wind and feel the spray on my cheeks. I can hear Luke's voice raised in excitement, calling out orders to Malachy who jumps about like an obedient terrier at his youngest son's command. I think of the laughter, the old jokes, the marvellous sense of ease created by knowledge and familiarity, knowing that you are known and understood, that one has one's place and everyone else theirs. Belonging, that's what I'm trying to say. The sense of belonging. If I give it up, will I ever know it again?

So I listened and said nothing. I didn't want to start a row. When he's in this mood, so high on optimism, he is impossible to deflate. I know he took my silence for a kind of consent, or the chance of it anyway. It's not hard to see why. From his point of view I really have no reason in the world to refuse. He assumes that things are over between you and me. Though he has seen you so recently and considers that you're still in love with me, he doesn't seem to feel it signifies much, I don't know why. He's used to thinking you so fickle, but you gave him the impression of being extremely secure and rooted there. Is he right? Of course, he also knows how I long to be with the boys and that I love new places. He knows, too, that I still care for him. So he must find it hard to see how I could want more.

How can I explain to him? Would he understand that I know I can't love him as he deserves to be loved? Not because of bad behaviour on his part – his outbursts of jealous anger, that he's trying so hard to make up for – but because of the way I love you. Whatever happens between you and me, there's no going back. Even if I were never to see you again, I am changed forever by my love for you. If I were to live with Malachy, every day of our lives together would be lived in your shadow. The best hours clouded by the knowledge of how far it fell short of my real potential. I'd be living always below my best. Making do. And he deserves more than that. Not because I don't love him, but because I once did.

I went up just now to the loft. I stood looking at him from the doorway while he slept. How long is it since I've done that? How long since I've really looked at him or let myself think about him?

Looking at him, I remembered how I used to feel. I remembered only the good things, his kindness, his unswerving love, the happiness he has given me. I still like the look of him, almost as much as the day we met. But it makes no difference. I am in love with somebody else. His good looks, his strength, his kindness, are no longer of any use to me. They've become pointless attributes. Something one might remark on in a stranger. After all, the world is full of handsome, decent men. What do they matter to me? There is nothing alive in me now but the pained consciousness of how I ought to feel for him. Of how much he deserves. When I was in love with him I didn't give his virtues a second thought. I took them for granted. It's only now, as I finally leave him, that I begin to rehearse his defence.

I sit with the curtains open to watch the sky. A pale silver wedge of moon hangs at the top right-hand corner of the sky above the lake. Every few minutes it is covered by black cloud, to be revealed a moment later, bright and delicate, whiter than the whitest star. The clocks ticks, the rafters creak. I hear the waves breaking on the lake shore. That's how quiet it is. I gaze into the dying fire. Little spurts of yellow flame still alive among the sunken wood. I think about the past. I think about the days leading up to this, the days with you and all the days before that – the days before I met you and the days after. My actions, my movements, my motives in loving you. The whole journey and process from my first laying eyes on you to this last separation. All that happened in my life to prepare me for you.

And all my life now, in retrospect, seems to have been a journey towards you. Towards the loving of you, the losing of you, and the refinding of you.

Do you remember the evening we met? Do you remember waiting in the casualty lounge, blood on your hands that I thought was your blood? Do you remember our first afternoon together? Do you remember sitting in the car at Sandymount, looking at the sea, while you kissed my hands? Do you remember clearing out the flat at Jan's? The mattress the last thing to go. Do you remember lying down and making love on it just before we carried it out the door? Not able to part from it without enjoying one more time? Do you remember parking the car at Monkstown only five minutes from home and making love in the back seat, not able to wait? Do you remember the day on the ferry coming back from France? Leaving the others, to rent a cabin, with only thirty minutes of the journey left. Do you remember that it cost twenty-five pounds? Do you remember who paid? Do you remember saying it was worth it? If it was twice as much.

I remember. I remember it all. Let that be enough for me.

I have written down the whole story. I've told what happened from beginning to end, and yet I've said nothing. Nothing that explains anything. Inadequate. Misleading. Understated. Overstated.

All of that. One of those things.

I will send this account to you. This record made without thought of your response. Set down in writing for my own eyes only. Written in blood. I'll send it to you because I want you to understand. All of it. I want you to feel as I did in this last week. To travel the same arduous journey, stumbling from one hour to the next, from one foothold to another. Arriving at what seems a vantage point to discover only another cliff-face, the path sliding from under foot. I want you to be patient as you read it. Without judgement.

Tomorrow I'll walk with Malachy where I'd planned to walk with you. By tomorrow, I'll know what I must say to him. I'll know how to say it.

But for now I like to imagine that it's you whose soft breathing I hear as I write these last words. You who lies asleep in the loft above my head. Here at last, and all the world changed by your presence. I let myself imagine that, in a few minutes more, I'll set down this book, put out the light and climb the stairs to bed. I will take off my clothes and lie silently beside you. Your body will welcome me even in sleep as it always does. I'll say nothing. Not wanting to wake you. Nothing except your name that I had thought I would not speak again in love. Softly, I'll whisper it in your ear while you sleep, your warm back turned to me, your hand reaching out to mine.

This is my story, Nina. The whole biography of my desire for you. Even now, a love story.

Chapter Thirty-Two

October, Dublin.

At home, Nina made a strong cup of tea and went out into the garden. She sat down on the wet grass. She could feel the dampness through the heavy cotton of her blue jeans. She could hear May's voice in her mind saying: "Don't sit on the wet grass – you'll get rheumatism." Well, it hadn't happened yet. Thirty-seven years of it and still not a touch of the dread disease. Solomon came and sat beside her, resting his long, pale muzzle on her foot, waiting for her to put her cup down so that he could drink the last few drops of the milky tea. She had finished the diary; the last page and still, she did not know how to answer it.

She smoked one cigarette and then went indoors to wake Lizzie. On her way, she stopped outside her own bedroom door where Paul was sleeping and listened. Not a sound. Softly she opened it and glanced inside. A few dark curls showed above the covers, one long, thin foot stuck out at the end of the bed. He was fast asleep. She could hear now, quiet, satisfied snoring. She moved on down the corridor to Lizzie's room. The second she opened the door Lizzie sat up in bed.

"Can I get up now?" she said pushing the duvet back and swivelling her feet to the floor.

"Will you come down and I'll make you breakfast?"

Before she had the kettle boiled, Lizzie was in the kitchen in her pyjamas and dressing-gown.

"Can we phone Elinor now?" she asked excitedly.

"No. Not just yet. There's something I want to tell you."

"You said that yesterday," the child said, looking at Nina doubtfully.

"Did I? Well, this is something different."

"What is it?" Lizzie sounded worried now. She had picked up a new tone in Nina's voice and knew that it meant bad news.

"Last night, after you went to bed, I got a phone call from a hospital." She paused, choosing her words carefully.

"What hospital?" the child asked in her literal way.

"St Mary's. A nurse phoned to tell me that Aunt May had been taken over to them because she had something wrong with her heart and needed to stay the night where doctors could look after her."

"What's wrong with her heart?"

"She had a small heart attack, that's all. But she's very well again. I went over there and stayed the night with her. And Paul came to look after you."

"Is she going to die?" Lizzie asked. She bit her underlip and her eyes opened wide with fear. Hearing her blunt question, Nina was struck by the harshness of the word and that Lizzie was the first person to use it. Is she going to die? No one had dared to say it in the hospital. In a place where people died every day, the word itself was taboo.

"No, she's not going to die. She's much too young and strong."

"Where's Elinor?" Lizzie asked, her mind moving from one anxiety to another.

"She's at the hospital with May. She came over this

morning to see her and she said I should bring you back with me after we've had breakfast and given Solomon a walk."

There was a sudden loud ringing of the front doorbell. Solomon raced into the hall barking furiously, closely followed by Lizzie who skated along the wooden floor in her stocking-feet. Nina walked after them

"Take it easy!" she called after him. "It's only the postman."

When she reached the hall, she saw three letters lying on the mat. Solomon, still barking madly, rushed into the sitting-room and up to the bow-window to catch the last glimpse of the postman as he walked down the path.

Nina picked up the letters. One was a bill from the telephone company. She put it in the hall table drawer, unopened. The second was a letter from Katherine and the third was a long envelope addressed in Elinor's unmistakable hand. Elizabeth appeared behind her.

"Is there anything for me?" she asked.

"No."

"Is there anything from Elinor?"

"No. They're all for me. Just bills and things," she said putting Katherine's letter into her shirt pocket.

"Can we take Solomon to the beach?" the child asked. She was sitting astride the dog's back and holding onto his ears.

"If you get dressed and have your breakfast on your own without disturbing me, I'll take you in ten minutes."

"All right."

Lizzie went into the kitchen. Nina went upstairs to her bedroom.

She closed the door and stood, leaning her back against it. A gesture she had seen so many times in films and thought to herself how unreal it was. A thing no one would do in ordinary life. She closed the door so that she could not see Lizzie. She leaned against it so that she could not be disturbed until she was ready. She needed to read these letters alone. She stood with the two unopened envelopes in her hand for a full minute before she decided which to read first. And another second or two before she dared to open it. Then she tore the fine paper roughly across the top. One sheet of the paper written in Katherine's closely-written script. She read it through, making herself take each word at a time.

"My love,

I've come to Galway with Malachy for a few days, to see the boys and to sort out our new arrangements. It's beautiful here – a whole city that smells of the sea. I think of you every minute. And long for you.

What more can I say? You know what I want. But it must be your choice. I won't try to cajole or persuade. There's been enough of that. If you can't come freely, it's better that you don't come at all.

I remember once, you said to me: "The heart that loves you is the same heart that loves Elinor. I can't grow another one." So, Nina, I won't ask you to cut out your heart. I ask only that you speak to me. That you look me in the eye and tell me what must happen.

Whatever happens, I'm changed forever by loving you. I regret everything. I regret nothing.

Katherine."

Nina's hand shook as she folded the page and stuffed it back into the envelope. She went to her desk, opened a drawer, and placed the envelope at the bottom, under a pile of letters and correspondence from work. She closed the drawer.

Then she took the other letter from her pocket. Her heart was racing. The sense of dread made her palms sweat. As she slit open the thick envelope, something fell out onto the floor. She knelt down. Two dried flowers lay on the polished wooden boards. A purple crocus. And a yellow one. She picked up the slightly stiffened blossoms and held them in her open palm. She looked at them in silence. Two small, stiff flowers – purple and yellow. She thought she remembered sending flowers like these to Elinor sometime last year. She touched the purple petals with one finger, warily. She felt a faint shiver pass over her. What did they mean? Why had she sent them?

Lizzie stood in the doorway, carefully dressed in blue jeans, leather boots and a denim jacket. Her face was scrubbed clean and her long hair brushed and tied back in a ponytail. She regarded Nina with the grave considering air that made her look so much like her mother.

"What have you got in your hand?" she asked quietly.

"Some flowers someone sent me."

"Who sent them?"

"A friend."

"A friend who loves you?"

"Yes, I think so."

"Why did they send you dead flowers then?"

"I'm not sure," Nina answered.

Lizzie looked at her with a doubtful expression. She seemed about to ask something else, but decided against it.

"I'll go out and get Solomon, will I?"

Nina put the two flowers into her pocket and turned away.

"Yes," Nina said absently.

She waited until she heard Lizzie's steps go down the stairs. Then she took the letter from the envelope she still held in her hand. She walked to the window and stood looking out. She took a deep breath, and began to read.

"I want to sleep for twenty-four hours without waking. I want to wake and not remember where I am. I want to wake and know myself somewhere else, and know myself in a time of life so good it went unnoticed. A time and place without fear and guilt. Without this ceaseless fretting over facts and half-facts. Without this constant need to analyse myself and our life. I want to wake in Spain or Greece. In a small village. On a beach in a place called Georgupoli. Woken at seven by the heat of the sun on my closed eyes. You waking beside me in the same instant. Not because I say a word, but because you always wake at the same moment. I want to kiss your hair and your forehead before you scramble from your sleeping bag and run naked down the beach and into the sea, the German visitors there before us. Loud and boastful. Proud of their perfect German bodies.

I want to swim out to sea, almost beyond earshot. And float, with eyes closed, the dazzled sea behind me. The water as cold as home, cold as the Atlantic. I swim against the waves, along the yellow path. The sun stretches to meet me. I taste its salt and rinse my mouth with it. I imagine the strong, milky coffee we will drink in a few minutes time, at our table under the olive trees, in the smallest café in the square.

I want to wake to this morning. A morning that begins a whole lazy day of idle pleasures. Of Greek wine and goat's cheese, of sunbathing, of walking among the vineyards. I want to stroll in the dark back streets of the village, and to listen while you talk to the old women, the lacemakers, who sell their wares outside the bare houses that are caves cut into the mountainside. You chat with them, in halting Greek and barter and they love you for it. And Mama

Lindos gives you a piece of exquisite delicacy for almost nothing, for your beautiful smile, she says. They wave and smile at us, friends for life, as we walk, arm in arm downhill.

It is time for another coffee or maybe a glass of retsina. We buy a loaf of hard, yellowish, unleavened bread, a jar of sour sheep's yoghurt and sweet honey to eat on the beach. But we are tired. Perhaps we'll doze for a while at our café table. Perhaps we could go back to the beach at evening and . . . your head is drooping, the sun scorches the back of my neck, the old men play backgammon at the table beside us while you sleep.

I want to wake in some great city, in Rome or New York. In Paris when the whole city is waking. Seven thirty and already the day well advanced. The shouting, the scurrying, the frantic work of preparing the whole drama. Of getting everything right all over again – exactly as a morning in Paris ought to be. Like yesterday and the day before. I dress quickly, because I'm hurrying to breakfast. The croissants must be fresh. The coffee newly made. We are meeting again at the Gare du Noré. I buy a paper at the corner stall. I order "café au lait" and "croissants au beurre." The waiter brings them with a flourish, with ceremony, as though for the first time on the first morning of their invention. He hovers for a second as though giving his blessing as I take the first sip from the wide, white china cup. I am there waiting for you. Waiting for the moment when this great panorama will narrow to the perfection of a cameo – your eyes, your mouth, your hand reaching out to my shoulder, your lips to mine.

I want to wake to that morning or any other we spent together during the last years. I would take back any one of them. I would give ten years of my life for the certainty of knowing that I could live one of them again, exactly as I lived it before. Here or in any other place we visited or dreamed of visiting.

I want to wake to any ordinary morning we spent together; in our house with the river at the end of the garden, to wake together, knowing Lizzie is asleep in the next room and that at any moment she'll come bursting in, Solomon at her heels and you will laugh delightedly and a new day will unwind before us, all three of us together. Routine. Unremarkable. I want to see again, your eyes, in the first second of waking – so startled to see me, full of pleasure. I want to hear you say my name and smile as if in astonishment that I'm there, once more, beside you. In that moment, I know that I belong to you for life. Possessed by that first look, that first act of naming.

How I am to forget this? Can you teach me?"

Nina felt her heart lurch with pain. She read over again the last sentences, her eyes clouded with scalding tears.

She folded the letter carefully and put it back into the torn envelope. As she did so, she saw a postscript on the back of the last page.

You sent these crocuses to me once. Choose one now and send it back to me.

Yes, she remembered. Elinor always preferred symbols to words.

She put them back into the envelope with the letter and put it in her pocket.

"Are you ready?" She heard Lizzie's voice from downstairs.

She hesitated before she called back. "I'll be down in a minute. I'm getting dressed."

When she went down Lizzie was waiting in the hall with

Solomon, ready to leave. She stood stiffly, her hands behind her back. Nina could see she felt nervous.

"What's wrong with your eyes?" she asked, glancing up at Nina's face. "They're all swollen."

"Nothing," Nina said and lowered her head.

"You look sick," Lizzie said. "Did you get sick in the hospital last night?"

"No, I didn't. I'm tired, that's all."

"Well, I'm not. And Solomon isn't either." She pulled at the black silken hair of the dog who was seated beside her, gazing upwards with adoring eyes, his tail beating a furious tattoo against the floor.

On an impulse Nina took the flowers from her pocket. She held them one in each hand and then tightened her fists about them. She put her right hand behind her back, then her left hand. She kept them there for a moment while Lizzie watched curiously. At last she stretched out both fists in front of her.

"Which hand do you want?" she said, offering them to Lizzie. Why not after all? It was only a game. It bound her to nothing. "Right or left?"

Slowy Lizzie walked over to her. She stood stiffly before her and after a moment's hesitation she reached out her hand to meet Nina's. It hovered over the right fist for a second. Then with a quick shake of the head she changed her mind and touched her fingers lightly to Nina's left hand instead.

"This one," she said loudly. The fist opened. Lying in the palm was a yellow crocus. Lizzie laughed in surprise. Then her expression became puzzled again.

"What's in the other one?" she asked with suspicion.

Nina opened her right fist and there lay the second flower, the purple crocus.

"I'm glad I didn't pick that one," Lizzie said at once. "I don't like that colour."

"Neither do I," Nina answered softly.

"Can I keep the yellow one?"

"I think I'm going to give it to Elinor."

"Why would she want an old dead flower?"

"She might . . . you never know. I'll ask her anyway," Nina said.

"What will you do with the other one?"

"I'll put it somewhere safe. Is that a good idea?"

"Yes."

Nina put the purple flower on the saucer beside her empty coffee cup. The other one she replaced in the envelope with Elinor's letter and shoved it deep into her coat pocket. Lizzie came and stood beside her.

"Now can we go to the beach?" she asked, pulling at Nina's sleeve.

Nina looked down at the pale, fine-featured face upturned to her's, with the dark blue eyes that were so like her mother's; grave and passionate. She remembered what Elinor had written: "In that moment, I know that I belong to you, for life. Possessed by that first look, that first act of naming." When she looked into Lizzie's face she looked into a mirror in which she saw Elinor reflected. So that loving one, she loved the other. It was the power of this reflected love that had held her rooted all these years.

Then she thought of Katherine's words: "I won't ask you to cut out your heart." No, that would not be asked of her. By anyone. She was safe. If she wanted to be safe. Forgiveness had been granted in advance.

She would go with Lizzie to the sea. She would stand on the shore in silence and let her mind empty. She would let all this wash away from her; break in slowly separating waves.

The past, the present, the future. She would look at the sea and stand on the shore. The shore that existed only at the water's edge; washed and gouged by the sea, bounded by it, enveloped, but remaining, always, itself. And the waves that broke against it, finding their end in their beginning, travelling, always, to extinction or transformation, to another place, another time.

She turned to the child at her side, waiting patiently for an answer.

"Yes," she said, at last.

"Yes what?"

"Yes, we can go to the beach."

"And after we go to see May," Lizzie persisted, "can we go for a walk together? With Elinor too?" she said. "And can we go the long way?"

Nina opened the door and stood on the threshold. She looked out across the street, past the gardens and pavements, wet and glistening after rain, beyond the patient, sentinel trees, out over the slated roofs towards the east where the light of early morning filled the sky.

She took Lizzie's uplifted hand in hers.

"Yes," she answered softly, "if that's what you want. We can go together. All the way to the sea."